Long

Past

Summer

Praise for *Long Past Summer*

"Kirwan's excellent debut brings charm, complexity, and plenty of heat…. This mature, steamy romance will have readers swooning."
—*Publishers Weekly*, starred review

"Noué Kirwan's debut novel, *Long Past Summer*, is more than a beautiful, scrappy and hard-won second chance romance. It's a story of the real, tangled and sometimes painful relationships of family, lovers and friendships. It also captures the empowering, healing relationship of a woman with herself. In a word? *Long Past Summer* is powerful."
—*USA TODAY* bestselling author Naima Simone

"A whip-smart, electrifying debut that marks Noué Kirwan as an author to watch."
—Yaffa S. Santos, author of *A Taste of Sage*

"Noué Kirwan is a welcome, smart new voice in romantic women's fiction. *Long Past Summer* delves into family, friendships, and romantic love, deftly examining how our childhood influences our perceptions, and how discrimination impacts women trying to strike a balance between their own ambitions and their personal relationships. Not only that, but every reader will swoon over the eminently lovable hero, Cam. A winning debut from an author to watch."
—*Wall Street Journal* and *USA TODAY* bestselling author Jamie Beck

"It is rare to find a romance that spans decades yet still leaves you craving more. *Long Past Summer* is that romance. Noué Kirwan's exquisitely written debut left me breathless."
—Farrah Rochon, *USA TODAY* bestselling author of *The Dating Playbook*

NOUÉ KIRWAN

Long Past Summer

Recycling programs
for this product may
not exist in your area.

ISBN-13: 978-1-335-44882-8

Long Past Summer

HQN
22 Adelaide St. West, 41st Floor
Toronto, Ontario M5H 4E3, Canada
www.Harlequin.com

Printed in U.S.A.

To Auntie 'Von, who *always* knew I could. I love you.

And to the Richonne Fandom, who gave me the courage to try.

Long Past Summer

one

NOW

Mikaela took a deep, cleansing breath and rolled her shoulders back.

Breathe, she chided herself. She hadn't even darkened the doorstep yet; a heart attack in advance of that seemed premature.

One of the doors to the gallery stood open in invitation, but it was the frigid air escaping from inside that was actually more enticing. It was unseasonably hot. A freak heat wave had made it a blazing, makeup-melting, fire-hydrant-opening, egg-sizzling-out-on-the-sidewalk day in New York City, in only early May. Still, Mikaela wouldn't reward herself with the tempting relief offered inside. Instead, she just stood on the bottom step for yet another moment, lingering as the various city dwellers went about their business. Another typical Saturday afternoon along a cobblestoned street in Soho.

Despite its swank location, this art gallery was more nondescript than any of the other storefronts that lined the street, rather anonymously tucked in between several ultra-high-end fashion boutiques. Its entrance, an open doorway like an ominous black hole, sat among a sea of gleaming white and vibrantly colored doors. In the single large plate-glass window hung a poster advertising a photographer's retrospective and the gallery's address. Adorning the poster was a small reproduction of a picture that even now bedeviled Mikaela from no less than a magazine cover, a thirty-foot sign in Times Square and numerous subway station advertisements across the City. But now, looking at the size of the relatively unremarkable gallery, she guessed most of the exhibit's undoubtedly extravagant budget must have gone to the rent on this place and the marketing for that poster alone.

The gallery itself was lo-fi, unassuming and minuscule, judging from her spot well outside of it. Mikaela pushed her sunglasses up off her face and peered through the dim doorway, head angling this way and that like an owl. Her feet remained rooted in place, fear-induced moisture popping out on her brow and nose, sweating through her carefully applied war paint. The problem was the sun made it hard to make out what further surprises might lie in wait for her on the other side of the door.

"It's okay," a voice said, startling Mikaela from behind.

Mikaela spun around. A young woman with a bright smile and a nearly white-blond ponytail stood on the sidewalk below. She squinted without the benefit of her sunglasses, which hung neatly tucked in between her breasts on her floral ditsy-print sundress. One open blue eye appraised Mikaela, top to bottom.

"We're open. They're just putting the final finishing touches on everything but it's all in there." She took a step up onto the old wooden stairs then paused, waiting to see if Mikaela would choose to enter.

Rather, Mikaela stepped aside to let her pass with two large iced coffees in her hands.

Indecision still gnawed at her nerves.

"Is the photographer in?" Mikaela gave a courteous smile as the young woman continued past.

"Yup, should be. This is for him." She raised one of the coffee cups. "He tries to come in for at least a couple of hours every day—he'll probably be coming in more often leading up to the opening."

Mikaela nodded as they changed places, backing down the steps as the young woman ascended. They continued to regard each other: the young woman with mild curiosity, Mikaela with acute wariness.

The young woman paused again at the top, just in the threshold. "Do you want me to get him?" She turned to the photo in the window then back to Mikaela. The beginnings of a smile curving the corners of her mouth. "Or tell him you stopped by? Miss…?"

For a split second, Mikaela saw the omnipresent photo in the window the way any stranger might.

Two girls on a swimmer's platform on a summer day.

"Oh no, that's not necessary." Mikaela stood on the cobblestones again, heart thumping, resolve faltering. Not only the full glare of the sun but also her own discomfort burned her up, urging her retreat. She shielded her face with a palm, partially from shame, and hurried down the street.

She was half a long block away the first time she heard her name. She hadn't heard his voice in over fifteen years, but she recognized it, quickening her steps.

"Mikaela!" he bellowed again over the ambient noises of the street.

It was still distant but closer.

Mikaela hazarded a quick glance over her shoulder. A figure made his way toward her, dodging pedestrians as he moved. Mikaela stepped into the street, raising her arm, waving her hand.

A passing yellow cab pulled over. She yanked open the door.

"Please drive," she commanded. "I'll tell you where to go in a second. Just pull off, okay?"

The cabbie eyed her through the rearview mirror then glanced farther down the street before understanding her hurry and doing as she requested.

A full minute later, he spoke, turning off the small bumpy street and merging into traffic on the smoother avenue. "Where to, Miss?"

"Downtown Brooklyn, please." Mikaela sighed. She swallowed through the lump forming in her throat trying to sort why his voice had upset her.

She had always imagined she would instinctively know if Cameron was in her city. Or that maybe they could walk past each other, simply another two strangers in a city of eight million. But today proved, for her, that wasn't possible.

He is Cameron Murphy and I am Mikaela Marchand and as long as we remain who we are, that will always be a patently ridiculous idea.

Mikaela pressed the button lowering the window nearest her, sinking into her seat. She closed her eyes and took a deep breath of the thick, pungent city air that blew into her face as her cab sped down the windy expressway along Manhattan's East River.

two

"Here."

A female sheriff's deputy handed Mikaela a moist towelette. Mikaela took it and wiped the black ink off her fingers.

"We've called your parents, who said they'd be here soon, but we haven't finished processing you yet." The deputy raised an arm and waved over an extremely tall young man in a dress shirt and khakis. "As soon as we're done with this, someone'll take you to stand in front of the judge and then your folks can spring you."

Mikaela nodded, meticulously removing every drop of ink from her fingertips.

"Stay here. Cam'll finish up with you," she instructed gruffly before switching places with the young man and walking away.

Mikaela and the photographer stood staring at one another for a moment before he leaned forward and whispered, "Judge came in special to arraign y'all. Your parents must be pretty important, huh?"

"Not mine, hers." Mikaela nodded down the hall in the direction of her best friend, Julie. Julie leaned against the high-top intake counter chatting with the desk sergeant and another deputy. "Her daddy's a judge too, but Georgia Supreme."

"Oh, so a real muckety-muck then?" He reached into a tub on a nearby desk and handed her several more wipes.

"I suppose." Mikaela eyed the stack of wet wipes in her hands.

The young man mimed wiping his own face in a circular motion.

"I gotta take your mug shot," he explained.

"You? Aren't you a little young to be a deputy?"

"I'm not… A deputy, I mean. Just takin' the pictures. Grade two, office support. But I can't photograph purple-faced perps."

"Oh." Mikaela obediently scrubbed at her face, yet every towelette came back with more purple paint. After the fifth one, she stopped.

"Can I please just wash my face in the bathroom?"

The photographer shrugged and directed her down the hall.

Inside the restroom, Mikaela made for the sink and the large mirror above it. She had a hard time, right then, remembering why she had been so obsessed with this "senior prank" for so many years. Although Mikaela could admit, up until she'd had breakfast that morning, she'd still been so excited. Even as she and Julie applied their purple-and-gold face paint, and Mikaela's little sister, Vanessa, affixed two glittery wigs of opposing colors onto their heads, they'd all giggled with an almost frothy enthusiasm.

"Trust me—no one will *ever* forget this!" Julie had promised, pulling Mikaela up the vaguely damp football tunnel to the thundering beat of the Harmon Spartans' fight song— and also Mikaela's heart.

"Yeah, 'cause we'll be laughingstocks."

"We'll be legends!"

Arm in arm, they'd marched toward the light as the shaggy foil tips of the itchy wig tickled Mikaela's face.

And as usually happened, Mikaela could feel Julie's seemingly limitless enthusiasm for high jinks begin to permeate the layers of her own innate reserve.

But now, standing under the harsh fluorescents of the police station bathroom, Mikaela just ripped off the moronic gold tinsel wig and ruffled her short brown hair trapped beneath it. It sprung wild, thick and curly from her scalp, freed from the loose plaits she'd had it in earlier. She took a deep breath and regarded herself, still covered in purple greasepaint. *Was it worth it?*

She knew that was going to be her father's first question for her and she didn't have an answer. Julie had been right— no one in this town would ever look at her the same again. Especially not after the two consecutive cartwheels and back handsprings she'd done on the fifty-yard line while school security chased Julie around the end zone during halftime at their high school's final football game of the season. At the time, more than half of the stands roared in appreciation. Mikaela stifled a little smirk remembering it.

Of course, that was probably because most of the Tri-County area now knew her better than her own gynecologist did.

But the truth was, for those two hundred and eleven seconds, it had been utterly wonderful. Mikaela let loose and was completely herself, joyful and free and brimming with the most intense hopefulness and excitement about what lay ahead after graduation. Not only for herself but every single young person there. In fact, it had been three and half of the finest minutes of her life.

That is until sheriff's deputies tackled her to the ground and dragged her off the field in handcuffs. Now, Mikaela stood in the mirror wearing only an extra-large Spartans T-shirt, her pink Keds, the remnants of particularly noxious paint on her face and a slightly lopsided Afro. She was a mess.

"Pull it together," Mikaela said to the grotesque, mocking face in the mirror.

She pressed the dispenser until there was a mound of soap in her palm. Then, using paper towels to scrub, she washed most of the face paint off in three cycles. Her face was tender from the effort by the time she emerged from the ladies' room.

"I was just about to come in there lookin' for you," the young man said as she stepped out. He stood in front of the door, facing it like a sentry.

"Sorry, it was a lot of paint."

"Yeah, no kidding. I had no idea what you looked like under all that stuff." He guided her back toward the intake area.

She glared up at him with lingering suspicion. "And what, were you taking bets?"

Mikaela had always been sensitive about her looks. A month from eighteen, she was still knobby kneed and gangly, with barely a B-cup. The only sizable things on her remained her hips and an ass that kept her from being one long, unbroken straight line from the back of her head to the back of her heels.

"Takin' bets on what? That you weren't a Purple People Eater?" He chuckled. "No, I just wondered. Step over there." He pointed to a plain wall notched with height markings, in front of which stood a camera tripod. "Take this." He handed her a placard to hold.

"I didn't know you guys really did this." She examined the slate with her name, the date and booking ID on it.

"We do."

Mikaela was not this person. Not a person who got arrested. She was not prepared to forever be identified as one.

"You misspelled my name. Tell me, is it like a parking ticket? You mess it up, and I get to go free?"

"I wish." He smirked. "You're funny. What's misspelled?" He walked up to her looking over her shoulder for the error.

Mikaela could tell what soap he liked to use and the fact that he'd brushed his teeth or eaten something cinnamony recently. She considered that as his eyes met hers briefly. This close, there were flecks of green in the blue of his irises.

"Um, it—it's actually *k* with an *a* before *e* in my first name. *M-i-k-a-e-l-a*."

"Well, Mikaela with a *k-a-e*, I'm Cameron." He underlined a small name tag on his crisp white shirt with a flourish of his hand before reaching for the placard.

Their fingers brushed as he took it from her, whisking it back to the booking desk as she stood waiting. She chewed on her nails, staring for a moment at the bulletin board on the far wall. A collection of real-life FBI wanted posters lined it. She paid particular attention to the mug shots and shook her head at the realization that she was about to have one of those too.

A wolf whistle pulled Mikaela's attention to Julie, standing down the hall. She laughed, galloping around the hall on an imaginary horse until one of the officers made her stop.

Cameron came back from around the desk to hand Mikaela the placard.

"Let's try that again," he said.

Julie made a face, mouthing the words *"He's hot"* and fanning herself while his back was turned.

Mikaela attempted to hold in a snicker. Cameron looked over his shoulder but saw nothing. "What?" He smiled, trying to read her expression.

Mikaela's stomach tensed, the kaleidoscope of butterflies that resided in there all suddenly banking hard left as his eyes searched her face for a clue. She shook her head, looking down for somewhere to put her eyes. Her fingers ran over the placard's velvety felt board and sharp white plastic letters.

"Are you ready?" Cameron asked.

"Seems the real question is—" she cocked her head "—are you?" The second the words were out of her mouth she wondered where they'd come from.

His eyes widened and he chuckled again.

Embarrassed, Mikaela nodded, averting her eyes and stepping back to the wall.

"Raise the placard and look at me."

He looked through the viewfinder and snapped the picture. "Now turn to your left. Keep the placard at your shoulder."

She did and he took the second picture.

How precisely weird is it that it feels like we're maybe making eyes at each other as he's booking me? Very, she decided.

There was a third snap as she turned to face him. Mikaela blinked and, with the unexpected flash in her eyes, it was over. Cameron straightened, walking up and taking the placard back.

"I'm sorry I moved, did I mess—"

"Course not. It's a mug shot," he scoffed. "Don't worry about it. We got it. Last one was just in case."

The intense melancholy and foreboding returned, leaden in the pit of Mikaela's stomach.

"Okay. Well, you're done with me. Lemme take you back to the folks in Holding," Cameron said, oblivious to the single tear that slipped along the side of Mikaela's nose. He placed a hand at her back, gently guiding her down the hall.

"What if I lose my chance for a scholarship?" she asked as they approached the small bench where Julie sat waiting.

He paused, putting a hand on her arm. "To where?"

"College… Early decision to NYU."

He weighed this, his head moving side to side, before he shook it. "For a prank?"

"For an *arrest*."

"Nah, I figure this is indecent exposure and misdemeanor trespassing, at best. From what I've seen, you'll do community service for a few months, but I promise you—you'll be goin' to school next fall."

"You think?" A couple more tears slipped down her cheeks.

He dug a tissue out of his pocket, handing it over.

"*I know*. If an arrest was enough to keep you out of college, half of Georgia would be without an education…including a couple of the deputies round here," he added sotto voce. "And you wouldn't be lookin' at what will be, *if I do say so myself*, a fine and upstandin' product of the University of Georgia. Class of 2003."

"You're only a junior," Mikaela stated glumly. "There's still time."

"O ye of little faith." He poked out his bottom lip. "C'mon now, 'Go Dawgs'?"

Cameron pulled a small set of keys with a key chain of

a flat, pewter bulldog on it from his back pocket and presented it to her.

"What's this supposed to be? You givin' me your car keys so I can make a break for it?" Mikaela sniffled, lifting her gaze to him before again finding him a little too painfully attractive to look at directly.

"Ah, no. This right here? I call him the Sagacious Uga. And he's a damn good dog."

Mikaela choked out something between a cough and a laugh at that. The guy might be horribly cute but he was also hopelessly corny and a bit weird... She kind of liked that.

"But more importantly, Uga knows *things.*"

"Things, huh?"

"Yes, and he says you'll be fine."

Mikaela rolled her eyes.

"What's the meaning of this?" Julie cut in from her seat as they approached. "You keeping my friend?"

Mikaela finally smiled then. "It was my fault. All that paint was hard to get off."

"Tell me about it," Julie commiserated, pushing back her veil of wavy, dark hair to show all the gold paint that still lined the edges of her scalp and her ears.

"Tommy, I mean, Deputy Sutton." Cameron motioned for one of the deputies, who came and squatted beside Mikaela.

"Sorry about this," Cameron said glumly.

They all watched as the deputy affixed a small set of cold, metal manacles to her ankle, linking her to a bar beneath the bench.

"Was that absolutely necessary?" Mikaela asked.

Cameron sighed, looking so pained by the question she almost wanted to apologize to him for asking.

"'Fraid it is, miss. It's policy, unless you wanna sit back

there in the drunk tank?" Deputy Sutton answered as he released Mikaela's ankle and stood.

He patted Cameron on the shoulder before walking away.

Mikaela shook her head, shamed as Julie extended her foot and shook identical prison jewelry around her ankle.

"I'm sure it won't be for long. The judge will call for y'all shortly. Just sit tight," Cameron attempted to reassure.

"We got nowhere else to go," Julie said in a singsong manner, batting her eyelashes at him.

Cameron stood there, waiting. Mikaela was sure he must have had somewhere else more pressing to be. More mug shots to take, maybe, but he just stood there blinking, eyes darting between the two of them, no doubt seeing what everyone else had all her life.

The odd couple: bubbly, wholesome, ridiculously pretty Julie, with her golden-hazel eyes and peaches and cream complexion, compared to circumspect, self-serious and off-beat Mikaela, with her own handsome face but witheringly incisive gaze. The fact that one of them was white and the other was black was barely their most obvious difference.

"Someone will come for you both soon," he offered again, looking from Mikaela to Julie.

Julie bent forward, dragging her fingers through her long hair. She shook it out, then flipped it over her shoulders impatiently. A move she'd done a million times, only five times out of ten to indicate any actual frustration. Julie's eyes ran the length of Cameron, chin resting in her palms, like he was her next meal.

"I sure hope so. I know y'all don't wanna have to babysit some high school girls all day." She smiled sweetly and nudged Mikaela with her thigh and shoulder.

As usual, she was doing a far more skillful job of flirting than Mikaela could ever hope to.

Mikaela elbowed her back instead of saying whatever Julie was hinting at.

"Oh! But in a few months, we won't be in high school anymore at all," Julie added as if prompted.

"That a fact?"

"Yup, UGA for me, but this one's leaving me behind to head all the way up to New York City." Julie pouted.

"No kidding?" he said, winking at Mikaela conspiratorially.

At this point, who knew? Mikaela lamented, shrugging. She peered at her feet, investigating new grass stains on the lacings of her tennis shoes.

"Well, I honestly don't think anyone minds anyway." He rested his hands on his waist, leaning in and lowering his voice. "What you girls did was 'bout *the* most excitin' thing to happen round here in months! And at the finals too?"

His eyes widened while Mikaela winced.

"Pretty legendary, right?" Julie nudged Mikaela again, giggling.

Mikaela didn't even look when she felt his eyes on her again.

"Ah, well, let's just say, people are definitely talkin'…"

Their voices dimmed to background noise as Mikaela retreated into her own thoughts. They had done this in front of their whole community, people they knew—parents, teachers, classmates, bandmates even. She didn't even know why she had ever wanted to do this to begin with.

But hadn't she been dying to be more than J.D. Marchand's quiet, nerdy "older girl"? Known for more than just being one of those "poor girls whose mama ran off"?

Well, be careful what you wish for, she chided herself.

There was a sudden ruckus in the holding tank. Mikaela,

Julie and Cameron all looked over the short half wall that separated them from the small cells in the back.

"Well, ladies, I better get goin'," Cameron said, excusing himself up the hall.

Julie grabbed Mikaela's shoulder, hissing directly into her ear from behind. "Oooh, what was his name? I forgot to look!"

"I don't know."

"What?" Julie spun Mikaela around to face her. "You mean you just spent twenty whole minutes with that hottie and didn't get his name?"

Mikaela shook her head.

"I think he was flirting with you! You gonna ask him out?"

"I seriously doubt he was interested. And this feels like, maybe, not the right time for that, y'know?"

"Is there ever a right time for anything? You haven't been with anyone since ole What's His Face left for college." Months later, Julie still refused to use Mikaela's ex-boyfriend's name, Mitchell.

Instead, she put a hand on Mikaela's shoulder and squeezed, fingers still stained with shiny gold paint. "What, are you trying to collect cobwebs?" Julie smirked impishly, arching an eyebrow. "And why shouldn't this guy be interested? I mean, he's already seen, um, the business."

Yeah, him and everyone else in Harmon. Mikaela cringed. *Who all saw us completely naked.*

"Come on, Mike, it could be exciting!"

"After today, I think I've had enough excitement to last me a while." Mikaela leaned her head on Julie's shoulder when they sat back down.

She blushed inwardly every time she thought of the prank yet a small part of her was still so proud of their brazen action. Lots of other senior girls had said they'd take part in the big senior prank. But in the end, only *she* and Julie had actually dared. Sure, Julie was no surprise, known as cooler, louder, more confident and outspoken than most, but in the end, it was "little Mikaela" that had been right there with her. This time Mikaela was a "wild" one too. At last, Mikaela Marchand had stamped her name on this town. Just the idea of it filled her with an odd exhilaration. Like for once, she was not only free but *seen* for who she truly was, and that was not just her dad's "good," *other* daughter.

"Well, if you don't go for it, I definitely will," Julie warned.

Mikaela shrugged. She didn't know why she had even bothered to lie about not knowing Cameron's name. Julie's threat was meaningless anyway. They both knew Mikaela would never "go for it"…and Julie *certainly* would. Not that it mattered anyway—it wasn't like she had a chance. He was a gorgeous college guy. And unlike Julie, who always got much further without trying very hard, Mikaela remained too awkward and oblivious to ever even try and shoot her shot.

Julie sighed, eyes rolling like she already knew what Mikaela was thinking.

"Girls?"

They both turned at the sound. Julie's parents, The Judge and Miss Liza, stood at the end of the hall with Mikaela's father. Chaos bloomed around them as a drunk tank scuffle turned into a true brawl while their parents watched. Their faces moved from concern to anger as both girls watched helplessly.

It was absolutely the wrong moment for them to have arrived.

"Aw, shit," Julie said, finally seeing what Mikaela had foreseen hours ago.

three

Mikaela poured some lemon juice into the top of the blender. It almost overflowed with kale, spinach, cucumbers, celery and Granny Smith apples. She certainly didn't need this much, especially when she could barely drink a couple of sips before the whole tart, green concoction activated her gag reflex. Still, she pressed the button and let it go around a few more cycles before pouring it into a steel travel mug.

When she heard the footsteps of her boyfriend, Rashad, coming down the stairs, she moved faster. Filling his flask to the brim, she capped it and wiped it clean. It was ready by the time he got into the kitchen.

"Vanessa suggested I add a little ginger this time. You tell me what you think tonight."

He came to a stop on the other side of the kitchen island and just looked at her.

She did the same. Standing there in his navy scrub pants

sans top, he was, as always, magnificent. Mikaela's assistant, Suze, frequently liked to remind her Rashad was "a whole snack," meaning the smooth, caramel brown skin of his intricately carved chest glowing in the natural light streaming in from the window behind her made him magazine-cover worthy. *In other words, the man was just hot.* The fact that he was a doctor didn't hurt either.

This morning, his lean athlete's build was on full display as he made his way around the space topless, preparing to go. And when Mikaela was ready for work early, like today, she could take time to really appreciate him, like her own personal all-male revue.

Rashad glanced from the mug to Mikaela's amused face before speaking. "Is this a peace offering?" His eyebrow arched in suspicion.

"No, why?" Mikaela smiled innocently, pushing her long, brandy-colored microbraids off one shoulder. "Should it be?"

Rashad smiled back, shaking his head, but still taking the steel mug from her. He took it to his messenger bag sitting on the dining table and tucked it into the side pocket.

"So, I can't take that to mean there's been any movement on my request then?"

"Who's the lawyer here?" She laughed. "You just asked last night—can I think about it?"

"No, I insisted you take a key last night, I've been asking you to move in for months. It's like you don't care. Is it so bad that I like having you here, in my house, in my bed? That I like seeing you when I get home, and when I wake up?" Rashad dug through his bag and then looked around the table. "My scrub hat?"

"The cute one with the little black-and-white Mickeys all over it?" She pointed toward the laundry room.

"You did my laundry? Wow, you must really feel bad."

He went into the laundry room, and emerged a moment later, with both the cap and his shirt on, to her disappointment.

"No. I was up late working. That's all." Mikaela's smile fell. "I don't feel bad. Why should I feel guilty for not being ready?"

Her past was checkered with relationships that went wrong. It all fell apart quickly when things weren't just right. Her whole misadventure a couple days earlier at Cameron's gallery could have told the truth of that story.

"I—I just can't move in with you, okay? We're not there yet."

Digging through his bag, Rashad snorted. "After two years? You have an ETA on when that might be then?"

Rashad was taking it in stride. Not every man she'd dated seriously had. According to her sister, Vanessa, that was part of what made this particular one a keeper. Still, Mikaela was unable to adequately explain the origins of her hesitation even to herself.

"Fine, Mikaela." He sighed. "Look, Dr. Butler is going to a game at Barclays on Wednesday, so I told him I'd take the extra shift in—"

"Uh-uh, that's the Yankee game with the partners. You promised me you'd come."

He tapped his forehead. "That's right. Sorry. Okay, I'll tell James I can't cover him."

Mikaela exhaled, releasing a tiny, panicked breath at the prospect of attending alone.

"Quid pro quo." He smiled widely then.

"You can't be for real? Agreeing to go to a client event with me is hardly the equivalent of us moving in together!"

"I agree." He frowned. "I was talking about my mother's gospel brunch on the thirtieth."

"Sorry, of course. Yes, yes, tell your mom, I'd love to go!" Mikaela pursed her lips, feeling contrite. "In fact, I'd rather go to your mom's thing than even plan this birthday party for mine. If you're up for a trade?"

Rashad stopped in his rush around the kitchen, right in the same spot he had been before, opposite her, looking concerned.

"You and your mom..." He paused when she gave him a rueful look for retreading such stale territory so early in the morning.

"But you know I love *your* mom!" she offered, deflecting. He shook his head.

"I'll see you tonight," Rashad said, swinging the messenger bag over his head and shoulder. He rounded the island and planted their usual, perfunctory kiss goodbye on her lips before walking out.

Mikaela inspected her soiled hands and the remnants of the disgusting green smoothie sitting in the blender in front of her, then gave the contents a brief sniff.

"Ugh." She gagged.

Vanessa and her health concoctions. At least she seemed to be right about the man.

"Morning," Mikaela greeted her assistant, Suze, as she strode into her office at Wexler, Welford and Bromley, the law firm she had worked at for the past twelve years.

"Boss." Suze looked up from her computer as Mikaela walked to the wide desk in her office.

"What's this?" Mikaela asked, stopping short, touching an elaborate bouquet of pink-and-white peonies and roses perched on the edge of her desk.

The cloying scent coming off the buds curled her lips with

a creeping revulsion. As she set her satchel down, she plucked out the card stuck in one corner of it.

"It's from Mr. Kang and the folks at Seo Labs," Suze called from the other room just as Mikaela read the signature on the card. "I try to tell 'em, boss. I swear I do." She came in then and hoisted the heavy vase off Mikaela's desk. "But I thought you'd at least want to see it before I threw 'em away."

Mikaela fussed with the pins keeping her tightly bunned braids in place, unsettled with the idea of that. "You don't want it?"

"Believe it or not, I still have Mr. Milbank's freesias from last week. I know you don't like 'em or whatever, but I put that mix they come with in the water and they're still going strong at home."

The irony was, Mikaela loved flowers. She just firmly believed they were meant to be enjoyed...outside growing somewhere. But she had learned over the years, she was of the minority opinion. That said, she also knew even hothouse flowers deserved their brief moment of adoration.

"Well, don't throw 'em away... Um, just take the card out and give them to Trish. She seemed a little down after our meeting yesterday."

"Good idea. After that dressing-down she got from Mr. Chamberlain, who can blame her? I heard she cried in her office for a half hour afterward," Suze shared.

A chill ran down Mikaela's spine.

Being caught crying at work was beyond a no-no; *it was a no, not-ever.* And though some partners seemed to pride themselves on how many of the associates under their supervision they could drive to the brink, the bottom line was, you were not supposed to let them.

Not at work.

Mikaela resolved she didn't want to be like that. It was just not the kind of equity partner she planned to be.

Provided things went according to plan.

"I'll drop them off with Trish then." Suze nodded before heading down the hall. "You have a one-on-one with Chamberlain in thirty minutes. Mr. Haig is expecting a call from you this morning. Oh, and don't forget, your mom's in town. You have lunch with her at one. I made a rez at Citron Cucina on Mott Street. She already has the details."

Mikaela smiled to herself, watching the young woman go. The deep purple ombré tips of her otherwise jet-black bob shone under the lights as she walked. Mikaela shook her head at yet another in the ever-changing, highly chic hairstyles Suze wore. It was one of the small ways Suze perpetually tested the firm's hard-won acceptance of the Crown Act and asserted her individuality in their overwhelmingly staid environment. And it was one of the myriad things Mikaela absolutely adored about her assistant.

Suzukea Williams was the perfect example of what a little faith, a smidgen of nurturing and a lot of guidance could cultivate. Suze had never been an executive assistant before, let alone a legal one, when Mikaela hired her. Fresh from undergrad with a bright red faux-hawk and a skintight leather skirt, she was not anyone's first choice from the pool of possible applicants. But with her formidable young mind, Mikaela had seen the proverbial spark of genius in Suze. And since then, she'd had the pleasure of watching Suze take on new challenges and excel. As another young, black woman in the firm, Suze's continued success filled Mikaela with an intense sense of pride. It convinced her that her investment in the young woman had been the right thing.

Mikaela didn't have children but watching Suze and the other young associates that she had mentored through their

early years at the firm find their footing was immensely grati-
fying. It was something she planned to further cultivate when
she got her promotion. She had a whole plan for their anemic so-called Diversity, Equity and Inclusion Program that
she was eager to unveil as soon as she got the news. Because
particularly when the "kids" became as competent and capable as Suze proved to be, she imagined the satisfaction she
felt was at least similar to a parent's.

What a parent was supposed to be like, at least.

Unlike her own mother.

four

"The party can start now!" a loud voice announced, drawing eyes to the speaker.

Mikaela exhaled as she saw her sister, Vanessa, making her way through the nearby tables of other diners. Normally, in a trendy, downtown restaurant like this one, Mikaela would have said something about making a scene. She was too relieved now.

Indifferent to the eyes that had followed her to their table, Vanessa swept her long, honey-blond locs over one shoulder and bent to kiss their mother.

"Nessa! What a nice surprise! You look beautiful, darlin'!" Her mother offered up her cheek for the kiss, caressing the side of Vanessa's face. She looked over both her daughters. "Such beautiful young women."

The words were almost like her complimenting herself.

As much as it annoyed Mikaela to admit it, she and her sister took after their mother. For Mikaela, it was like looking into dual mirrors. They all had the same big, lovely brown eyes, pronounced cheekbones, full lips and toothy smiles.

But where Mikaela had her father's wider nose, Vanessa lay claim to Natalee's pert one and amber brown coloring, shades lighter than Mikaela's own. And today with Natalee's taut, flawless skin accented by a relaxed bob, dyed a chic golden brown to complement her coloring, she and Vanessa were more like twins than mother and daughter.

Mikaela checked her watch. Vanessa had made excellent time. Mikaela sent an SOS when they picked up their menus. The food hadn't even come yet.

Vanessa sat between them.

"Sweetheart, what are you doing here?"

"You're in town!" Vanessa glanced at Mikaela. "And I, uh, just wanted to hang out with my two favorite ladies."

Natalee Franklin eyed both of her daughters.

"You know, I've always wanted to be one of those 'ladies who lunch!'" Vanessa insisted.

"Aren't they going to miss you at school?" Natalee clasped her hands together in her lap, skewering her daughter.

"Ehh." Vanessa waved that off. "It's high school. If the kids can play hooky, surely I, as their teacher, can too. At least for a period."

Natalee's eyebrows knitted together. She looked to Mikaela. "She didn't actually skip a class, right?"

Mikaela hadn't given much thought to Vanessa's circumstance, just begging for the rescue.

"Course not, relax, Mama. I have what's called a prep period, which is basically a free period. Added to my lunch break, I'm as free as a bird for the next hundred minutes!"

Natalee exhaled, satisfied.

"Interesting that you weren't concerned if *I had* two hours to spend at lunch today!" Mikaela snarked.

Vanessa cleared her throat, tapping Mikaela lightly with a foot under the table.

"Don't be ridiculous, I spoke with your assist—"

"Clearing it with Suze is *not* the same as—"

"You know what *I* saw the other day?" Vanessa announced, voice raised, speaking over them both. Her mouth curled into a smile that made Mikaela suddenly wary.

"What?" Their mother dragged her eyes away from Mikaela.

"Cam's picture!"

"What picture?"

"Oh, you mean Kaela hasn't mentioned the giant photo of her up in Times Square?"

"No!" Natalee glanced between her daughters, eyes widening.

"It's nothing." Mikaela played with the condensation on the outside of her water goblet with a finger.

"It's huge! *Literally!*"

"Something for the firm?" their mother asked excitedly.

"No, not for the firm—"

"It's one of Cameron's pictures of Mikaela." Vanessa smirked.

"It is not *of me!*"

"Wait." Natalee had lost the plot, looking back and forth. "Who's Cameron again?"

Vanessa closed her eyes, pressing her lips together as Mikaela bore holes into the side of her sister's face.

"He was a boy from back in Georgia," Mikaela answered.

Natalee frowned. Still, no bells ringing...of course.

"The white boy," Vanessa clarified.

Mikaela choked on her sip of seltzer.

"Well, wait...that hardly tells you anything back then," Vanessa amended. *"The blond one."*

As if that would help illuminate things any further for

their mother. Natalee never paid attention to Mikaela's relationships.

"Oh! You mean, the one Luke and I met when you were in college? He was nice. Good-looking too, if I recall. Somehow you always end up having the most handsome beaux, Kaela. It's a shame none of them stick."

Vanessa winced, stifling a laugh. Mikaela took a deep breath through her nose.

"Why must you act like there's some endless parade of men? Rashad and I have been together for two years!"

"I wasn't acting like anything, sweetheart." Her mother forced a smile and a light laugh, smoothing out a section of tablecloth in front of her. "My goodness, can't say a word around you girls."

"Why am *I* in it?" Vanessa chimed in then.

"I just wish you would stop acting like my bedroom's some revolving door!" Mikaela spoke over them both. "I don't know, perhaps, had a stable home life been modeled for me…"

Mikaela deliberately aimed low, but Natalee was an old pro. She simply took a sip from her gimlet before she spoke again.

"Ah yes, I know, I know. *It's all my fault.* I'm the reason neither of you can seem to settle down. Why you both haven't found love. Well, in my own defense, *again*, I did not leave you, I left your father. I've supported you girls your entire lives. I just made the decision to leave John in order to live *my life*. And I understood my choice wouldn't win me any parenting awards and that people—*apparently including my own daughters*—would judge me for it, though, let's face it, society would *never* judge a man…"

Mikaela breathed a heavy sigh, rolling her eyes. She'd

heard her mother jump up on her faux-feminist soapbox before.

Vanessa just grinned, intent on being wholly unhelpful.

"A great regret of mine is that you're such a people-pleaser, Kaela. Just another thing you can blame me for, I suppose. But remember this—when your focus is on pleasing everyone else, you'll inevitably end up pleasing no one, yourself included."

"I don't even understand what that means," Mikaela said, looking at her sister again. "I'm happy with my life."

"Don't look at me." Vanessa shrugged. "According to my therapist, my problem is the fact that I lost my virginity to my closeted best friend and, *my brief marriage notwithstanding*, that's *still* the most honest, loving and equitable relationship I've ever managed to have."

Mikaela rolled her eyes again, fighting a snicker as Vanessa crossed her eyes and stuck out her tongue.

Natalee just continued on as if the girls weren't speaking. Truth was, this was all pretty typical for the three of them.

"All it means is, I see you take care of everyone else. Ever since you were a child. You tie yourself in knots to be perfect, but no one gets the real you. You never let anyone even remotely close enough! That's why Rashad won't last. Like the man before him. Or the one that'll be after. You're quick to lure them in with all that sweet, sweet honey you've got, but there's a bear trap around your heart."

Everyone sat up straight, falling quiet. Even Vanessa, who had scarcely been serious, took on a more solemn expression, her arms dropping off the table.

When he came, the waiter placed two plates in front of them.

"Can I get you something for yourself?" he asked Vanessa.

"Just a drink, please. What she's having." Vanessa pointed at Natalee's gimlet.

"Sugar, aren't you going back to class?" she asked.

"Right, make that a screwdriver."

"And you're sure I can't get you anything else?" the waiter confirmed.

"I'll just pick off their plates."

"Pick off hers." Mikaela gestured toward their mother. "Shockingly, I'm not feeling all that *generous*."

"That's fine, darling. I couldn't possibly eat it all anyway!" Natalee said, long impervious to Mikaela's daggers. "I think I might have put on a pound or two. Can you even imagine? Anyway, we're here to talk about my party…"

Natalee continued chattering as Mikaela stabbed at her lunch with her fork.

Stewing.

five

THEN
May 2002

"Take your sister."

Mikaela and Vanessa sat at the breakfast counter. They regarded each other, then their father.

"No," they replied in unison then smirked.

"You don't want to go?" J.D. Marchand asked his youngest, pulling his Professional Taster cooking apron off and tossing it on the counter.

"I'm good," Vanessa declared, resuming with the buttons on her Game Boy.

Mikaela sighed, shrugging at her father. That was just fine with her.

"You're in those doggone games too much," their father chided. "Sitting inside the house is gonna rot your brain and rob you of your pretty color."

Mikaela nibbled at a toast triangle.

At that moment, Julie slid open the glass door from the

backyard, walking in wearing her bikini top, shorts and flip-flops. She'd come across the yard from her house with a tote bag and towel slung over her shoulder.

"I'm here to spring you, kid!" she announced, sliding the door shut behind her. "Your parole came through." She turned. "Mornin', Mr. Marchand."

"Juliette," he said, clearing the dishes from the table.

Julie hustled over to him and stole a couple of pieces of bacon off Vanessa's discarded plate before it all went into the garbage disposal.

"I thought your parents were vegetarians now? Isn't that why your garden now needs an extra foot into my east yard?"

"Mmm." Julie nodded, munching on the crunchy strip. "Yup, they are, on account of my dad's cholesterol, but me and Gabe aren't."

"Nessa! Is that where all my deli-sliced ham has been going? To feeding your little boyfriend?" Mr. Marchand questioned his younger daughter.

"Don't leave me!" Vanessa slid off the stool. "Lemme go get my towel, I'll meet you guys outside!"

The abandoned portable game system was the only evidence she'd been there.

Mr. Marchand shook his head.

Julie shot Mikaela a look then eyed him.

"Daddy, don't make me take her!" Mikaela pleaded as he washed the dishes. "She doesn't listen to me and she doesn't ever wanna do what we wanna do! She's just gonna stand around and scowl."

"She didn't have a problem participating in all y'all's foolishness last fall."

The extended plea Mikaela had planned ended abruptly.

"Uh-huh. That's what I thought."

Julie picked an apple out of the basket at the center of the island and buffed it on her shorts, stuffing it in her mouth to stay conspicuously silent. She made a face at Mikaela, to which Mikaela shrugged back in frustration.

"Um, I'm gonna go make sure Vanessa picks out an *actual* bathing suit and not just that Oasis T-shirt she likes," Julie announced.

When she was on their creaky steps, Mr. Marchand spoke in the lowest registers of his voice. Mikaela already knew what was coming.

He turned to her. "I don't know what goes on in Mr. and Mrs. Robertson's house but in *here*, you have got to act better because you know better! They expect her to cut up, and when she does, they think it's cute. They laugh and call it 'high jinks.' But they look down on you for the very same thing. You have three more months until you're off to college. I will not let that little girl lead you astray."

Mikaela bit her lip to refrain from asking who the mysterious "they" always were. Because she knew, as she'd always known, for as long as her family had lived in this town.

"If making you drag your little sister around all summer is what I have to do to ensure that there will be no more of this nonsense, then that's what's gonna happen, y'hear me?"

Mikaela nodded.

"If you prove to me that you can conduct yourself with some sense, I might change my mind…" He trailed off for a moment before beginning again. "Julie is a nice girl, but she has neither the sense God gave her *nor* aspirations like you do—"

"She's going to UGA."

Her father glared at Mikaela for interrupting. Her mouth snapped shut.

He snorted. "We'll see how far that goes. That girl has Pampered Housewife written over every inch of her. But like

I said, *you girl*, you have plans. Don't make me regret having ever let her into my house."

The sound of footsteps rushing back downstairs ended their conversation. Mr. Marchand returned to the sink.

"Julie." Mr. Marchand wiped his hands on a dishcloth. "You havin' dinner with us tonight?"

Julie nodded. "Can Gabe too? Mama has a women's auxiliary meeting."

"I don't see why not? Apparently, I've been feeding him anyway."

"I'm outside," Vanessa announced from the mouth of the kitchen before disappearing.

"Let's jet," Julie said.

Mikaela gathered her gear, stuffing it into the tote sitting on the table.

"You have some of that sunscreen, Mike?"

"She can borrow mine, Mr. M," Julie called over her shoulder, walking toward the front door.

Mikaela placed a quick kiss on her father's cheek before following.

"You heard what I said?"

"Yes, sir." Mikaela nodded as she left.

The sun was almost directly overhead when Mikaela and Julie finally reached the lake with Vanessa trailing farther behind. The sand burned as they made their way across the shore to the exact spot Julie desired. Mikaela and Julie spread their towels out and sat down.

"Good spot. I thought we might have been too late to get one," Mikaela said, relaxing on her own towel.

"Oh, everybody's stopping at Meg's first now. She's giving out two-for-one shakes till Fourth of July."

"What?" Mikaela sat up. "Then why didn't we go there first?"

"Calm down," Julie said. "'Cause I wanted a good spot, duh?"

Julie kicked off her flip-flops, scooted out of her shorts and tossed her sunscreen bottle at Mikaela. "But don't worry, I have someone delivering some for us."

"Of course you do. Who?"

"Corey…or Rory, one of the two. They seem to think we're dating or something." Julie shrugged.

"One of them?"

"Or both…" Julie smiled as Mikaela sighed.

It was like she'd been out of the loop for decades. Mikaela's grounding for the streaking had been epic, like her dad's wrath. And significantly longer than Julie's. She missed her last prom. She lost the chance to be valedictorian, disqualified from giving the customary commencement address. *She didn't care since her grades ended up making her the valedictorian on paper anyway.* But there was also the matter of community service—*being a member of the chamber of commerce's beautification program.* It had eaten up every weekend of her final semester of high school, walking around town in a neon orange vest, picking up trash and cleaning graffiti for three hundred hours or roughly seventy-five days, whichever came first. Julie's father worked a cushy deal where Julie just spent her court-mandated time working for his colleagues in the courthouse instead.

He had offered Mikaela the same opportunity, but Mr. Marchand shot it down immediately. Naturally, because "the purpose of punishment is to *punish*."

The only superior benefit proved to be that while Julie would be working off her hours clean through the summer; Mikaela was already free. Still, the end result was that this was Mikaela's first genuine outing in months. She was like a bear coming out of hibernation. Everything old was new all over again.

"Don't you worry about them. Now, rub it in," Julie mocked, eyeing the tube of lotion. "I don't want your dad hollerin' at me."

She always gave Mikaela a hard time about using sunblock as if a black girl with a tan was somehow a scientific impossibility.

"This is wack." Vanessa plopped herself down in the sand on the other side of Mikaela, kicking it up. "No one's here yet."

The grains splashed up on Mikaela mingling with the greasy lotion she'd just applied.

"Damn it, Nessa!" Mikaela said, attempting in vain to wipe it off but just adding more.

"What? This?" Vanessa deliberately flipped more onto Mikaela's towel.

Mikaela cried out, slapping Vanessa on the shoulder.

"Ow!" Vanessa rubbed her arm as if wounded. "Calm down, you nut!"

"Mike, just go wash it off." Julie sighed, seeing Mikaela was unusually upset. "You okay?"

"Yeah." Mikaela nodded. "I just want to read my book in peace."

"Only you would come to the beach to read a book. *Loser.*" Vanessa made an L against her forehead with her thumb and forefinger.

"This isn't a beach. You see an ocean somewhere, bitch?"

"Whoa, whoa! Time out!" Julie sat up. "What the heck, M.?"

Mikaela shook the loose sand off as she stood, glaring at Vanessa, who ignored her.

"What is up with you two?"

"Ask her, I'm just sitting here." Vanessa shrugged.

"Nothing," Mikaela said simultaneously.

Mr. Marchand had decided that even though Vanessa didn't have to participate in the court-mandated community service part of Mikaela's punishment, she should have to suffer for giving aid and comfort to Mikaela's little act of rebellion. *She had to give it to him; the man knew how to turn allies into enemies.* For months now, Mikaela and Vanessa's only reprieve from each other was their respective school days in high school and middle school.

Both had hoped this would finally be their first day of liberty, from the house and each other... No such luck.

"I'm just gonna go rinse this off," Mikaela said.

"Maybe you should cool down too."

Mikaela walked to the shore's edge and put a foot into the murky blue-green water. The one good thing about having been grounded was missing those first few days after the lake opened for the season in late April when it was still ice-cold. She looked out at the swimmers' platform over two hundred feet away near the center of the large lake.

The Platform was a summer tradition.

Mikaela remembered the numerous summers as a child when her only goal, the same as half the children in her town, had been just to swim there and back. Followed by summers when it was the coolest place in the world to be. It would be so full of kids that there was no place to stand and the unfortunate children and teens who were last to reach just had to stay there, treading water and hovering around, hoping someone would eventually leave.

For that reason, Mikaela learned to be a strong swimmer, and then a fast one.

Julie never had to worry about that. Guys used to jump in the lake just to give her a place to sit or stand.

Mikaela had always had to earn her place.

She dove into the lake and swam leisurely to the platform. Because it was early yet, there was still plenty of room. She and her friends had largely ceded the struggle to be first to the platform to the next generation of kids coming up. Still, it hadn't stopped her from occasionally swimming over just to prove to herself she still could.

Mikaela pulled herself out of the water using the metal bar and stood on the old, algae-caked, greenish-brown, wooden platform. It bobbed slightly on a gentle current but was largely stationary, as permanent a fixture where it floated as it was in the imaginations of the community's youth. All who spent their summers at Lake Shelburne knew the location and nature of the platform like they knew their own home addresses. As she stood there, feeling oddly triumphant, Mikaela looked around at the still water and lush green tree line on the opposite side. A massive and sheer rock face behind the trees made the lake a crescent shape and provided it with excellent acoustics. At night, if you put a radio on the platform, the music could fill the entire shoreline. Mikaela had attended many a nighttime party organized just like that. She'd miss that when she went to school that fall. Pondering her future, she sat down on the edge of the platform.

"Don't jump."

Someone stood behind her. She peered all the way up his tall, broad body until she saw his face. It was the guy from the sheriff's station months ago, Cameron. Shielding her eyes with her palm, Mikaela could just barely make out his face framed by the sun behind him. He was shirtless, his light hair slicked back by the water, wearing swimming trunks and carrying a strange boxlike contraption hanging by a rope around his neck.

"It's a camera in a homemade waterproof case before you ask."

"So, they have you taking mug shots out here now too?" Mikaela squinted up at him, looking through one eye.

"Only of the usual suspects," he said, easing down beside her. "Now, say cheese."

"Ha ha." Mikaela moved her legs in the water, peering at her toes floating in the clearish green liquid.

"No, the platform is the best place to get good shots of the lake and its wildlife. Human and otherwise."

As if to prove his point, a cliff swallow flew close overhead, buzzing around the platform. They both watched it go.

"You keeping out of trouble?" he asked a moment later.

She looked at him, not appreciating his humor. "Model citizen."

"Glad to hear it, the aim is to avoid recidivism."

"No need to worry about that. I'm outta here soon."

"So still New York–bound then?"

Mikaela was surprised he still remembered it months later. "Uh, yeah."

"See, told ya. Uga's never wrong."

"I guess." She laughed.

When there was a brief silence, Cameron opened the box around his neck and took an old camera out. "I'm a photographer," he announced.

A rectangular box with two vertical lenses, the camera looked like an antique, just like the case itself, which was a weathered brown wood. The box interior, from Mikaela's vantage point, was lined with some sort of rubber.

"My granddaddy's old Rolleiflex," Cameron offered, again unbidden. "Then my dad's, now mine."

"I thought you worked at the sheriff's station?"

"That's just so I can eat and stuff…you know, live." He shielded his lens from the glare coming off the water with his hand.

"Your livelihood. Got it. But this is where your heart is."

"Yeah, but as my uncle Steve likes to say, 'you can't eat *pictures* of hamburgers.' Hence the day job." His expression flattened as if beaten down by just repeating the words.

"Nice uncle… Wait, Steve? Steve Davenport? Sheriff Davenport is your uncle?"

He nodded, watching Mikaela and angling the camera toward her. "Well, he's really my mom's second cousin."

"Guess nepotism is alive and well in Harmon."

He laughed. "Yeah, I guess so…fortunately or unfortunately."

He managed a lopsided smile that seemed to encompass his lukewarm feelings on the matter.

It was still a nice smile.

"I haven't seen you around lately," he said as he snapped off a couple of shots without even looking through the viewfinder, cupping the camera in his hands in front of his chest and rolling a crank on its side.

"Well, you know, streaking naked through the regional football finals can kinda put a dent in your social calendar for a while."

At least for some people. She looked out at the distant spot then, where Julie held court on the shore.

"And getting arrested for it can sort of kill it, you know how that is."

"I do," he chuckled.

There was a click as she noticed where his camera was pointed, at a dragonfly that had alighted on the tip of her toe, floating just above the waterline. It flitted on as she dropped her foot back into the water.

"Wait, you had before?" She asked as his previous words dawned on her.

"I had what, before?"

"Seen me around?" A half smile played on her lips.

"Uh, um…" He gave an awkward truncated chuckle. "Ah, just a figure of speech."

"Well, I've never seen you around before either."

"We just moved here. I'm from Larkspur, over on the other side of Mercer County. But this is where the job was. I live down on Orchard now."

"I'm on Magnolia. We're practically neighbors! I guess I'll have to make you a pecan pie."

"Really?" His eyebrows rose.

"No, not really. You're across town…and I don't bake." She laughed, shaking her head. "You really are new, huh?"

"Very. I'm actually in school getting my bachelor's in fine arts."

"Yeah, over at UGA, I remember," she admitted as his eyebrows rose a little more. "But a degree in fine arts only to come back and work for your play uncle in Harmon? That's kinda weird."

His face fell a little.

Mikaela had been told before she could have a careless tongue…and here it was, right on schedule, like the Atlanta-bound Greyhound.

He cleared his throat. "My mama got sick. So, I needed to be able to work *and* commute to school. Athens is still seventy miles away but closer than being in Larkspur."

"Oh wow. I'm so sorry."

He shook his head. "It's okay, she's in remission. She lives here with me. I mean, we live together, I guess." He chuck-led again, more strained this time.

They both looked out at the shore. It was filling up.

"You guys liking our fun little town so far?" Mikaela re-sumed, with her usual twinge of sarcasm.

"Yeah, we are," he answered with an odd earnestness that made Mikaela instantly feel guilty.

"It definitely has its charms." Their eyes met as he grinned.

Mikaela cleared her throat, focusing her gaze back out onto the water and the people floating around a few yards away.

"She works at the flower shop on Main, her name is Anne," he added out of the blue. "My mother, I mean. If you ever happen in there."

"I'm not big on cut flowers, but you know, good to know," she said, tapping her temple.

Cameron looked around and took another few pictures, adjusting his lenses between each snap.

"You think you got any good shots today?" Mikaela asked a few minutes later just for something to say.

More people were swimming up to the platform now and it was beginning to fill.

"A few. I like water, and I like watching how everyone interacts with the water, near the water. So, I'll take these and see what I see."

Cameron scanned the platform as people popped up on all sides of it, pulling themselves out of the lake all around them. He took a couple of shots as they did. Finally, he low-ered his camera, his eyes settling back on her.

"And of those, maybe I'll actually be happy with one. Gotta develop it all to tell."

"*Develop?* You're still using film? I hear everything is gonna be totally digital in a couple of years."

His eyes brightened at her words. "Maybe they will, but I won't. My dad used film. Film is my medium too. Plus, I'm a simple guy and digital sounds too complicated."

Somehow, instead of making him sound like a technophobe, his declaration was thoughtful, principled. There was depth there; he would require further consideration.

"Yeah…and think of all the development labs that would go under if everyone up and went digital," she concurred. "Plus, how ya gonna be the next Ansel Adams without real film, right?"

He smiled slowly, cocking his head to the side.

Mikaela didn't bother to mention that Adams and Annie Leibovitz were the only photographers she knew by name. It pleased her just to watch the corners of his mouth rise as they looked into each other's eyes. Then he looked up at something behind her.

"Your shake is melting!" Julie appeared over Mikaela's head, dripping fresh lake water onto her. She sat down heavily in the small space between Mikaela and Cameron, slapping Mikaela on the thigh with her wet palm while doing it. "You want to go over to the farm tonight? The girls are having a party. Their dad's away overnight… Cor and Ror are bringing a keg."

Mikaela shook her head.

"Hiya! You didn't hear any of that, right?" Julie said, turning to finally acknowledge Cameron sitting there.

"As long as no cows get tipped, I have nothing to tell my boss." Cameron gave a Boy Scout salute and pulled his legs out of the water, standing.

"In that case, you could always join us," Julie sang melodiously, flipping her hair and unintentionally lashing Mikaela in the face with it.

Mikaela spit Julie's wet hair out of her mouth, peeling some of it off her shoulder.

"Uh, I think I might have aged out of high school keggers a couple of years back."

As Julie flirted more and more shamelessly, they became the definition of "three's a crowd," although technically, there had to be about twenty or thirty people on and around the platform by then. When she had a guy in her sights, Julie just turned it on—*whatever it was*—and Mikaela tried to steer clear as she cast her spell. Generally, guys never knew what hit them. And Mikaela couldn't warn them, having fallen for it herself long ago. Now, whether Cameron knew it yet or not, he had made Julie's hit list.

Mikaela's expression gently collapsed in on itself like a day-blooming flower at dusk.

Normally she didn't care, but for some reason, being a third wheel was just a bit too much today. She wondered whether Julie was embarrassing herself now or if she had been embarrassing herself earlier with her pathetically inept version of flirtation. Try as she might, Mikaela never did understand how that worked or how to do it right. Although as she watched Julie work expertly now, the answer seemed clear to Mikaela: she'd been the one to mess it up.

Julie's laugh was lilting, her eyes wide and expressive, engaged. "No waaay, you can't be older than, what do you think, Mike? Eighteen? Nineteen?"

Mikaela glanced up as Julie elbowed her.

Then with a shrug, she returned to her feet in the turbid water. *Julie always does this.* Pushing or prodding Mikaela to assert herself, be bolder more like she was. As if Mikaela wasn't aware that there could only ever be one Julie Robertson.

Besides, Mikaela's comfort zone was where she had always been…comfortable.

"I don't know, thirty," Mikaela posited, tossing the words over her shoulder though she knew Julie had to be closer to the truth.

Cameron had looked like a baby from the first moment she laid eyes on him. As likely to be in her and Julie's old homeroom as in his third year of college.

"Close, I'm twenty-one," he said with a chuckle.

"See? You don't age out of a good rager for another couple of years, at least." Julie pushed.

"Ah…" He looked from Julie to Mikaela again. "Still don't think so. But, um, have fun, ladies."

Mikaela wiggled her toes, focusing on that, pulling her foot out of the water to inspect it.

Julie flipped her hair again; being nearly dry it bounced off the side of Mikaela's face this time. "Well, it's at the old Brown farm, if you change your— Hey!" Julie squeaked in indignation.

Mikaela turned just as Cameron lowered his camera. He put it back into the box hanging around his neck and snapped it shut.

"Don't you have to, I don't know, ask my permission first? I didn't say you could take that picture!"

Julie's mouth complained but Mikaela could tell from her tone she was still flirting.

"Can I at least see it when you develop it?" Julie was absolutely transparent always.

"Sure," he said, but a roguish smile played at his lips. He glanced at Mikaela with a brief wink.

She shook her head, grinning at her feet.

Then Cameron took a step off the platform holding his camera box and sinking like a stone.

Julie gasped…as if dozens of primarily boys hadn't departed in the exact same melodramatic manner for a million summers before.

"So, I was asking if you got his name this time?" Julie asked after they both watched for a moment in silence.

Again, for reasons she couldn't yet identify, Mikaela just shrugged.

A minute later, as Julie waited breathlessly, Cameron and his box popped up a few yards away and he swam all the way back to shore using a strong, elegant backstroke.

six

"You aren't angry, right?" Rashad asked loudly through the phone so Mikaela could hear him over the sound of a cheering crowd inside the stadium.

The game had started as she sat in a town car outside waiting for him. She bit the side of her nail looking out of the lowered window.

"How can I be?" Mikaela took the phone off speaker as she finally stepped out of the car. "You save the lives of toddlers. What am I, heartless?"

Mikaela stood on the concrete sidewalk; the massive edifice that was Yankee Stadium loomed above her. The numerous championship pennants lining the stadium floated gently in the breeze.

"I know you needed me there, honey." Rashad's voice dipped, mirroring her disappointment.

Even though this event had been on his calendar for weeks, he still had to cancel in the end anyway. It wasn't new, just disappointing. Tonight, Mikaela was supposed to close the deal that would have her firm represent the North American interests of a gigantic multinational media conglomerate. One she had courted and wooed away from their current representation. Now, she was walking in all alone.

"I'm so, so sorry," he said as her shoulders fell a little.

"Rashad, Rashad, it's—it's okay. No sweat." She hustled up the stairs to the landing of the suite elevator.

"Really?" Rashad asked. "So, I'll check you later?"

"Definitely," she reassured him. "In fact, if you get out of surgery before midnight, come over."

Mikaela checked her appearance quickly in the glass doors. Her braids were still in their tight, daytime chignon and her makeup was still light, but she'd traded the simple shift dress from work for a sleeveless chartreuse, silk jumper cinched at the waist and covered by a black blazer for a business-glamorous look. She was definitely not dressed for the average day at the ballpark, but this wasn't one of those anyway. Now however, she worried that the chunky gold necklace and matching belt she wore made it look like she was trying a bit too hard. It was one thing to look like a million dollars on the arm of a handsome doctor, a little much for watching the game with her boss and colleagues in The Bronx.

"How can you tell the difference between a good lawyer and bad one?"

Mikaela shrugged, baring her teeth in a decent approximation of a smile. In law school, she and her classmates had traded lawyer jokes as a pastime; she doubted there was one she hadn't already heard.

"With a bad lawyer, a case might drag on for several years. But a good one knows how to make it last even longer!"

The group of men standing with Mikaela all laughed. Her

boss and the managing partner of the firm, Art Chamberlain, guffawed the loudest.

"Aw, Mr. Proctor, good lawyers are a dime a dozen. They know the law." Mikaela smiled, taking a sip of her beer. "But great lawyers…"

Mikaela paused and the men around her hung on her next words.

"…*know the judge.*" Her grin grew as they all roared around her.

Her prospect, Burt Proctor, raised his glass to her as the Yankees scored another run, putting them in the lead. In the seats just outside the doors, the group watching the game erupted. Several men and the few other women in the suite jumped to their feet.

"A lawyer is in the elevator," Mikaela began, unspooling her showstopper. "And someone runs for the door. Unusually, something tells him to hold it. Who gets on? It's Satan…"

Mikaela's eyes swept the room, absently glancing through the glass doorway to the box seats outside. The game happened in the diamond beneath them as the men of her group followed her words carefully.

Schmoozing was one of the many acquired gifts Mikaela was most proud of having developed. Along with a thicker skin and a supposedly sunny disposition, she'd learned to tell a great joke with charm. And this particular joke, she could tell in her sleep. Even Art leaned back on his heels smiling in anticipation. But this time, her voice caught. She glanced at the doors again, sure she had made some sort of mistake.

"And?" Art's second-in-command, a brownnoser named Todd Hoover, prompted her.

She narrowed her gaze on him before plastering a closed-mouth smile back onto her face for Mr. Proctor and his associates.

"*And* he's thankful that the lawyer held the door. 'Very few people are that considerate anymore,' the Devil says. So, he makes the lawyer an offer. He says, 'I will make you a winner—every argument, every brief, every case, for the rest of your life. Your clients will adore you, your colleagues will worship you and you'll be rich beyond your imaginings. But, in return, you must give me your soul, the souls of your wife and children, parents, grandparents and all of your friends...'"

She turned to the outdoor box again, scanning the faces for familiarity...*until she saw him.*

"Uh-oh, I feel like I know where this is going," Proctor said, smiling at the other members of their group.

Mikaela tried to stay focused, but she'd been thrown off.

"And?" Art asked when she paused a second time.

"I'm sorry." Mikaela shook her head, phony laugh at the ready, trying desperately to stay on track. "The lawyer thought about it for a moment, then asked, 'Okay...but wait, what's the catch?'"

The men surrounding her broke out in another round of laughs. Mikaela grinned, pleased to have made it through, but still felt distressed. Art's recent Aruba tan kept him a sort of reddish color that threw her off in gauging his feelings. Usually when he was concerned or excited, he turned a little pink in the cheeks.

"Mike, you okay? You seem off."

"Maybe she has her money on Baltimore," Todd snickered.

"I'd never bet against the home team," Mikaela remarked, skewering Todd with a look that said *shut up.* "Gentlemen, I'm going to refresh my drink and check out the hors d'oeuvres." She raised her half-full beer cup.

But before she stepped away, she leaned into Todd's shoulder, for his ears only. "Nice try. And I can see why you'd get confused."

"Oh yeah, why?" Todd gave a smug smile, glancing at the other men.

"'Cause if I added you to all forty of the Orioles, I'd still just have forty-one men that couldn't do shit."

As her perennial competition, she understood where Todd's motivation to undermine her was coming from. *She did that too.* Always checking for cracks in Todd's smarmy, mediocre but practiced facade to chip away at. Still, it didn't stop it from being annoying as hell.

"Yeah okay, Mike," he chuckled uneasily, guiltily glancing around. He smirked when he knew no one else had overheard.

She gripped her clutch under her arm as she walked away. Mikaela despised conflict but years in this field and the boys' club at her firm had taught her the hard way to give as good as she got. Still, her stomach roiled and hands shook as she struggled to keep them still. Mikaela turned toward her group still speaking companionably together. She knew she wouldn't be able to hide out at the bar long before she had to reassert herself. It wasn't just that Todd couldn't be trusted—she knew in her heart Art couldn't be either. She always had to be on point.

Just then, there was another cheer outside, drawing her attention again to the window. Through the glass partition separating the box lounge from the box's stadium seats, the man on the other side was now clear. And definitely who she thought he was. Being this close was like jumping from the frying pan into the fire. If he just turned, he would see her too. Clear as day.

Cameron Murphy stood right there as a girl—*maybe even*

the one from the gallery—beside him cheered wildly, high-fiving him.

Mikaela scowled as the unbidden thought came to her.

He didn't even like the Yankees.

No, not only that, he hated them. He was a proud Georgia boy and Braves fan.

As his neighbors cheered, Cameron's eyes passed over the seats around them, then into the suite just as Mikaela had dreaded, until they fell upon her. It was like slow motion when their eyes met. Then the car wreck. His eyes squinted before widening in shock.

Mikaela spun to face the bar. "I'm gonna need something stronger than this." She pointed at her abandoned cup of beer. "Bourbon? Can you do that here?"

"Absolutely." The bartender nodded with a grin.

A minute later, Mikaela glanced over her shoulder again. Cameron was beginning the near-glacial shuffle past all the other people seated in his row.

"Could we make it a double please? Neat." Mikaela put the plastic cup to her lips as soon as the bartender handed it over.

"Imagine seeing you here of all places." Cameron cast a shadow over her. His baritone, as mellow as the bourbon, was a familiar stab in the heart. "For the second time in a week, wow."

Mikaela paused midswallow, her eyes tracing Cameron head to foot as he reclined against the bar. He wore a gunmetal-blue dress shirt that disastrously—*for her*—matched his eyes. It was open at the collar and neatly tucked into a pair of dark slacks. He was not dressed for the ball game any more than she was.

Throwing an elbow onto the bar, he motioned to the bartender with a finger, his face breaking into a full-out grin.

It was that smile she had dreaded most.

"I don't know how I missed that you were here." He wagged the finger at her, tutting.

"I wasn't hiding. I didn't see you either." Mikaela glanced around, making sure no one was watching.

She backed up as he straightened to his full height.

"Guess you were always a little bit wily though, weren't you?" He leaned in slightly to intimate. "Hard to pin down."

That was a jab.

She sighed. "Let's dispense with—with whatever it is you think you're doing right now. New York is a very big city. So, I'm asking you nicely, please stay away from my side of it."

Cameron raised his arms, palms up, falling back as if in defense, before reaching for a beer the bartender pushed his way.

"Now, excuse me, *please*."

For some reason, she waited for any sort of response from him. But only his eyebrows and those piercing, frosty blue eyes of his seemed to react at all. He didn't even move or speak when, with a sigh, she just took her drink and walked away.

Still, a flush from the encounter heated Mikaela.

"Mikaela? Are you okay?" Mr. Proctor asked as she rejoined the group.

"I'm fine," she said, lips curving into an unconvincing smile. "What were we saying?"

But as much as Mikaela wanted to stay focused, she just couldn't. She'd been able to maintain her composure, seeing Cameron there, completely out of any reasonable context after not having laid eyes on him for over fifteen years. So, she supposed, she was doing well, reaction-wise. But having Cameron there, mingling among her coworkers and others—*for reasons he hadn't even bothered to say*—rattled her.

"You know what, gentlemen?" Mikaela spoke up after standing there for a long while, only halfway engaged in the conversations happening around her. "I'm sorry but I think I might have to duck out a little early. I know I should hang around till at least the top of the ninth to support our boys, but I have faith the Yanks will pull this one out without me."

A few of the men chuckled.

Art frowned with concern. "You sure?"

Mikaela nodded. "Do you mind?"

In unison, they all shook their heads, murmuring various consolations, the way men did when they didn't know what was wrong with a woman.

She took Mr. Proctor's hands in her own, giving them a farewell squeeze. "We'll talk tomorrow. Enjoy the rest of the game." She smiled as everyone said their good nights.

"Do you need me to call a car for you?" Art asked anxiously, as he took her by the elbow, walking her toward the entrance of the suite.

"No, of course not. This isn't the dark side of the moon. It's The Bronx." She approximated a chuckle for him.

Art was always at his chivalrous best when he thought there was a damsel in distress. Mikaela struggled to control her irritation. She hated seeming weak in his eyes…and sometimes even seeming female.

"I'm so sorry," she said again. "But I'll follow up with Mr. Proctor in the morning."

"I'm sure you will," he said although his face didn't change from the previous concerned expression. "This Yankees box was deliberately chosen, Mike. You're our Mariano Rivera, you're our closer. You'll bring it all home. I have no doubt."

She was glad at least he believed it.

Mikaela stood waiting for the elevator for a few minutes before deciding to just make her way to the wide cement staircases general admissions used. Unfortunately, wearing her usual five-inch heels, she wasn't nearly as nimble as she thought she'd be heading down. A seeming eternity later, after rounding the final set of stairs to the ground level, she nearly ran directly into someone standing there.

"The elevator is faster than you think," he said, smirking.

"Cameron." She sighed, weary of continuing what started upstairs.

"I just wanted you to know I didn't follow you here, if that's your concern."

Mikaela's eyebrows rose. "You didn't just follow me down here?"

He grinned. "Well, what I mean is, *after* I saw you last week, I didn't follow you. I didn't know where you'd gone. And I still don't know how to reach you…"

"Good."

He stopped short for a second, speechless at her response.

"I'm still fairly certain I was the injured party the last time we saw each other, unless you remember something I don't."

"That depends on—" Mikaela began to rebut before catching herself. "No, you know what? I'm not going there with you." She shook her head. "I don't know what you were doing up there."

He opened his mouth, but Mikaela cut him off before he had a chance to speak.

"And I don't want to know! Just do as I ask and stay out of my way."

She recognized that request was unnecessarily frantic as her heart raced somewhere near her throat.

"O-okay." Cameron nodded.

"Okay?" she said, regaining her composure as she stepped around him and headed toward the exit to that gate. "Great."

"It was nice seeing you, Kaela! It's been too long," he called over his shoulder.

Not long enough, she thought, pushing her way through the heavy glass doors and into the muggy night air.

seven

THEN
May 2002

"Hey, Nessa!"
Someone called out from the street as Mikaela pulled open the door to the local diner, Meg's. She sighed, trying to recall why she hadn't stayed home to rewatch her VHS of *A Few Good Men* or *The Firm* for the millionth time. Hanging out at the mall or at Meg's with her friends was fairly typical for a Friday during the summer, but tonight, Mikaela wasn't in the mood.

Mikaela, with Vanessa right behind her, turned at the sound. A gang of kids on dirt bikes cycled down the road.

"Hey, Nessa! Hey, Nessa's big sister!" a kid called Bug shouted from the center.

One kid broke away from the pack as they rode down the empty street, past the diner. He rolled all the way into the parking lot up to the curb where Mikaela and Vanessa stood waiting.

"Hey, what's up?" Vanessa said giddily, her attitude always doing a complete one-eighty when Julie's little brother, Gabe, appeared.

Mikaela crossed her arms.

Vanessa and Gabe went to school together, like Mikaela and Julie did. But somewhere along the line, they had started dating off and on. Yet, they still acted like buddies, all roughhousing and video game battles. Par for the course, Mikaela supposed, for a pair of fourteen-year-olds.

"We're all going to Scott's to play a *Super Smash Bros.* round-robin. Wanna come?"

"You're with me tonight," Mikaela cut Vanessa off before she could answer.

This was the last remnant of their punishment from their father, still having Vanessa as her shadow. At this point, Mikaela was no longer sure if this was their punishment or just *hers.*

Vanessa sucked her teeth. "Seriously?"

Honestly, Mikaela was as eager to see the back of Vanessa as Vanessa was to leave. She just felt like dragging it out.

"Gimme a break, can I go?"

Gabe put his hands together as if in prayer, beseeching her.

"What time will you be home?"

Vanessa eyed Gabe for a moment before returning to Mikaela.

"Eleven on the dot. Okay?" Vanessa huffed. "Can I go?"

"Fine! Fine, go! Get out of here but make sure you're on the porch by eleven."

"Whatever, Kaela." Vanessa climbed up on the back wheel of Gabe's bike and put her hands on his shoulders.

"Thank you, Mike," Gabe said with his trademark ingratiating sweetness as he rolled his bike backward and pedaled them out of the parking lot and onto the street.

Mikaela sighed to herself.

"That was impressive." Cameron walked up from a squad car parked at the side of the diner. "I have to say, that right there made me grateful my parents kept me an only child."

She glanced around the car for the accompanying deputy.

"I stole it," Cameron answered, grabbing the front door for her.

Her eyebrows shot up. "Who's gonna need the mug shot now?"

"I'm joking." He smiled. "He's inside waiting on our order."

"You were eavesdropping," she accused but smiled, stepping through the first door in front of him. Mikaela paused in the glass-encased vestibule. Julie and their group hadn't shown up yet.

"Sorry, I was," Cameron said, opening the second door politely, as if that was what she had been waiting for.

"Tsk, tsk, tsk," she teased.

"My younger cousin, Morris, stayed with us one year. He was my responsibility that whole summer. By the end, I thought I was going to kill him."

Mikaela chuckled. "Yeah, it can be like that."

He was close, mere inches away, leaning right over her shoulder as he held the second door open.

"I'd say."

Cameron was taller than she remembered, towering over her even as she stepped up into the diner and he stood a step lower. They exchanged a look and she blinked, trying to free herself from his gaze like a butterfly caught in netting.

"Thank you," she muttered, tearing her eyes away as he followed her through. "Sheriff Davenport's nephew-cousin, right?" She joked, pretending she didn't remember his name.

"I forgot you were funny." He chuckled, shaking his head. "Please just call me Cam."

"Mikaela."

"Yeah, I remember."

He did? "You do?"

He grinned at that.

Her stomach did an unexpected somersault.

"*K-a* before *e*," he recited, popping a stick of gum into his mouth, then tipped the packet her way. His smile hadn't lost any of its potency since the last time she'd seen it.

She declined, now understanding the faint but not unpleasant scent of cinnamon that emanated from him. "Most people just call me Mike."

"Mike?" he said between chews of his gum, and with just the way he said it and the way his lips moved with her name on them, it suddenly became her new favorite word ever. "Really? Why would you let them call you that?"

It was like the record scratched on the romantic ballad that was beginning to play inside her head. The butterflies in her stomach dropped dead and the hearts in her eyes cracked.

"Excuse you?"

"No, no, I'm sorry. I didn't mean that the way it sounded." Streaks of red crept from his cheeks toward his ears.

"Okay?"

"Didn't your sister just call you Kaela—"

"Only my family calls me that," she snapped, even as the words were still coming out of his mouth.

That was her mother's nickname for her.

"I just meant that you're so... I mean, your name, Kaela, it's so pret—"

Mikaela didn't need to ask if she was being hostile. Cam's frantic stammering told the tale.

"I'm sorry." He stopped and took a beat. "I really didn't mean offense."

"Mike, what're you doing over here? Did you get us a

table?" Julie came up, wrapping her arms around Mikaela's waist from behind.

Nicole, Emma, twins Corey and Rory and about ten of Mikaela's former classmates all piled noisily through the diner's doors behind her, flooding the entryway with bodies.

"Hey there!" Julie tossed her hair over a shoulder as she acknowledged Cameron standing there, and the group chattered around them all.

"There she is," he declared then. "Your other half."

"Better half," Julie laughed with the girls behind her.

Mikaela glared over her shoulder.

"That remains to be seen." Cameron leaned into Mikaela's shoulder to whisper, *"I doubt it."*

Mikaela snickered, scandalized. No one ever spoke about Julie that way.

"I'm ordering ten burgers!" one of the boys boomed through the cacophony of other voices surrounding them at that exact same moment, leading the group down the aisle toward the booths.

"Kidding!" Julie hugged Mikaela tighter and leaned her head on Mikaela's shoulder. Even after she'd outgrown Mikaela by three inches, it hadn't stopped her from doing that. "I was kidding, M."

"I know." She nodded. "Nessa's left with Gabe, so I was hanging with Cameron…"

"Call me Cam, please."

"Okay, *Cam*." Julie straightened, striking a studied, quizzical expression. "Well, *we* have to get a table. Can't keep the guys waiting."

For whatever reason, Julie was a firm believer that you couldn't gain one guy's interest without insinuating there was another one just waiting in the wings. Mikaela didn't understand the logic. Still, she couldn't argue with Julie's results. Mikaela could attribute almost her entire dating life to Julie's efforts and methods.

One of Cameron's eyebrows rose. "Well, far be it from me to hold y'all up."

"No hold up." Julie smiled, looking him over. "You just have to wait your turn."

Mikaela didn't know what to do first: apologize or die.

But he only laughed as Julie led her away, pushing her toward the group by the shoulders. Cameron waggled his fingers as a goodbye.

"Were you arguing with him when we came in?" Julie whispered as they slipped into one of two crowded booths alongside their friends.

"No, of course not!" Mikaela said, aggrieved by the idea. She never argued with anyone…except Vanessa.

"It sure looked like it. Looked like you were about to take his head off his shoulders."

"That's silly. It was nothing."

Although the more she thought about it, the more it did seem like *something*.

A minute later, that deputy Tommy emerged from the kitchen doors laden with bags. Miss Meg Whatley, the proprietress of the diner, was right behind him talking his ear off. Mikaela watched Cameron walk up to his friend, reaching to help with their bags. She also saw the brief moment when he caught her watching.

He smiled again before she could look away.

eight

Seeing Cameron again prevented Mikaela from getting any sleep that night. Rashad's peacefully sleeping form at her side didn't help either. Just thinking of Cameron with Rashad lying there made her uncomfortable.

So, the next morning, Mikaela attempted to make an early start of it, getting into her office at 5:00 a.m. She sat down at her desk for two hours making calls to the UK, wearing her gym clothes with her microbraids pulled into a ponytail and clearing work from her desk before the first of the other partners came in.

But as soon as she was sure he was in, Mikaela made a beeline for Art Chamberlain's office.

"Bad sushi was the culprit," she lied with a shellacked smile on her face. "It's too humiliating to even tell you how the rest of my night went."

Art's expression hovered somewhere between pity and disgust, shaking his head. "No need, Mike, no need."

Mikaela stood in front of Art's desk and fiddled with the wrist strap of her fitness watch as he stood at the window looking out at the skyline. Art had one of the best views, from his corner office high atop 4 World Trade Center, facing the Hudson River with sight lines to the Statue of Liberty, Ellis Island and Jersey City across the water; it was spectacular. The unspoken truth, however, was that Mikaela, not Todd or one of the more senior partners, had the second-best view, owed to her work two years ago on their LynQ Technologies account. It was unofficially when Mikaela became Art's favorite too. Boasting a view of Brooklyn Heights and both the Brooklyn and Manhattan Bridges, her office rivaled Art's, though not nearly in size. Such were the perks of being Art's pet. And she didn't intend to jeopardize them.

"We have them!" He turned and smiled suddenly. "They absolutely love you! Proctor gushed when you left."

Mikaela exhaled, relieved that two years of flattery, courting and schmoozing hadn't been undone in a single evening's folly. She still couldn't account for how much seeing Cameron had upset her after fifteen years.

And after not wanting to see him in at least…ten.

She shook her head trying to dislodge that thought and refocus on what her boss was saying.

"…they're gonna give us some work on spec."

Mikaela's shoulders fell.

"No, no," Art said, catching her motion. "We're still getting paid, but Altcera's a large company and we're a medium-sized firm. They just want to make sure we can handle the volume before they turn it all over to us. Right now, they're giving us the collective bargaining agreement for Zenigent, a wrongful termination suit at Splendure, a purchase and sale agreement for Colorrblur's new headquarters and some little *Glamazon* magazine litigation. Todd, Slocum, Fredrickson and Max Bailey are Zenigent, Splendure and Colorrblur. I want you on the *Glamazon* case. We can't have anything going wrong with that. Of course, you know their editor-in-chief, Jacqueline Dampierre, is the queen bee over in Altcera's publishing arm and that recent *Glamazon* merger was her baby. Now, they're in the middle of some nuisance suit with one of her favorite photographers. And if that little lady's not happy, no one is. Proctor says she has the CEO's ear. So, we're gonna make sure that gets done right for her, no sweat. I want every *i* dotted and every *t* crossed and I know you are the only one who can help me do that."

Mikaela tried to stop her eyes from involuntarily rolling all the way into the back of her head at Art's mild chauvinism and flagrant blandishment. She hid her disappointment with a tight smile that strained her jaw.

Glamazon was a well-established glossy fashion magazine but besides the fact that she was female, Mikaela didn't know what made that brand more of a lock for her services than those of her male counterparts. If it was so easy, why not put one of the other guys on it? She handled twice the regular workload of Todd, had three times the billables of Slocum or Fredrickson, and Bailey was just a senior associate. Their acquisition of Altcera's North American legal interests was her thing. It was supposed to be the thing that took her to the next level, from junior to equity partner. She'd been saving up for the $700,000 partnership buy-in since she first got her job at this firm twelve years ago. She was a planner and this was to be the final phase of her plan.

Mikaela let the smile drop and bit into her thumbnail when he turned back to gazing out at the river.

Not to mention, all the scut work she had already done on three mergers in the last fourteen months, plus she had five cases of her own on her desk and the five additional that other partners had roped her into recently because she couldn't ever say no. As much as she was happy and eager to bring this deal home to the "family," she had hoped that this victory could mean having her pick of the legal work involved in rolling it over. The grinding, relentless, meticulous work of overseeing the nuts and bolts of a litigation meant another few months of work—weeks where she might as well bring a pillow and blanket into the office with her and temporarily change her mailing address to her desk.

"Sound good?"

Art turned back to Mikaela and she nodded reflexively, tight smile automatically affixed.

"Great, the *Glamazon* people will be here tomorrow."

Even all these years later, why are other people's opinions of me always so important? she chided herself. It seemed both her mother and her therapist, Ximena, were right; she was an inveterate people-pleaser. *How am I still this person?*

It was as if she couldn't find it within herself to say the word *no.* As a junior partner, she tried to remind herself often she was within her rights to do so. Still, each time someone asked, she couldn't form the word.

"You did good." Art beamed at her.

Mikaela fixed her face into some version of convincing happiness.

"You should be proud, kid, you did really good."

nine

"No problem, I'll tell her," Suze was saying when Mikaela walked back into her office from her meeting with Art. Mikaela mimed a telephone in her fist, shaking it. *"Who?"*

"Your sister," Suze mouthed.

Mikaela shook her head and waved no, crossing both hands over each other in a flurry.

She hustled in her door and closed it, changing quickly into a short-sleeved blouse, a pair of palazzo pants and her usual sky-high heels.

"Your sister wants to make sure you didn't forget you're supposed to be helping her," Suze said through the intercom minutes later as Mikaela was putting on her lipstick.

She was silent trying to recall, looking from her compact mirror around the room as if she could snatch a clue from the air.

"With your mom's birthday thing," Suze said when Mikaela didn't reply. "You're supposed to be going with her this weekend to check out venues?"

"Oh yeah," Mikaela said, mildly embarrassed by the oversight. Suze's recall for the minutiae of her life had gotten better than her own.

"Dr. Guerrero also called to ask you to pick up some take-out on your way over tonight, he's going to be late. And someone else called. *Twice.* A Mr. Murphy. Said he would call back again in twenty minutes or so."

Mikaela glanced at a photo that sat innocently—*and anonymously*—on the credenza behind her desk. It was as if it had come to life. She squeezed her eyes closed for a moment before reopening them. As expected, it hadn't transmogrified or even moved.

To anyone who looked at it, it remained as it always had, just an artfully composed black-and-white silhouette of an unidentified male standing among a field of flowers. Most, whoever even noticed it sitting there, thought it might possibly be the picture the simple silver Tiffany frame came with. But for umpteen years, it had framed her only photo of him…

"What?" Mikaela shook the sudden panic off.

"Mr. Cameron Murphy, he said he knew you?" Suze was skeptical.

The intercom clicked off and a moment later Suze knocked on the door, poking her head into the room.

"Was I wrong to tell him you were in?"

He claimed he didn't know how to reach me.

"N-no, it's fine." Mikaela stood from her desk and walked to the window, attempting to coax her diaphragm into taking deeper breaths.

"So should I put him through when he calls again?"

"Absolutely not!" Mikaela's voice was shrill even to her own ears. She gathered herself. "I mean, no. Um, just tell him I'm in meetings all day."

Mikaela regarded the faceless subject of the photograph again.

She was being silly. It was a ridiculous notion that a two-summer-long fling could have constituted the love affair of her life, and its subject, her greatest love. Still, some tiny part of her maintained that it was true. That the duration had been irrelevant. That she had loved the man in this picture…and at least for a short while, he had loved her too.

Suze headed back to her desk with a short nod and a puzzled look on her face that was not lost on Mikaela.

"Suze?"

The young woman promptly reappeared in the doorway.

"In fact, instead, why don't you just let that number go to voice mail."

Facing due north, over sixty floors up, the firm's largest conference room had the Empire State, MetLife and Chrysler Buildings as its backdrop. Because of that and Mikaela's natural penchant for stargazing, she preferred getting into meetings a little early to scout a seat that kept her back to the large floor-to-ceiling windows.

Today, Mikaela was engrossed with her cell phone as people trickled in.

Suze: Heads up. They're on the way.

The text from Suze hit her screen and Mikaela's head popped up as Margaret Tillerson, the firm's most senior female equity partner walked up to her.

"Mike!" The woman smiled. "Congratulations."

"Thank you, Peg."

"How long have you been talking with Altcera?" Deb Harris, the newest junior partner, asked sitting down nearby.

"Ah, about two years," Mikaela said, as if she didn't know the answer down to the day, hour and minute. "Give or take."

"May be your year?" Lincoln Hayes, one of only a pair of black senior partners, the man who recruited her years ago, threw out there as if he didn't have a direct say in whether or not that would be the case.

Still, he looked up from his seat and smiled brightly as if he hadn't seen her sitting there the whole time. How their relationship had gone from mild idol worship to mildly collegial was one of the great unsolved mysteries of her life...and why she knew the POC staff needed new and better leadership in the form of her and her proposed mentorship program.

"Or maybe not," Todd cut in under his breath as he moved into the seat beside her, smirking.

Mikaela fought to keep from rolling her eyes, a regular and visceral reaction to the nauseating smell of stale coffee constantly on his breath.

She and Todd had joined the firm together, he from Yale and she from Columbia, both with their Ivy-covered pedigree. They came up through the ranks together too. But because Todd didn't have to carry as much water and eat as much crow as Mikaela had over the years, his failure to ascend to the highest ranks had never particularly bothered her. She wasn't naïve enough to believe the firm was a true meritocracy, but realities were just realities.

It made sense that Todd never managed to make the cut.

Still, Todd and others—*he certainly wasn't the only one*—initially rose faster there. But that was no surprise either, having been forewarned by every female mentor or lawyer of color she'd ever met that this would inevitably be the case. However, through sheer hard work, tenacity and diligence, Mikaela had caught up anyway. This promotion, though, was to be the confirmation that hard work too paid off and that she deserved not only to catch up but to excel.

She. Could. Not. Wait to wipe the floor with Todd's irritating, egotistical ass at this fall's partnership announcement.

Mikaela cut her eyes at Todd's male-pattern balding and pompous face-having self when he turned to the person to his left. Meanwhile, as was typical after the acquisition of any new business, numerous partners saluted her, some crossing the room to literally pat her on the back until Art arrived.

"Let's get started, people," he said, finding his place at the large table.

The room fell silent.

"Our fiscal year is on track to look very good thanks to Todd and his team and all their hard work with Savantix." Art paused as the round of applause for their big end-of-year bonuses filled the room then subsided.

"Hear, hear!" someone called out.

"Just doing my bit for Wexler, Welford and Bromley!" Todd clicked his teeth, imitating hitting a home run as various partners chuckled and a few friends drummed the table for him.

"And Mike," Art said as if he'd just remembered she was there, "who has gotten her foot in the door over at Altcera."

Foot in the door? We already have five cases…

Her chin rose and she sat up ramrod straight nonetheless, enduring their attention as all heads turned her way. She clasped her hands together until they ached as her heartbeat resounded in her ears. Mikaela despised being the focus of attention.

But on the verge of everything she'd ever wanted, if it meant being under the microscope as The Token Black Woman in the room, it was the price she would gladly pay. *And* this was what she constantly reminded herself.

"Well done…" Art said, clapping. Polite applause circled the room like a wave.

She nodded to Art. "Thank yo—"

"And now that the easy part is out of the way, it's time to do the *real* work," he announced, moving on and causing the room to fall dead silent. "To that end, this spring WW&B bought a table at this year's L&LGala."

A riot of murmurs erupted. Eyebrows rose and fell around the table. Mikaela had to hold her mouth shut to keep it from falling open.

"A whole table?" Someone whistled, no doubt at the price tag.

Art nodded. "We're pulling out all the stops."

Altcera's Lymphoma and Leukemia Gala was one of the premier charity events in the City's social calendar annually. It lay at the rarefied nexus of high society and pop culture, attended by both the doyennes of the moneyed classes and the newest Hollywood starlets and other celebrities. Hosted every year by *Glamazon*'s editor-in-chief under the auspices of its high-fashion sister publication *Du Monde*, it was the who's-who, who-wore-what and who-was-seen-with-whom event of the year, held at Central Park's Museum of Contemporary Art.

"Gotta spend money to make money, right?" Todd leaned in to whisper as Mikaela struggled not to cringe.

"I want us to be a notable presence there. This is Jackie Dampierre's baby. So now it's ours."

Mikaela sighed, examining her nails in her lap and holding her tongue as usual.

All Art's plans seemed painfully transparent... But that was Art.

Jacqueline Dampierre was no dummy. What she was, was the Grande Dame of Fashion, New York media maven so widely known and highly feared that numerous, notorious romans à clef about life inside one of her magazines were all authored by the same person: *Anonymous*. And if she had to guess, Mikaela would imagine no one ever called her Jackie to her face.

Margaret glanced in Mikaela's direction from a few seats away and shook her head, laughing.

"Sixteen invites. My girl will be sending out the emails this afternoon with invitations. Everybody gets a plus-one *we expect you to use*."

"That means you, and imaginary Dr. BoyToy." Todd elbowed Mikaela. "Guess he'll have to clear his calendar for real this time, huh?"

Mikaela shrugged Todd off.

"He'll be there," she said, trying to guess how slipping an event less than two weeks away onto Rashad's calendar was going to work for him.

ten

On Thursday afternoon at precisely two thirty, Mikaela gathered up her tablet and her cup of coffee and headed into a conference room. But when she got there, part of the *Glamazon* team had beaten her to her preferred seats, facing away from the windows. There were only supposed to be four visitors: *Glamazon's* in-house counsel, co-counsel and two associates, which would still be okay. So, Mikaela was surprised when she saw five people there instead. It left her with the choice of either taking one of the seats at either end of the table or sitting in the one remaining seat on the *Glamazon* side. Not that there were really sides, they were all on the same team today.

She sighed.

"Hope you don't mind, Mr. Murphy found the view a little distracting," the *Glamazon* in-house counsel, Cecilia Albright, said with a smile.

Mikaela blinked, hoping that when her eyes opened, he would be gone.

Cameron turned in his seat from the view to her, smiling.

Only seeing him stroke a cat in his lap could have made the moment any more bizarre. She felt faint, as if her blood sugar had plummeted, shaky and off-balance. *What is he doing here?*

"Ah, that—that's fine," Mikaela said, placing her things on the opposite side but that left her facing not only a glorious skyline but his face.

Mikaela reconsidered, sliding her things over to the head of the table opposite Art's assumed seat, which would still leave her sitting a seat away from Cameron.

Cameron's eyes tracked her avidly, watching her choose. Ms. Albright and her associates were too busy talking to each other to notice Mikaela's game of musical chairs.

Now she moved back to the opposing side, which again was diagonally across from him.

Cameron actually laughed as Mikaela's face grew hot.

She abandoned her things and picked up her coffee cup. "I'm getting myself another cup—can I get anyone anything?" she asked, with a challenging gaze fixed on Cameron.

The *Glamazon* quartet declined, deep in conversation. Mikaela tilted her head back and toward the door.

Death-gripping her cup, which was thankfully made of sturdy ceramic or she might have crushed it, Mikaela headed to the door. Outside the doorway, she paused and Cameron bumped right into her back. His hands, encircling her hips, braced her as their bodies collided.

"Shit," Mikaela gasped, her coffee spilling onto her blouse. "Goddamn it."

"Oh man, I'm so sorry, Mikaela," Cameron said, falling back, hands raised.

They both looked around.

The quartet were still deep in conference and barely

looked up. The only person who seemed to have noticed their collision was the assistant stationed in front of an office down the hall. But she dipped her head back behind her computer a moment later.

"What are you doing here?" Mikaela gruffly whispered, wiping the coffee out of her cowl-neck blouse. "I thought you said you didn't know how to reach me?" She hurled the question like an accusation.

"Before the game I didn't." Cameron stayed safely a few steps away, trailing her down the hall.

"This is my job, Cam!"

"I know that." A deep line bisected his brow.

They walked through the spacious executive dining room to the kitchenette at the far side.

"Look, I didn't intend to ambush you."

"It sure feels like an ambush! Didn't I ask you to stay to your side of Manhattan?"

"Oh? Only Manhattan? I actually thought you meant all five boroughs."

Mikaela stopped wiping her shirt. Cameron's glacial blue eyes danced at the sight of her, roaming her face with a small smile playing at his lips.

This all pleased him.

As Mikaela watched him watch her, the same old butterflies, their zombied, petrified selves, all rose from their long-dead state to flutter and beat their wings about in her belly. It seemed impossible that she could still harbor the ancient attraction to him that she'd had as a teen…but there it was.

Mikaela blinked rapidly then, turning away to wet her napkin again and catch her breath. "You're *not* funny."

"I used to make you laugh," Cameron said, encroaching on her personal space.

"It's been a long time since then."

She could feel his body easing up behind her and took another deep breath to balance herself.

"I have a carafe of scalding hot coffee right here, Cameron. It's inches away. So, back off."

He chuckled. "I guess we're acting like we don't know each other again… Reminds me of old times."

Mikaela winced.

A second later, two of her colleagues walked into the room as Cameron stepped away. She nodded and they nodded back. Mikaela and Cameron watched silently as the other couple took turns filling their cups from one of the coffee-pots and added their condiments, not breaking their conversation with each other.

"How do you take it, Mr. Murphy?" Mikaela turned to him with a pot in one hand and a paper cup in the other.

Cameron shoved his hands deep into his pants pockets, rocking back on his heels. "Black." He grinned. "And strong."

Mikaela rolled her eyes, but a corner of her mouth curled, fighting the urge to laugh at his dumbass joke.

Cameron raised his eyebrows, looking at the cup pointedly.

Just seeing him made Mikaela forget what she was doing and where they were.

"Oh." She began to fill it, before pushing it at him. "Uh, here."

Their fingers brushed. It wasn't exactly bolts of electricity, but staring into his eyes, Mikaela could feel it: there was still a spark between them. Parts of her that should have remained unaffected, like her heart, thudded riotously at his touch.

"I think you can find your own way back to the conference room, right, Mr. Murphy?" She turned her back on him and poured her own cup, adding cream and sugar.

Her colleagues smiled and Mikaela gave a tight smile back, watching out of the corner of her eye as they all left, then exhaling. Alone, she gripped the counter edge for a moment to steady herself, and finally let her shoulders drop. The ache that was building at her temples eased a bit. In a matter of ten minutes, Cameron had shown up, touched her twice and now she was walking around like her insides were on the outside. She didn't need the distraction of him in her space.

Sipping from her cup, she turned. Cameron was seated at a nearby table drinking his coffee, waiting.

"Christ!" She jerked, narrowly missing getting more coffee on her blouse. She sighed, grateful it was made of a beige charmeuse. She could camouflage for now and change later. "I thought you left."

Cameron shook his head. "I didn't think we were done yet."

"Oh, that's right, according to you, we'll never be finished," Mikaela said under her breath, stirring her cup, before Cameron's flabbergasted face revealed he'd heard her.

He cleared his throat and continued evenly. "I did try to call. And had three very pleasant conversations with your assistant, Susan."

"Suze...as in Suzukea. It's Japanese."

"My bad."

Mikaela raised an eyebrow. *"My bad?"*

"My son's thirteen. He says it all the time." Cameron sighed, shaking his head woefully. "I can't *not* say it at this point."

That's right, she remembered hearing about the existence of a son.

Mikaela sobered, checking her watch. "We need to get back."

Cameron stood but allowed her to lead the way out of the break room.

"Please, Cam." She paused at the door and he barely avoided running into her again. "You still haven't explained what you're doing here but—"

"I got it, stay out of your way. I'm not sure how well I can accomplish that, but I'll try my utmost."

The amused, sort of mocking tone in his voice returned, making Mikaela's shoulders tense again.

They reentered a much fuller conference room, where only a few seats were still open. Mikaela's belongings had been pushed along to the seat directly next to Cameron's... which of course someone on his side had saved for him. In her previous seat, Todd sat attentively waiting for Art to begin.

"Ah, I think Ms. Marchand was sitting there," Cameron said, standing directly over him.

Cameron was a big guy but always too gentle and unassuming to be an innately imposing presence. However, Mikaela had somehow forgotten that sometimes, by virtue of his size, he could take on that bearing whenever he wanted to...*like now.*

Todd's eyes traveled up Cameron's long-limbed and solid form for an extended moment, mouth agape before beginning to gather his things. Mikaela had to cover her mouth to hide a delighted smirk.

"No, it's fine. Todd, you stay where you are," Art instructed, unconcerned with the showdown occurring. "Everyone on this side, move one seat down. Mike, I want you up here anyway."

Art spoke to their whole team while pointing at the seat immediately to his right. They all shifted obediently as Mikaela gathered her things and moved as she was bid. The meeting started and after introducing the eight other people in the room, all eyes fell on Cameron Murphy.

Their *Glamazon* client.

Mikaela had to bite her cheek to keep from laughing as everything clicked into place.

Well, Cameron certainly wasn't stalking her.

He was being sued.

As Cameron spoke, Mikaela watched him in his natty, navy suit sans tie, and her eyes strayed all over, seeing the things she'd overlooked earlier, while periodically refocusing on his mouth.

It was true: he was older now and a little grayer at the temples. There was no escaping the laws of gravity and the march of time no matter how well-preserved you were, but Cameron was essentially the same. There were the hints of crow's-feet near his eyes when he smiled. His hair was cut exceedingly short at the temples and around the back to hide the impending gray. But he still had a mass of that wavy, dirty-blond hair on the top of his head that she used to love to run her fingers through and passionately tug. He also had a more robust five-o'clock shadow than he'd had before as if his baby face had finally figured that facial hair thing out. And his fashionable stubble was a little gray now as well. Overall, however, the years had been incredibly kind to Cameron and he looked as good at forty-one as he had at twenty-one, if a little leaner in some places and more nicely filled out in others.

"Not only Mr. Murphy himself but *Glamazon* are being named in the lawsuit," Ms. Albright was explaining when Mikaela tuned back into the conversation.

"And as you can imagine, we were saddened that the plaintiffs were not amenable to the initial settlement offer," Cecilia's assistant counsel, Monica Yee, chimed in. "But we're trying to convince opposing counsel that this matter would be best served in arbitration."

"She won't see reason," Cameron added.

The familiarity with which Cameron was speaking and the delicacy the *Glamazon* counselors were using gave Mikaela pause.

Was she missing something?

"I'm sorry, can you repeat that? You said this was a misappropriation claim, for which work?" Mikaela spoke up to ask. "And the plaintiff in the case is who exactly?"

She flipped back through the pages of the complaint. Mikaela was technically little more than an interested party in the actual suit itself. It was the aftermath with *Glamazon* that affected her, insomuch as the suit's outcome affected their relationship with the parent company, Altcera. Which everyone knew was Mikaela's baby: to be either nurtured to its fruition or mired by an unwieldy, capricious, but more crucially, *expensive and embarrassing* litigation. So, the fact that they were hopefully well on the way to arbitration was an excellent sign.

Ms. Yee nodded to one of the firm's summer interns seated against the back wall. He dimmed the lights and turned on the large flat screen sitting on the opposite wall.

Mikaela turned to face it, scratching at a space above her ear between two braids when she saw the photo:

The one Vanessa wouldn't stop harassing her about.

The one hanging in the art gallery.

The one gracing a massive billboard in Times Square.

The same one advertised all over as posted bills, and also evidently, in subway ads all over the City, boasting a retrospective at a new gallery.

It was the forty-fifth-anniversary cover of *Glamazon* magazine...

And it was the photo that secretly included her face as well.

"The plaintiff is my wife." Cameron answered that question himself.

Mikaela turned.

"My *ex*-wife." He addressed Mikaela directly, his face pained. "Juliette Murphy."

eleven

THEN
June 2002

"Marchand Custom Autobody, how can I help you?" Mikaela affected her most polite phone voice to counteract her general annoyance. She'd already sat in her father's hot back office uneventfully for an hour. Mikaela had drawn the short straw that morning right as she meant to head to the lake. Halfway out the door with her bathing suit, shorts and tote, her father had waylaid her in the kitchen.

"Kaela, it's Mom."

Only the creaking of Mikaela's ancient office chair and the steady oscillation of a large fan in the corner sounded in the room.

"Kaela?" Her mother's tone was light, almost tuneful as she asked again.

Mikaela's traitorous heart always fluttered in her chest, both thrilled and pained by the sound of her mother's voice.

"Yeah?" She cleared her throat. "Ah, I mean, hi, Mama. How can I help you?"

"I called— I mean, I wanted to—" *There was a slight tremor in her mother's voice then.* "Um, did you get the backpack?"

"Yes, I did. Thank you," Mikaela answered.

The backpack was a graduation gift delivered in a lavish box. A tanned, buttery soft leather with a pungent but not entirely unpleasant odor. Gilded letters were ornately embossed on the monogrammed flap. It was beautiful, and as a gift, it had been both practical and thoughtful. Everyone at her graduation party said so. But later, Mikaela put the bag back into its box and tossed it into her closet, where it remained even a month later.

"I can just see you wandering around Manhattan with it…filling it with all your books and papers and writings." Her mother spoke rapidly as if she knew Mikaela was about to stop her.

Mikaela sighed heavily in her mother's ear, which the woman didn't seem to hear, rambling on.

"When I saw it, I just knew it was for you! Oh, sugar, I'm so, so proud and excited for you…"

"Can I help you with something, Mama?" Mikaela asked, speaking over her.

Her mother fell silent on the other end of the line. Mikaela sighed again, imagining in her silence the same wounded-animal look her mother always wore.

As if she wasn't the one who had deliberately chosen to become a stranger.

Still, Mikaela softened. "You called for something, right?"

"Y-yes. Your father." Her mother's answer was subdued. "Hold on."

"I love yo—"

"Dad!" Mikaela put a hand over the receiver, bellowing out the open office door right as Julie walked in.

Julie started at that. Seeing Mikaela's expression, she mouthed the words, *"Who's that?"*

Mikaela made a face. "It's Mom! Line one!"

Julie nodded before slouching into one of the seats in front of Mikaela's desk. She crossed her feet, one over the other on the armrest of the chair. Mikaela put the call on hold and slammed down the receiver, rolling her eyes.

"What did she want?"

"Who knows," Mikaela said.

She could ask her father later but as frequently happened where relations with her mother were concerned, he was extraordinarily tight-lipped. Vanessa and Mikaela hadn't even known their parents were divorcing until they accidentally found the paperwork among their father's things.

Julie shrugged in sympathy, acquainted enough with the dynamic that she didn't even bother to press. "Did you thank her for that backpack?"

Mikaela nodded. "I did."

"Did you tell her I want one exactly like it for my birthday in August?" Julie smiled broadly as she dangled her flip-flop off one toe.

"You can have mine," Mikaela offered.

"Your name's on it."

"So, scrape it off. It's just gonna go to waste otherwise."

Julie cut her eyes at her best friend. "You're gonna let a perfectly nice bag sit in your closet, for what? To spite your mama?"

Julie said it like there was something wrong with that. It seemed perfectly reasonable to Mikaela.

"Why can't you just pretend your dad gave it to you?"

Julie asked. "This is what The Judge calls, 'Cutting off your nose to spite your face.'"

Mikaela wrinkled her nose, touching it lightly. "Look, I just don't want anything she has to give. I don't think there's anything wrong with that."

"Don't be stupid. Every time your mother gives you stuff, you return it or don't use it. I just don't get it. Nessa doesn't have this problem."

"'Cause Nessa's easy. She doesn't see that the woman's just trying to buy us."

"There's nothing wrong with being bought. And face it, she's your mama, Mike," Julie spoke softly, her face taking on the infuriatingly sympathetic look she sometimes wore when discussing war or homelessness...*or girls without boyfriends*. "She's always gonna be your mama. Not accepting her gifts won't change that. You do realize that, right?"

A warm sensation licked at the back of Mikaela's neck, tensing her shoulders and throbbing at her temples.

Julie would never understand.

She had her mother and father together and yet still managed to have tons of opinions and "advice" about Mikaela and her broken home. But Mikaela knew she should be grateful. Julie had been there when no one else cared. Wiping the tears when her mother left and being an ear as Mikaela raged against the unfairness of it all. As her best friend, Julie had earned her right to an opinion, even if Mikaela didn't necessarily care to hear it.

"Anyway, what's up with you?" Mikaela asked pointedly, but with a smile plastered across her face.

Julie straightened in the seat, bringing her feet back down to the ground. "I think Cam is gonna be at the lake today," she announced, grinning broadly.

Mikaela stopped breathing for a second.

"Are you gonna be getting outta here anytime soon? Nicki, Emma and I want to stake out our spots by the water and make sure we're there when the guys arrive."

"How, um, how do you know he'll be there?" Mikaela asked, attempting a blasé air.

She was trying to figure out a way to ward Julie off Cameron or gently suggest that perhaps she should place her interest elsewhere. They'd never really had a problem like this before, and certainly not where *Mikaela* was the one asking *Julie* to stand down.

"You're really in a funk over this thing with your mama, huh?" Julie asked.

Mikaela looked at her askance.

"Well, you're not listening to me—you're off in your own world. *I said*, he likes to do his photography thing on Saturdays. He's really serious about it. I went by his house and saw all these other great pictures. His mama's really nice too. I love that he works at the sheriff's station but he's actually a sensitive artist—" Julie's voice grew soft and breathless, beginning her usual rhapsodizing.

"Well, he seems about as tough as a cotton ball, so…" Mikaela cut her off peevishly.

"Why are you so bad?" Julie giggled.

Mikaela smirked at her friend, a little unnerved that Julie had already been to his house. She couldn't say that. She'd only ever seen him a few times. Had she somehow misinterpreted his interest?

"His mom was having this tag sale." Julie plowed ahead, unaware of Mikaela's darkening mood. "Mostly junk honestly, but she was showing off some of his pictures too. And now I wanna see more so bad. You think if I just ask, he'd show them to me? Maybe I could show him some of my sketches too…"

Mikaela listened with one ear while her mind wandered. Maybe she *wasn't* the one he actually liked?

"So?"

"So what?"

Julie cocked her head, eyes hitting the ceiling before settling back on Mikaela with a pronounced sigh. "*Oh. My. God.* Mike. Are you coming soon or not?"

Mikaela shook her head, for the first time that day, actually a little relieved she was stuck at the auto shop for another few hours.

It was midafternoon by the time Vanessa came in to relieve Mikaela.

It hadn't been that bad, considering Saturdays were her dad's busiest day. And Mikaela wasn't terribly unhappy to be there. She foresaw what might have been a very awkward afternoon by the lake watching Julie making a play for Cameron's attention in front of her and was grateful to be elsewhere. So, freed for the rest of the day, Mikaela struck out in the opposite direction of the lakefront entirely. Not interested in going home, she strolled through town. The scent of honeysuckle wafting on the breeze eventually made her pause in her wandering. But it took a full minute before Mikaela realized where she was, standing almost directly in front of the local community garden. An errant blue butterfly fluttered by and Mikaela followed it.

She hadn't thought of this place since she was a child. And she was astonished that, though empty, it was clear the space was still being well-tended. Situated far from the center of town in what used to be an abandoned parcel of land willed back to the township of Harmon, it abutted the edge of a forest and spanned outskirts bordering three nearby towns. Most of the kids Mikaela's age probably didn't even remember it existed, if they were ever familiar with it at all. But looking around, it was apparent somebody still was.

The rust-colored brick path was still lined in daisies and marigolds the way she remembered. Mikaela hadn't walked through this garden since her mother had been a full and active member of the garden club that supported it. But she still knew all the names and could identify the assortment of flowers just as her mom had taught her. Flowering trees, like purple magnolias, golden laburnums and red chestnuts provided colorful shade for the red cedar visitor benches. Pink hollyhocks, white oleander and rhododendrons sat along the edges of the garden. And as she watched, at least four hummingbirds attended to fuchsia garden phlox. Bees buzzed in and out of vividly blue-purple coneflowers and tall verbena plants as Mikaela marveled.

She could still recall lying on her back among the flowers and calling out the shapes of clouds as her mother pruned the camellias at the center of the garden, laughing at Mikaela's wild imagination.

She sought out the small handmade bench her mother had donated to the club years ago. It took her a moment to locate it, shaded and hidden by a magnolia that had been half its size the last time Mikaela saw it. Made from the vinyl bench seat of an old AMC Rambler placed atop stacks of old tires, her mother's donation had seen better days. Still, it possessed a personality that all the plain old red benches with their golden plaques lacked. It had always been her favorite and not just because her father made it. Obscured by an outgrowth of Russian sage that nearly covered it, it was left alone by the benign neglect of the garden club.

Mikaela took a deep breath and exhaled, trying to control the wistfulness coursing through her like a current. She dusted magnolia petals, pollen and debris off the old seat with a towel from her tote bag before sitting. The years hadn't made it any less comfortable or sturdy though, she was pleased to discover. She pulled out one of her library books and began to read, surrounded by the splendor she had completely to herself.

Mikaela had lost time until she heard a snap.

"Please don't tell me you took a picture of me like this?" she asked once she recognized who it was standing there, no less embarrassed than she was when she thought it might be a random stranger.

"Don't worry, I won't," Cameron answered, holding his camera at his chest.

She grinned, wiping her eyes and pulling herself together. "How'd you find me?"

"I wasn't looking for you."

He took another one of those pictures where he snapped it without looking through the viewfinder.

"No more pictures," she said, then heard another click. "What are you doing here?"

He was wearing shorts, a white U2: *Joshua Tree* tour T-shirt and tennis shoes.

"I come here sometimes. I get great pictures. Flowers, birds…"

"Butterflies, yeah. It is pretty nice, but shouldn't you be over at the lake?"

Julie was going to be so disappointed. Mikaela tried unsuccessfully not to be gleeful.

Cameron blinked, a smile curving the corners of his mouth. "I try to go early. It gets too crowded by midday."

Mikaela nodded. That it did.

A sea of people as far as the eye could see for eight to ten hours each and every day, all summer long. It could be over-whelming if you hadn't grown up with it.

"I like this place. There's rarely any people here and it's never the same experience twice. You're actually in my fa-vorite spot."

Mikaela glanced at her seat, opening her mouth to brag.

"This gnarly, broken-down old bench. Somebody loved this tacky thing once upon a time but then just left it here to rot."

Her mouth snapped closed and she shrugged instead. "Yeah, I guess. It's definitely comfortable though."

"I can tell," he replied with a smirk. "You're perfect there."

"On the 'broken-down old bench'? Gee, thanks."

Cameron reddened. "That's not what I meant."

"Yeah?"

"I meant among the flowers, with your book. Like Sleep-ing Beauty, kinda."

"Oh." Mikaela was genuinely tongue-tied, trying to mem-orize everything about this moment. Cameron's words. The hazy glow of the setting sun. The few straggling humming-birds flitting from blossom to blossom on the daylilies clos-ing nearby.

Somehow, she knew, everything about this was going to be unforgettable later.

Cameron stepped up into the sage and extended his hand to her.

"What?" She looked at it, then up at him.

Cameron didn't answer, holding his hand out and smiling until she took it. He pulled her to her feet and down through the thicket of blooms, onto the walkway beside him. Then picked a small stalk from the purple flowers around their feet.

He avoided her eyes. "I like lavender," he announced, of-fering it to her. "The color and the plant."

She smiled without accepting it. She pushed the stalk back toward him, explaining, "This isn't lavender. Smell it."

Cameron's eyes widened in surprise, smelling the pungent difference.

"It's sage." She pointed to an almost identical patch of purple flowers a few feet back behind him. "*That*. That's lavender."

Mikaela took the stem from him and retrieved another stalk of real lavender to replace it. She went back to grab her tote off the bench. But instead of tossing the sprig of sage aside as she might normally, she put it in her bag for safekeeping.

Cameron took her hand again to help her out of the brush. "You need me to walk you home?"

Mikaela laughed. She'd been walking the streets of Harmon unaccompanied since she was eight years old. She shook her head. "No, I'll be okay."

He nodded.

She decided not to tease him...*too much*. "But you get on home safe now, y'hear? Don't you stay out here too late with yer little pictures. Get yerself in trouble with these neighborhood girls."

"I see what you're doing." He laughed, growing a little red. "Alright now."

"Alright now," she repeated, charmed by how wonderfully awkward he was.

They walked to the entrance of the garden together. Then Mikaela said a quiet goodbye, turning off in the opposite direction.

"It's cool I ran into you here," he called after her.

"Yeah," she agreed, backing away from him and down the street. "A surprise..."

A pleasant one, but a surprise nonetheless. That this kept happening, even in a town of ten thousand, defied reason.

"I love surprises," he said, grinning. "But maybe we can make it less of one next time?"

"Maybe… Seventy-three Magnolia Way," she added unprompted, but it felt like a logical progression. "My father has two daughters and a shotgun. I'm just warning you."

Cameron's smile widened, fixed on her. "So noted."

She turned away then to laugh unobserved. But once she'd calmly turned the corner, she ran the whole rest of the way home.

twelve

NOW

It wasn't as if Mikaela hadn't already attended a half-dozen deposition prep meetings with Cameron in the two weeks since her firm had come aboard this *Glamazon* case. And it wasn't as if her best, up-and-coming, young midlevel associate Jackson wouldn't be joining them in ten minutes—or at least that's how far behind he'd said he was when she texted him earlier. Still, when Mikaela walked into the restaurant Art's assistant had chosen for their lunch meeting, she stopped in her tracks before catching herself, seeing Cameron was the only one seated at their table.

Sitting with Cameron for ten seconds, let alone ten minutes, was less than ideal.

Mikaela dropped her shoulders, willing away her nerves as she made her way through the other patrons behind the host. He pulled out the seat she pointed at when they arrived and Cameron rose politely for her.

"Hey," Mikaela said from the seat farthest on the other side of the six-person rectangle from him.

Cameron smirked at her choice. "How ya doin', Mikaela?"

Mikaela put her purse on the table and fished through it. She needed to tell Jack to hurry it up.

"Good, you?" she asked as she pulled her cell phone out of her bag and began typing.

"I'm great."

"Terrific."

She scrolled through items from her daily punch list on her phone and checked her email to avoid engaging further. To his credit, Cameron just sat there as Mikaela busied herself with anything but him. She glanced around the room once.

Where was everyone? One would have thought they'd want to get here on time to enjoy the opulence of this restaurant.

It was full and buzzing. A hive of stylish, well-heeled patrons and bustling, attractive, young waitstaff. Curious lookie-loos peered in from the street as the A-listers vied for attention. Snagging this large table at midday was probably a minor coup for Art's assistant. Lunch at the Plum Iris, a Michelin-starred establishment, was an event in and of itself. Just another part of Art's plan to wine and dine the whole Altcera group. Cameron wasn't the least bit out of place there, striking in his dark suit and white shirt with two buttons open at the collar, gazing around. Meanwhile, Mikaela, in her puce sheath dress, wished she didn't have to be such an active participant. The Altcera workload she could handle; the three-martini lunches and attendant sycophantic schmoozing were always a chore.

Eventually, the excruciating silence got the best of her. She leaned back in her chair, crossing her arms and legs. It caught Cameron's attention and he reclined too, matching her, another slight smirk playing at his lips.

"What?"

"Nothing." He smiled fully, raising his arm to signal for the waiter then. "You look good, Mikaela."

"I know." She checked her watch as her knee wobbled under the table, her heel clicking against the tiling underfoot. "Uh, you do too."

It wasn't the simple pleasantry it sounded like. He did look good. He looked so good, in fact, that it had already distracted her in meetings, unsettled her as they passed in hallways and unnerved her anytime they found themselves as close as they were now. She couldn't understand it. He was still just a regular man...but then again, he wasn't; *he was Cameron.* In her younger days, she'd not been able to take her eyes off him, unable to fully fathom that he was hers. Now, she was horrified to discover that was still the case.

Long ago, she daydreamed of scenarios where she was successful and fabulously attired and would just happen to run into him. In those dreams, it was *her* magnificence that would cause him to stammer. To lament his decisions once upon a time, the way she still did hers all the time.

Yet, the reality was proving to be something else entirely.

When the waiter arrived, Cameron ordered a Scotch and soda for himself and menus for the table.

"For you, miss?" the waiter asked, bending to hear over the din of the lunch rush.

"Ginger ale with a splash of lime juice," Mikaela said as the waiter nodded.

Cameron shook his head, leaning forward. "You still don't drink?"

Mikaela had been avoiding his eyes, willing her knee to stop moving, but she eyed him then, incredulous. "Uh, it's noon? I can't afford to get sloppy in front of my colleagues, like you."

"It's a glass of soda with a finger of whiskey, not a wine flight. You sure you're okay?" he asked, without dropping the smile.

"Yup," she started before pivoting with annoyance. "You know what? No, I have better things to do right now than be out of my damn office in the middle of the day. Especially when no one else can seem to be on time!"

Cameron choked back a laugh. "You do remember that I'm your client so these are all billable hours, right?"

Mikaela shrank a little in her seat. "You're right…but only technically. You're Celia Albright's client, *not mine.*" She paused and gripped her thigh to still it. "But I'm sorry, that was rude."

This was not the way Mikaela normally treated valued clients… She was usually sugar and spice, professionally speaking. Everything nice, the "perfect" woman.

"No worries." Cameron shook his head.

Mikaela scanned the room, peering through the picture windows to the street scene beyond, searching for someone, *anyone* she might recognize to come in and rescue her. Her infernal shoe heel continued rapping sharply against the tiles.

"They'll get here when they get here." Cameron shrugged, twisting a lemon wedge over his ice water. "And in the meantime, let's bury the hatchet."

She turned back to him then. "We aren't at war."

"Aren't we?" He took a sip of his drink.

Mikaela considered her recent behavior. It was true: she had been hostile. And perhaps Cameron hadn't quite earned all of that.

"C'mon," he coaxed. "I don't bite."

Mikaela rolled her eyes at his knowing toothy grin. "Well,

I certainly recall evidence to the contrary." It slipped out of her mouth before she could stop it.

Cameron's eyes widened a second before a geyser of water spurted from his mouth and nose, dribbling down his chin and into his lap as he grabbed the cloth napkin under his silverware to catch it.

Mikaela snorted loudly. He coughed and laughed, covering his face with the cloth.

"Mikaela!" Cameron choked out, his face florid.

Just looking at his scandalized expression made Mikaela giggle until her own face burned and eyes watered. Soon, she too needed her napkin to prevent her mascara from running.

The waiter came back to give them their drinks, a smile already on his face. Mikaela briefly rested her forehead on the table, staring at her shoes as Cameron sank into his seat, head thrown back, howling with laughter.

"I can practically hear you guys from the door," Jackson informed them, whispering as he walked up to the table a minute later. "What's so funny?"

Mikaela shook her head trying to compose herself.

"Don't mind us," Cameron said, clearing his throat but still struggling to keep a straight face. "Ms. Marchand and I just discovered that we have similar senses of humor."

Mikaela snorted again, which set Cameron off further, as Jackson tried in vain to discern the joke.

thirteen

Mikaela: I'm bored. 🙁 Miss u

Rashad: ...same.

Mikaela: Wish u were here

Rashad: You looked hot in that dress!! 😈

Mikaela: TY 😀

Rashad: Tell all the guys to stay away! 😊 Youre mine!

Mikaela: Ur stupid! 😜 See u at home later?

Rashad: ...

"Oh my God! I was just in a bathroom selfie with Alexis Ruhle, Kween Kitty and Black Rose!" Suze deposited her clear Lucite clutch on the table and slid into her seat beside Mikaela, whispering in her ear. "Game over! Turn off the internet, I have attained the social media pinnacle!"

Mikaela closed her texts with Rashad, still waiting on a response. Her assistant hung on her arm, peeking over Mikaela's shoulder and around the massive, ornately decorated atrium. Mikaela listened with one ear as Suze indiscreetly pointed out notables and celebrities as she saw them with the delight of a small child.

"I was standing at the sink washing my hands when Alexis Ruhle asked me if I had some gum. I couldn't breathe! I just saw her new movie *last week*!" Suze gushed. "I will never thank you enough for letting me tag along!"

Mikaela's mouth flattened, thinking of Rashad's overnight shift that had prevented him from attending Altcera's Lymphoma and Leukemia Gala. Without her intended plus-one, this was just another work event where she'd rather be at home watching TV or catching up on casework in her pajamas.

Mikaela and Suze were seated at one of the dozens of tables lining the large dance floor with both a DJ booth and a live band at its center. Despite the lively music that made the room almost vibrate with energy, Mikaela barely looked up from her phone screen. In truth, other than when they first entered, Mikaela hadn't spared as much time appreciating their exclusive surroundings as Suze had.

Themed after van Gogh's *Starry Night* and located in the art museum's immense rotunda, the L&L Gala was like an art canvas itself with everything draped in lavish indigo-blue-gold-and-onyx fabrics, gilded filigree and crystal decor. Everywhere fashionably attired black-tie attendees roamed the room. And van Gogh's work inspired not only the backdrop but also the attendees' sartorial interpretations, channeling their favorite celestial bodies. Still, Mikaela just wore a simple, one-shouldered, wine-colored evening gown with her hair done up in a sideswept chignon. Suze, however, chose to skirt the line as usual, with her voluptuous body poured into a tuxedo-inspired black-and-white dress with a deep plunging back and a single long, black, rope-style braid in her hair.

"Heads up." Suze issued her favorite warning, before standing and moving toward coworkers seated in the opposite direction.

In Pavlovian style, Mikaela's head rose as Mr. Proctor approached with Jacqueline Dampierre and Cameron in tow. Mikaela licked her lips and painted a broad smile on them instantly.

Art, a few seats away, followed suit, rising to receive them. Mikaela joined him.

"Art, Mike," Mr. Proctor said, handling introductions. "You know Mr. Murphy—"

"Cameron, please," Cameron corrected, reaching for Art's hand and shaking it firmly. "Ms. Marchand." He acknowledged Mikaela with a nod as his eyes traveled the length of her body, before darting back to Art with a smile.

"Let me introduce you to Jacqueline Dampierre. Jacqueline, this is Arthur Chamberlain and Mikaela Marchand from Wexler, Welford and Bromley."

Everyone exchanged pleasantries as Mikaela struggled to avoid Cameron's eyes, instead focusing on Jacqueline. The older woman was everything Mikaela had heard and seen in magazines. Petite, fine boned and chic, tonight she wore her infamous silver pixie cut and crimson red lips with a magenta-colored, popover crepe gown that fluttered around her arms as she moved.

"This is an amazing event, Ms. Dampierre." Mikaela waved her hand in a wide arc as if to illustrate. "It's so beautiful!"

"Thank you, Ms. Marchand," Jacqueline said in her distinctive and melodic French-tinged voice. "Twentieth annual." She exchanged a warm look with Cameron, squeezing his forearm.

"Every year, we wonder how Jacqueline and her staff will outdo themselves, and still every year, they manage it," Mr. Proctor gushed.

"It's remarkable. We thank you so much for the invitation," Art concurred.

Jacqueline smiled demurely.

"The social event of the year! My wife, Countess, wakes up on the eighth dying to see what everyone wore on the red carpet. This time we'll know!"

"Ms. Dampierre, if you don't mind me asking, what's the significance?" Mikaela asked. "Of the date?"

Jacqueline exchanged another look with Cameron before answering. "June seventh was my baby brother's birthday. He died of lymphocytic leukemia at twenty-four."

Mikaela covered her mouth. "I—I—"

"It's on all of our literature." Jacqueline pointed out the thick, elegantly embossed booklets that had sat at each place setting on all the tables all night.

Art frowned and Mikaela's stomach lurched.

"Oh." Mikaela put a fluttery hand to her forehead. "I'm so— I apologize."

She hadn't even picked one up, other than to briefly peruse the dining options for the evening.

Rookie move.

Jacqueline glanced at Cameron before she shook her head, dismissing it. "Never mind, it's dissertation length."

But it wasn't okay.

Proctor cleared his throat. Cameron gave her a lopsided grin.

"Countess?" Art turned then to his seated wife, encouraging the young woman to her feet. His lovely, model-esque, German third wife, *who was several inches taller than any of them there, aside from Cameron*, immediately commanded all the attention, to Mikaela's relief. "Nastassja, let me introduce you…"

"It's okay." Cameron leaned sideways to whisper to Mikaela as Art moved to introduce Jacqueline to other assorted Wexler, Welford and Bromley partners and their guests seated at the table.

"I can't believe I did that." Mikaela sulked. "She hates me now."

"She doesn't."

"How would you know?" she snapped.

"I just do, I promise. Care to dance?"

"Huh?" Complete mortification occupied Mikaela's thoughts.

Proctor looked their way briefly and Mikaela flashed him a strained smile.

"Ms. Marchand," Cameron repeated louder, putting out a hand to her. "Would you like to *dance*?" He pointed into the air, looking upward, and she noticed then that the music had slowed from a faster-paced tempo that played before.

Art, Proctor and Jacqueline were already gone before Mikaela could redeem herself, speaking to Todd and his wife, Anita, a few seats away. Then Art whisked Nastassja out onto the dance floor.

"We've never danced together before," Mikaela whispered under the music.

She tracked the room, conscious of any possible eyes on them. But only Suze seemed interested, although she tried valiantly to appear otherwise.

"You know, you're right." Cameron cocked his head to

the side. "With everything so hush-hush, we never attended any parties together, did we?"

Mikaela shook her head, shamed by his casual reference to her one great and lasting regret.

"No time like the present then." Cameron smiled in the way that historically Mikaela found hard to resist. Then extended his palm to her again.

Mikaela clenched her fist, steeling herself before taking it. "I'm not great. Just warning you."

"Don't worry, I am," he said, walking her through the crowd with one hand resting on the small of her back.

The warmth of his palm seeped through the thin material of her raw-silk dress. Mikaela tried not to stare at him, debonair in a tailored jet-black tuxedo that accentuated his broad shoulders and slim waist. Cameron led her out onto the crowded dance floor before taking her by the hand as they arrived. He gently raised it and she spun in a fluid motion into his arms. Placing his hand delicately on her back, he pulled her closer. Mikaela cringed slightly at the surprise of his touch, clutching the back of his suit jacket in her fist. She scanned the room again, just barely seeing over his shoulders even in her heels.

He looked down at her. "Relax," he chided as they began to sway together.

"Easy for you to say, your job isn't on—"

"And quit leading."

"What?"

"You're leading." He shook the palm he held, making her whole arm wobble. "Stop it and just trust me," he said softly, pulling her closer and resuming their small sway. "See?"

Mikaela nodded, glancing around the crowd trying to spot Art and his wife.

"Don't worry about them. Worry about me. You don't

want me stepping on your toes and I don't want you stepping on mine. Not in those things."

Both their eyes fell onto the strappy stilettos she had on as he led her through a conservative box step.

"Wow, you are really light on your feet."

One song had already flowed into another as they moved in a small square, buoyed by the music.

"Blame Anne Murphy and Saturday afternoons at Larkspur Dance Academy, from eight years old to eleven when I washed out. I can fox-trot and Viennese waltz too."

"Uh-oh, watch out!" She laughed, growing more comfortable. "Don't let the music change to 'The Blue Danube.'"

"You wouldn't be in any real trouble, until they put on a rumba." He chuckled along with her.

"Don't you worry, I'd leave your ass right here on the dance floor."

"Oh, I *know*." One eyebrow rose. "You'd absolutely abandon me, wouldn't you?"

Mikaela stiffened, attempting to pull away but he held on.

"Kaela, it was a joke."

"It wasn't funny."

"It was to me."

"Then maybe you should be out here alone." She let the hand on his shoulder drop.

Just then, Jacqueline, on the arm of Proctor, danced into view. Mikaela returned the smile to her face and her arm to his shoulder, resuming as Cameron searched around until he saw Jacqueline too. He smiled and yet another look passed between them. Jacqueline appraised Mikaela pointedly, giving them both a nod.

"What is up with you two?" Mikaela asked.

He grinned down at her. "You jealous?"

She scoffed. "Besides the fact that she's married to the head of the whole Manhattan Stock Exchange, nope."

"Ouch."

"So, you're one of her favorite photographers. But it's obviously more than that, right?"

"Well, we've been good friends...for a long time."

Mikaela's eyebrows shot up.

"*Not like that.* We met, through *this* charity, actually." Cameron inhaled as if bracing himself. "My daughter, Robin, had acute lymphocytic leukemia as a kid."

"Like Jacqueline's brother?" Mikaela gasped.

"*Marcel.* Yes." He nodded. "Exactly like him. But the survival rate is much better in children. Like ninety percent."

"How old was Robin when she was diagnosed?"

"Three. When she went into full remission, six." Cameron exhaled deeply as if the relief of that moment remained with him all these years later.

Mikaela was stunned. At three? She couldn't imagine what that must have been like for Cameron...and Julie too. Back then, she was fresh out of law school, renting a tiny studio apartment in West Harlem and living on ramen and coffee. It was hard to fathom having had to deal with a sick child.

"Cam, I'm so sorry."

"Wasn't your fault. Wasn't anybody's fault...even though for a long time I did blame myself. Just the luck of the draw, I guess."

Mikaela fell silent. Knowing what happened to Cameron's mother and father, she knew Robin's illness must have been a particularly terrifying period of his life. She squeezed his palm, giving him a wan smile.

Cameron returned it in kind, continuing on. "Anyway, in addition to funding research, the L&L Foundation sponsors treatment for sick kids. And Robin ended up being one of those kids."

"Thank God. So, how'd you end up working for Jacqueline?"

"Jacqueline takes an interest in the foundation's families. Because of Marcel, it's more than charity for her," he said. "We got to be friends and she saw my photos."

"And the rest is history?" She snapped her fingers. "Just like that?"

"She encouraged me to try." He stilled for a moment. "In my life, I've had three women who believed in me—my mother, Jacqueline..." His eyes were aflame like sapphires in the ambient light. *"And you."*

Mikaela's face warmed under his intensifying gaze. She dropped her arms and stepped back from him abruptly.

"What is it?" Cameron looked around, confused.

All around them, people continued to dance. But Mikaela couldn't, frozen in place. It was as if more than just the crowd swayed around her. At his words, she struggled to correct the little capsizing boat that held all her emotions, attempting to right herself.

"I can't dance to this," she lied, convinced everyone, but him especially, could see her reel.

"It's an easy two-step." He illustrated, putting one foot, then the other in front of him, snapping on the one and three.

She shook her head ruefully. Dance lessons or not, Cameron barely had the hang of a faster drum-heavy R & B beat the music had changed to. Mikaela was far more proficient in this than the slow dance. It was the only other thing she had in her back pocket besides the *Electric Slide*, and she knew that was too much to hope for at a gala.

"Here." She took his hand, trying to shake off the queer feeling he'd given her and help him find the rhythm, moving on the two and four. "We got it. Now, what were you saying?"

"I was saying," Cameron continued, oblivious to the fact that the way he looked at her made Mikaela feel like the ground had fallen out from beneath her, "Jacqueline got me commercial work—ads, some fashion photography."

"I thought you did black-and-white landscapes and people and stuff?"

"I did. I do." He leaned in to answer. "But that's become my more personal work. My editorial stuff? The stuff I'm known for, is all fashion."

"Known for?" Mikaela scoffed, the sound carrying above the music, then instantly regretted the incredulity in her voice. "I mean…sorry. I guess I don't really know what it is you do anymore. So, you're no journeyman photographer then?"

"Nope." Cameron smiled, and a moment later, took Mikaela's hand, raising an arm to encourage her into a little spin before pulling her back to him, causing her dress to flare around her ankles.

She hadn't wanted to know about Cameron's life once it had bifurcated from hers. Now, the flutters in her stomach reminded her of precisely why that was.

It was by design.

"I should have guessed that, huh?" She tried to laugh it off.

He averted his eyes for a moment as if thinking on something while the music slowed down again. Then he paused, holding her to him, and leaned in to speak directly into her ear. "I didn't intend on any of this." He referred to the opulence that surrounded them.

There was an affecting earnestness in his voice. Mikaela's heart thudded with him this close, his thumb absently caressing the base of her spine like he used to.

"But it would've been like looking a gift horse in the mouth. Jacqueline's been in my corner, like a godmother, a big sister. She's been my most vocal champion since day one. But the catch is she generally demands access to everything. All my work. So, when I give *Glamazon* permission to use my photos, I ask that they agree to represent me through any related legal issues. It wasn't my idea, my good friend's a lawyer, and he decided if anyone wants to use not only my commercial or commissioned stuff, but the personal work too, then they have to at least agree to that. I didn't ask him to do it. And I don't know if they don't read it or what, but the companies…they just usually do. You see?"

She nodded, eyebrows rising. "I do see."

"Honestly, you know me, it's not like I set out to be a diva, or the next Avedon or Testino."

She pulled back. "*You're* comparing yourself to…?"

"No! I'm just saying…the fashion editorial stuff, I didn't pick it." He shrugged. "I fell into it."

"Of course you did." Mikaela's eyes rolled from him up to the pretty glass dome of the atrium high above them, with the faintest smile playing at her lips. "Yup, sure. Fashion photography, beautiful women, sumptuous locales, a real hardship, huh? Bet you 'fell into' your fair share of models too."

She nodded as Cameron laughed and shook his head.

"Maybe," he admitted. "In a manner of speaking, but only when I was newly a bachelor."

"I'm sure you had it rough," she teased. "Compromising your principles."

"Who said *anything* about principles? Those were lean times. I had to work to eat, right?"

"Oh, so you ate models, did you?" Mikaela adjusted the slightly crooked knot in his bow tie as the song overhead changed again.

Cameron's eyes widened, his finger pointing upward at the sound. It was the classic Prince slow jam "Adore." A grin crept over his face, enraptured by the music. His arm stiffened at Mikaela's back, pulling her closer again, his hand tightening around hers as he sang the tune under his breath, gazing down on her face. She didn't need to look at his lips as she'd come to know the words by heart over the years.

"I mean, makes sense…" she mused over the music to distract herself from his humming, instead appraising the dozens of models that happened to share the dance floor with them at that very moment. The problem with that was, as much as she fought it, it seemed impossible that any of those women could feel as beautiful as Cameron was making her feel right then. "They look high in fiber, being twigs and beanpoles and whatnot. Good roughage."

Cameron burst out laughing as Mikaela chuckled along with him.

It was so similar to old times. Mikaela could practically smell the flowers in their community garden back home.

Just then, he spun her out once again and she squealed in delight. And as the room whirled around them both, Mikaela truly enjoyed herself for the first time in a long while.

fourteen

"So, that's the old guy from *Gunsmoke*?" Cameron asked, looking up at the screen. "I used to love watching the reruns with my dad."

He spoke in a hushed tone, leaning into Mikaela. But a shushing noise came from a few rows off to their left anyway. For a moment, that stopped Mikaela from responding.

This week, Mikaela met Cameron at the movies for a Man vs. Nature matinee—which was a double feature of *Them!* and a personal favorite of hers, *Kingdom of the Spiders* with William Shatner. She liked that the theater was a safe and easy place to meet in public during the day. The matinee was after work for her but before work for him. But most importantly, it was while Julie was occupied with her job at the courthouse.

"Yup," Mikaela whispered back quickly, trying not to be distracted from the scene.

As far as she was concerned, James Arness, of Marshal Dillon fame, looked younger but not so much younger as he attempted to save costar Joan Weldon from a giant, bus-sized ant. She didn't understand Cameron's confusion, but then again, not everyone lived for that kind of movie mi-nutia like she did.

Cameron put his hand over Mikaela's on the armrest they shared, rubbing the back of it gently with his thumb. She held her breath, enjoying its unexpected softness and the lightness of his fingers. There were small calluses that, in a passing moment, she almost asked him about. She glanced over and saw he was staring at her.

Mikaela couldn't pretend anymore. It was obvious; he was only there for her.

She held her chin up and directed her eyes back to the screen. But as he held her hand and whispered gently to her in the dark, the movie was doing a bad job of keeping her at-tention. This was the third matinee they'd seen together but now every time she saw Cameron, all Mikaela could imagine was his mouth and hands on her. It wasn't even Cameron's fault either. So far, he'd been a perfect gentleman.

Yet, she was already beside herself with anticipation.

"And him?" Cameron asked, pulling Mikaela back from her straying thoughts, with his breath feathering the side of her face.

With him this close, she was no longer sure it wasn't de-liberate on his part. She crossed her legs in front of her.

"That's the guy who played Brooks in *Shawshank*. Re-member? The old guy with the little bird?" She saw Cam-eron looking at her in the dark. "What?"

Mikaela leaned away, thinking of the sort of adoring way Cameron seemed to always be watching her now, praying for the strength to not jump all over him for it.

"You are such a nerd."

"Hey, you're here too!"

"Agreed. I just think it's so cool that you know that. I don't know many other girls who liked *The Shawshank Redemption*."

The way Cameron seemed thrilled by every word she uttered was like catnip.

"Many?"

He chuckled. "Any."

Mikaela shook her head. "You don't know the right girls then. Julie and I love that movie. We watched it three times in this theater."

A person two rows ahead of them turned to put her finger to her lips. Mikaela made an apologetic gesture as Cameron reached over and tickled her side. Mikaela squirmed.

"You're ticklish!"

"Seventy-three percent of the population is ticklish, big whoop."

"Well, I think it's cute. I also think it's cute that you can probably quote Morgan Freeman after seeing *Shawshank* three times."

Cameron reached over and tickled her again. Mikaela shifted away, trying to stifle a high-pitched squeal. "Stop it!"

She giggled as a man near the back shushed them again.

"These nice people are trying to watch the movie, sir. And we're probably driving them insane."

"You know what *else* can drive someone insane?" Cameron asked with his mouth near her jawbone.

"You wish!" Mikaela's cheeks burned where his lips hovered. She pushed him off playfully and snorted, scandalized.

"I do." In the glow of the screen, a slow smile crept across Cameron's face, as his eyes rose to meet hers again.

The heat in the apples of her cheeks burned as he watched her smiling an identical smile to his.

"You're blushing, aren't you!" Mikaela declared.

Cameron's smile grew. "You are too."

"How could you ever tell?" Mikaela challenged, though he was right.

"I can tell."

They both snickered like schoolkids telling naughty jokes. Somewhere in the audience someone shushed them again.

"Well, you're far too easy to impress if Morgan Freeman does it for you," she teased him.

"You might be right."

"I guess you're lucky you found me then."

Cameron guffawed, earning himself a few more scattered glances and shushes from other members of the small audience. "I suspect you're bein' sarcastic, but yeah, I am."

Mikaela sighed, gripping the armrest they shared in case she'd float away with delight. There was something so sweet and strangely guileless about Cameron.

Mikaela knew then with a rising panic, *this* was going to become a problem.

"Kaela!"

Mikaela and Vanessa both paused, waiting for their father's chastisement yet again. They'd been loudly going back and forth all afternoon and he'd been refereeing in lackluster fashion from downstairs.

Mikaela lowered her voice automatically. "You're nuts if you think you're gonna turn my room and my stuff into your own personal yard sale!" She snatched the contested T-shirt out of her sister's hands.

"C'mon, Kae. Quit being a bitch. You aren't taking all this stuff with you."

"But I am taking this," Mikaela huffed. "I already gave you a ton of my stuff. You can't have everything!"

Vanessa's face said she believed Mikaela was the stupidest person who ever lived. "Oh please—"

"Miss Marchand!" their father called again.

They both froze.

"The elder!"

Mikaela rushed to her door, sticking her head out into the hallway. "Yes, Daddy?"

"Kiss ass." Vanessa snickered behind her.

Mikaela scowled at her sister, moving to the top of the stairs. "Yes?"

"You have a guest," her father announced from below.

"Don't touch any more of my shit, Nessa. I mean it," Mikaela commanded in a harsh whisper, pointing at Vanessa's little head poking out of her bedroom door like a shy groundhog. "I'll give you what *I* want you to have. In fact, get out of my room!"

Mikaela hustled down the stairs, past her father standing at the front door. She only stopped short when she got onto the porch.

"Do you know this boy?" J.D. asked, arms crossed and frowning.

Cameron stood there in a dress shirt and slacks with a baseball cap in a strangle hold between his hands.

"Uh…" Mikaela hesitated. "Um, Dad, this is Cameron Murphy. Sheriff Davenport's nephew," she added.

"Sheriff Davenport?" The furrow in J.D.'s brow deepened. "His nephew, you say?"

"I'm his cousin, actually. An' Cam's fine, Mr. Marchand." He stepped forward from the edge of the porch to reach out and shake her father's hand.

"He send you here? Did he need somethin'?" Mikaela's father eyed the outstretched hand with suspicion before taking it. "I warned him that that rear axle wouldn't last much longer."

Mikaela gave an audible sigh of relief as their hands clasped. With remarkable speed, this surprise visit had been on the verge of taking a hard left.

"No, sir. I just wanted to talk with Mikaela for a minute. If I may?"

"Wait, is this Julie's Cameron?" her father said as if cylinders had begun falling into place. He pumped Cameron's arm cheerfully. "Oh hello!"

Mikaela wanted the ground to split open and swallow her…or preferably her dad.

Cameron frowned, as deeply puzzled as she was mortified. *"Daddy!"*

Mr. Marchand looked between them, grinning.

"Dad, I—" Mikaela stopped, too flustered to continue.

"Isn't this the young man Julie was going to the lake to—" he began.

Mikaela forced an awkward smile in Cameron's direction before stopping her father. "Thank you for calling me, Daddy! We'll be just out here on the steps, okay?" She grabbed the front doorknob, pulling it slowly but firmly closed in her father's face.

Unfortunately, the ground had not opened to envelop her when she turned to see Cameron still standing there.

"What are you doing here?" Mikaela sighed, giving a tight smile.

All she needed in her otherwise uncomplicated life was for Julie to see her on the porch with Cameron. Mikaela looked up and down her empty street, still debating taking him inside, but there was zero privacy there either. At least on the porch no one could sneak up behind them without somehow announcing themselves.

Cameron chuckled. "What was your dad saying?"

"What?" She offered him a seat on the top step of the porch, sitting down beside him. "N-nothing."

"Something about your friend Julie?" His face was still but from his tone it was clear Cameron was amused, razzing her.

"Ah, well…" She shrugged, trying to drift off topic. "W-why are you here?"

"Uh-uh." He shook his head. "'*Julie's* Cameron'?"

Mikaela stammered. Admitting this would not only break her best friend's confidence but be spectacularly awkward. She clasped her hands together, averting Cameron's gaze.

But remaining quiet as Julie rhapsodized nonstop about Cameron incessantly for weeks had been wearing on her nerves anyway. "She… Well, she may or may not have a little, tiny—" *not so tiny* "—crush on you."

Mikaela sighed, somewhat relieved, imagining then that it was better he knew the truth now. That way, he would know he had his choice between them, he'd pick Julie—*naturally*—and that would be that. Mikaela's feelings might be a little hurt, of course. Sure, she'd be a bit mopey for a while, but ultimately, she'd be just fine. And maybe knowing this now, they could all get on with the rest of their summer. Then Mikaela could head off to an exciting new life in New York City in a matter of two short months and forget it all. Off to bigger, better things…she hoped.

Cameron smiled, a bashful slant on an otherwise straight face. "Aw, that's cute. And do you too?"

Cute? Mikaela mulled that, almost missing his question. "Me?"

"Do you have a crush on me too?"

The resounding yes that was dying to shoot out of her mouth found resistance, making her face burn. But there was no point in denying it. She nodded instead.

"Well, that's a relief, since I'm here to see *you*." Cameron exhaled, moving on as if there was nothing else to be said about it. He hit her with the full force of his thousand-plus-watt smile then.

Mikaela's heart lurched, feeling liable to burst out of her chest and flop around on the porch like a fish.

"I mean, I realized, I wanted to see your face…"

She'd already noticed how Cameron smiled effortlessly, unaware of how debilitating it was to those he inflicted those smiles upon. He deployed them in a charm offensive that she was constantly fending off. Mikaela sighed as he did it yet again and slid away from him on the step.

"Since you gave me your address, I came to call on you."

"Call on me?" She laughed, glancing over her shoulder at the frosted glass pane in her front door. She slid farther away when she saw her father's shadow move across it. "From which century exactly are you?"

"Oh, so you're one of those who believes that chivalry is dead, huh?" Cameron said, clueless about their audience.

"*And buried*. Yup," she declared with a nod. "A man's as likely to be a serial killer as a gentleman, these days."

"Wow, that's an opinion," he remarked. "So says you, huh? Well, we'll need to do something about that."

He'd stupefied her again. She paused, unsure of what next to say, given the certitude with which he'd declared this intention. She was just flirting in her usual off-color and combative way. Cameron, however, was being perfectly serious.

"I was being hyperbolic."

"You ruin the joke if you explain it." He nudged her shoe with his own.

Mikaela closed her mouth, focusing on her legs and feet in her dirty shorts and old sneakers. She tapped them together absently, checking behind her again for their eavesdropper, but the shadow had finally gone.

"Do you like *Under the Cherry Moon*?" Cameron asked, pulling her attention his way.

"Pardon?"

"The movie?"

Mikaela blinked at Cameron, confused.

"'Anotherloverholenyohead'?"

Her eyes widened as he gazed right back at her.

"Okay, 'Kiss'?"

"I'm sorry, *what*?" Mikaela choked out as if he'd been speaking in tongues, or worse yet, making a request.

"Prince and the Revolution? The *Parade* album?" Cameron said, pointing to the T-shirt Mikaela had draped over her shoulder. "'Anotherloverholenyohead'? It's my favorite song by him."

Mikaela followed his finger, having forgotten the shirt was there, being kept from Vanessa's covetous hands. She pulled it off her shoulder and opened it. Cameron pointed to Prince's usual eccentric countenance staring back at them from the front.

"I went to his *Love 4 One Another* tour a few years ago. I had to mow lawns a whole summer to afford those tickets. Amazing seats."

"*You're* a Prince fan?" Mikaela asked incredulously. "You don't seem like the type to be a Prince fan."

"What does *that* mean?"

Mikaela stopped herself from saying "white" out loud.

Which was stupid, lots of white people loved Prince. But was that true of a lot of the white folks in her town who looked like Cameron? He seemed like he was more of a Radiohead or Foo Fighters fan.

…Or maybe even Garth Brooks and Toby Keith, for all

she knew. Which, incidentally, would have put him in company with her dad.

"His Purple Highness?" He scoffed. "Who exists that isn't a Prince fan?"

Mikaela nipped at her bottom lip, silently examining the shirt open in her lap, staring at the jagged purple lettering on it: "Prince and the Revolution: Purple Rain Tour '85."

"You?" He laughed as if baffled by the very thought. "You aren't, *really*?"

She shook her head sheepishly.

"Then what's up with the shirt?"

Mikaela shrugged. "I mean, I've seen the movie, heard the album. It's just 'eh.'"

"Blasphemy! So, wait a minute, this shirt's an heirloom. Who's the fan? Your dad?"

She shook her head, keeping her expression even but her hands betrayed her by twisting the tee as if she was wringing it out.

Cameron nodded with slow awareness. "Well, in my house, *my mom* couldn't care less. My dad was the real fan. His gateways to the Purple One were Hendrix, Clapton and Santana. Had a weakness for a wicked axe-man." He did an impromptu air-guitar solo for her until she laughed.

"*I* liked that the lyrics were dirty," he admitted. "Have you ever listened to the lyrics to 'Darling Nikki'?"

She shook her head.

"Good, don't," he chuckled. "My mom nearly murdered my dad when she caught me singing 'Erotic City' in my room. He thought it was hilarious…but then, he thought everything was freakin' hilarious."

Cameron grew pensive. Mikaela watched him fiddle with his ball cap, crunching the brim in his hands, curling the well-worn beak more.

"Thought? He's gone, he passed?"

"If you're asking if he died, yes. A year ago, this past spring," Cameron said, tapping the cap against his knee then. "I hate talking about death euphemistically."

"Sorry."

He touched her arm. "No, I'm sorry. I didn't mean anything by that. I just get frustrated when people make it sound like he went out for a pack of cigarettes and didn't come back."

"My mother left and never came back so…"

"But she didn't die though?" He seemed agonized by the thought.

"No, but she might as well have." Mikaela sighed with exasperation.

Cameron frowned. "Don't say that. Seriously, Mikaela, don't *ever* say that. You don't know what it's like."

It wasn't a rebuke; he wasn't angry with her. His tone hadn't changed, even if he was a little pained by her carelessness.

"Losing my dad was like, like losing an arm or an eye or something. One minute, I could reach out and touch him, talk to him, ask him a question and then the next, poof, he literally didn't exist anymore."

"I'm so sorry I said that, Cam."

"Forget it." He shook it off. "I don't know what you and your mom's deal is. I just know that losing my dad and almost losing my mother in the span of only two years nearly killed me… *And I'm not being hyperbolic.*"

Mikaela was honored that he'd chosen to confide in her but ashamed of her callousness.

"Cam, I—"

Cameron took her hand and smiled again, using a little

more effort this time than normal, drawing in a deep breath. "Um, I'm sorry. Can we start over?"

"Sure." Mikaela squeezed his long fingers sitting in her palm.

"Good." It seemed as if his whole upper body shuddered under a weight.

Mikaela scooted closer now, resisting the very real fight-or-flight instinct that was screaming at her to do the opposite.

Cameron was the kind of guy Mikaela could easily fall for. And though she knew perfection was objectively impossible; already her heart couldn't tell the difference. But she was leaving for school. What good was it meeting a guy who seemed perfect now?

"Hi, Mikaela," he said, starting again, staring into her eyes.

"You can call me Kaela."

The corners of Cameron's mouth rose then. They both grinned at each other, hands clasped and knees touching.

"I think I need to take you on a real date, Kaela."

She giggled.

He was so officious about it. Previously, most of her "dates" were group outings where there were at least two or three other couples with them. Julie was the only girl Mikaela knew of that had been legitimately picked up at her front door and accompanied to a venue for any event besides prom and homecoming. She didn't know what to say.

"Okay." Her grin grew outsize, thrilled by the idea of it... until she remembered Julie. How would she react to the idea of Cameron dating Mikaela?

Not well, was Mikaela's first thought.

Though she was almost too giddy to care, there was the matter of her recent relationship history. Even a year after Mikaela's last ex, Mitchell, left for college, their relationship was still a bone of contention between her and Julie. For as long as the girls had been friends, the boys that followed Julie around tolerated Mikaela's near-constant presence as long as it meant spending time with the girl they adored. And as far as Julie was concerned, Mikaela owed her that same consideration. Those boys, the ones who adored Julie, clamoring to be whomever she needed them to be—boyfriend, chauffeur, open wallet—had all just gotten in wherever they fit in, happy to vie for Julie's undivided attention. None earning it. But when Mikaela was with Mitchell, she wasn't the same. She hadn't been available to constantly cater to Julie's whims, when Julie was bored, or sad, or lonely, or just plain wanted her around. And though, even to this day, she still wasn't sure she agreed with it, Mikaela spent months afterward apologizing to Julie for that anyway.

Which left the matter of Cameron…

"How about Angelino's in Dunwoody?" Mikaela suggested.

"Out of town? Okay." Cameron grinned, squeezing her hands in his. "You pick the day and time."

"Could I meet you there?"

"Sounds good."

Mikaela flung glances up and down the block, making sure the street was empty. Then, leaning forward as Cameron did, they met in the middle. He brushed his smooth cheek against hers once and then again on the other side, grazing the tip of her nose with his own, before pressing his lips chastely to hers. A second later, she fell back, jumping to her feet.

Cameron startled, scanning the porch and the yard, eyes wide as the front door swung open and Vanessa appeared in the doorway.

"PRIVACY?" Mikaela bellowed.

"Yeah, okay, out on the front porch?" Vanessa spit back, turning her attention on their visitor. "What's his deal?"

"Nessa, that's rude," Mikaela chastised. "Cameron—"

"Cam," he interjected.

"Cam, this is my little sister, Vanessa."

"Hi there," he said, with a broad, nonthreatening grin like Vanessa was a cranky toddler.

Vanessa scowled at him, deep lines of suspicion etching themselves into her brow.

"Yes?" Mikaela prompted, fidgeting guiltily as her sister stared.

Vanessa pried her eyes away with a roll, back to Mikaela. "Dad says he's free to join us for lunch...?"

Mikaela shrugged at Cameron apologetically. But he was beatific, not nearly as put out by being dismissed by Vanessa as Mikaela was on his behalf.

"Tell Mr. Marchand thank you, but I have to run. This was my lunch break." He directed this at Vanessa as he got up and dusted off his pants with his hands.

"Whatever," she muttered, retreating into the house, but leaving the door ajar.

"Your dad doesn't *really* keep a gun in the house, does he?" Cameron asked then. "'Cause I did see him lurking earlier and your sister looks like she's got an itchy trigger finger."

They stared at each other for a long moment before breaking into giggles.

"Hush." Mikaela shook her head and, cupping his face between her palms, she stretched to kiss him again.

fifteen

NOW

"There's another one," Vanessa said, sticking a sharp elbow in Mikaela's ribs as she tried to say goodbye to the concierge of the Soho Luxor.

Mikaela thanked the older woman yet again, with a tight smile before turning to her sister.

"Are we gonna do this every time you see one?"

"Maybe, I haven't decided."

As they pushed through the lobby's extravagantly gilded revolving door, Mikaela squinted at the waiting sun. She tracked her sister's singular line of sight across the street. And sure enough, there it was. Yet another of the posters featuring her face, now on a wooden shed surrounding a construction site. Tucked between dozens of posted bills for new films, Broadway openings and new album releases.

Mikaela scowled, feeling for her sunglasses on top of her head and pulling them down.

The photo from the *Glamazon* cover was plastered all over

the City, which should have inured her to it by now. Even more so once these gallery posters with the same image seemed to become ubiquitous, popping up all over the City like mushrooms.

Vanessa ran across the street, indifferent to the blaring horns of annoyed drivers. Mikaela shook her head, apologizing as she followed behind.

"Oooh, it's right down the street!" Vanessa squealed, perusing the image and pointing at the address listed.

"Let's not." Mikaela had a hard time shaking what had happened the last time she dared to stop by Cameron's gallery. "We have to meet the guy at Tribeca Loft in an hour and then go see Pearl of the Seaport at four."

"I suppose I should be grateful that you're finally taking Mom's birthday seriously, actually interested in checking out the venues. It's been like pulling teeth to get you to do this. And I would be, if I didn't know it's just an excuse not to see what's up in that gallery!" Vanessa cackled at Mikaela's expense. "This is your ex-man, girl! Ain't you even *a little* curious?"

"Not even a little bit." Mikaela maintained a blank expression, despite the fact that, as usual, Vanessa was speaking the absolute truth.

Cameron had been good enough, so far, to not mention it. But the shame of her past aborted snooping operation had not dissipated. That was still a low-water mark, too embarrassing to even think about for long. Even her therapist, Ximena, had considerable difficulty prying many details about it from her.

"Oh, come on! We'll be quick," Vanessa chided. "You may not care, but I'm dying to see what Cam's been up to." She grabbed Mikaela's clenched fist and dragged her along the long block.

Mikaela was surprised, when they arrived, to find she'd entirely misjudged the space. She peered around, stepping through the darkened threshold.

It was much bigger on the inside than she'd originally thought. It opened up into a far larger space toward the back. Gray slab cement floors, exposed terra-cotta-colored brick walls, strobe lighting in ironwork fixtures and reclaimed-wood support beams flagged it as the trendy, downtown gallery it was. The gallery was empty, save a single well-dressed man seated at a glass table in the back. But the whole space still exuded money.

There was no sign of the young woman from before, to Mikaela's great relief.

"We're just passing through," Vanessa announced as they stepped inside. "That okay?"

"Please," the man said with a big smile. "Just let me know if I can help you with anything."

Vanessa was the first to ooh and ahh as she examined the multitude of different-sized pictures hanging on the walls. Some were framed, made for display, while others were pasted directly onto the brick walls like street posters. And Mikaela passed the variety of images with a genuine sense of awe that matched her sister's.

Cameron's photos were an impressive combination of portraiture, landscapes and candids. Some were in black-and-white but others were magnificent editorial photographs in vivid color. There were shots of women and men from the covers of numerous magazines. Celebrities she'd watched countless times on television or the big screen. Some photos were parts of advertisement campaigns from most of the major fashion houses and perfumeries in the world. Spreads from some of the biggest publications. Cameron had been being ridiculously modest when she'd asked him about his work.

The photos were gorgeous. And standing there now, Mikaela could admit it was kind of amazing that she knew the man who brought these images to life when he was just some guy shooting pictures of wildflowers and waterfowl. A glance in Vanessa's direction told the same story. Her sister remained a few steps ahead, smiling to herself as they walked around the room. It wasn't long before they both recognized some of the locales in them too. Businesses long shuttered and people long dead were alive in these images.

"Look, Talbert's!" Vanessa exclaimed. A sense of nostalgia, as vivid as the photos, overcame Mikaela. "Aw, and old Dr. and Mrs. Brookhaven."

A black man married to a Latina woman, the Brookhavens were the first interracial couple Mikaela had ever seen.

Mikaela actually gasped, her eyes welling with tears. "Judge Robertson's old Camaro."

Vanessa nodded at the black-and-white image of Julie's father's beloved classic muscle car sitting on a block in the yard at their father's garage for maintenance.

Cameron's picture evoked a nostalgic sadness that was surprisingly visceral even after all these years. Mikaela trailed by a few paces, crisscrossing the room behind her sister, reading the didactic panels beside each photograph.

Cameron had transitioned to digital despite swearing he wouldn't. Mikaela smiled to herself.

Promises made full of conviction didn't always hold up twenty years later. She was going to have to remind him of that the next time they met.

A photo of a child's footprint in the sand at the moment the small foot left and the water returned to fill it caught her attention, intriguing her. Mikaela paused in front of the accompanying triptych. Even in black-and-white, she recognized Julie's abundant brown hair billowing in the breeze in the next picture, though her face wasn't visible. She held a grinning little towheaded girl over her shoulder, who had the same entrancing smile as her father.

"You recognize where they are?" Vanessa asked, glancing back at her. "Over on Capt'n Sam's…"

"These must have been from when the whole family was still going to Kiawah."

Vanessa nodded.

Mikaela remembered hearing about that at the time and wistfully thinking how they must have had it all figured out. That Julie and Cameron were living some sort of dream she had scarcely dared to have as she struggled through her lonely, challenging first years after law school. Now knowing what Cameron had told her and seeing these images, she understood appearances could be very deceiving.

"Oooh, look at these…" Vanessa cooed, moving into another section of new photos.

These were divorced from anything Mikaela recognized but indicative of the amazing life Cameron must have led now. Vanessa read aloud from the panels.

"Goa, Cuba, Bali, Lima… Girl, hold the phone! He been to the Seychelles!"

"He was always taken with the water," Mikaela explained. "Always wanted to travel."

"Didn't you too?" Vanessa asked.

Mikaela shrugged in response.

Cameron's newest work remained as preoccupied with the beaches, marine wildlife and the everyday activities of coastal and island communities as he had ever been.

She was envious.

"Hmm, well, I'm jealous." Vanessa again spoke Mikaela's truth aloud. "I mean, Salvador de Bahia is a long way from Lake Shelburne or landlocked ole Harmon. Good for him."

That it was. Mikaela adjusted her sunglasses, blinking back tears.

"Time," Mikaela declared, checking her watch. "Let's go."

"Y'all were so good together." Vanessa's voice gained a wistful quality. "Did you ever wonder—"

"No, I didn't." Mikaela cut her off forcefully. "And what do you know about how 'good' we were?"

"Girl, please." Vanessa sucked her teeth as she headed for the door.

Mikaela followed her little sister down the steps back onto the street, taking a deep breath of car-exhaust-tainted air.

"Not everyone was as blind as Julie was," Vanessa said, putting on her own sunglasses and taking the lead down the busy sidewalk.

sixteen

"Okay, give me the three elements of the complaint," Mikaela stated before biting into her sandwich and moaning.

As far as she was concerned, in New York City, the perfect lunch date consisted of just three things: a good spot, some good company and a marinated chicken breast sandwich with chipotle mayo on focaccia from Olive's in Battery Park City. Sitting on a park bench next to Suze, on a beautifully sunny day, looking out over the Hudson River, she had all those things.

Unfortunately, amid this final push ahead of the fall partnership announcement, Mikaela often didn't have the time to do this anymore. But she still tried to carve out a lunch or two outside the office with her young assistant. Over their four years together, it was their only tradition. And through it, Suze had become not only her favorite mentee but also her girlfriend. And not only that, her inspiration.

Thanks to scholarships and her mother's money, Mikaela had not had to do law school the way Suze currently did it: at night, while holding down a demanding full-time job. Still, Mikaela knew, eccentric hair and daring sartorial choices included, Suze was a force to be reckoned with and so, watching and helping her come into her own made Mikaela happy.

"Um," Suze spoke while piling leafy greens onto a fork. "The jurisdiction, the statement of the claim and the relief?"

"Good. Now, identify types of motions against the complaint."

"I can defend against the validity of the complaint..." Suze stuffed the heaping fork into her mouth.

"How?"

"If I knew this is how I'd be spending my lunch hour, I'd have stayed in the office," Suze said between chews.

"You have a test tonight. And I know you already know this stuff. But Civ Pro is foundational. You gotta know this backward and forward," Mikaela said. "Now, c'mon. Your defenses?"

Suze sighed. "I do this, and we can get back to this being a lunch where you'll answer some of *my* questions?"

Mikaela shrugged. "Sure. Like what?"

"You promise?" Suze paused, skewering Mikaela with a doubtful look.

Mikaela wondered at the young woman's sudden evasiveness. "Yeah, of course."

"About Mr. Murphy."

Mikaela picked up her water bottle and took a long pull from the straw before answering. "What could I possibly tell you about Cam—" she sputtered. "Cameron, I mean, uh, Mr. Murphy?"

Suze broke into a broad self-satisfied grin as Mikaela groaned internally. "Oh, you and he just seemed cozy the other night, that's all. Like you were getting along *really* well."

"Suzukea!" Mikaela scoffed. "Did you forget? I have a man."

"A cute one too. That you hardly ever see." Suze rolled her eyes. "So?"

"That I'm happy with…"

"If you say so." Suze pursed her lips, digging into her bowl. "I'm just saying, Dr. Guerrero ain't put a ring on it, yet. And Mr. Murphy's fine—you seem to like each other."

"Mr. Murphy is a client."

"Only technically. He's your *client's* client." Suze punctuated her statement with her fork, her mouth full of greens. "You're always on me about legal 'technicalities.' Well, that's one, the way I see it."

The way Mikaela saw it too. Unfortunately for her.

"You think so, huh?" Mikaela asked, unsure of how much she could or should share with her assistant. "And it's just that easy?"

The truth danced on her tongue, desperate to leap free. It had been stressful enough keeping it from her colleagues. Still, was it fair of Mikaela to burden Suze with the truth then swear her to secrecy?

"I watched y'all the other night. And I mean, I like Dr. Guerrero and everything, but woo!" Suze fanned herself. "You and Mr. Murphy…" She hissed, imitating a sizzle.

Mikaela groaned out loud this time. "It's that obvious?"

Suze smiled. "Obvious? I mean *I* noticed that y'all had enough chemistry to need hosing down by a hazmat team but, you know, I'm an empath."

Mikaela snorted.

Suze cut her eyes in her boss's direction, affronted, but she continued. "But the white folks in our office? They wouldn't notice if you started wearing a hot-pink habit and speaking in tongues as long as you kept that work flowin' and dem billables up."

"True." Mikaela rolled her eyes.

"So?"

"So what?"

"The deets, give 'em to me."

"Uh-uh, you first." Mikaela crossed her arms and legs, leaning back on the bench.

"Fine. Defenses against the complaint—lack of subject-matter jurisdiction, lack of personal jurisdiction, improper venue, insufficient process, insufficient service of process."

"And?"

"Uh…" Suze closed her eyes as if she was envisioning it. "And failure to state a claim upon which relief can be granted."

"Huh." Mikaela mulled. "Why do I suddenly feel like I just got hustled?"

"I don't know what you're talking about. *But* from now on, I wouldn't make any more risky deals with chicks from Flatbush. Just sayin'," Suze offered as Mikaela giggled. "Now spill."

seventeen

Mikaela shuddered. Closing her mouth, she made a little gasping noise, nearly headbutting Cameron above her.

"I've never gotten that kind of a reaction before." Cameron rolled away. "Bless you... I think?"

"Sorry," Mikaela said, trying not to laugh and failing, "but, I think it was obvious that that was a sneeze."

"Not really."

Mikaela rose to her side and hit him lightly on the shoulder as he chuckled.

"So, a sneeze, huh? That's okay, I guess."

She looked him over, eyebrow raised. "I don't know what you expected to happen when we're in a field of flowers."

"I thought you liked it here? I thought you thought it was romantic? Girls like this, don't they...a field of flowers?"

Mikaela sighed audibly.

"Do you have hay fever? Is that the problem?"

"I don't but look around you, we're literally rolling around in dirt and pollen regularly."

Flat on his back, Cameron's mouth eased upward into a smirk at the sky. "But I enjoy getting dirty with you." Cameron rose up onto one elbow to face her, drawing his eyes and a hand down the slope of Mikaela's bare shoulder along her side, coming to a stop on her hip.

He may have had numerous qualities she cherished, but being a natural Romeo was not one.

Mikaela shook her head, flipping onto her stomach. The blades of grass sticking through the blanket were itchy against her skin. She reached into the picnic basket, extracting a small Nikon camera Cameron had gifted her. He was teaching her form and composition, but so far all she had were lots of pictures of the flowers in this garden.

They were both nude in the middle of a small wildflower-filled clearing among some trees in the most forgotten corner of her mother's community garden. Lying together on Cameron's mother's old picnic blanket, it was a place they found themselves more and more frequently as the hot summer dragged on. On the outskirts of town, far away from any possible risk of detection.

Mikaela sneezed and then sighed.

Cameron patted her hip. "I'll bring an antihistamine next time."

"Next time, huh?" Mikaela laughed. "Did you even hear me?"

Cameron winked at her.

"Damn." He glanced at his watch, sitting up and reaching for his clothes.

They always seemed to be on borrowed time, either his or hers. And for today, their time was nearly up. His shift started in an hour and Julie would be off work, looking for Mikaela soon.

Mikaela sighed again at the thought.

Secret moments like these, when she'd been able to steal away with Cameron, had become their respite. The only times and places where they weren't responsible for anyone else's happiness or subject to anyone's needs above their own. No demanding friends or sick parents. For Mikaela, Cameron detailed his plans to take a cross-country trip as soon as his mother recovered fully, shooting pictures of the different people and new places he encountered. And Mikaela told Cameron her dreams of clerking for a Supreme Court justice. They imagined exploring the world together; she was adventurous with him and he was ambitious with her. And only together did they express these thoughts and dreams freely, not editing themselves like Mikaela tended to do among her friends, even sometimes Julie. But the summer was almost over and when it ended, Mikaela knew precious moments like these would go with it.

Mikaela played with the camera lens, focusing it like Cameron had taught her as she lay on her stomach, unconcerned with her own nudity, propped up on her elbows, watching while he dressed.

"What?" he asked when he saw her watching.

She framed him in her viewfinder as he turned toward her.

"Just checking out the goods."

He grinned. His bronzed and muscled stomach strained as he leaned back to scoot into his shorts, dragging them up his legs then over his slim hips and firm backside.

"You enjoying your exclusive ticket to the gun show?" Cameron flexed an arm. He jumped to his feet in front of her. "Cannons!" he announced like a carnival barker, flexing the other arm.

"Eh, looks like a small-arms affair to me," she deadpanned, snapping a shot.

"You love it!"

He was right: she did love it.

Mikaela framed him, pressing the shutter button numerous times, capturing Cameron as he played around. Through her camera lens, the abundant sunlight broke through the trees, bouncing off his body and dancing in strands of his light, wavy hair.

"Where's your f-stop?" He paused to quiz her, referring to the aperture of her camera's lens.

"Um, eight?"

He squinted up over his shoulder. "Stop down to sixteen."

With the sun directly behind him, visible air particles floated in the beams that seemed to frame him beautifully. Sweat still glistened on his broad shoulders and shimmered in the fine blond hairs on his chest, making him look quite literally golden.

"Mr. Olympia," she called out to him, taking repeated shots while he struck a series of exaggerated bodybuilding poses. "You're a fool!"

Cameron deflated theatrically, pouting at Mikaela's words. She giggled at him.

"Only for you." He bowed deeply, dropping to his knees. Then, bending forward, Cameron grabbed her with both hands and bit her bottom. As his teeth sank into the tender flesh of her cheek, Mikaela screeched in surprise...a little louder than she intended.

"Hello? Is someone here?"

Cameron's head popped up behind Mikaela and they exchanged panicked, wide-eyed glances. Mikaela dropped the camera in the grass.

"*Sorry!*" he mouthed as she glared at him, scrambling onto her hands and knees.

"Hello?"

"Yes?" Mikaela responded reflexively as Cameron frowned.

He sprang to his feet, grabbing her sundress from the ground a few feet away and whipping the balled-up fabric at her. She pulled it over her head as he did the same with his polo shirt, stumbling into his tennis shoes. She shooed him forward, continuing to straighten herself up.

"Hello?" The voice, bird sweet and feminine, called again from another part of the garden, closer this time. "Who's here?"

"Hi, Mrs. Silberling, it's just me, Cam," Cameron called back, stepping through the small thicket of trees and shrubbery that shielded them from the main garden.

Mikaela grabbed their incriminating detritus—*like her underwear*—and stuffed them into Cameron's picnic basket. She touched the small cornrows in her hair, brushing out the leaves and flower blossoms he'd stuck in them, running to catch up.

"Oh, Cam, it is you!" The woman clasped her hands together, an outsize smile practically splitting her face in two.

Mrs. Silberling was an old-guard member of the gardening club and one of its longest, strongest and most vocal advocates. She always looked like a combination between a wood sprite and a schoolmarm. Both ethereal and wise, in her two long, silver-white braids under a floppy sun hat.

"And who's that with you?" The woman pulled her glasses up from the chain hanging around her neck to place on her nose. "My goodness, little Kaela, is that you?"

Mikaela's cheeks grew warmer than they already were under Mrs. Silberling's gaze.

"Yes." Mikaela smoothed down the sides of her dress with shaky hands. "Hi, Mrs. S."

"Come on over here. Let me see you!"

Mikaela struggled for a smile as she sidestepped various flower patches down the circuitous stone path to where the woman stood. Mrs. Silberling opened her arms and enveloped Mikaela. Mikaela tried to hold her breath but it was no use. Even after all these years, Mrs. Silberling still smelled of roses, gardenia and sage. But far worse than that, she reeked of an acrid citrus.

Citronella.

Mikaela couldn't smell it without thinking of her mother. She had covered herself and Mikaela in it religiously to keep the bugs away during their times tending the garden. Now, the scent nauseated her.

"It's been an age."

That was true and not entirely unintentional.

"How's your mother? Tell Nattie Veronica says hello!"

Mikaela managed a wan smile, dying to escape that overpowering scent.

"I didn't know you two knew each other?"

It was as if Mrs. Silberling's brain had finally caught up with her eyes.

"Is everything okay?" she continued. "I heard a scream."

The couple exchanged a look.

"A bee…bit me."

"*Stung,*" Cameron corrected. "A bee stung her."

"Oh." Mrs. Silberling nodded. "Well, a little prick never hurt anyone."

"It was a big one."

Mikaela's face fell as Cameron snorted, pleased with himself.

"Ah well, even still, just ice it. You'll be fine." She patted

Mikaela's shoulder, moving on. "I wish more of you kids would make use of the space, instead of letting it languish."

Mikaela held in a laugh as Cameron smirked.

If Mrs. Silberling had any idea what they were using the garden for, she might not feel the same.

"We try, Mrs. S., but Mikaela and I kinda like keeping it as our little secret." He winked at the older woman and she giggled like a girl.

"Yes, I can understand that." Mrs. Silberling took up Mikaela's hand, staying infuriatingly close. "*Ah, I see*, no sense in introducing you to my granddaughter then, I don't suppose?"

Cameron smiled, one of the crooked kinds that generally made Mikaela's stomach do a loop-de-loop. "No, don't s'pose so."

She patted Mikaela's hand, beaming. "The girls of the gardening club will be so sorry to hear that, I can tell you. I think a number of us had designs on you for our own girls."

Cameron chuckled, turning that beet red he frequently did when anyone dared notice he was an attractive, eligible young man.

"Good for you," Mrs. Silberling whispered only for Mikaela's ears.

Mikaela fretted. Half the gardening club, as she knew it to be, also belonged to the women's auxiliary...where Julie's mother, Miss Liza, was the queen bee.

After two months of keeping their relationship all secret, Julie finding out like that, right before they left for school, would be a nightmare.

"Um, if you don't mind, Mrs. S., we'd appreciate it if you kept this between us."

Cameron frowned but didn't contradict her.

"A good boy like Cam? In this town? I would think you'd want to proclaim from the mountaintops that he's spoken for?"

Mikaela chuckled uneasily as Cameron watched, awaiting her response too.

"Well... Cam should keep his options open. I'm off to
school soon, then what will he do for warmth all winter?"
Mikaela tried a weak joke but neither person it was intended
for laughed.

"Yeah, I guess I don't want to put my access to all those
peach cobblers y'all keep promising me in jeopardy," Cameron responded gamely even as the frown lines deepened in
his face. "Excuse me, ladies."

A second later, he turned, walking back up the path
through the trees.

"You sure about that, sugar?" Mrs. Silberling eyed the
empty space Cameron just occupied.

Mikaela sighed before nodding. "Can you, um, not say
anything?"

"Don't worry." She squeezed Mikaela's hand more vigorously. "I'll tell 'em he's gay or sumthin'."

Mikaela smiled weakly, distracted and eager to get back
to Cameron and undo some of the damage she'd just done.
"No, ma'am, I don't think that's what—"

"Just go get him, sweetie," the older woman said, releasing Mikaela's hand and shooing her in the direction Cameron fled.

"Uh, thanks."

Surprising both Mrs. Silberling and herself, Mikaela bent
forward and kissed the woman's cheek before taking off after
her boyfriend.

He was gathering their things together, placing soda bot-
tles and burger wrappers into the basket, when Mikaela came
back into the clearing.

"Make sure you empty that out before you give it back to

your mom. I put the condoms and stuff in there," she said, attempting another joke.

"I know, I saw." Cameron swept the Frisbee they'd played with earlier off the grass without looking at her. "The whole summer, Mikaela… Is this really all we've been doing?" he asked after a prolonged silence, plucking her underwear out of the wicker basket and holding them up for a second before tossing them at her.

"Of course not, I—"

"Just tell me if I've wasted my time." He cut her off. "Are you embarrassed of me? Just some dumb hick livin' with his mama? I'm not stupid, I know you have plans beyond this. I do too."

"I know that. Why would I be embarrassed? No, I love…" Mikaela paused.

Cameron's eyes widened at her words, but she caught herself.

"…s-spending time with you."

To Mikaela, her feelings were so obvious. The polar opposite of what Cameron perhaps thought, she was terrified of being too caught up with him so soon before she left. Her feelings *of love.* She was confused by how plainly she cared for him. How did he not know this?

"I just kinda want to keep things the same. Keep it to ourselves."

"So, what? We're just hooking up?" He gestured around the area that they had lain as evidence of his words. "Fucking around?"

Mikaela was appalled by how crude the question was, and how hurt Cameron clearly was. She came up to him, pulling the basket out of his hands to stop him. He watched her without moving or speaking as she took his hands.

They had become so much more than a fling.

"Julie and I share everything," she started, trying to find the words. "Always have, always will. We tell each other everything. There's nothing about her I don't know and vice versa...*until now*. I haven't shared you. All summer you've been mine."

"Mikaela, I don't want to write our names in the sky." Cameron intertwined their fingers. "I want to hold your hand in public without you breaking into a cold sweat, or maybe take you out to eat somewhere within town limits. Why is that a problem?"

"It's not..." she muttered.

"What? 'Not' what? Tell me." His voice was plaintive yet forthright. "I want us to have a chance, but I know we won't as a secret."

"I want that too." She sighed. "Just not now... It's not something that I can do right now."

"Then when?"

She slipped her hands out of his, going to pick her sandals and camera out of the grass.

"You don't get it. You don't know Julie like I do. She won't understand."

"I don't get what Julie has to do with us at all."

"C'mon. She's my best friend."

"So then shouldn't she be happy for you? I mean, if we make each other happy, you'd think she'd be glad, right?"

"You'd think, but Julie loves me and likes you, so our relationship would be weird for her."

Cameron didn't understand Julie the way Mikaela did.

Julie was someone who, without intending to, always found some reason to be around, sucking the air out of every room. She was someone who craved attention, any kind, and thrived on being the focus of everyone's energies. It was fun at parties, but could be oppressive otherwise. And Mikaela and Cameron's exclusive interest in each other would threaten that.

Once upon a time, having Julie's love was like living in a sunbeam or floating in starlight. Back when they were children, it was one of the things Mikaela loved most about Julie—how she was the only person in the world that made Mikaela feel special. *Interesting. Worthy. Wanted.* Until they grew up and it became something else.

Cameron couldn't understand how jealously Julie guarded Mikaela's attention. And how it became a wedge between Mikaela and basically everybody else. Particularly every boy Mikaela had ever dated. Mikaela knew it was selfish and dishonest to keep them a secret. But it just didn't seem so wrong, in her last summer at home, if she chose not to deal with all of that.

"You gotta understand, Julie is possessive and competitive," she tried to explain.

"No, I don't," Cameron answered combatively.

"I can see that. Because no one cares what you do, so you don't have to either, do you?"

"You're wrong if you think no one would have anything to say about the fact that you're in high school."

"I'm not in high school—" her voice got reedy and thin, her pitch rising "—anymore!"

His mouth quirked with a raised eyebrow. "Well, you're sure acting like a teenager."

"I am a teenager, you asshole! What's your excuse?" She stepped back, out of his reach. "'Cause I mean, if I'm such a teenager, what are you even doing with me?"

"Right this second, I'm wondering that myself."

Mikaela's breath caught. "I can't believe you said that to me." Her chest tightened, cymbals crashing at her temples.

"I'm sorry. You know I didn't mean that."

Arguing with anyone was hard for Mikaela. With Cameron, it was almost unbearable. Her pulse raced.

"You're three years older but you spend all your free time messing with that camera and fantasizing about leaving here. Is *that* supposed to be adult? You're so worried about me and what I'm doin', maybe you need to get a life!"

As they both stood dazed, it was difficult to judge who drew first blood.

Mikaela sighed. "You just don't understand how it is with girls."

"Girls, or you and Julie? 'Cause seems like you're just invested in staying her sidekick. Tell me somethin', how's that gonna work when you're up in New York? She gonna boss you around over the phone?"

He might have done less damage if he'd struck her. Cameron was supposed to be the one person in this town who saw Mikaela as more than the pitiful creature that lived in Julie's long shadow. Her whole body actually shook after the words left his mouth.

"Kaela." Cameron backtracked. "I'm sorry."

"Don't you dare—"

"It's just— It's like I'm the only one who wants this to work."

"So insulting me was your way of showing that?" Mikaela pulled farther away as Cameron reached for her. "I'm walking away now."

"Fine." He threw his hands up. "Go."

She gave a flippant shrug, heading toward the trees.

"Like you said, you're leaving soon. Why don't we just call it?"

She spun on him. "Fine."

The ease of her reply hurt him. He blinked.

"Let's forget the whole thing!" he shouted after her as she stomped across the small clearing. "Why bother?"

"Yup." Mikaela pushed leaves and branches out of her face without looking back.

"Okay!"

This was the only and quite probably last real argument they would ever have. School started back for Cameron next week and Mikaela was set to leave for New York in three weeks.

Still, she could already feel her heart sinking with regret.

eighteen

"Mr. Murphy, would you say that the photo in question—"

The speakerphone in the center of the conference table beeped. "Boss?"

Suze's voice rang out in the room.

"Yes?" Mikaela answered as the four people seated around it all turned to look at her.

"I'm on my way out but Ms. Albright asked that I alert her when it was eight."

"Mike, Murphy, I'm so sorry. But it's time for me to take off." Cecilia perked up, gathering her things into a black satchel. "I gotta go put my kids to bed, or they'll riot. It's my night for the bedtime routine."

"I remember those days," Cameron commiserated. "Full-scale insurrection at bedtime."

Everyone chuckled.

"You ready to wrap it up for the night?" Monica asked.

Mikaela frowned.

"I gotta run too." Mikaela's associate, Jackson, made a regretful face, mouth turned down in the corners. But she knew his social and dating life was too busy for him to be truly sorry.

They'd been at this for hours. Honing Cameron's planned testimony to a refined near monologue. Badgering him with leading questions until he wouldn't even confirm the color of his tie for opposing counsel without careful consideration and the tacit approval of someone from their team.

Mikaela checked her watch, not ready to call it a night. But just because she was in no rush to go home didn't mean they weren't. Tonight, Rashad was scheduled to be on call. So, it wasn't exactly her schedule keeping them apart this evening.

"I'm ready, Coach," Cameron said, eliciting more chuckles from around the room.

"Yes, you are." Mikaela rose as they all began pulling together papers and their things. "Good night, team."

Cecilia, Monica and Jackson cleared out fastest, rushing for the exit with assorted goodbyes thrown over their shoulders.

Cameron caught Mikaela's eye as she held her tablet and notepad to her chest. "You got plans tonight?"

"Not exactly," she admitted. "You?"

"Maybe later."

Her eyebrows bobbed in surprise she kept to herself.

It was fully evening now, the sun vanishing. And the city outside began to glitter like a constellation of colored lights in the dusk beyond their wall of glass. She sighed. She would never tire of this city. Particularly in the summer, at night.

It made her wish she did have plans.

"Could you eat?" As if he'd heard her, Cameron's question floated between them.

Mikaela hesitated. "Uh, food was in my plans."

"Then how's about breaking bread together? My treat."

Dropping her things into a bag, she picked up her purse, licking her lips as she mulled it over.

"Consider it a peace offering," Cameron said waiting, leaning in the doorway.

Dressed in his usual impeccable designer suit and wearing boxy-framed glasses that made him look remarkably urbane, he was a long way from the cute boy in jeans and a Joy Division tee she used to know.

Mikaela blinked to short-circuit that line of thinking.

"C'mon, we've already established, I don't bite," Cameron coaxed.

"Anymore." They both snickered in unison.

She glanced around as she exited past him, alert to eavesdroppers—though at that point, even Suze had probably taken off. Mikaela knew she just needed to go home, even while she reached for her cell to text Rashad her new plans.

As they stood before the elevators, waiting, she finally nodded discreetly. "I could eat."

"That's my girl! Now just promise you'll stay away from anything that says 'market price,' okay?" He laughed, winking.

On their best behavior the whole meal, Cameron and Mikaela walked a fine line. Deftly avoiding any specific recollections of their previous selves. Mikaela only realized Cameron had coaxed her into spending sixty minutes talking about nothing but herself after the fact. She never talked about herself to anyone, let alone clients. But Cameron just seemed to eat it up, wheedling more and more out of her until he'd learned as much in an hour as Rashad had learned in twelve months. And they were only at the after-dinner coffee.

"...then at long last, you accepted their offer. And they

made you a partner with the corner office." Cameron leaned back, throwing his arm over the top rail of the chair next to him. "Cue the triumphant Carly Simon ballad."

"It was hardly the ending of *Working Girl*, and I don't have a corner office yet," Mikaela corrected but then grinned proudly. "But it is pretty nice."

Cameron peered thoughtfully into his drink, a whiskey sour in a crystal lowball glass. "That whole building is something else."

"You have to come through the next time, if for no other reason than the view. It's beautiful!"

"Oh, I'm sure, but I can find other reasons to come through."

Mikaela stopped, her stomach dropping as it always did around him. She swallowed her cappuccino with difficulty.

"Like to sign all that paperwork and whatnot..." His eyes twinkled the way they did when he used to tease her.

Mikaela forgot herself for the briefest of moments staring into them.

"Yup," she mumbled, looking away abashed. A familiar fluttering began in the pit of her stomach. "So, in addition to Robin, you guys have a boy too, right?"

She changed the subject to curb her sudden jitteriness.

"Yup, my bookends, Robin and Kit. *Christopher*."

"Aw, Julie loved that name," Mikaela laughed, tickled. "She always wanted to name a son Christopher just so she could call him Kit."

"I know, after Kit Marlowe. Is it bad to admit I was really impressed with her for that?"

"Ah, after Rupert Everett's character Kit Marlowe in the movie *Shakespeare in Love*," Mikaela countered. "Julie had been obsessed with him after *My Best Friend's Wedding*."

They exchanged a look before dissolving into laughter, shaking their heads.

"I should have known. Well, either way, she was pretty insistent. To be honest, it wasn't my first choice," Cameron confided, after clearing his throat. "But then he came out all tiny with this tuft of spiky hair and it just fit." Cameron cupped his hands together as he recollected it, smiling. "Now he's almost as tall as me!" He sighed wistfully.

Mikaela marveled at the thought. She'd never asked but best guess, Cameron was at least six-three.

"They're grown in a flash…and dating." He put his elbow on the table, propping his chin up glumly. "When did we get so old?"

"Speak for yourself, old man. I'm only twenty-nine." Mikaela grinned, stirring her cup daintily.

"Yeah, for the tenth time maybe."

"Hey! *Ninth* for six more months." She feigned outrage. "And how's that? Is Robin driving the boys crazy like her mom did?"

Cameron smiled, tapping his fingers along the side of his face. "She's wonderful, so the answer is *yes*… Her current crush is eighteen going on nineteen. They work at the mall together." He sighed deeply. "I told her no way! She didn't speak to me for a week. But Juliette is much too permissive."

Mikaela sat back with a raised eyebrow. "Really?"

"What? She's *sixteen*!"

"And I was eighteen when we met, same three-year age difference—or did you forget?" Mikaela clasped her hands together on the table. "And you were…older than nineteen."

Cameron sat up, dropping his hand onto the table. "It was different then. My parents were five years apart. They met when my mom was sixteen!"

"And my parents were seven years apart, what's your point?"

"That it was different. We had a more serious relat— Wait a minute." He leaned in, speaking low, his eyes widening. "Mikaela, do you feel li-like, I took advantage of you? That I *preyed* on you?"

He was clearly troubled by that. But, for her part, Mikaela was merely surprised that this was the first time the thought had ever even occurred to him.

"No," she answered after a moment.

He exhaled deeply.

"I think you're right; I do think it was different then. Back then no one gave enough thought to what adult relationships could potentially do to young people who weren't ready."

"You weren't ready?" Cameron's face was pinched, pained by the thought.

Mikaela leaned forward now too, placing a gentle hand over of his. "Put it this way, I wasn't as ready as I thought I was. As I might have been a few years later, for a relationship as important to me as ours was. And guess what? *Neither were you.*" She smiled at him. "Maybe if we'd both been a little bit older, things might have turned out a bit differently."

Cameron's eyes revealed the briefest flash of regret. She knew he was seeing the same thing in her. His thumb swept over her fingers and she slid her hand away, reaching for her cup again.

"Still, I think you should meet the boy before you issue any edicts one way or the other," Mikaela added. "Have you?"

"Nope, and don't care to."

"Cam," she chided. "Is that fair? What if my father had been that hard on you?"

"In the end, I seem to remember he was."

"And you did more than enough, arriving unannounced on my porch that night, to deserve it."

Cameron cleared his throat, leaning away.

Mikaela did similarly. They'd broken their unspoken pact to steer clear of this stuff.

Cameron checked his watch, lifting his hands and miming a scribble to the waiter.

Mikaela was relieved by how nice their one-on-one dinner had been. No need to ruin it all now.

"See? You're still all in one piece," he said, as if he'd heard her inner thoughts, just as the waiter brought the check and placed it in front of him.

"And while I've got you in such a receptive mood..." He smiled at his own joke as he scribbled his big, swooping signature onto the receipt. "Robin's got a dance recital coming up, I'd love it if you'd consider coming?"

He glanced up then and caught her staring wide-eyed. "Me?"

He looked around. "Yeah, you." He chuckled. "She's up in the City this summer dancing with Manhattan Ballet Company's school. I'd love for you to come see her perform."

Yes, Mikaela wondered, *but what would Julie think having me there? Is it even a good idea?*

"Can I check my schedule?"

Cameron's face broke out in what must have been a painfully wide smile. It nearly hurt Mikaela to look directly at it. He was just too easily pleased, and she didn't want to think about how much that always delighted her in turn.

"Great," he exclaimed on an exhale, like a job well done.

Cameron escorted Mikaela out, holding the door open for her as they left. He checked his watch again, scratching his five-o'clock shadow and looking around just as Mikaela turned to face him.

"Time for the other hot date?" She laughed.

"Not *another* date, no," he corrected her smugly.

Mikaela's mouth closed as she pulled her phone out of her purse. She knew this wasn't a date.

"I already called you a car," he said, glancing at his phone before stepping off the curb just as a black sedan pulled up. Cameron greeted the driver, then opened the back door for her.

He reached out a hand and waited like that, as her stomach bottomed out at the sudden flash of a memory.

Guiding her into the car, Cameron instructed the driver. "Wherever the lady wants to go."

"Kaela." Standing in the doorway, he spoke her name gently, as if the word slipped over his tongue and through his lips like exhaling.

She remembered when she used to love hearing him say it. Back then, she loved her name all the more for the way it sounded coming out of his mouth.

"This was good. We should do it again."

"Mm-hmm." She nodded.

He dipped his head into the car and pressed his prickly cheek to hers as she inhaled audibly. A deliciously piquant, musky aftershave wafted around them. But more potently, for her, that scent was him, the way she remembered him.

"Relax," he whispered into her ear a second before pressing his warm lips into her cheekbone.

Her skin heated where his lips had just been. "Night, Cam."

She slipped her feet in as he closed the door behind her. Tapping the hood, he stood back from the curb and watched the car pull away. Mikaela turned to watch him too, with his hands in his pockets as the car moved up the avenue, until it caught the first light.

It was difficult to make out the finer points, but a moment later, a petite blonde bounded out of the shadows and nearly leaped on Cameron from behind. She looked like the young gallerist from weeks earlier. Cameron spun her around and kissed her on the cheek right under the streetlamp. Mikaela fumed. She had never before taken Cam as someone who could end up being such a total fucking cliché...

She turned in her seat having seen enough. Lambasting herself for being so gullible, for so easily succumbing to Cameron's charm and how they so comfortably fell back into old rhythms, if only temporarily.

nineteen

The Brooklyn Bridge was backed up today.

Mikaela sighed, rubbing her neck. She stood at her enormous picture window in the catbird seat feeling pity for the undoubtedly livid folks below. But her mind kept creeping back to her dinner with Cameron.

Her intercom beeped and she couldn't account for how much time she'd spent standing at her window staring. Her morning had only just begun and she'd already spent minutes of it in a funk. She'd almost been late as it was, just staring at a pigeon roosting on her kitchen windowsill. Rashad had to snap her out of it.

But she just couldn't let the other night go. Since then, she'd been unable to even look Cameron in the eyes. The two occasions he'd been in the office since, she'd stayed as far away from him as she could, refusing to make even polite conversation. *He'd played her.* There was no other way to say it than that. Made an appeal to the side of her that longed to be friends with him again and then left her to cavort with someone half his age.

Mikaela hated to admit it but she was as disgusted with herself for falling for it as she was with him for doing it. No, she would not be sparing him any more of her precious time. No, she would not pretend they were alright. Just no. And she made it clear with her actions if not words. Her time was far too expensive for this nonsense. And Cameron Murphy couldn't afford it.

Her intercom beeped again, before she heard Suze speak. "Hello?"

"Yes?"

"Ms. Marchand?" Suze's crispest diction poured out of the speaker, letting Mikaela know whoever she was about to discuss was standing right there. "Mr. Murphy is here with a guest. He says he knows he doesn't have an appointment but hoped he could pop in anyway."

"Uh…? Yes, just give me a moment."

Mikaela ran to the credenza behind her desk, turning down the small silver picture frame before dropping back into her seat. She hit her keyboard to wake her laptop screen up, but then rose again.

"He must want to talk about the case," she volunteered, before realizing Suze hadn't asked. "Tell him to come in."

She smoothed out the wrinkles in her linen tunic as Suze escorted him inside.

"I know it's early," Cameron was saying as they walked in, not waiting for a greeting. His casual outfit, a departure from what she was now accustomed to seeing him in, sockless in loafers, with a navy print, Cuban-collared shirt and light chinos, belied this urgency. "But we have a long day ahead of us and I didn't know if there was any good time for this."

"Time for what?" Mikaela came around her desk calmly but then stepped back as Cameron advanced farther into the room, approaching her.

Suze stood at the door watching and waiting as a young lady stepped through the door behind him also.

Mikaela sealed her lips shut, pulling the corners up into an awkward smile. Curiously, the young woman, in a cyan-blue shirtwaist dress that complemented her similarly colored eyes, carried a small potted plant in her hands. It was the young lady from the gallery...and the other night.

"Time to do what?" Mikaela asked again, dragging her eyes from the young woman back to Cameron.

He paused and turned slightly. Catching his signal, Suze began to pull the door closed.

"No, Suze is cool. She can hear this," Mikaela pronounced. "Stay."

Cameron's eyes brightened, smiling as he spoke. "Okay, well, um, Mikaela Marchand, I'd like you to meet Robin Leigh Murphy."

He presented the young woman then, encouraging her forward as Mikaela stood there stunned.

"*Th-this* is your daughter, Robin?" Mikaela turned to Cameron.

"Yup." He grinned knowingly. "I thought you might like to finally meet her."

Mikaela bit her lip, grateful she couldn't turn as crimson as she felt.

"Was this your 'date' the other night?"

"I told you it wasn't a date." Cameron smirked.

Robin smiled, watching their exchange. It was an effort-less motion that illuminated her already beautiful young face. It reminded Mikaela of her father so completely that she felt silly for not having considered that possibility.

"Yes, you did say that." Mikaela nodded sheepishly.

Interestingly, Robin looked nothing like her father. From her short stature to her hair, a glossy ash-blond that judging from her russet roots was probably only achieved with chemical help. It was only that easy smile and her eyes, a dazzling Mediterranean blue like her father's, that suggested Cameron at all. Her face—the shape of it, the squareness of her jaw, the length of her nose, the tiny dimples when she smiled—that was all Julie, now that she got to see the girl up close, with context.

"Oh my goodness!" Mikaela gushed. "You're so big! I feel so old!"

Mikaela looked to Suze then, who turned and pulled the door shut behind her while smirking. Mikaela rushed forward to reach for Robin's hand, shaking it vigorously. She turned toward Cameron and grinned with him.

"I think the last time I saw you you were only a few months old." Mikaela offered them seats as she perched on the edge of her desk in front of them.

She refrained from letting on the circumstances or the very awkward standoff it had entailed in a supermarket shopping aisle. That had been an excruciating experience, made worse by staring into the same pair of round clear eyes that currently looked at her now, only then swaddled in a stroller.

Mikaela's eyes strayed to Cameron, looking very pleased with himself in the chair next to his daughter. He watched Robin as she spoke.

"Dad says you went to high school with my mom?"

His head tilted ever so slightly to the side as if intrigued by the answer she would provide.

"Yes." Mikaela popped up off the corner then, clearing her throat and retreating back behind her desk. "Ah, *and* middle school *and* elementary... Me and your mom go way back. We were neighbors back home."

Mikaela marveled; she hadn't really thought of Harmon as home in dog years. Back then, Julie had liked to say their friendship was fated, but Mikaela always knew the truth. It had been merely an accident of circumstance, of geography. Two girls whose backyards abutted one another, with parents too busy or distracted or disinterested to construct a proper fence between them. Attracted opposites, they'd become a local oddity like unusual interspecies friendships you'd read about in the local penny-saver. A dog and a chicken, partners in crime, thick as thieves. Completely inseparable. *Until one ate the other.*

Cameron knew a little about that…although clearly, he'd chosen not to share with his daughter.

"Yeah, Dad said you even knew Grampa Robertson?" Robin asked, pulling Mikaela's attention back from its sojourn.

"The Judge?" Mikaela chuckled. "Oh yeah… Lee was great. You know he's the reason that I got into the law in the first place? I've got him to thank for this." She waved a hand around her office as Robin grinned. "He used to drag us to court once a season to sit in on one of his bench trials. *Your. Mother. Hated. Every. Minute.* Meanwhile, I was rapt."

"Sounds like Mom." Robin looked to her father. "She can't even stand courtroom dramas on TV."

"Your mother seems to like court just fine," Cameron groused and Robin's face fell a bit.

Mikaela cleared her throat again, poking her cell phone screen with a finger to get the time. "So, what's brought you guys in so bright and early this morning?"

"Oh!" Robin rose from her seat and presented Mikaela with the plant. "Here."

Mikaela was puzzled as she reached across the large desk, taking it from the young woman's hands. "What's this?"

"An inducement," Cameron interrupted.

"An invitation." Robin shot a dagger at her father before addressing Mikaela. "To my recital."

The recital again. It was dirty pool bringing in Robin to try and persuade her.

"You never gave me that answer," Cameron added. "And you know, she's the youngest they've ever accepted into their corps de ballet."

"Wow, that's quite an accomplishment! I used to go to their *Nutcracker* every Christmas." Mikaela directed the words to Cameron, remembering how much her own father viewed every one of her accolades and diplomas as another notch in his belt.

"I keep telling her she's the next Misty Copeland."

"Dad." Robin rolled her eyes.

Mikaela smiled. Robin had clearly inherited her father's bashfulness.

"They're doing a summer showcase of Balanchine's *Jewels* as their culminating event of the season. And gave her some tickets for family…and friends."

"If you were going to do it yourself, then why'd you ask me?" Robin snapped.

Numerous crimson-colored splotches bloomed on Cameron's cheeks, meeting by his ears as Mikaela pressed her lips shut and glanced between father and daughter.

"Sorry." He sucked in his cheeks, amusingly chastened. "Busted."

"Anyway, my uncle and grandma can't make it in from Arizona. She's sick."

Cameron interrupted yet again, eager and rushed, watching Mikaela's face. "The idea was we might convince you to come instead?"

"Since, you know, you're an old friend of the family." Robin watched her father with good-natured amusement.

She was, in fact, her father's daughter.

Mikaela was a bit stunned. She definitely would not have called herself that—not in a very long time.

The African violet sat in her hands. She stroked one of its fuzzy leaves.

"I knew you'd prefer a potted one," Cameron explained, eyeing her fingers.

Mikaela smiled, appreciating his thoughtfulness, warming to her guests, if still not to their proposition.

That blinding smile that reminded Mikaela so much of Cameron returned to Robin's face, delivering an effective wallop to her reticence.

"I do adore the ballet…" Mikaela hedged.

Cameron beamed then in anticipation.

"I'll tell you what, give the date and time to Suze, and I'll see what I can do," Mikaela answered, setting the plant aside.

Cameron and Robin turned to each other, pleased, and all three rose from their seats together to say goodbye.

"Maybe you can even bring Vanessa? I haven't seen her in forever," he said to Mikaela as they walked toward the door. "Oh, and very nice."

"What?"

"The office, the view." Cameron grinned, winking at her.

Once she'd walked them all the way to the elevators and returned, she told Suze to add the graduation to her calendar as she watched Mikaela grinning ear to ear. Then Mikaela went to her window again. She straightened, noting with pleasure that all the traffic on the bridge had finally cleared up.

twenty

Mikaela sat at the desk of her roommate, Eleanor, working on the term paper for her ethics class. The last thing she had to do for the semester. Three separate philosophy books sat open around her and the blinking cursor of Eleanor's little purple iMac stared back at her. It was the one thing between her and freedom for the next four weeks and it was due in two days. But Eleanor was leaving the following morning and taking the nifty little iMac back home to Shaker Heights with her. Sometimes Mikaela could see how Julie was right and she was only spiting herself when she declined the things her mother offered—for instance, a new computer.

In the open door, Penny, a girl from down the hall, was speaking.

"I'M SORRY. WHAT?" Mikaela shouted before modulating her voice.

Mikaela pushed her headphones off her head, allowing the pulsing beat from Prince's "When Doves Cry" to flood into the room.

Penny smiled. "I said—" she dragged out the word in her thick Bronx accent "—I'm headed out! Merry Christmas!"

"Oh! Already?" Mikaela ran to the door and gave the young woman a hug.

They weren't great friends exactly yet, but Mikaela had gone out with her a few times in the last couple of months. Being one of only five native New Yorkers on their floor, Penelope Narvaez had been the only one willing to play tour guide to anyone.

"Now I'm only a phone call away. And you can take the 4 straight up to my house on Christmas Day if you change your mind, okay?"

Mikaela nodded.

This was the third time Penny had offered to host Mikaela for Christmas and it was the seventh invitation overall. Something about hearing a person was choosing to stay in the dorms over the holidays inspired a remarkable amount of pity. One of the invites had even come from a professor. No one understood that, though finances had played a part in her decision to stay—*the cost of a ticket out of New York Christmas week being exorbitant*—Mikaela was actually excited for the opportunity to stay in the City over the holidays. She'd watched *Home Alone 2, Miracle on 34th Street* and *Scrooged* a million times each. She was desperate to see the Christmas tree at Rockefeller Center and go ice skating, to watch the ball drop in Times Square from somewhere closer than her TV screen. And more than anything else, she wanted to walk over the Bow Bridge in Central Park as a light dusting of snow covered it and her eyelashes.

The thing was, there had been no significant snowfall yet,

the Christmas-tree-lighting ceremony had been on a week-night and ice skating alone was just pathetic. So, Mikaela hadn't done anything she wanted to, yet. Remaining in the City over winter break would give her that time.

"We're still on for Rockefeller, right?" Mikaela asked, walking back to her desk.

Penny huffed an exaggerated breath before relenting. "I'll go see the tree with you, 'cause I never do shit like that. But I'm not waiting on that long-ass line with a bunch of tourists to skate at that tiny-ass rink. We make it Wollman Rink and I'm there."

Mikaela pouted for a second before acquiescing. "That's the one in Central Park, right?"

"Yup, not a long walk from that bridge either." Penny had heard her little fantasy; it amused her. "And to think, I didn't know that damn bridge had a fucking name before you told me."

Penny chuckled. They had bonded over the fact that Penny almost knew less about famous New York iconography than Mikaela did. Their adventures were essentially as educational for Penny as for her.

"Okay, girl, I'm off. But that's a standing invitation to come up to Tremont and have some of my *abuelita*'s coquito, alright?"

Mikaela nodded. "Merry Christmas!"

She slipped her headphones back on her head just as "I Would Die 4 U" ended but hit the repeat button on her stereo. A couple of minutes later, however, Penny flagged her down again.

"Um," Penny started, with the most peculiar look on her face. "Ah, there's a guy downstairs asking for you?" Her whole demeanor was different than previously. Her face danced between puzzlement and suspicion.

"A guy?" Mikaela repeated, completely confused.

Mikala had gone on exactly two dates since she'd been in New York. She hadn't been ready for anyone after Cameron. Their breakup hurt her more intensely than she was prepared for. And trying to get back on that particular horse had been more difficult than she anticipated. Especially when Julie had been only too happy to keep Mikaela thoroughly apprised of all the goings-on over at UGA: She was great, things were fabulous and life in Athens was awesome. There was no parallel to that on Mikaela's end, no progressing relationships, romantic or otherwise, no upbeat dispatches from the field, no one else she knew. New York was different, college was hard and Mikaela was lonely.

Maybe she should have gone home for the month?

"Mike?"

She looked up at Penny, confused again.

"I said, a *white* guy." Penny lowered her voice, eyeing Mikaela like her fly was open.

"Where?" Mikaela bounded out of her chair.

"Downstairs, I said." Penny watched her. "He said he was trying to get security to let him up as a surprise. But I'm sure they thought he was full of shit like I did. But I promised to come tell you. And you do know him, don't you?"

Mikaela nodded, moving toward the elevator, with Penny at her heels.

"I see you, girl. 'Cause I get down with the vanilla swirl occasionally too but I thought y'all Southerners didn't play that. He is a cutie though," Penny commented on the elevator. "You're what they call a dark horse, huh?"

Mikaela made a face, shrugging.

The elevator doors opened after an interminable period. Mikaela tried to compose herself. She walked through the lobby, passing the flurry of students with duffel bags and cardboard boxes decamping for the holiday. When she finally saw Cameron standing at the guard station, chatting up the security guard, she nearly cried. He was beautiful. He wore a ball cap and bomber jacket, with dark blue denim beneath. And had never looked better. Mikaela couldn't help it; she smiled, big and bright. She hadn't realized how much she longed for someone from home, a familiar face. As such, there couldn't have been a better one.

"Cam?"

He turned and his face lit up when he saw her, making Mikaela's stomach flip. It almost nauseated her. Unlike any sensation she'd ever had before, she was queasy with happiness. The other people present and watching were the only things that stopped her from running into his arms. Still, she closed the distance between them quickly and gave him a hug, then stepped back despite the fact that she could feel he hoped to hang on a little longer.

"Happy Belated Birthday! I came to surprise you!"

"You did that."

She glanced at Penny, who was now standing at her side.

"Penny, this is Cameron…" She struggled with the next part, having rarely said the words out loud. "My boyfriend."

Cameron looked at her with surprise as he greeted Penny.

"Ex. *Ex*-boyfriend, I mean."

"*Nice.* My ex wouldn't even take the subway to visit me from Bedford Park. Yours came all the way up from Georgia. Y'all just do things different down there, I guess." She nodded. "Well, I'm off…again. Nice to have met you."

"Merry Christmas," Mikaela said, giving her another quick giddy hug.

"Happy Holidays!" Penny gave Cameron a last long appraising look while releasing her.

"Merry Christmas and thank you for your help."

As he spoke, Mikaela noticed how thick his accent was for the first time ever, and it was so good to hear. It was like a piece of home.

"What are you doing here?" she asked after she'd signed him in and pulled him toward the elevator.

"I heard you weren't coming home for Christmas," he explained as if that made more sense.

"You heard?"

"Vanessa told me."

Mikaela frowned.

"I may or may not frequent QuarterWorld." He gave a sheepish shrug, averting his eyes, referring to the local video game arcade in their town.

Mikaela chuckled, leading him off the elevator to her room.

"And you just took that as an invitation to come up?"

"I took it as an excuse to visit New York City," he amended, sitting on her bed while she sat at her desk. "Since I know someone up here now."

Mikaela licked her lips, crossing her arms, listening.

"And I was upset that you weren't coming home," he admitted under her gaze.

"Well, I was home for Thanksgiving." She chose to avoid sharing her "New York at Christmas" fantasies. "And I couldn't afford to do both."

"See? You should have taken the car your mom offered you."

Mikaela held up a hand. "If you wanna talk about my mom you can go back home now."

He chuckled. "Okay, how 'bout we talk about my mom then?"

"Your mom? Is she okay?"

"Who do you think encouraged me to take time off and come? She told me to stop worrying about her, give you a big hug and tell you 'Happy birthday' when I saw you."

Mikaela laughed. She did have a way with Cameron's mother; Miss Anne liked her a lot.

"So how long do I have you for?"

He grinned at her words. "Six fun-filled days."

Mikaela couldn't help giggling as he quoted from her favorite movie of all time, *Splash*.

"I have to finish my paper," she whined, remembering the blinking cursor waiting for her on Eleanor's desk.

"Well, you'll need to eat at some point, right?" He stood. "I'll go out, find something to do for a while, then come back later, okay?"

Mikaela nodded, still looking at him in slight disbelief.

Cameron was here, standing in front of her, *in New York*.

twenty-one

Mikaela wrote as much of the rest of the paper as she could, considering the fact that somewhere outside her door, Cameron waited for her to be free.

It took a half hour after he'd gone for Mikaela to settle down enough to write anything. Then, roughly four hours before she gave up and came downstairs searching. Mikaela saw Cameron through the glass door after stepping off the elevator, sitting in the student lounge flipping through a magazine. And when she opened the lounge door and he smiled up at her, indescribable happiness filled her all over again.

Later, at a random Indian restaurant, one among many on the Lower East Side near the school, she watched him pick through his tikka masala. They sat together in the gaudily decorated restaurant; with its colorful paper garland and shiny walls, it was like being inside a wrapped Christmas present. While Cameron talked about home and his mother and college, catching her up on the peculiarities of that place and his life, he pushed large cardamom seeds onto the sides of his plate. And Mikaela thought about nothing but him. Not about her love for him, or how handsome he looked sitting there charmingly oblivious to her close inspection, but about him, being there, at that very moment. It wasn't that what he was saying wasn't interesting or funny; it was just that seeing him there across from her was so suddenly incongruous. This was New York, this was the rest and now *real* portion of her new life, divorced from Harmon and home and who Mike Marchand was back there. To her, seeing Cameron here was like having dinner with Bugs Bunny, the cartoon character himself, after watching a lifetime of *Looney Tunes* on TV. She was delighted but perplexed equally.

"You're happy to see me, right?" He spoke through a mouthful of food, trying to read her face.

She laughed, since it was a little bit late to be asking. "Isn't it obvious?"

"I can't tell. Sometimes you look happy and other times—" he said this, pausing to take a sip of water as Mikaela fixated on his mouth "—I don't know."

"I am. I'm also surprised. You broke up with me. We agreed not to bother with the long-distance thing? *That happened, right?*"

Cameron swallowed. His Adam's apple, which she rarely noticed, bounced a little.

"Yeah, but in that letter you sent, you said you missed me."

Mikaela sat back.

It wasn't a letter.

It was a note. A slip of paper accompanying an "I ♥ NY" T-shirt she'd sent to him on a whim. But admittedly, it was driven by loneliness more than any other single emotion. It was also sent almost two months ago.

"I didn't know you got that."

He avoided her eyes. "I was working up to saying something about it at Thanksgiving."

She shook her head, confounded. "I didn't even *see* you at Thanksgiving."

"I know. I'm sorry. That's why I thought I'd make it up now, when you got home...but then Vanessa said you weren't coming."

Mikaela sighed with frustration and he did the same.

"I almost got busted by Julie and Nicole," he offered up hopefully, like another little college anecdote.

Cameron chuckled until he saw Mikaela wasn't laughing along. She knew how much time Julie and Nicki had been spending trying to chat up Cameron and his friends. Julie made a point of punctuating their increasingly infrequent phone calls with yet another detailed account.

"They caught me at Bolton dining hall in your shirt. I had to make up a Yankee cousin."

Mikaela rolled her eyes, peeved by the idea that their paths ever even crossed. Julie was a freshman, Cameron a senior—they should have nothing in common, including classes. She was annoyed by how gullible he was. His big, pretty, ice-blue eyes, and obvious eagerness to please suddenly so puppylike, irritated her.

"Where are you staying?"

"At the Y," he answered, reaching into his pocket for his wallet.

"The YMCA?" She almost laughed. She didn't know people even did that anymore. "The big one on 14th Street?"

"No, only the one in Harlem rents rooms nowadays."

Mikaela pursed her lips, bemused. "*You're* staying in Harlem?"

Cameron smiled, pleased with himself.

Mikaela's silence was her response. As if there was ever a planet on which she would congratulate him for willingly sleeping in a black neighborhood.

Quietly, however, she was a *little* bit impressed that he

wasn't like so many others who found any situation in which he might be the only white person an automatic, off-the-top no-go.

"I'm on 135th Street near Strivers' Row. You heard of it?"

"Yes, of course I have," she scoffed, omitting the fact that she only recently learned of the affluent black enclave because of Penelope.

Mikaela's exposure to Harlem and black culture in the City's resident black mecca started at Zora Neale Hurston and James Baldwin and ended at Langston Hughes with virtually no stops in between.

"I wanted to eat at Sylvia's before I go," Cameron explained as he counted out the cash for the bill and placed it on the table, rising. "And my funds are limited but I wanted to be in the same borough as you."

As he spoke, his earnest words made the little glass shards of irritation that prickled Mikaela's skin dissipate.

She followed him out.

"You're not really upset, are you?" He shivered a little, outside in the cold.

The garish Christmas lights that Mikaela had recently learned the restaurants kept up year-round, reflected different colors onto his face, so for a moment he was red, then yellow and then green.

"I needed to see you," Cameron admitted quietly.

There was something pitiable in the way he said it that made Mikaela feel potent and enigmatic and yet monstrous in her sudden power over him. She smiled to herself, wickedly. And he smiled back, mistaking this as charitable.

"I wanted to see you too." She acceded to the unspoken plea in his eyes, instantly neutering the monster.

For a moment, she'd allowed herself the fantasy that she was the one in control between them. But the more they looked at each other, the more she knew that it just wasn't true. And though she hadn't said so in the note, he'd read it between the lines anyway. Sitting all alone in her dorm room tearfully scribbling onto a sheet of loose-leaf before shoving it into a tiny box with a T-shirt and shipping it to him.

She had needed him too.

twenty-two

"So, this old boyfriend of yours is now your client?" Rashad asked, his brow furrowing as his hand closed over Mikaela's in the crook of his elbow.

He steadied her in her heels on the cracks in the pavement as they attempted to walk faster. They jogged, at his urging, across the wide avenue to the park. Mikaela looked him over, before answering. Rashad always looked good but now in his charcoal gray suit, periwinkle shirt, pink tie and his fresh from the barber shape-up, he looked festively good.

Mikaela hesitated for another minute to gather her thoughts, a little droplet of sweat breaking out on her top lip. "Yes, but I wish you'd stop calling him 'my old boyfriend.'"

Rashad's eyebrows rose as they fell in with the excited throng of others: dance enthusiasts, parents, and assorted family and friends, all converging on the park from all corners. She was glad she chose to bring him. Looking around, she was also glad she'd chosen to wear a complimentary cheerful cantaloupe-colored tea-length wrap dress. The bright color palette accentuated both of their skin tones, making his copper-toned and her cocoa-brown skin nearly gleam in the sun. Together, they looked very cute...*but then they always did*. Vanessa teased that they looked like the epitome of "Black Love."

"Am I somehow misstating things? Didn't you say the other night that you dated this guy or something back in the day?"

"What's relevant is he's a *client* now. Well really, his bosses are, but yes, I knew him back in Georgia," she explained again, handing over their entrance tickets and walking past the ticket-takers. "We kinda dated, true, but years ago. Eons ago."

Mikaela had given Rashad the broad strokes when she asked him to accompany her...but was necessarily vague about certain aspects. For her own comfort, if not Rashad's.

"I understand. But if he's just a client, what are we doing here?"

"They asked me. It would've been rude to say no." She said it like it was perfectly rational and as if she hadn't asked herself that same question at least a dozen times in the past week. "...And his ex is an old family friend too."

Rashad's elbow clamped down on her interlocked arm as if he knew she might find a way to wriggle away.

"Of yours and Vanessa's?" The bemusement in his voice was apparent.

Mikaela nodded as they stepped onto the smooth, wide tiles among a sea of white folding chairs. "What can I say? We all lived in the same town."

"Hmm, that's a small world," he remarked. "And a messy one."

Mikaela took off her sunglasses and squinted at Rashad

in the blazing sun directly above. "Small towns are. Why do you think I left?"

She inspected their surroundings as they settled in near the middle of the audience. The small Upper Westside park was originally conceived of as an open-air ballroom and performance space, so while it was lined with leafy green trees and abundant flower beds, at its head stood a stark white stone band shell and stage.

Taking Rashad's hand, intertwining their fingers in her lap, Mikaela squeezed. "Thank you for this. I know you probably had other things to do today."

"Just buying back some goodwill from when I left you high and dry at the Yankees game…" He leaned into Mikaela and gave her a little peck on the lips. "And the gala," he continued between kisses, giving her another and another as she chuckled at his amorous attention. "Besides, who doesn't love being arm candy, huh?"

"Sexy chocolate at that!" She wiggled her eyebrows, smiling suggestively at him as he sat back in his seat, laughing.

When his head and shoulders moved, the field of people revealed Cameron standing there, milling around in front of them. He was directly in her line of sight, searching for seats with his son, Christopher, and Julie. They were all holding their programs and standing in the adjacent aisle to the section where she and Rashad sat. A second later, Cameron glanced up as if he could sense it, finding her eyes immediately. The smiles slipped off each of their faces simultaneously as they saw the other's companion.

"You okay?" Rashad turned to follow her gaze but Cameron had already slipped his sunglasses down and turned away. "You look like you just saw a ghost."

"Of course I am."

But in a way, it was as if she had.

Cameron, standing there with his supremely photogenic family, gave her visions of what they must have been like over the years. Once again, she was confronted by how unprepared she was for this. And again she questioned what silly notion had come over her when she'd agreed to come and subject herself to it. But just as quickly, she was awash with such tenderness for Cameron as he smoothed a hand over his son's chestnut hair. Cameron kissed the boy's forehead and watched as he followed his mother, while unstringing his camera from around his neck.

"It's a beautiful day, I'm here, you're here." Mikaela smiled, patting Rashad's hands but still watching the Murphys. "I don't think we've been to this park since you dragged me to Midsummer Night Swing, when was that?"

Rashad chuckled, unaware of her distraction. "Our fifth date, I think."

"That long ago?" She turned to him in surprise. "I just remember my sheer terror watching all those people doing the Lindy Hop…"

"Yeah, I made a mental note ever-after: no dancing for Mikaela."

An involuntary pang of guilt clawed at Mikaela remembering how much fun she'd had at the recent gala.

She sought out Cameron's family again. Julie stood beside her son, looking nearly the same as the last time Mikaela had seen her. Still remarkably beautiful but in a more adult, refined, way. Her face wasn't as full as it had been in their youth, the apple cheeks had vanished but the small, cute dimples remained when she laughed. Julie's skin was taut with cheekbones and a jaw that could still cut glass. Stick-thin with small hips and the long legs of a thoroughbred, her sable brown hair rolled in waves over her shoulders nearly to the middle of her back.

Mikaela had seen the occasional picture because Vanessa and Julie's little brother, Gabe, had improbably remained friends. So, she already knew that time and childbirth had been incredibly kind to Julie. Still, she was unprepared for the truth of that borne out in the flesh. Now wearing a stylish cream-colored, tailored pantsuit with a garnet-red blouse underneath, Julie even had that same vaguely patrician look about her. It was almost comforting, as if nothing at all had changed.

So, maybe it was only Mikaela that was different.

Before long, everyone was seated, except for Cameron, a few other professional photographers and some amateurs. Each staking out their own corners and angles. And as interesting as the performance was, as skilled as all the dancers were, Mikaela found her eyes repeatedly drawn back to where Cameron had situated himself—although that itself changed frequently. He unobtrusively flowed and moved with the performance as the performers did.

Mikaela's heart throbbed as she watched.

She'd seen Cameron in his element before, taking multiple rapid-fire shots, his head bobbing up and down as he framed a picture visually then captured it with a camera that was like an extension of his arm. Still, she was surprised by how comforting she found this experience, like in that moment he'd finally revealed himself to be the man she formerly knew. The one she'd fallen for so many years ago. It was as if the fog of years had dissipated and the person she recognized reappeared in its place.

Mikaela's mouth dried as she shifted in her seat. Rashad offered her a half-finished bottle of water he'd stuck in his suit pocket, which she accepted with gratitude as guilt plagued her.

I shouldn't be here. Not watching this and definitely not watching Cameron.

She gripped Rashad's arm and leaned her head against his shoulder, forcing herself to stay engaged with the performance.

"You good?" Rashad whispered under an orchestral movement reaching its crescendo.

She nodded. "It's so lovely."

That was true; the ballet company made elegant, acrobatic feats look simple. In groups of ten and twelve, they ran on- and offstage in billowy bejeweled costumes, engaging one another with pirouettes, cabrioles and grand jetés. To her dismay, for the majority of the performance, Mikaela hadn't made out which of the many young women onstage was Robin. Until she spotted Cameron focusing his camera on a particular couple among a trio of other demi-soloists.

Mikaela leaned into Rashad to whisper and point, identifying the young girl with delight, as Robin moved downstage with her partner. When Cameron straightened, at last resting his camera against his stomach to enjoy his daughter's performance, mesmerized, Mikaela recognized that expression too. The pride was evident in the faint smile painted across his face, which made her smile as well.

"Oh, there they are," Mikaela lied later, after the performance ended. While strains of Stravinsky and Tchaikovsky played over the loudspeakers, she nudged Rashad with an elbow in the direction Julie, Cameron and their children stood.

Mikaela had observed them minutes earlier as they rose from their seats to embrace Robin when she emerged from backstage. But she wanted to take time to watch them unobserved. She wanted—*no, needed*—to witness their family dynamic. What her callousness eighteen years ago had helped create. Because whether Mikaela liked it or not, two people existed on the planet because of her. They probably didn't know it, and of course she certainly didn't want to be thanked for it, but she was instrumental in their coming to be. It was a weird thought, to say the least, but now, for some reason, it stuck with her.

As Julie doted on her daughter, peppering her face with effusive kisses, Mikaela grinned. Julie was the same as ever, affectionate to the point of obnoxiousness.

"They're just there." Mikaela pointed, sliding her arm back into Rashad's as they stood from their seats.

Of their little group, Julie spotted Mikaela first, as she huddled mid-conversation with her two children. Her eyes wandered past Mikaela before returning, her expression showing she believed she'd made a mistake. Mikaela held her breath. Then Julie must have said something to Robin because the girl spun around, her face still covered in heavy character makeup, grinning. She waved them over and Cameron, standing a few feet away snapping a number of pictures in various directions, looked over too.

In a dark suit with sunglasses sitting on his head, Cameron had been standing slightly to the side, only speaking when directly spoken to. Not in a hostile way, Mikaela could tell, but taken with the ambiance of the event, the people, the surroundings, a small park in a valley of tall buildings. She remembered that from their shared past, his tendency to silently take things in. Sometimes, if you watched him, Cameron looked like a space-cadet, completely checked out of a conversation, a little bored even, but then later, Mikaela could rely on him to give the full accounting. He didn't ever miss a beat.

Deciding to meet the moment head-on, Mikaela spoke first. "Juliette," she said, as soon as she was close enough to be heard.

Julie licked her lips, her eyes traveling all the way from the strappy heels on Mikaela's feet to the very top of her head, before responding.

Her mouth curled to a smile. *"Mike!"* She stepped forward, pulling Mikaela into a hug. "Oh my God, it's been so long!" She rubbed Mikaela's back, drawing her into her side.

Mikaela was at a loss. She hadn't expected to be received like this.

"How is everybody? Mr. M? Nessa? Your mama?"

"Fine, y-you know, good, great."

"Yeah?" Julie frowned, skeptical, leaning back slightly to catch Mikaela's eyes, arm draped over her shoulder, rubbing her upper arm in a way she recognized instantly.

This was an unspoken question about the state of her relationship with Natalee. It was almost amazing how a simple word unlocked a floodgate of things Mikaela hadn't confided—and hadn't wanted to confide—in a single soul in years, other than her therapist. A multitude within a word and a look.

Only fucking Julie.

"Yeah," Mikaela cleared her throat, nodding with an enthusiasm that was entirely counterfeit. "Oh yeah," she said, waving a hand as if all of that was long forgotten.

Julie released her, but not before giving her shoulders another small squeeze. Mikaela was then immediately crushed in Robin's tiny but strong embrace. The unanticipated emotion of Julie's question still disquieted her, and Mikaela struggled to keep it together as even Christopher hugged her. Cameron's eyes tracked her throughout, she knew, as the only other person who understood what had just transpired. Then they each took turns shaking Rashad's hand.

"Everyone, this is Dr. Rashad Guerrero," Mikaela said as Cameron took his hand.

Their shake wasn't unfriendly, but Mikaela noticed Cameron's face lost the vaguely charmed look it had before and even the mildly concerned expression from just a moment earlier. He pulled his glasses down onto his nose to obscure an appraisal of Rashad that rivaled his ex-wife's.

"Rashad, this is Cameron Murphy. My..." She hesitated. It was only a second, but long enough to catch Cameron's attention, if no one else's. *"Client."*

His eyebrows rose behind the sunglasses, turning back from Rashad to her.

Mikaela thanked God his dark frames obscured his expression as she moved on rapidly in an exhalation of words. "And this is my very old friend, Juliette Robertson—"

"Murphy," Julie corrected her.

Cameron's mouth tightened, his jaw clenching.

"My bad," Mikaela's eyes darted to Cameron's face. "My bad, Julie Murphy. And this is their son Christopher, and their daughter, the talented ballerina, Robin."

Rashad smiled at them all as Mikaela grinned at Cameron. Her words had the hoped-for effect as now he smiled slyly at her too.

"You were lovely up there, Robin," Rashad said, playing his part with aplomb. As the handsome doctor boyfriend, he was always...impressive. But when he really turned it on, Mikaela almost envied herself. It was an ongoing crime that the people at the firm had yet to meet him.

They moved with the crowd, en masse, out of the park, spilling back out onto the streets just as they had gathered, seemingly from every direction, earlier. Rashad kept his arm low, wrapped around Mikaela's waist as they walked abreast the Murphys. Mikaela was intrigued. Julie was much taller than her daughter. She wondered how two such statuesque people managed to make such a little pixie in Robin. Meanwhile, Christopher resembled his parents entirely. Tall for thirteen, he had a similar build as a young Cameron, with the same angular face. And his carefree, loose gait, shaggy light brown hair and a similarly sunny temperament made him virtually identical to his uncle Gabe at that age.

It was eerie. Being there in the City, so firmly rooted in the present, while simultaneously confronted by so many signposts from her past. Mikaela glanced over her shoulder in Cameron's direction. He walked a step behind his son with his hands in his pockets and a serious expression on his face, watching her and Rashad.

Cameron's eyes connected with hers, a sudden pall falling between them, leaving her uneasy. Mikaela turned away, leaning further into Rashad's shoulder as they made their way down the city street.

twenty-three

To Mikaela's surprise, Robin had asked them to join some of the families of other dancers as they all went to a steak house for a celebratory dinner. The families rented the entire back portion of the restaurant and assured her two additional people were more than welcome. Still, Mikaela only accepted because she noticed something happening with Cameron's darkening mood that she hoped to keep an eye on over the course of the afternoon. If not for his sake, for her firm's.

And even as she panned the large table while they talked now, Mikaela's eyes fell on Cameron. Seated diagonally across from her, he watched them all stone-faced. Self-consciously, she dropped her hand beneath the table onto Rashad's thigh. Rashad was engaged in conversation with Robin's dance partner's father about the local basketball team's recent losing streak while Mikaela spoke with Julie.

"Now, Mike." Julie leveled her with an even gaze, as if sizing her up. "You mean to tell me you and that handsome doctor right there don't have any children yet?"

Mikaela straightened in her seat a bit. "Ah, no. But it—it's only been two years…"

It was suddenly like talking to Natalee and her dad, like she was justifying herself. Defending her life choices and her decision not to grab Rashad and do the "traditional" thing.

"Who cares how long it's been?" Julie laughed.

"I do," Mikaela asserted. "I think we both do."

"You were always so brave."

Brave? What's that supposed to mean? Mikaela thought. She forced a polite smile at the invasive comment but chose not to take the bait. "Well, there are always, um, *considerations*. Getting pregnant is usually a two-person operation. And I'm busy a lot."

"Of course. When Cam and I decided it was time to give Robbie a sibling, within a few months of me coming off the pill, bam, there was Kit! But I was a Fertile Myrtle back then and y'know." She winked. "We also tried a lot." Julie chuckled at her own joke. "The advantages of youth."

"Well, I'm glad for you," Mikaela fibbed, flabbergasted and still struggling to regain her balance in the conversation. She took a large swig of Jack and Coke to settle her roiling stomach.

"Oh, Mike, for as much as we've grown up, you have to admit one thing's still true—we've always had the same taste."

Mikaela choked, forcing herself not to glance at Cameron. "W-what do you mean?"

Julie lifted her own glass, filled with the same rich amber liquid as Mikaela's. "I remember our first drink like it was yesterday. Jack and Coke…and too heavy on the Jack."

Mikaela laughed with relief. "You said you liked that I

gave a heavy pour. Though of course The Judge was less than impressed."

"Especially after finding us passed out in his study!"

"Up to a one-thousand-dollar fine for underage drinking!" Julie and Mikaela quoted together, dissolving into a fit of giggles.

Mikaela could feel someone staring, and her eyes strayed in Cameron's direction. He watched them both, jaw rolling sullenly.

Mikaela reminded herself she was there to keep an eye on Cameron and did her best to shake off the nostalgia. "So, do I understand that you and the kids live in Charleston now?" Mikaela asked, changing subjects.

In an effort to prevent awkwardness in their conversation, Mikaela acted as if Vanessa hadn't kept her abreast of select happenings in the Robertson clan for years. Mikaela asked questions instead of making statements, but she also knew from the suit's briefing documents that Julie had retained a very old and well-respected law firm based in Charleston.

"Ah, close, Mt. Pleasant," Julie corrected, smiling. "We tried living in Savannah for a while. But once I was..." She trailed off, avoiding the *d*-word before starting again energetically, "I—I just decided, 'whatever,' you know? As Kit likes to say, 'I gotta do me.' What's best for me. And you know I had always loved the Low Country. So, I picked up stakes and left Georgia. That was, goodness, about five years ago."

"Well, you know, Juliette has never had trouble doing what's best for herself," Cameron said.

Nearly every other conversation at the table came to a momentary halt. But he didn't say anything else.

Cameron had been drinking all afternoon, on his third Scotch on the rocks in two hours. Not enough to make him drunk, but enough to become annoying. Every so often,

Cameron lobbed little bon mots at Julie throughout the meal that were, if nothing else, petty.

"All the Robertsons are out that way anyway," Julie continued. "If you remember?"

"Yup."

Mikaela definitely remembered the numerous summers spent in and out of lavish Kiawah Island beach houses belonging to numerous members of the Robertson clan or their cadet branches. Uniformly wealthy people largely from the Savannah area originally, they all paradoxically converged once a year on the Carolinian beachfront instead. And Mikaela, Julie, Gabe and Vanessa, along with assorted little Robertson cousins, had their run of the place. But Mikaela also *vividly* recalled she and her sister being among the few black people there that weren't "the help."

For nostalgia's sake, Mikaela didn't mention that part.

"Yeah, originally Cam and I both thought we'd like Savannah. Bit more culture, bigger city, stuff we were dying for, but it was still a little too, um—" Julie paused "—*Old Dixie* for me."

She leaned in and spoke that final part behind her hand as if intimating a dirty secret. She laid on the accent extra thick for emphasis and it was as if she'd seen into Mikaela's mind...or maybe just read her face.

Mikaela cracked up and Julie did right along with her.

Suddenly, it was like old times.

Cameron snorted, spinning the brown liquid in his lowball glass.

Mikaela stuck an errant braid back behind her ear and squinted, trying to focus on Julie's words and ignore Cameron's not-so-quiet grousing in the background.

A few minutes later, after a short, whispered conversation

with Robin, Mikaela saw out of the corner of her eye when Cameron got up and walked out, tossing his napkin on the table as he went. Mikaela exhaled watching his departure.

It was five thirty when the first people began to leave the celebration, a slow trickle until only a core few remained.

And for some reason, Mikaela still found herself among them, genuinely enjoying herself in Julie's company again and charmed by Robin and her friends. A handful of the men, including Rashad, adjourned to the steakhouse's lounge, where a game was playing on the four large flat-screen TVs above the bar. The women had all moved closer to one another at the long banquet table and were talking over coffee and dessert when Mikaela decided to take a moment to herself.

She stepped out onto the street, taking a deep, restorative breath. People walked, cars drove and bicyclists rode past her along the avenue. It was still sunny and hot even though it was already evening, and Mikaela was tired. This day had been a lot, emotionally taxing, yet somewhat remarkable. She hadn't spent any time, not in a long time, thinking about what reuniting with Julie could be like but it was still astonishingly different from anything she would have imagined...

And good.

"You finally had enough?"

Cameron was there when Mikaela turned around. Hunched over, elbows on knees, his suit jacket off and laid beside him, he sat on the bench in front of the restaurant. He dragged a palm across his sweaty brow, pushing hair out of his face. A cigarette burned, nearly down to his knuckles, between his index and middle fingers.

"You're still here? I thought you left."

"I did. Walked over to Central Park, bought a pack of

cigarettes, took two." He brandished the one in his hand. "Threw the rest away."

"And got some more to drink somewhere from the look of you." Mikaela's lip curled into a sneer. "Since when do you do *that*?"

"What?"

She rolled her eyes. "Smoke."

"It was a bad habit I picked up when shit was especially awful and I thought possibly dying of lung cancer might not be the worst thing ever."

Given what happened with his mother and daughter, Mikaela couldn't tell if he was joking.

"What the hell?"

"Don't worry, I quit a few years later. It's just these two, this once. The rest of the pack is in a garbage on the corner of Columbus and 63rd, if you wanna go check." As he said it, he flicked the butt in a high arc into the street.

"No, I meant why are you acting like this? You look a mess. What are you doing?" She smoothed out her knitted eyebrows, rubbing the pads of her index finger and thumb across them, toward her temple repeatedly, massaging it.

"What are *you* doing, Mikaela?"

"I'm here like y'all asked me to be."

"No, you're kissing Juliette's ass again like you did when you were eighteen!" He stood then, speaking in a harsh whisper. "I don't understand how she does this to you."

"W-what?" Mikaela stepped back when he was within striking distance, giving herself space.

"I've been watching you all afternoon—"

"Yes, I noticed that. What the hell is your problem?"

"She's playing you," Cameron said ominously.

"What are you talking about?"

"She knows you're my lawyer, Robin told her. But Julie hasn't mentioned it once, has she?"

"And she's not supposed to, as no doubt *her* lawyer told her." He scoffed, rolling his eyes.

"Cameron, I know Celia informed you. You're not supposed to discuss the case either. Even though you've spent the whole afternoon making stupid little snide comments."

"What, am I supposed to pretend like she's not fucking suing me for every goddamn cent I have in this world?" he spat back.

"*You cannot discuss the details of this case with her!* Here! Now!"

This being New York, despite their scene, very few people even stopped. Those that did moved along after Mikaela glared at them.

Cameron's eyes widened. "Since when do you yell?" Splotches of red bloomed across his face.

"Since, contrary to what you apparently think, I stopped being some little eighteen-year-old sycophant that follows behind people mindlessly!"

Cameron's eyes scanned her face as if seeing her anew. "I shouldn't have said that," he said, examining his feet, contrite. "I didn't mean it."

"Yeah, yeah, I'm sure you didn't. But do you understand the legal advice I've just provided you, Mr. Murphy?"

He turned away, nodding once. "I didn't pay for that volume though."

"*You* don't pay at all. And if you sobered up maybe you'd realize that's why I'm still here. Why I came at all. To make sure that you didn't say something you shouldn't and screw up our case."

Cameron's head jerked at that. "Are you saying you only

came to *my daughter's recital* to make sure that Juliette and I didn't say anything to each other that would jeopardize your deal?"

It was Mikaela's turn to look as if she'd been scolded.

"No, I didn't mean it like that. Of course not, I just—"

"But it is one of the reasons why you came?"

"It's one of the reasons why I *stayed*."

"That's a distinction without a difference."

"What do you want me to tell you?"

"That you came because I asked you to share this moment with me and my family."

Mikaela was stunned by the intimacy of the statement. "I—I—"

"And that's also why you brought *him*?" Cameron looked past her into the restaurant through the large plate glass.

She didn't turn around but knew he looked to where Rashad sat with the others watching the game.

"Rashad is my boyfriend! Of course I brought him. What was I gonna do, come alone?"

"Kaela," Cameron sighed deeply. "You wouldn't have been alone."

Mikaela worried her bottom lip and Cameron's eyes fell to her mouth.

"I don't understand you and I *definitely* don't know what you thought this was gonna be."

"Do you have any idea what it's been like all afternoon seeing you with *him*? Hmm?" Cameron licked his own lips as Mikaela willed her eyes elsewhere. "Then you and her, thick as thieves again? To be standing on the outside of all that, just watching? When *I* asked you to be here?"

"You're drunk and way outta line. And *Robin* asked me to come."

He narrowed his eyes, crossing his arms. "I think you know full well that I'm the one who wanted you here."

Mikaela sighed. "Julie and I were just making conversation."

"Listen to me, you *cannot* trust her. Juliette is a liar and a phony. She'll say or do whatever is most convenient at the moment. Then the story will change in the next. She's not the person you remember... *Or maybe she is?* I don't know." He shrugged. "Imagine being married to someone like that for ten years only to realize you had no idea who they really were. I mean, who they *ever* were?"

Mikaela put her hand to her mouth, to stop herself from saying anything.

Cameron's eyes bore into her. "And then imagine realizing you'd forfeited one of the most important relationships of your life...*for that?*"

Mikaela's eyes began to burn.

This was precisely why she hadn't wanted to come to the recital, or really, to even see Cameron again. To become entangled in any part of his life that wasn't directly related to her job or his case. She had left this all behind years ago, particularly Cameron and Julie and the person she was with them back then, conflicted, needy, wanting of their attention or approval—along with the rest of these old attendant feelings. She hadn't wanted to come and face any of it again. She knew now she should have followed the impulse for self-preservation that had screamed in warning to her. Mikaela turned away just as Rashad came through the door and out onto the sidewalk.

She wiped forming tears from her lashes quickly, hoping she was fast enough.

From Rashad's expression, it was obvious she wasn't.

"Kaela, baby, you okay?"

"I guess you let just anyone call you that now, huh?"

"Excuse me?" Rashad said, placing himself between them. "What?"

"What?" Cameron repeated, but stepped back, wisely.

Rashad was not bigger than Cameron, but he was a broader man. And though they never talked about it because he swore it didn't matter, he was younger than Mikaela too. By three years, making him six years Cameron's junior. Mikaela prayed they didn't go any further with this.

"Everything's fine, Rah, I was just having a disagreement with my client."

"Your client?" Rashad turned to her. "Your clients frequently leave you in tears?"

"She just told you to mind your own goddamn business! You said you're a doctor so I'm guessing you're smart enough to get that."

"Cam!"

"Listen, man, I will wreck—"

"RASHAD!" Mikaela grabbed his arm as he stepped forward. "Rashad, please."

She tugged on the lapels of his suit jacket to get him to turn away from Cameron and down to her. "This man is my client and he has had too much to drink. Please don't help me make this situation worse. Please go back inside. I'll be in in a second."

Rashad stopped, looking from one of them to the other, as if he were comprehending the whole scene finally.

"An old *friend*, huh?"

Rashad lifted Mikaela's palms off his jacket with his fingers and dropped them. Then he stalked down the street, not back into the restaurant.

"Quite the boyfriend," Cameron quipped from behind her.

"You happy?" Mikaela rounded on him.

"Very."

"Well, if you're smart—" she poked him in the chest "—you'll get yourself some coffee, sober up, go back in there and apologize to your son and daughter for making an ass of yourself!"

Cameron closed his mouth.

Mikaela went back inside and left Cameron standing on the sidewalk as the rest of the world moved all around.

twenty-four

Mikaela didn't actually get to Harlem until three days after Cameron's arrival.

On Christmas Day, for the first time in a couple of years to hear the locals tell it, it snowed. Not a lot, barely enough to sink their whole boots down into, but for Mikaela it was enough. The City was sufficiently covered to make everything a gleaming white and hush the cars on the street for a little while.

She had finished her paper at the university library, *just in time for them to close for the semester,* and was finally free. Which meant, at last, she and Cameron could indulge her little Christmas-in-New-York-City fantasy.

Without fully intending to, they walked all the way from her dorm at West 3rd Street, through the Village, up into Midtown. They wandered around Rockefeller Center, where she allowed Cameron to take a single picture of her peering up at the enormous tree. Although, *allowed* wasn't quite the right word since she was only aware he'd done it after the fact. They lunched on hot chocolate and roasted peanuts from one of the street carts that cast off heavenly toasted-honey-nut-scented steam. Then they walked up the wide avenue that dead-ended into the 59th Street entrance of Central Park.

Inside the park, Cameron, with a suspicious lack of false starts, led her to the Bow Bridge—*not anywhere near where Penny claimed it was.* He admitted then that he'd spent the whole time she'd been locked away in the library exploring the city. It meant this, their adventure, was no longer new for him. And Mikaela was genuinely surprised by how slighted this information made her feel. Still, they stopped a jogger at the crest of the bridge requesting a picture. He took three, before jogging away as Cameron grumbled under his breath that none would likely be any good. Mikaela teased him about his snobbery afterward. Nevertheless, despite being completely different than she expected—the birds had largely flown away for the season, the water was a muddy brown with opaque, white chunks floating in it and the trees were bare—they couldn't have been any happier.

This was *exactly* the Christmas Day she had hoped for.

It was late afternoon and already dark by the time they reached 110th Street and the Harlem Meer, the small lake at the upper terminus of the park. From there, they walked until they found an open restaurant—*Chinese*—and an open venue—*a movie theater on 125th Street*—before finally heading up to the Y late. It was after ten when they hustled up the narrow stairwell and down the hall to Cameron's room. The building was very nearly silent around them, except for Johnny Mathis's rendition of "It's the Most Wonderful Time of the Year" playing low behind someone else's door.

Once inside, Mikaela considered the small, sparse room. It was modest but not as run-down as she'd imagined. Cheerfully painted and refurbished at least in the same decade, the room pleasantly surprised her. Cameron stood by the door, as she walked the step or two it took to circumnavigate it.

The window was open, making the space chilly.

"They give good heat," he explained, rushing to close it again. "I had to open the windows in the middle of the night."

Mikaela took off her coat and draped it across the back of the single chair beside a small desk.

"Do you need any water? They have a vending machine on the next floor," he asked, jamming his hands into his pockets for coins.

Though he'd been there for three days already, this was the first time they'd truly been alone. The first night Cameron arrived, Mikaela's roommate, Eleanor, had returned by the time they got back to her dorm after dinner. And though Cameron stayed there that night, they'd only fallen asleep in each other's arms watching an old episode of *Star Trek: The Next Generation* as Ellie struggled not to stare from across the room. The two days leading up to Christmas were lost to Mikaela's paper. She holed up in the library writing frantically until the librarians put her out, and paused only for food Cameron provided before heading back uptown alone each night. So, this was it. Their first time alone in a long time.

She turned. Cameron stood fidgeting by the door as if searching for a reason to escape.

Mikaela walked back to him. Catching hold of the still-cold lapel of his bomber jacket and pulling his face down on top of hers, she kissed him.

His heart was beating fast against her knuckles.

Hers too.

She'd been waiting for this for a while—if she was honest, ever since she'd seen him in the lobby of her dorm.

"C'mon." She grasped his hand, pulling him away from the door.

Mikaela stripped out of her clothing one item at a time and placed everything neatly on the chair before her confidence finally drained from her like the waning end of an adrenaline rush.

"You okay?" She took a seat on the bed.

"You know, this means a lot to me." Cameron's expression was solemn, severe in its thoughtfulness. "I didn't come all this way just to get laid."

"I never thought that." Mikaela smirked, tucking her chin. "Why would you?"

"I overheard some of the old-timers round here talkin'. Sayin' that's all white guys are after. They think that the girls that fall for it are kidding themselves. I wasn't sure I even wanted to bring you up here. I didn't want you to hear that but you said you wanted to come."

"You think I haven't heard that before?"

Cameron's forehead furrowed.

Anytime they weren't in Harmon, where both the black and white people knew her from birth, Mikaela had heard some version of it. In equal measure from blacks and whites, albeit for different reasons. One, with a familial concern, the other, in poorly disguised distaste.

It was kind of a shock to realize now Cameron hadn't heard any of those comments himself. Obviously, he had just not been listening.

Mikaela wrapped herself in the threadbare, drab, sky blue comforter covering the bed and sat up straight. Something in his eyes told her that this had somehow become more important than even their first time, than all the times during the summer, in fact.

"I love you, Mikaela."

Mikaela's breathing sped up as Cameron sat down beside her, softly whispering.

"I hope you realize that."

He'd never said that before, though she knew he felt it. Taking a deep breath, Mikaela smiled, trying to act like it was nothing. But with Cameron's words, everything about this now felt strangely consequential. Though she was the only one in her underwear in the chilly room, Cameron sat beside her uncertain, hunched and like her...starkly vulnerable.

"I know." She nodded. "I do."

Cameron kissed her tenderly, delicate fingertips along her jaw, his lips almost skimming over hers. Mikaela fell back onto the flattened pillows of the small bed stiffly as he leaned over her. Cradling her head in the crook of his arm, he eased onto the bed to lie at her side.

"I've had time to think about it." He pulled back to gaze into her eyes. "I think our breakup was a mistake."

Mikaela was conflicted. "We broke up because I was leaving for school."

"We broke up because you refused to tell Julie."

She began to speak but he cut her off.

"But I don't care anymore."

"Long distance is hard."

"I know, but I *really* don't want this."

"It was your ide—"

"Kaela," he interrupted her again. "Because I thought *you* wanted it. You told Mrs. S. that you thought it was better for me, better for us both to be free...but I hate it."

There in his arms, Mikaela agreed.

In her loneliest moments, walking through Washington

Square Park on the weekends as couples frolicked on the lawn, grabbing a slice by herself at Patsy's Pizzeria nearby, watching Ellie pack her things to go visit her boyfriend for the weekend upstate in Syracuse, Mikaela wondered at what she had traded in to come all this way from home, alone. But the feeling wasn't constant; it ebbed and flowed as she made her way around, learned to switch from the 4-train to the 6-train to avoid missing her stop, struck up conversations with classmates, psyched herself up for her first trip to Coney Island with Penny.

Yet she nodded as Cameron dipped his face to kiss her again anyway.

She loved his kisses, how they always tasted like cinnamon and how his familiarity made her feel content, safe, like sitting on her porch swing at home. His eyes adored her. His mouth made her forget her apprehension and the questions of Julie's ongoing infatuation with him, and possessiveness over her. His tongue made her forget the rest of anything else, of everything else. And his hands on her made her forget she was forgetting at all.

Mikaela closed her eyes, enjoying it as he caressed her. He drew a hand down the length of her body as she relaxed into his touch. He pulled back briefly to linger over her, crossing her brow ridge with his thumb, running it along her cheek and jaw, as if memorizing her face. His hand moved over her shoulder, his thumb slipping her bra strap down, before pausing to unclasp its front fastenings. He kissed her breasts before moving lower, past her rib cage, tickling her stomach, moving toward her hip and thigh while she held her breath, waiting.

Cameron paused to stare up into her eyes again, and Mikaela gasped lightly when he ventured further, moving his hand lower. She inhaled and shuddered, as he touched the downy vertex between her thighs. They both breathed heavily as he rained kisses on her belly, hips and thighs and slipped off her underwear.

"Good?" he asked as she moaned softly at the feel of his exploratory hand.

Mikaela whimpered, nodding, unable to speak.

She pulled him back up to face her, taking his shirt in her hands. He obliged quickly, stripping it off. Mikaela ran her hand down Cameron's chest and he cringed at her cold fingers when she stroked his stomach. He trembled slightly and she paused.

"Oooh, you're ticklish too." She delighted in discovering this so belatedly as Cameron tried to remove her hand.

He laughed at himself as she made him squirm a little, her hand skimming lightly along, playing with the smattering of hair descending from his chest in a trail she followed.

"You're as ticklish as a little kid…" Mikaela mocked him in a singsong voice, taking strands of his hair between her fingers and pulling them until he winced a little.

Cameron hissed at her, which she enjoyed, then exhaled audibly when she released him, brushing her hand away.

Returning to his face, she ran her index finger along his jawbone before arriving at his chin. Mikaela touched it, lingering under his cute, full bottom lip, staring at it. He had a charmingly bowed mouth. She opened her mouth to say it, when he spoke instead.

"I want to marry you someday."

Even though she was unnerved, the apprehension in his eyes and uncertain quaver in his voice made the declaration touching, but at the same time, somehow quaint.

Mikaela kissed him, lacking an adequate response. She tried to quiet the sudden fear his words elicited by focusing on the things she loved about him.

Cameron turned away to strip off his jeans and put on a condom as Mikaela stroked the back of his neck and slid her open palm over his broad, sloping shoulders, appreciating his large form. She'd fantasized about this on so many nights, alone in her dorm room wondering if he or any of the things they had shared over the summer had been real. Thinking of how their quiet moments—like when they had just sat together on her parents' donated bench in the community garden, or lain together and stargazed at midnight in the middle of the high school's football field—were their finer moments, some of the best moments of her life, in fact.

But now that Cameron was here and though he still intoxicated her, the smell of him, the heaviness of his body inches above hers, the feel of him between her legs, the sensation of his mouth tracing her contours, boldly kissing her most delicate parts, something was strangely different.

They both slipped under the thin sheets and Cameron's slightly callused fingertips tickled as they skimmed the smooth surface of Mikaela's skin, moving from her waist, down toward her bottom, gliding along the curvature of her hip and thigh. His touch was featherlight, making her aware of every place his hands moved. With his encouragement, Mikaela lifted one leg, then the other, wrapping her thighs around his waist. And after long leisurely minutes where they kissed deeply and molded their bodies together, he entered her. Mikaela gasped, closing her eyes and burying her head in his neck. She wrapped her arms around him as he moved, clinging to this euphoric moment and this exquisite manifestation of their feelings for one another. Eventually, they both shuddered, one tumbling over the other as they sighed with release.

Afterward, as they lay together quietly, whispering and giggling and listening to the Christmas music wafting in from another room, Mikaela let her new misgivings drift away on the melody. Yet all the while, something small and tight wrapped itself around Mikaela's heart and squeezed.

twenty-five

"*I knew* I didn't like the look of his ass! White boys always wanna hit it and quit it. My girl Tiff met this dude last year at that big bookstore on 82nd and Broadway. Next thing you know, he got her into all this transcendental meditation and Ayurveda and whatnot, even had me snowed for a minute. But after he knocked her up, *poof*, his ass vanished like David Copperfield," Penny droned on outside the door of the bathroom stall Mikaela occupied. "She had a full ride to Seton Hall but instead she's up in Co-op City with half a degree and a little boy. Meanwhile, this dude's back up at Colgate or Cornell or wherever."

"It's not like that." Mikaela's voice hardly carried over to the other side of the door.

Penny acted as if it hadn't, continuing undeterred. "Mm-hmm, I'm sure. But he still came up for some of that good-good and left you with what? An October Surprise?"

Mikaela gripped the white, plastic stick between her fingers, willing it to say what she wanted. Otherwise, she had no idea what she would tell her father...

Or even her mother.

This was precisely what Natalee warned them about, when she could find the time to expend a few moments of breath on her daughters. It was literally the story of their lives. The perils of "getting caught up."

And left unsaid was that Natalee had firsthand experience "getting caught up."

But Mikaela and Cameron *had* been careful. More than careful, *meticulous*. Even though Mikaela wasn't on the pill, all summer they'd gotten by without it, just being conscientious.

Then over Christmas…

There just hadn't been enough time together and so every moment after the first was frantic, as if they were racing against a ticking clock. Each time had flowed excitedly into the next until they must have just gotten comfortable and careless. Now, Mikaela was peeing on a stick and dreading a one-way ticket back to Harmon in three months sporting a rounded belly and facing a life sentence.

The idea of it made her sick. She hadn't been able to sleep for the past week.

But it was only when Penny caught her crying in her room that she'd actually done anything about it—or at least Penny had.

So, a trip to the drugstore later, here she was with a white stick and her anxiety.

"Time's up!"

Mikaela startled when the stall door rattled.

"What's it say?" Penny demanded from behind it.

"It's two lines," Mikaela gasped. "What does that mean?"

But Mikaela knew.

In her heart, she already knew. She wiped the tears crowding her eyes with the back of her arm until they came too fast and numerous to be controlled.

There was an extended silence before Penny spoke again. "Um, well, box says positive, but here, let's use the other one. Just in case." Penny's hand appeared from underneath the door wagging another foil-covered stick that Mikaela snatched from her.

twenty-six

"Still no calls from Dr. Guerrero," Suze, today crowned in twin coppery hair buns and looking like an Afro-Japanese Princess Leia, informed Mikaela in a whisper.

Mikaela swatted at her like a fly.

The deposition hadn't officially started so it wasn't inappropriate, technically, for Suze to have wheeled her chair over to Mikaela from the conference room wall to deliver this information directly into her ear. But it wasn't germane to the proceedings and Mikaela certainly had not asked Suze to give her a minute-by-minute accounting of whether or not Rashad had reached out. Suze was just voluntarily providing the service, checking their call log on her tablet, as the minutes ticked by waiting for Julie and her counselors to arrive.

Cameron glanced over at Mikaela from his space farther down the table next to the assistant general counsel, Monica. He quirked his head, but Mikaela sat, face impassible instead, giving him nothing.

He'd caused her enough trouble this weekend. While Mikaela had been calling Rashad nonstop and he'd refused to pick up or call her back, Cameron had been ringing her phone off the hook, multiple calls per day until she nearly picked up just to tell him to stop calling. And today, he even had the audacity to try to speak to her in the hall before the meeting started.

Now, she closed her eyes to keep herself from glaring at him.

"Are we late?" Julie swept into the already seated room breathlessly moments later.

Two three-piece-suit-wearing gentlemen followed her in and took seats at either side of her opposite Cameron.

Mikaela checked her watch as the men in the room reassured her that her timing was fine.

They were twenty minutes late.

When Julie sat, Mikaela smiled, small and easy. Yes, they were officially on opposing sides today, but she saw no need to make it unnecessarily awkward. They had seen and spoken at length just the previous Friday. However, Julie's face didn't register the greeting, remaining a mask. She only gave a tight toothless smile to Monica, Cecilia and the rest of the *Glamazon* faction before staring blankly into the middle distance. Still, Mikaela shrugged it off as the proceeding began. And the whole deposition went as it should—*uneventful salvos in a protracted and warlike afternoon*—until Mikaela heard her name coming out of the mouth of one of Julie's lawyers.

Mikaela's eyebrows went up, pulling her attention to the speaker. She shook her head to make sure she wasn't hearing things, shooting a glance at Cameron. His perplexed expression told her he'd heard it too. Unfortunately, it was not her imagination.

"I—I'm sorry, what?" Mikaela stammered as all the eyes at the table swiveled her way.

"I asked if Mr. Murphy is your client?" It was the pasty-faced man named Meyers seated to Julie's left, whose red hair, sad eyes and jowls reminded Mikaela of an Irish Setter.

Mikaela knew enough to recognize something was up.

"Ah, not technically." She clicked the top of her pen repeatedly as her knee bounced beneath the table. "Technically, Ms. Albright and Ms. Yee represent his interests. I am just observing on behalf of the parent company, Altcera."

"So that's the extent of your interests here?"

Julie's eyes finally met Mikaela's, probably for the first time that day. It was startling the way they sought Mikaela's out from across the room. Her hazel irises seemed to brighten, crackling to sudden life as her head, which until then had been tipped ever so slightly to the side in boredom, straightened. The rest of her face stayed blank. It was like an automaton powering on.

"I'm sorry, what does that have to do with anything? Mr. Meyers remembers that this is not court. There are no benefits to 'shocking revelations' and 'surprise witnesses.'" Cecilia made air quotes with her fingers and laughed.

"Yes, Mr. Meyers." Monica smiled mildly and nodded. "Is there a point?"

Julie's lawyer smiled too. In fact, Mikaela noted, *both of them did.*

"We're trying to ascertain Ms. Marchand's interest in the outcome of this litigation. Forgive me, *arbitration.*"

Monica scoffed. "What else could it be?"

She had walked right into that.

Cameron's eyes closed as the corners of Julie's mouth curved fractionally upward.

"My client was concerned that Ms. Marchand's personal

relationship with Mr. Murphy gave her an interest in the outcome beyond strictly looking out for the interests of *Glamazon*'s parent company."

With at least seventy-five years of legal experience combined among them, only Mikaela's associate was foolish enough to look at all surprised. Although, Cecilia Albright did put a finger to the flat line that had become her mouth, as Monica's head rolled slowly around from Mr. Meyers and Julie to Mikaela awaiting a response.

Mikaela cleared her throat, straightening from a tiny slouch in her seat she assumed as this gut-punch approached. She rolled the pen between her fingers. "I do know Mr. Murphy personally but I still have no interest in this, other than that of my client, which again, is Altcera."

"I understand what you've said. But can you elaborate on the nature of this relationship?"

"Relationship?"

"With Mr. Murphy," Julie's other lawyer, Webster, clarified. *"For the record."*

The stenographer's fingers clicking across his stenotype and Cecilia tapping her front tooth with a nail, sounds that would normally have been so minute as to escape notice, were clearly audible in the dead silence.

"If she won't say it, I can," Julie's high, musical Georgian cadence rang out, cutting into the near-complete quiet.

"Is this necessary?" Cameron cast around to the assorted bewildered faces with desperation.

"Before we were married, they were lovers."

"Jesus Christ, Juliette!" Cameron interjected, glowering at her.

Mikaela sucked in an irate breath, holding stock-still. She fought the impulse to scramble across the tabletop, grab Julie by her double strand of pearls and throttle her. But what did she expect? Wasn't it the height of stupidity that she hadn't predicted exactly this would happen? Cameron had even warned her, albeit drunkenly.

"What?" Julie shrugged. "So, we're gon' pretend it's not true? I mean, is it even *legal* that she's in here?"

"Um, can we stop?" Monica said then, placing her hands flat on the table as if holding it down. "We're going to go off the record now."

The stenographer at the head of the table looked up, busy fingers pausing.

"Yes, please." Cecilia cleared her throat, adding in a low, but dire tone, "Let's take a break to, uh, stretch our legs."

Mikaela fixed her gaze out the plate-glass windows, onto the City below. She sought refuge in the view because she couldn't bear to turn her head. Not to face Monica, Cecilia or anyone else there as they all rose to leave. Especially not Cameron, who throughout had wrung his hands, turning them over and over until even from her distance she could see them redden.

She was too afraid of the *told-you-so* she knew would be written across his face.

twenty-seven

As Art looked out his window with his back to Mikaela, everything from his balding scalp to the tips of his ears was red. No amount of Aruba tan could make her mistake that.

He was pissed.

Mikaela sank farther into her seat in the large cushioned chair in front of his desk.

She'd already told Art as much of the truth as she could bear: Julie was an old friend, Cameron, a former boyfriend—the ins and outs of which were too convoluted for her boss, thankfully—but she had not seen nor heard from either of them in years. Julie's lawyers had tried to make hay with the connection when they reconvened, but Cecilia made quick work of their insinuations, confirming that a decades-old relationship would not affect the outcome of the case. Still, in the end, Cecilia and Monica were so upset they made a beeline from the conference room to Art's office as soon as the deposition adjourned for the day. Mikaela, meanwhile, nearly ran to her own office, even as she saw Cameron approach-

ing her, heedless of how it would look. She only emerged
thirty minutes later when Suze knocked to say she'd been
summoned.

Now, Mikaela had been in with Art for over an hour.

Art took a labored breath before speaking. "You didn't
think it was worth disclosing, in all these weeks, that Murphy was your ex-boyfriend?"

She bristled. "It wasn't like we dated yesterday. I was something like twenty years old the last time I set eyes on him.
It really didn't feel like an omission."

"*Feel?*" It was Art's turn to scoff. "As if how it 'feels' mat-
ters. And the picture? You didn't think that would come up
either?"

Julie's group didn't miss a trick, trotting out the photo to
highlight that a young Mikaela was indeed there, sitting in
the background, right under everyone's nose. It was a real
gambit, assuming Mikaela hadn't already disclosed that to
her colleagues. But, Mikaela realized, maybe the truth was
she hadn't actually changed that much at all. And Julie had
learned from experience that betting Mikaela would keep
an inconvenient secret to herself was apparently sure money.

Mikaela sighed. "It wasn't relevant. I'm hardly noticeable.
And I signed a model release for that twenty years ago, before Mr. Murphy first started selling his work."

Or at least she thought she did. But it didn't really matter
anyway since she wasn't the one suing Cameron for misap-
propriating her image.

"And now?"

"And now what?" Mikaela said, shrugging as if she didn't
know exactly what he was asking.

And now, who was Cameron to her?

She didn't know the answer to that any better than Art did.

"Celia and Monica want you out." Art said it plainly, but it hit Mikaela like a two-by-four.

She inhaled sharply. "And you?" She dug her nails into her palms then opened them to examine all the little red half-moons that crisscrossed the brown lines in them.

"I told you I needed you on this case because I did. You didn't tell me this was a potential conflict for you, but I also didn't give you the chance to say no."

Some of the immense tightness that was beginning to constrict Mikaela's breathing eased.

"Be that as it may, Mike, I know this was more babysitting and hand-holding than even you are used to doing for us. But it's just that you have that magic touch. You make everyone comfortable, you make the clients content."

Mikaela listened, suddenly perturbed by how much the phenomenon he was describing made her sound like the firm nursemaid. She'd never noticed that before.

"Not disclosing our past was a mistake, but I was only doing what I thought was best to protect Mr. Murphy's privacy. Now that everything's out in the open, I can assure you there won't be any other surprises. We can keep the case moving forward as planned. I can speak to Celia and Monica if they have questions, but I don't see any reason we shouldn't just put this all behind us."

Art shook his head. "Mike...they were blindsided today. To be honest, I was too. No ground was truly lost, but we just can't let it happen again. So, maybe you take a step back and we have Todd take over now. There's no harm done— you'll be fine, the ladies will get over it."

A queer, scratchy feeling came to Mikaela's throat and her eyes suddenly ached. This was not happening. Mikaela was never reprimanded. She never failed. She was never replaced or relieved.

"But Mr. Proctor wanted an update on Monday. Do you want to discuss how you'd like me to broach this change with him?"

"Oh, no. I'll handle Proctor," Art said, coming around the wide desk and ushering Mikaela to her feet. "I'm quite sure Celia will give him an earful in the meantime, but I'll set things right."

"Maybe he should hear it from me though?" Mikaela said, moving with Art toward the door as he led her.

"I'm sure I can handle it." He laughed as if he wasn't crushing Mikaela's spirit like a little bug on a windshield. "Just turn your notes over to Todd and I'll have him send you his Zenigent contract negotiation files."

He patted Mikaela on the shoulder.

"Mike," Art said, looking into her face. "This is fine. You're still in the game. We're gonna get this all done. It's a team effort. And we're still a long way away from handing out the MVP trophies."

Mikaela nodded as her eyes filled, infuriatingly, with liquid. She pressed her lips shut and swallowed, annoyed at how Art could make light of what was supposed to be the biggest move in her career. She was the MVP. She was *already* the MVP when she landed this whole goddamn deal!

"Okay?" Art coaxed, trying to catch Mikaela's eyes as she looked away.

Mikaela nodded again reluctantly, struggling to smile for him. She did not want to cry in front of her boss. She couldn't.

"When this is all done, you, me and Countess, we'll go to Le Bernardin to celebrate."

Even hearing Art call his wife, Nastassja, by her ludicrous nickname didn't cheer her as it normally did.

"In fact, let's invite Todd and Anita too. Why not make

it a party! God knows by then we'll deserve it." Art made it sound like a reward, when inviting Todd to anything that involved her was without question a punishment. This was all going from bad to worse.

Especially when she realized Art had deposited her on the other side of his office door.

She'd fucked up.

twenty-eight

THEN
May 2003

The doorbell rang but Mikaela's father just beamed at her instead, making no effort to move.

He'd been smiling at Mikaela like that for the four days she'd been back home.

Meanwhile, Mikaela tried to pretend that everything didn't feel different.

Even the town itself, as her dad drove her through, seemed odd and surreal. There was a new store on the main street, just one, but it was enough to throw her off-balance and make the configuration of the entire block novel again. Vanessa was annoying as usual, but things were off. Her dad was acting funny as well. But it was not just the two of them; the feeling pervaded everything. Even Mikaela was like a stranger. Attending her first party back in town had been weird; Mikaela was dragged there by Nicole since Julie begged off. And there, with kids she knew, filling rooms she knew, in houses she knew, it was all somehow foreign.

So, while Mikaela was ecstatic to be home for the summer break, there was a small part of her that wasn't. Particularly after months of dreading it, worried she would have to do so harboring a secret. But even though she'd lost the baby, things were still different. And even a month later, it was still that way. She was no longer the same Mikaela that had left Harmon nine months earlier.

"So?" J.D. pressed, leaning against the breakfast bar as Mikaela inhaled one of his famous candied-banana PB&Js.

She forced a smile. Like everything else now, even the sandwich was tainted and bittersweet, since while pregnant she'd actually dreamed about having them.

Still, her father grinned proudly while she attempted to speak and chew simultaneously. "Swallow first."

She swallowed as directed but paused before taking another bite. "I don't know, Daddy. I'll still help if you need me, but I already promised Mrs. Ogilvy that I'd come back to my library job, and I still wanna have some free time for myself."

"For yourself or for Cameron?" Her father's cat-that-ate-the-canary smile didn't leave much room on his face for the even smugger *I got you, didn't I?* element also present.

Mikaela counterfeited amusement.

Cameron was both the first and last person she wanted to see. She hadn't called him in the near week she'd been home and in actuality, they hadn't spoken as much as they'd planned since Christmas. After their "accident," calls decreased in frequency, because keeping it all a secret from him made talking too difficult and hearing his voice even more so. Particularly knowing, after she'd lost their baby... *that she'd wanted to.*

"What about Vanessa?" Mikaela offered, knowing full well that working at their father's shop was Vanessa's version of a circle of hell. But no less than she deserved for ratting her and Cameron out to their father.

"Am I the only one who realizes someone's at the door?" Vanessa yelled down the stairs, just before flying by to answer it.

Mikaela and her father paused as Vanessa opened the door. Then both saw Tommy Sutton, Cameron's best friend, out of uniform in jeans and a T-shirt, stepping into the foyer. He held his ball cap in his hands.

J.D. rose first. "Deputy?"

Tommy turned at hearing J.D.'s voice but his solemn gaze fell on Mikaela first.

Her stomach dropped, heart crashing against her rib cage, threatening to break out of her chest.

"Tommy?" Mikaela's voice trembled as she tripped off her bar stool. Only her dad's firm grip applied to her shoulders held her steady.

Cameron.

Yes, she'd only sent a couple of letters, more travelogues of her adventures with Penny in New York than missives. And he'd replied with long heartfelt notes on unfortunately sappy greeting cards featuring hugging teddy bears or portly white cupids that made Mikaela want to roll her eyes. But she did love them...and him.

"Tommy?" Mikaela said again, grateful for her father's support right then. "Is Cam alright?"

Tommy's brown eyes were dull and his mouth grimly set as he shook his head. "It's Miss Anne."

Once she was inside the hospital, relief eased Mikaela's nerves when she learned Mrs. Murphy had been admitted not to the hospice wing as she feared but onto the opposite side of the floor, the acute care unit.

That's what she missed when she decided not to reach out immediately upon returning home. Being there when Cameron needed her.

When she got upstairs, Cameron was sitting hunched over his mother's bed, slipping ice chips into her mouth from a small pink plastic bucket on her bedside table. They whispered to each other, a conspiracy of two, with him doing the majority of the talking as Mikaela observed from the doorway. Using her one unfettered hand, Mrs. Murphy stroked her son's cheek, while concern etched newly drawn lines into her face. After a moment, she spied Mikaela beyond him and smiled.

"Look," she whispered to her son, pleased, and he turned.

Mikaela's breath caught. Cameron's normally frosty azure eyes were a sooty gray and encircled by dark shadows, ringed in red from strain and sunken into his head. The harsh artificial light gave both mother and son identical waxen, pallid complexions.

"Hi, Miss Anne, Cam. I hope I'm not interrupting."

Cameron's eyes widened seeing her there and then filled with tears even as he tried to blink them away.

"Hi, Mikaela," he said simply.

Mikaela came to him then, wrapping her arms around his head, and he buried his face in her stomach and sobbed. She stood perfectly still as he clung to her, anxiety making her heart throb. His shoulders shook and though the sound was muffled, Mikaela could feel his gasps against her navel and the wetness of his tears soaking through the flimsy T-shirt into her skin.

"Thank…you…" Mrs. Murphy's voice was low and hollow. The words lethargic and ragged as if they battered about her chest before escaping. Still, she managed to hold Mikaela's gaze between long, drowsy blinks. "For coming to see me... Mike."

That short sentiment took effort. Mikaela gave the woman an anemic smile in return, staggering back against the agonized tears that racked Cameron's body. She rubbed Cameron's neck with her hands as she watched his mother.

"It's okay." Mikaela bent forward and kissed Cameron's head, shushing him. "My dad says he's going to stop by tomorrow, if that's alright?"

She spoke to Mrs. Murphy quietly, rather than acknowledging their current situation.

The woman nodded before gathering her strength to answer with words. "That'll be...nice," she said after a long pause where she breathed deeply from an oxygen mask. "Provided you...can get Cam to...bring me my face."

As usual she acted as if nothing was wrong and Mikaela played along for lack of an alternative.

But this didn't seem to be the same woman that Mikaela knew lying in that bed, barely able to speak. This woman was skeletal beneath the floral quilt, obviously from home, that dwarfed her. She had multiple wires tethering her to the bed, monitoring her heart rate and her oxygen intake, feeding her fluids, pumping air into large booties on her feet, heating another blanket stretched across them. Mikaela knew that lymphoma had ravaged Mrs. Murphy previously, having already stolen some of one lung, but every time Mikaela saw the woman, she had been upbeat and sprightly.

Whether puttering around her extensive vegetable garden behind their house, playing solitaire at the kitchen table or watching her soap operas on the couch, Mrs. Murphy seemed full of life. Sometimes at her own expense, but often at Cameron's, and occasionally just with a fun story, Mrs.

Murphy was a hoot. In those moments, it was hard to glean that she'd ever been sick, except from the exceedingly tender ways Cameron cared for her. Mikaela had witnessed Cameron rushing around to make sure his mother didn't, and solicitous to the point of her irritation. Mrs. Murphy frequently shooed him away to do things for herself.

"I always…told my boy—" Anne sucked heavily from her mask "—I believe in…painting…my self-esteem…directly onto my face."

Mikaela attempted a chuckle. Even now Mrs. Murphy was still quick with a quip.

"See? She's gonna be fine." Mikaela bent her head to whisper into Cameron's ear as Mrs. Murphy's eyes drooped, exhausted from this small expenditure of her reserves.

Her eyes, when they opened periodically, stayed on Mikaela, watching as she held on to Cameron, stroking his head. Mrs. Murphy smiled wanly at Mikaela while they waited for Cameron's grief to exhaust itself. And Mikaela stood there, kneading his neck and watching as Mrs. Murphy's breathing slowly evened out until eventually, she fell asleep.

Later, they stepped out into the hall.

"Thank you for coming," Cameron croaked, his voice rubbed raw.

Mikaela frowned. Cameron said it like it was some gesture of largesse on her part. She didn't understand where that was coming from.

"I'm just so sorry I didn't come sooner," she countered.

"It's alright," he said, shaking his head as if it was nothing.

But even now Mikaela was still shaken by the level of anguish she'd witnessed. Cameron's tears sluiced from a reserve of grief he'd clearly been keeping at bay for days, possibly she suspected, even years.

"Tommy just told me what happened." She hugged his arm, staying close, holding him up until they could make their way to a bench down the hall, near the elevators.

He just nodded without replying.

As they sat, Cameron put an arm around her shoulders, leaning his head against hers, his other hand crossed over her thigh. They sat in silence intertwined for long minutes as he breathed and his heart beat against her arm until she thought he'd fallen asleep.

"I had wondered if you would come at all." His voice cut through the silence that only the occasional staff member walking by infringed upon.

"Why wouldn't I?" She continued to rub the hand that was draped across her lap, pushing her fingers between his.

He eased away slightly, straightening so he could look down at her. "Because you stopped calling, writing. You've been home for a week and I haven't heard from you."

"It hasn't been a week. Just a few days. I—I just wanted a couple days to myself first."

"I get that. Doesn't mean you couldn't call though?" Cameron's hand fell out of hers as did his arm from her shoulders, retreating to his side. "I thought at least you might stop by when Julie told you."

Mikaela twisted in her seat. "Julie knows?"

"Julie's been here every day since Mama was admitted. She didn't tell you?"

"I haven't seen her since I've been back either."

"It was one of her mother's friends that found Mama on the floor at the flower shop. Called the ambulance for her."

"We never saw each other, I'm sorry." She reached into his lap and squeezed his hand. "I promise if we had, I would have come sooner."

Mikaela hadn't considered what it meant that Julie wasn't

waiting for her to get home. Their relationship had begun to change anyway. All the previous summer's covert splitting of their normally unadulterated girl-time with Cameron had strained things. Then when they hadn't even spent Christmas together it didn't help. In truth, though they spoke, they'd barely seen each other at all since Mikaela left for college. But that didn't seem strange. Julie was busy at college herself; they were just moving in different directions. So Mikaela had hardly noticed when one day back home flowed into four still incommunicado. Even when Julie missed the big end-of-year high school blowout that even Mikaela attended, she still didn't wonder what was really going on…

Cameron took her hand in his and brought it to his mouth, sighing. "I was out taking stupid pictures when this happened. All the way off on the Creek Trail, out past the garden." He stared at the opposite blank wall.

"Uh-uh, you know better than that." Mikaela turned his chin with a finger, trying to catch his attention. "That one photo you sent me last month? Of my parents' chair under the big magnolia? I loved it."

"When I look at it, it makes me think of you," he whispered. "Thank you for coming. *Really*."

She hated that he was thanking her. And the relief in his voice embarrassed her.

His shoulders fell and his eyes welled with tears again.

"What if this is it? What if I lose her now?" Cameron's head dropped into his hands. He pressed the heels of his palms into his eyes as if he was trying to push the bad thoughts back in. "This is how it happened with my dad. One day he collapsed at work. They took him to the hospital and he never came home again."

He rocked in the seat, and a frantic edge crept into his words. "They said he'd been lucky, that it wasn't that bad.

That he'd recover. He just needed a routine angioplasty. He'd be out of the hospital in a couple of days."

Mikaela had never heard this before. Cameron had no problem talking about his father generally but had never shared anything about his death.

"Mama told me it was fine. To not even bother coming home. So, I didn't. He died while I was in a damn color and composition class. Now, what if it's her turn?"

His voice cracked as he leaned farther forward, his back and shoulders shaking. Mikaela grabbed him around the shoulders to hold him up.

"If she goes, I'll be alone. And I won't... I won't have anybody left." He collapsed onto her lap, moaning. "I don't want to be alone."

Mikaela rubbed Cameron's back and whispered to him. "She's gonna be okay. I just know it'll be okay." She said it again and again, a soothing refrain until his tears subsided.

When he finally sat up a long while later, sweaty and flushed, his eyes red-tinged and hair wild, he chuckled. "I'm so sorry, Kaela. Now you're here I can't seem to stop. I must look crazy. Cryin' in front of you."

"No." She shook her head, pushing moist strands of hair back from his scarlet face with her fingers. "You can cry if you need to."

He laughed at himself, sniffling, trapping his hands underneath his knees awkwardly. He searched her face and she saw the same desperate yearning for reassurance in his eyes he'd had at Christmas. Her heart constricted at the sight and suddenly his anguish was her agony too.

She eyed him squarely. "Cameron, it's gonna be alright, I promise."

"You don't know that." He shook his head, looking impossibly young, silent tears overflowing his lashes and stream-ing down his face.

"I do." She nodded.

She took his head between her hands and pulled him down to kiss his forehead and then his wet cheeks, before delicately settling on his lips.

"Because you won't be alone, 'cause I'm not going any-where."

twenty-nine

THEN
June 2003

Mikaela perused a menu as she shifted in her seat in a booth at Meg's diner. Her knee shook. She scanned the thick laminated menu, flipping through the pages for something to do with her hands and eyes instead of glancing at the doors repeatedly. She already knew the whole list by heart. It never changed and every item was good to excellent; years as a patron had taught her that. But she'd never bothered to marvel at how that was possible until now. It was just something she knew, something so familiar it was second nature.

Like her friendship with Julie.

Nothing was off-limits or too personal to discuss, so why Mikaela had lived in fear of telling this secret—so sure Julie would disown her once it was out—was still something she had yet to fully understand.

And now Mikaela had to try and explain that to Julie.

When Julie finally arrived, forty minutes late, she had her

hair up in a high ponytail with a pair of sunglasses propped up against it. She wore a teal one-piece bathing suit under a pair of white pedal pushers with flip-flops.

Clearly, she intended to go to the lake after this, and didn't intend to stay long.

Julie spotted Mikaela and her hazel eyes went dark, mouth flattening into a straight line.

At least this meant Mikaela wouldn't have to start from the beginning; Julie somehow already knew. But the cheer in her voice contradicted her previous expression.

"Hey!"

Mikaela sucked in a deep breath to steady herself, returning her best friend's greeting. "How're you doing?"

"Great, can't complain," Julie declared as she slid into the booth, her voice almost challenging Mikaela to say differently.

Mikaela blinked, leaning back in her seat. *But maybe she doesn't realize I know she knows?*

"Uh, that's good."

Julie looked Mikaela over. "Where's your bathing suit?"

"What?"

Someone who didn't know Julie as well, and hadn't spent as many years organizing their life around Julie's feelings as Mikaela had, would have missed Julie's "mean look": her eyes widened as if in surprise while the corners of her mouth curled almost imperceptibly. This was the look when Julie "nice-nastied" someone with a sweet-seeming, backhanded compliment or a snide remark that would have a girl crying hours later when she realized what Julie had truly meant. Mikaela coined the term herself. She didn't particularly like this side of Julie and had worked hard for years to be a counterbalance to it. To soothe feelings, not just between them but even in their friend group when someone was hurt. Be the sweet one when Julie got caustic, the forgiving one when Julie chose to be vindictive. The thing was Julie never ever actually *looked* angry or bothered, and she definitely never looked vicious or vindictive, though she could be all of those things…at the same time even.

"For the lake? Hello? I told Nicki we'd be there by twelve thirty."

Mikaela checked her watch. It was twelve ten. Julie was late for lunch and she had barely even given them the fifteen minutes it was going to take to get to Lake Shelburne from the diner.

She didn't plan to make this any easier after all.

"Look, Jules, I wasn't planning on going to the lake today. I'm headed back to the hospital." Mikaela's voice dipped, a tremor going through it. "To be with Cameron."

It was even possible her bowels loosened.

Julie's lips pulled tight across her face, less a smile than a grimace as her eyes grew as wide as platters. Mikaela had no idea what an outsider might have seen, but Mikaela knew Julie was incensed.

"Oh really?" Julie ground out between her teeth, still affixed with the faux smile.

"He told me you knew…" Mikaela swallowed hard. "That, um, Miss Anne, is sick?"

"He did?" Julie brought her hands up onto the table and clasped them in front of her. "When you spoke with him?"

It was as if Mikaela stood at a precipice with jagged rocks at either side on the way down. And it told her: *Just jump in now or be broken up in a fall later.*

"I'm dating him."

"Are you? For how long? How long exactly were you two going out behind my back?"

Mikaela glanced around at the other diners enjoying their

meals, wishing desperately she could be sitting with any one of them now.

"Since last summer." Mikaela paused then, hearing herself finally. "I—I, uh… We'd been seeing each other…" Mikaela bit her lip, struggling to get it out. "A-all summer."

Mikaela choked on the words, finally hearing what Cameron had been trying to say to her. How horrible it had been keeping such a big secret from someone she claimed to care so much about. Here were the awful words she'd been dreading for months. They were exactly as bad as she'd always feared they would be.

"And you never said anything? Why?"

"It was just that you wouldn't stop talking about him, you just seemed to like him so much. We thought it would be awkward." Mikaela spit the lie out with her guts churning and her tongue burning. Cameron couldn't have cared less what Julie thought.

"You are not trying to tell me that you told him not to say anything, right?" Julie glowered at her, able to read Mikaela's face. "And Tommy?"

"He wasn't supposed to know either." Mikaela was suddenly irritated that it all kept getting worse because Cameron had confided in his own best friend.

"What about Nicki and the boys?"

Mikaela shook her head, holding back tears. It certainly seemed now like Julie didn't know anything. Guilt tore through her.

"I can't believe this." Julie's eyes shone with unshed tears too, voice cracking. "So what, you both spent months making a complete ass of me?"

Mikaela cringed. That was the other thing Julie didn't do: she never cried. Not even when she broke an arm falling from the top of the cheerleaders' pyramid or when her grandma died. Julie was a rock. *Usually Mikaela's rock.*

Julie raised her hand before Mikaela could object.

"Or at the very least, y'all watched me make an ass of myself without ever saying a damn word! So, y'all were what? Off somewhere together laughing at poor, stupid, lovesick Juliette?"

"We wouldn't do that! We didn't!" Mikaela tried to explain. "I wanted to tell you but you were always gushing, going on about Cam!"

Julie's eyes narrowed, clearly offended at Mikaela's description of the countless hours she'd spent in paroxysms of ecstasy about even the most mundane aspects of Cameron and his life. Which was regular for them about a celebrity crush but odd for a real-life boy they actually knew. Julie was usually unflappably cool on the opposite sex.

All the better to lure them in with.

"I didn't know how you would react if you knew he liked me and not you." Mikaela felt like she was sinking. There was no angle from which to approach this that didn't insult or aggrieve Julie.

"'Cause of what? Like, pity or somethin'? Since when has that ever happened? Since when have I ever needed you to feel sorry for me?"

Mikaela fell back wounded by the disdain embedded in the question, by how pathetic it made her seem by comparison.

"Honestly?" Julie rose, grabbing her tote bag from beside her to scoot out of the seat. "It's his loss."

Mikaela grabbed her wrist. "We— I didn't do this to hurt you, I swear."

Julie icily inspected Mikaela's hand for a moment before she sat back down.

"Don't worry, you didn't," Julie said after she took a long

moment. "It was always the secret that pissed me off." Then the shadow lifted from Julie's face like a cloud passing.

"W-what?" Mikaela felt like she'd lost a crucial piece of a puzzle.

"I mean what am I, an idiot?" Julie flipped her ponytail over one shoulder and turned to her fully, looking Mikaela squarely in the face. "Do you think I couldn't guess you were going with someone? At first, I was hurt you were keeping it a secret. Suddenly you're always coming back from some-where, or off doing something when I wanted you. Like what the heck, Mike? *All summer?* We always tell each other everything. You didn't think I could work it out?"

"Jules—"

"It just took a while to figure out *who* you were sneaking off with. You've always been so finicky and weird about dat-ing. If I didn't know better, I'd have thought your dad slapped a chastity belt on you after What's His Face, *Mitchell*, left."

Mikaela didn't bother being offended.

"But when Cam's mom told my mom's friend what a great time her son had had in New York over Christmas with his girlfriend, I knew."

An incessant throb behind Mikaela's eyes grew. That damn women's auxiliary.

"So what was all this? Just trying to draw me out?" Mi-kaela suddenly imagined Julie like a ferret, trying to burrow into her brain and unearth her secrets, get to the bottom of things.

"It wasn't like you didn't deserve it." Julie pouted. "You're *my best friend*, he's just a boy."

This cat-and-mouse game was far more true to Julie's nature than all the months she'd supposedly spent blithely mooning over Cameron. Trying to harass Mikaela into a confession was much more Julie's style than guilting her into one. In retrospect, that had always been the strangest part. Julie never liked anyone as much as she claimed to like Cameron, even her exes. It made far more sense now that she'd done it to get under Mikaela's skin than anything else.

The only snag in Julie's explanation now was that her crush on Cameron and all her antics had started well before Christmas. But that was Julie too. Always trying to save face. She'd never allow it to seem like she was playing second fiddle to Mikaela. And honestly, Mikaela didn't care; she was just relieved they could put this all behind them.

She took a bracing breath before speaking. "I am so sorry, Jules."

Julie pouted in a theatrical way. "You broke girl code."

Mikaela rolled her eyes. "Right, 'Bros before hoes'?" She deliberately tried to inject some humor. She didn't think she'd ever heard Julie openly invoke girl code into the rules of their friendship before—and she had doubts Julie, in all her romantic entanglements, seriously believed in it either.

Julie resisted a smirk. "No, stupid. 'Ovaries before brovaries.'"

Mikaela snorted. "Juliette Marie Robertson, there is no such thing as a 'brovary.'"

They broke into a round of giggles, laughing for a good long time. Finally, when it subsided, Julie appraised Mikaela. "So, you and Cam, huh?"

Mikaela nodded tentatively, holding her breath.

Julie rolled her eyes and sighed. "Whatever. Tommy's the cuter one anyway."

Mikaela exhaled. She could accept that, even with the distinct sour-grapes tinge to Julie's words. Finally, Mikaela felt like she could breathe again for the first time in over a year.

"So, I guess that means you're gonna be at the hospital a lot for a while, huh?"

Mikaela didn't bother to say that Cameron told her Julie had been at the hospital every day herself. She just nodded.

"He can't have all your time, Mike. Not like last summer."

"Julie, his mother is sick."

"I get it, but he has his own best friend. You're mine. And I need you too."

There was a petulant whine threaded through Julie's otherwise demanding tone but as always Mikaela took her point. "I promise I'll be better this year."

"Look, I don't know, but maybe you could bring him around?"

Mikaela nodded again, though she suspected Cameron would have little interest in hanging out with her friends.

"Well—" Julie looked out the window "—come by the house later, 'kay?"

Mikaela followed her eyes out to the parking lot where Corey waited patiently for Julie in his car.

"Meg's doing the two-for-one shakes again until Independence Day," Mikaela offered.

Julie's mouth twisted. "I'm trying to cut down on my carbs."

"But what about Corey?"

"What about him? If he wanted one, he coulda come in and got one himself."

Mikaela shook her head as they both slipped out of the booth.

Julie reached out and pulled Mikaela to her. Squeezing her tightly, Julie whispered into her ear, "You're still in the doghouse. You know that, right?"

Yeah, Mikaela thought as she squeezed Julie back. She did.

thirty

"You *are* kidding, right?"

Cameron was reclined against Suze's desk when Mikaela finally emerged from her bout of tears in a stall in the executive washroom and ventured back to her desk. She had to struggle not to shout at them both chatting so amiably in front of her office.

Suze appeared utterly charmed. She practically batted her eyelashes up at Cameron from her seat.

"You do realize I shouldn't even be *seen* with you? You were both in that meeting, right?"

Mikaela looked from one to the other as they stared back, faces blank and slack-jawed.

"Go away, Cam," Mikaela said, stalking into her office.

She plopped down on her couch, pulling her heels off her aching feet as Cameron walked in casually, his hands in his suit pockets.

"Leave me alone, I said." She chucked her red-bottomed shoes across the room.

Cameron paused as they sailed from her hands. One knocked over an empty sterling silver vase that was decoratively placed on a side table. The other hit her bookshelf and bounced off. Cameron was close and agile enough to catch it.

He examined it for a moment, before going to pick up its mate and right the toppled vase. "These shoes are way too expensive to be treated like this."

"What could you possibly know about women's footwear?" she griped, pulling her feet up off the floor to rub them.

"You'd be surprised." He brought the shoes back, placing them on the floor neatly in front of her.

She groaned as she sat cross-legged kneading her aching soles.

Cameron dragged one of the chairs nearby over to sit opposite her. Then, he leaned forward, gazing into her eyes. Mikaela sat up straight under the intensity of his stare.

"Mikaela." He said her name in that hushed and honeyed way he used to that went through her, like he was breathing it.

"Stop." She put up a hand. "I'm not working on *Glamazon* anymore. Art kicked me off. So, spare me the Uga-says-pick-myself-up-and-dust-myself-off speech."

He grinned but was undeterred. "Mikaela, I spoke with Monica and Celia before they left. And I told them that I asked you not to say anything so that you could continue to oversee things."

Mikaela began to object.

"Listen, I knew that you'd be removed if we said anything. So, it wasn't technically a lie. And I can speak with Jacqueline too?"

"Thank you, Cameron. I appreciate you doing that. But it's not about whether or not I'm working on this case. The account—I brought it in. It's *mine*. A win for you is a win in my column regardless," she said firmly, willing it to be true. "It's the optics. And the optics of this are that either I'm so foolish I'm having an affair with a client or I'm so dissolute, I've got my firm mixed up in my ex-boyfriend's marital spat."

"We're divorced," he interjected.

"You won't be by the time this thing has had its run through the office rumor mill."

Cameron sat back, silent.

And then the stupid tears were back.

Mikaela did not cry at work. Sure, there had been plenty of moments here or there where she could probably have drowned herself in tears but she never allowed them to see her fall apart. She was breaking her cardinal rule. Yet today, she couldn't seem to help herself.

Cameron looked to the window, giving her personal space as she wiped her face again. But Mikaela saw when he spied his silver frame on the credenza. His eyes narrowed.

"You get it, right?" she said quickly to distract him from his discovery.

"Get what?" He turned back to her.

"The fact that this *stuff*..." She started gesticulating, letting her hands tumble one over the other, unable to find words for the jumble of emotions just seeing his face elicited in her. "It has to stop. My judgment is not the best around you. History has borne that out, and now it's repeating itself."

He began to say something.

"It's not you. I'm not blaming you." She cut him off to add, "I'm at fault."

Cameron crossed his arms and leaned back but refrained from speaking.

"This has got to be a failure of character on my part. I

don't know why I wasn't just up-front from the get-go. I should have admitted the conflict."

Mikaela wiped away the last few stray tears still streaking her face and took a couple of deep breaths, willing herself to get it back together.

"Shall I get you a cat-o'-nine-tails too? Self-flagellation works best with one, or so I've heard."

Rather than say something snarky, Mikaela fell over sideways into her cushions and groaned.

"Forget it. You don't get it. You never will." Her voice was muffled by the pillow in front of her face that she was using to smother herself.

"Why not? All I'm saying is you're beating yourself up for no reason."

"No reason?" She set the pillow aside and raised her head. "See? You *don't* get it. Not looking like you do, being who you are. Unlike you, I have *no* margin of error… Zero, zip, zilch."

"Who am I? What does that mean?"

"I have to say it?" She flung out her hand, sweeping the length of him as he watched, bewildered. "A white, heterosexual, cisgender man. C'mon!"

"Oh."

Mikaela rolled her eyes. "Me? *I. Cannot. Make. A. Mistake.* Couldn't back home, still can't. Ever since I was a child, I've known that. I've known what was expected of me. I must be perfect because I don't just represent myself. I always represent everyone who walks through those doors and looks like me. When I lose we all lose. Every door I can't kick down, that little girl out there—" *she pointed toward the door and Suze beyond it, her voice cracking* "—is gonna have to break her shoulders trying to bust down after me."

"But—"

"No! Anything I want, I have to *prove* I deserve. I have to scrape and claw to make happen. I want to be an associate? I have to sacrifice my social life to be at everyone's beck and call, 24/7. I want to be a junior partner? I have to accept the crappiest assignments and act like they're gifts. And I can't be the Angry Black Woman railing at the injustice of that fact either. And I certainly can't get caught doing something stupid like, replying-all *company-wide* on a pornographic email that was supposed to be just for 'the boys.'"

Cameron looked at her blankly.

She mouthed the name *"Todd"* before continuing.

"If I want the big title and the bigger office, I have to prove that I'm one thousand percent worthy, one thousand percent infallible, one thousand percent unimpeachable. So, let's say I also can't get caught having an affair with a twenty-five-year-old receptionist."

Cameron was shocked. *"Who?"*

"Art," she intimated in silence. "But then he married her, so that made it all magically okay."

He rolled his eyes.

"All the time. I want to be offered an equity stake, right? To get that, I have to slay the dragon and lay its charred corpse at their feet. And I do it! Potential millions of dollars in billables annually, that I charmed and cajoled and flattered and lured, then presented to them on a platter. *On. My. Own.* All by myself. Just to be considered. *Considered!* To have someone tell me, *to my face,* that my name is in the damn running. That there's *still* time for me to *prove* I'm the MV-fucking-P!"

"Well, that's not fair—"

"Who said shit about fair?" she snapped.

Cameron closed his mouth.

"To do this job successfully in this here skin—" she pointed to her dark brown cheek "—I have to be unassailable. Personally and professionally. *Impeccable.* A flawless fucking paragon!"

"That's not possible, Kaela. Everyone makes mistakes, has lapses in judgment."

She glared at him, her laugh disdainful, more of a harsh bark. "Not me! For twelve years, I have been flawless. I don't misjudge or mistake or miscalculate, or mis- anything else. I am *Miss Perfect.* Then *you* came along." She didn't finish, leaving the unintentional accusation where it was. Hanging between them.

"Sounds tiring," he said eventually.

"It is." She sat up and cut her eyes at him. "You think you're being funny, but it is and it's absolutely *demoralizing* to watch as the things that they laugh about among themselves threaten to become firing offenses for me."

"So, fight. Don't let them take you for granted."

She stilled a moment.

"You just don't understand, do you? You can't understand."

"You're right but I do sympathize."

"Okay, then you understand why this has to stop?"

"This, what?" he asked, eyes widening innocently. "We're just old friends."

Mikaela nudged him with her bare foot as he smirked.

"I'm being serious, Cam." She took a deep breath and they fell into silence. The sun began to set, creating an orange-violet tableau in the sky outside her wall of windows.

"Ow!" Mikaela said later, looking down at her feet, now lying in Cameron's lap, across his thigh. She wasn't sure how long they'd been there, but it felt too good now to stop him, though she knew she should.

"Sorry." He pressed his thumbs into the arches of her feet and it was exquisite.

Mikaela let her head fall against the backrest as she relaxed into the sensation of his large hands kneading her feet. Her toes flexed as his fingers made small concentric circles across her soles.

"Oh God," she moaned, watching his fingers move.

He smiled, pleased. "I did always know how to make you feel good."

She raised her head to look at him in warning before returning to the bliss of his skillful hands, eyes closed.

Cameron clipped their extended silence short. "Mikaela?"

"What?"

She just wanted him to shut up and keep moving his fingers as her head lolled boneless against the couch.

"Mikaela?"

"I said, *what*?" She raised her head again.

"Why does the bar's code of ethics prevent sex between attorneys and their clients?"

Her eyebrow shot up at his innuendo. She tugged at her feet but he refused to relinquish them.

Why was it that people always felt the need to tell lawyers lawyer jokes?

She licked her lips not even bothering to keep up the pretense of novelty with him. *This was Cameron.*

"To prevent clients from getting *fucked* twice." As she spoke, her eyes lingered on his and he grinned mischievously at her stern expression.

They both smiled, breaking into belly laughs.

He pressed harder into the balls of her feet and she groaned, which he seemed to enjoy, judging from the way his lips curled.

"For real, Kaela. Don't take this thing lying down," he spoke after another few wonderfully silent minutes.

"What am I gonna say? Claim it's not true? I did lie. I

didn't recuse myself. This thing between us is potentially a probl—"

"Dr. Guerrero!" Suze's voice came through the intercom.

Mikaela jerked herself out of Cameron's hands, jumping to her feet as Rashad walked into the room.

"Look, baby, I'm sor—" He stopped when he saw Cameron seated there in front of her.

Rashad held a gigantic bouquet in both arms. They drooped slightly as he looked between Mikaela and Cameron.

"Nice flowers." Cameron snorted, and Mikaela could have kicked him for it.

She parted her lips in a forced smile. Mikaela honestly didn't know how many times she'd gently declined flowers from suitors. The fact that she didn't care for them just went in one ear and out the other. And as always, seeing all the dead flowers in Rashad's arms nettled her. Despite his intent, she still couldn't help making an accounting of the hot-pink roses, the pale alstroemeria, the orange lilies and peach carnations there, all soon to be brown and desiccated. The idea turned her stomach.

"I came to apologize for overreacting." Rashad spoke slowly, as if he was trying to catch up on something he missed. "I think."

He frowned as Mikaela stepped into her heels and rose five painful inches.

"Should I come back?" he asked, although it was clear from his tone, he had no intention of doing that.

"No, of course not!" Mikaela walked around Cameron, still seated.

She came up to Rashad and kissed him on the cheek as his eyes stayed on Cameron, allowing him to put the heavily fragrant and lavish bouquet in her hands.

"I was just leaving," Cameron spoke finally, his eyes on Mikaela.

Cameron stood, pushing his chair back over to its proper place before walking up to Rashad.

"But before I go, I wanted to sincerely apologize for my behavior on Friday. I was outta line. I am *deeply* regretful." Cameron laid on his accent so thick Mikaela wanted to squint into his mouth to see who was in there. "I won't blame the alcohol. Though I get a little liquor in me and…woo buddy! Let me tell you! I'll argue with a fence post!" He shook his head woefully. "But seriously, I was just one poorly behaved son of a bitch. Quite frankly, there's *no excuse* for the way I spoke to you, Dr. Guerrero, sir. No excuse a'tall. I truly, *truly* hope you can find it somewhere in your heart to forgive me."

Both Mikaela and Rashad fell silent, frowning as Cameron offered Rashad his hand.

"Um, okay?" Rashad's brows furrowed and he shot Mikaela a bewildered glance as he accepted Cameron's handshake.

"I'm so appreciative of that, Doc." Cameron placed his other hand over them both and shook them again, once, firmly.

Then just that quickly, he let go.

"Mikaela," he acknowledged her with a nod, heading to the door.

"Let me give these to Suze to put in some water, and then walk him to the elevators," Mikaela said to Rashad. "We just need to finish up."

"Didn't he say he was just leaving?" Rashad asked before assenting with a weary nod and a sigh.

"Sit down, I'll be right back. *Promise.* Just give me a second."

As she rushed out the door, Suze met her in front of her desk looking stricken.

"I am *so* sorry, boss," she whispered, "I didn't have any time to say anything else."

"It's okay." Mikaela deposited the multitude of flower blooms in her assistant's arms, trying to track Cameron's progress as he strolled through the halls.

"Put these in some water in the silver vase. When he leaves, *you know what to do*," she instructed sotto voce, before rushing off.

She caught Cameron near the elevator bank.

"What was that?" She grabbed at his sleeve to slow him down.

"An apology. You said I owed everybody one."

"I said you owed *your children* one! And you know that's not what you did. That overly effusive *performance* now has Rashad wondering just what exactly you were apologizing for!"

"That's his problem." Cameron smiled to himself, as if he was hearing a joke no one else was privy to. "Don't sound so guilty."

Mikaela choked on her retort. "Damn it, you're not funny!"

He smirked, clearly delighted by flustering her.

"And I have nothing to feel guilty for." She shook her head. "But what was already wonderfully awkward, you've now made ten times worse. So, thanks for that." She lifted a scolding finger and leveled it at him. "And just for future reference, that good ole boy shtick works better when you're not wearing a four-thousand-dollar suit!"

Cameron glanced down at himself, considering that before shoving his hands into his pockets. His eyes rose to the call display overhead, as he waited for one of the elevators to reach their floor.

The lobby was empty and the receptionist had already left for the day. So, she took a step closer to him.

"Now, what the hell was that about?" she whispered.

Cameron turned his full attention on her and Mikaela's stomach dropped, but she didn't step back, afraid to cede ground in this contest, though she knew she probably should have.

"Just had a realization."

"Oh yeah?" she challenged. *What possible realization could he have had in the span of ten minutes?*

"My dad always said, 'Be gracious in both victory and defeat.'"

"And what does *that* mean?" Mikaela's head jerked. "You're admitting you're defeated? I don't get it?"

He stepped closer. *"Not me."*

Mikaela stopped breathing. Taking in his casual cool and entirely unruffled mien, it felt like everything around them stopped too.

Then the bell announcing one of the elevators arriving rang out. Its sound, sharp and loud, startled them both out of their standoff.

Doors behind them opened onto an empty car and Cameron stepped in, leaving her behind. Without thinking, she chased him.

"No, you're not leaving until you've answered me."

"I'm not, huh?" He turned, sizing both her and the elevator up. It was a distressingly small box with only the two of them in it.

"We aren't done yet." Mikaela faltered as he leaned in and reached to hit the ground floor button. "Are we?"

"I guess not." Cameron chuckled, infuriatingly amused and as surprised to see her still there with him as she was to be there.

"Listen, I like Dr. Guerrero. He seems nice enough," he answered evenly as if he were actually contemplating this.

"Like a smart, *decent* guy. But he's not the guy for you, and he doesn't even know you. Now, whose fault is that?"

"W-what?" Mikaela's voice trembled.

"Whose fault is it that he doesn't know that you hate bouquets of cut flowers? Why doesn't he know you hate that they're so temporary and they die so fast? That you prefer them growing in a garden?" He took another step, then another, until he loomed over her. "On Friday, you said you've been together for two years? Shouldn't he know by now that you hate that sickly sweet smell they get as they die? So, I'm asking, whose fault is it that he doesn't, yours or his?"

Mikaela's mouth dried up and she closed it when it fell open. But she gathered strength to attempt what she already knew would be a half-hearted retort. "It's none of—"

"You know you were right about this, Kaela. What we're doing." Cameron turned to her again, cutting her off.

"What we're, what?" Mikaela started, but she did know.

"You're going to pretend now?"

"I'm not prete—" She tried again but couldn't even continue, the way Cameron unflinchingly held her gaze, flustered her, demanding truth.

His head tilted then, something turning feral in his eyes. In the way he tracked her body as if he was contemplating how to devour her whole. From her peep-toed shoes to the topknot of her bun, it was like he'd begun making mental calculations and adjustments to accomplish the task. It was inscrutable and beyond unnerving.

"What?"

Cameron's eyes settled on her face again in answer and she stepped backward, daunted, hitting the corner of their little metal box with a resounding thud that echoed through the elevator shaft. Her elbow accidentally dragged across other floor buttons, lighting up the panel as he cornered her. Placing a hand above her shoulder, Cameron braced the wall behind her with his palm. The other held down the door-close button, effectively boxing her in between.

He was so close; they breathed the same air.

"Aren't you tired of pretending this isn't happening?" he whispered, inclining his head down toward her. "I am."

Mikaela knew what Cameron wanted to do and somewhere deep within her consciousness, she knew she should want to stop him—yet she didn't. He held her eyes with blatant desire. And in that moment, she feared what hers gave away too.

Though her hands remained at her sides, automatically, as if of its own volition, Mikaela's head tilted back as Cameron gazed at her closed mouth.

"You have no idea how much I want to kiss you." He spoke the words to her lips, echoing her suddenly disloyal mind.

"Cam, we can't. I can't. Rashad is just upstairs. I could never do that to him." She said it even as her resolve wavered.

I couldn't, could I?

Cameron didn't test her though, stepping back, nodding as if he agreed. *No, of course not.* But then he pinned her to the wall with a penetrating gaze and Mikaela's cheeks burned, her whole body flushed boiling hot, breath holding.

"But you do want to?" Cameron's dilated pupils, an ink black that nearly overtook the narrow blue-gray halo around them, provided his own answer to this provocative question.

He needed her to say it.

"Yes."

"As much as I want you to?"

"More."

Cameron's face tinted red at her frankness. His nostrils flared and jaw tightened, notching with clenched teeth. He kept staring at her face, focused on her mouth. And the yearning lingered, hanging there between them. They remained separate but joined in the knowledge that they felt the same thing, and both wanted, if only briefly, to give in to it.

In the silence, only the dings of each descending floor and their labored breathing passed between them.

When they reached the ground floor, the car bounced once smoothly before coming to a stop. Facing the doors, Cameron fixed his shirtsleeves, then straightened and ran a hand down his tie, though not a thread of fabric was displaced.

"So then, I guess I was right. In fact, we *both* had something to apologize to Rashad for, didn't we?" Cameron held the door open and pressed the 61 button again. "And now it's your turn."

Then he stepped off the elevator, leaving Mikaela alone, in silence and in thought all the way back up.

thirty-one

"Have you been back over there? Seen them setting up for this evening? They've brought in more. *It's grotesque.* It's not natural to have so much food. People are starving in this world. And there's so much meat!"

"You did have meat at your last barbecue," Mikaela reminded Julie as they swayed on her porch swing.

It had been like this for a while. Just the two of them. A sporadic sentence here or there to break up the silence, the sounds of cicadas vibrating their wings in the distance and the metal-on-metal creak of the rusty swing beneath them.

They were still wearing their black church clothes from earlier, all wrinkled and sweaty from the oppressive July heat, with their feet up on the seat hugging their knees. Julie's head rested on Mikaela's shoulder.

Mikaela was still having trouble making the news fit into the world as she knew it only days before. Julie's father.

Judge Robertson. Lee. Dead. A titan not only in Harmon but within her own life. As much a permanent fixture as any family member. Gone. After a massive heart attack on the bench. On what seemed like an ordinary day. Mikaela had just spoken to him the day before by the back fence as he picked snap peas and carrots for Miss Liza's pasta primavera, wearing his wife's big straw hat and pink gardening gloves. Tears flooded Mikaela's eyes thinking of it.

"Of course! That was a barbecue!" Julie declared, startling Mikaela out of their silence. "What red-blooded American would serve anything other than big, fat slabs of meat at a barbecue? But this is not a barbecue! This is a funeral. Show some respect, we're vegetarians."

"Oh 'cause that makes sense," Mikaela said under her breath.

Julie nudged her hard in the side, making a sound that perhaps in a few years could have evolved into a chuckle.

"Well, my nana says you know how much you were loved by how long you can live off the food people bring."

"He musta been a great man then," Julie cracked, still attempting humor, though her voice was detached.

"The greatest!"

"Monumental!"

They joked without laughing.

"I'm just saying that's how people pay their respects…with food." Mikaela crooked her neck to the side, laying her head on her knees, and looked at Julie out of the corner of her eye. "*Aaand* also because we all know you and your brother will eat all the pork products not nailed down or hidden. So *err'body* knows it won't really go to waste."

"Hey! I resemble that comment!" Julie snorted, finally sounding like an approximation of her old self.

They both grinned.

Mikaela put one foot on the ground to push them off as they relaxed. The gentle swaying lulled them back into another contemplative silence.

Julie raised her head.

"Do you know my mother doesn't even know how to balance a checkbook?"

Mikaela glanced her way.

"Do you?"

"That's not the point," Julie said, pouting. "Apparently, all my mother knows how to operate is a platinum card." Julie rolled her eyes. "Mrs. Coles had to go with us to the funeral parlor to write the check."

Mikaela doubted that was the only reason Mrs. Coles went along. She had seen Miss Liza in the past week, struggling. Today was the first day she seemed herself, composed, elegant...lucid. Mikaela knew for a fact taking care of the Robertsons over the past few days had become a neighborhood preoccupation. While her mother was nearly catatonic and inconsolable, sequestered in her bedroom, Julie and Mikaela had spent the last week making dozens of phone calls to family and friends. The women's auxiliary organized the details for the funeral and repast, and Mikaela's father and Gabe spent the morning putting out folding chairs and tables. Even Mikaela's mother had come back into town to do what she could for the funeral.

"She didn't even know where any of our papers were. Not the life insurance, bank statements, the deed. *Nothing*. Sheriff Davenport and Cameron came over to pay their respects and find some paperwork in Daddy's office. They ended up having to help me break into his safe. Go through his legal papers and whatnot. Mama didn't even remember what the combination was. Can you believe that?"

Thinking of how The Judge had always prided himself on

spoiling "his girls," Mikaela was tempted to say yes. She'd seen how Julie didn't even know how to iron a shirt or do her own laundry or change a tire, all things Mikaela's dad had insisted she and Vanessa knew by the time they were twelve. Her dad had always griped that Julie's big problem was The Judge had spoiled her by giving her everything, *except the ability to do things for herself.* But Mikaela had never guessed until this moment that The Judge had done the same thing to his wife too.

"Is it horrible that since then I've been thinking about Cameron? Like, of all times, now? You know, with his mama and everything..." Julie's head popped up, turning to Mikaela. "How did he manage when his father died? 'Cause I don't know what my mama is gonna do without Daddy. I already feel like I'm dying myself."

Mikaela considered the question seriously as bumblebees chased each other from one yarrow flower to another in her mother's flower patch in the front yard.

Cameron was all she could think about too. In light of Mrs. Murphy's illness, the ladies of the women's auxiliary had been doting on him, bringing him meals. And with their constant presence for the past few weeks, it was possible they saw him more than Mikaela did. Up until The Judge's passing, Cameron had been all Mikaela thought of too. So, if the same was somehow also now true for Julie, that weirdly seemed perfectly reasonable.

After a minute, Mikaela shrugged. "I mean we've never really spoken about it," she lied, still constantly trying to downplay the extent of their relationship to spare Julie's feelings. "But I think he's still getting over it, what, two years later?"

"So, is that really how long it's gonna take me to feel better? Feel like I can breathe again?" There was a desperation in Julie's voice, her forehead creasing. "Two whole *years*?"

"Jules, I have no idea how long it takes. That's Cameron, this is you. The Judge was your dad."

Mikaela wished she had an answer that Julie could hold on to. Could give her something to help her through this. But she was useless, to Julie *and* to Cameron. He was right: this was nothing like what happened with her and her mom. Mikaela knew nothing about how it felt to lose a parent. Between this and Mrs. Murphy's illness, it was nothing close to how she had imagined her first summer back from college would go.

Mikaela shook her head, ashamed of the ridiculous, self-centered obliviousness of that thought. She was sure this wasn't the way Julie had imagined the rest of her whole *life* going either. Without her father.

"I know, *I know*, it was a stupid question." Julie laughed at herself, misunderstanding Mikaela's reaction.

She covered her face with her hands and a moment later, the laughter morphed into sobs. Julie's shoulders shook and she moaned until Mikaela's heart ached for her, the pain of it all tearing at her insides. Cameron's agonized description of losing his own father echoed in her mind. *Like losing a limb*.

Mikaela rubbed Julie's back, soothing her until the crying jag subsided. In that moment she knew she had nothing to offer. Nothing for either of them and the gaping maw of their grief and need seemed frighteningly deep and wide.

"Do you think Cameron coming by again would make you feel better?"

Julie raised her head, hugging her legs closer to herself.

He knew what Julie was going through, while Mikaela had no idea. She felt utterly helpless in the face of her best friend's anguish.

Julie considered the question, putting her chin on her knees. "Honestly?"

"I don't see why not? He helped you the other night. I can ask him?"

"Would you?" Julie grinned at Mikaela, with a glint in her golden eyes for the first time in days.

thirty-two

NOW

The key in the front door woke Mikaela up as two exonerated marines saluted Tom Cruise on Rashad's giant sixty-five-inch flat-screen television.

Mikaela stretched as a moment later Rashad appeared in the entryway to his living room.

"You're here," he said with surprise, coming around the couch to lay a sloppy kiss on her lips.

The distinct earthy tang and odor of hops lingered in her nose and on her lips as he collapsed beside her on the couch. He wasn't wearing his scrubs as usual after a late shift but instead had on his old blue-and-orange Mike Piazza Mets jersey.

Nothing about Rashad was as offensive to Mikaela's sensibilities as his love for that team. At times, as a Yankee fan for her years in the City, it was like being in an interfaith relationship. But he was from Long Island, so, she rationalized, he couldn't help himself.

"I didn't know you were going to a game tonight?"

"Got last-minute tickets," he said, grabbing the remote off the coffee table and switching channels. "I didn't tell you?"

"No. If you had, I would have just stayed home."

He glanced at her before shrugging. "What's the difference?"

"The difference is," Mikaela said, bristling, "I left my work and my laptop at home because we were supposed to hang out tonight. So, all I could do was sit around watching TV while I waited."

Rashad seemed to think about that for a moment. "Well, if you lived here, you'd be home already." He snickered at his own joke.

Mikaela sighed. "Or…you could tell me when you don't plan to come home like we agreed, so I can plan my life accordingly."

"Fine, fine, I'll have my person call your person to put it on the calendar from now on." Rashad's tone was snide and mocking.

He'd been drinking. Though she doubted he was drunk—practicing emergency medicine, it was something he avoided—he was probably pretty well lubricated.

"We don't have to schedule to see each other, Rah. I just need you to tell me what's up."

He harrumphed, turning the television to the baseball highlights.

"Didn't you just watch this at Citi Field?"

When Rashad didn't answer, Mikaela gathered her plate and cup, heading into the kitchen. Washing the dishes in the sink, she noted the spacious kitchen and all its appointments: the double oven, subzero refrigerator, professional-grade range. Guilt tore at her; Rashad had invested so much care and attention into remodeling the kitchen and the entire house. In the beginning, he had plans for it. When he was just thirty-three, he had inherited the old house from his great-aunt and decided to do a gut-renovation with the objective of starting a family…before, a year later, he met Mikaela and her oldish ovaries.

Now, it was just a large, Central Harlem, mint-condition brownstone where, to Rashad's frequent objection, he rattled around alone. In truth, it was a far bigger and nicer home than Mikaela's modest little duplex. She actually even liked it there. So why didn't she ever want to be there if Rashad didn't insist? And why was she so resistant to moving her life up to Harlem permanently? She'd lived in Harlem before when she was in grad school. His neighborhood was equidistant from her job. This was where his recent frustration was coming from and she couldn't blame him. She honestly didn't know why she couldn't just say yes.

Mikaela sighed, drying the dishes before going back into the living room to say good-night. But when she entered, the television was off and Rashad was perched on the edge of the couch, waiting.

"You said you want me to tell you what's up." A vein pulsed in his temple. "So why didn't you?"

"What are you talking about?" She pursed her lips.

"I waited for you to tell me the whole truth, after last weekend, to just fess up. It would have been nothing if you had just been honest about it."

Mikaela's pulse began to race. She wouldn't lie.

"How'd you find out?"

"That's your concern?" Rashad shook his head.

Mikaela pressed her hands together, squeezing them.

"The mother, Juliette? She made a comment when you were arguing outside."

Julie. *Of course, she did.* Not satisfied to merely damage

her career, she was now trying to wreck Mikaela's personal life too.

"Not that I couldn't tell something was off immediately. Your whole vibe was different around him." He waved his hand at her. "You were tense the whole time. And I thought, 'Oh, she's just nervous because he's both a friend and her client.' But then you're outside shouting at each other, and I knew. She really didn't even have to say anything."

"*That's* what made you think there was something more between me and him?" Mikaela's eyes widened with incredulity.

"No, that's what made me *know* something more was going on with you two."

Mikaela's voice shook with indignation. "I am not cheating on you with my ex-boyfriend from a million years ago!"

"Mikaela, interestingly enough, I'm not jealous." Rashad folded his arms across his chest. "But I do know what I saw. That you exhibited more passion arguing with that man, Cameron, than you do nowadays even when we make love."

Mikaela fell back against the dining table, as if pushed, her mouth falling open.

"It's like you're there and I'm there but we're both checked out. Does that make sense? That we have to break out our calendars to make time to even see each other?"

"We're both busy."

"So then move in with me."

There it was.

And Mikaela hesitated yet again, shying away from an answer.

With that, Rashad's shoulders fell, his head drooping.

"We've got to admit it, Kaela, we've neglected this relationship. You've prioritized your work over us and I have too. I'm not a resident anymore. I don't need to work back-to-back nights, I don't *have to* be on call all the time. I am because I have no reason not to be."

At his words, the air emptied out of her.

"It wasn't always like that. Once upon a time, I'd come to your house off a sixteen-hour shift and we'd still make love. Or we'd just make out in a cab on the way to work the next day. We used to talk about things, debate things, hang out, laugh."

"Nothing is like it was in the beginning forever. We're just content. We're happy. We're compatible," Mikaela insisted.

"We're bored and we're complacent. It's not the same thing. We don't even disagree!" Rashad frowned, shaking his head.

"My parents argued about everything! Arguing is *not* a sign of happiness."

"No, but it is a sign of life! I'm trained by profession to search for those. Signs of viability. Shit, I'd even take investment. Interest, maybe. *But they're all gone.* Tell me, how much do your folks argue now? Not at all, 'cause they divorced instead."

"That's ridiculous," she laughed scornfully. "They don't argue now because they've been divorced for *over twenty years!*"

"Okay, so then how is it that a man you haven't even *seen* in fifteen is able to elicit that kind of emotional response from you, huh? Whereas with me, you're indifferent, you're like ice."

"I'm not indifferent." Her voice hitched. "I'm committed."

"No, you're dug in. You're settled. *Or settling.*"

Mikaela sucked in a breath, biting into her cheek before throwing up her arms. "Well, we're definitely arguing now!"

"No." Rashad stood, coming up to her and taking her by the hand, his voice tender. "We're breaking up now, aren't we?"

Mikaela followed him over to the couch, her eyes welling with tears. They sat there, holding hands, fingers intertwined, until at last she nodded.

Three days later, and a day after she returned Rashad's house keys to him, a large potted star jasmine came to Mikaela's office by messenger. Suze seemed suspiciously unsurprised by the delivery.

Pulling the envelope out of a clip attached to its wire trellis, Mikaela read the card and smiled as Suze sat it on a side table.

"What's it say?" Suze asked, moving the plant until it sat perfectly situated in a sunbeam. She turned, watching her boss with her hands on her hips, smiling widely. "Mr. Murphy?"

Mikaela licked her lips, fighting to remain circumspect as a smile strained her cheeks. She nodded.

"And?"

"It's Hemingway. It says, 'Eventually, the world breaks everyone, but afterward, some are stronger in the broken places.'"

thirty-three

The Drifters sang "White Christmas" overhead via piped-in Muzak that echoed throughout the upper deck of the Tri-County's newest cavernous megamall. It was Mikaela's first visit to the jam-packed, blindingly white and pristine Oglethorpe Mall. This would have been a decision she regretted, if she wasn't aware that on Christmas Eve, everywhere else was just as bad. She sucked her teeth but kept her peace, dragging herself through the mall like a pack mule behind Vanessa, carrying numerous shopping bags.

It was her own fault. She hadn't done any Christmas shopping beforehand either.

Had she been willing to go a week earlier, she could have flown home with Vanessa and avoided the last-minute shopping trip. Returning from her freshman year at Columbia, Vanessa was eager to leave New York. Mikaela wished she could say the same. But as it stood, flying in the day before meant needing a lift *in her own car* from Hartsfield-Jackson and finding herself subject to any and all of Vanessa's little whims on the way back home.

But this was Mikaela's habit now. Her visits to Georgia generally, but Harmon specifically, had become like surgical strikes. She arrived within hours of the event she was attending, stayed long enough to be seen, then made an appearance at her mother's home in Atlanta before catching the first thing smoking back to New York. The less time spent in Harmon the better, was Mikaela's abiding philosophy.

This visit was to be the first time in a year and a half that she actually overnighted in Harmon, having been given the all-clear from Vanessa that it was safe to return. Yes, it would still be difficult looking out the back window and seeing the Robertson house all lit up from afar or dealing with the possibility of running into Gabe sitting in their kitchen waiting on Vanessa, but that was a cakewalk as far as she was concerned. Compared to the alternative of seeing *them*.

"Y'all still okay?" Mikaela asked suddenly.

"Who?" Vanessa pried her eyes away from the price tag on a tan cardigan to frown.

"You and Gabe," Mikaela whispered as if they might be overheard.

She was exposed here. Not just in the brightly lit store with its festive holiday bunting and assortment of garishly decorated Christmas trees, but anywhere in Georgia now. That feeling was wildly paranoid but she couldn't shake it.

"Of course we're fine." Vanessa waved a hand, pshawing with an impressive lack of sadness. "Just not dating anymore. He's, like, still my best friend though."

After they graduated from high school, Vanessa and Gabe handled their breakup maturely. Just the natural result of one going to college in New York while the other went to Arizona. Mikaela not only admired them for it, but she also envied them. Their relationship had managed to be four times the length of anything she'd ever experienced, yet they didn't seem the least bit broken up about its end.

"That's nice," Mikaela replied, preoccupied, heart thumping.

More than anything else, she wished to avoid running into any old friends or classmates. The idea of having to endure either the awkward pretending not to see each other or the even more awkward forced catch-up filled her with dread. The catch-up always inevitably devolved into a cross-examination.

At this point, everyone in Harmon knew some version, usually *their own*, of what transpired.

The irony of which wasn't lost on Mikaela.

That something she'd worked so hard to keep secret had become the hottest piece of gossip coming out of their graduating class was an embarrassment. Why was it that Mikaela Marchand and Julie Robertson, best friends practically since birth, no longer spoke? Where was it Mikaela ran off to? What part did Sheriff Davenport's nephew Cameron Murphy play in the entire mess? Mikaela had no interest in setting any records straight. It was just better for all involved that she'd made herself scarce.

But, she decided, the good news was she was no longer either J.D. Marchand's little nerd or the girl who showed her cooter to the whole entire county anymore...*for all that served her.*

"I'm tired. Let's go," Vanessa announced an hour later, stopping unceremoniously in the middle of a walkway on the third floor, overlooking the mall's atrium.

Mikaela almost ran into her back, trudging a step behind,

sucking the dregs from her Orange Julius cup. Vanessa caused a minor pedestrian backup as she spun on Mikaela; people swarmed on all sides.

"You sure there isn't something in Claire's or Hot Topic that you've forgotten?" Mikaela teased, gnawing on the end of her straw and grinning.

It had taken a while for her pulse and anxiety to level out, but going on hour five back in Georgia, Mikaela was no longer waiting for something awful to happen.

Which, of course, meant something was going to.

"Mikaela." Vanessa barked her name humorlessly. "Let's go."

Her sister's eyes narrowed, brows knitted together, signaling a mood change so abrupt goose bumps begin to prickle Mikaela's skin.

"What?" Her voice rose, eyes scanning the faces of people walking by, her heart thrashing madly against her breast.

"Kaela, *please*." Vanessa's face fell, her voice taking on a plaintive tone it never got.

Then she saw: it was Cameron.

On the opposite side of the glass-and-steel atrium, separated by the massive hundred-foot drop to the food court below. They'd been walking parallel to one another along the glass railing, going in opposite directions. It was hard to imagine, but they hadn't laid eyes on each other in almost two years. And somehow, she had begun to think she would never see him again. In one way, she hoped for that, but in another, she had prayed it wouldn't be true.

So, this was both the dream and a nightmare.

He was the same; she didn't know why she expected different. *Maybe because everything was so different now...like they were strangers.* Cameron held shopping bags in one hand and an oversize, bow-tied and monocled chocolate-brown teddy bear in the other. He stood there staring at Mikaela until she couldn't take it any longer.

"Okay," she muttered to her sister, turning away and hustling toward the nearest exit.

They'd broken through the second set of double doors into the brisk, pine-scented air outside, before Mikaela could breathe again. But they were on the opposite side of the mall from their car.

"Shit," Vanessa said. "We gotta go back in."

"No." Mikaela shook her head.

The idea of that seemed a physical impossibility, like her legs couldn't move in that way again.

"You wanna walk all the way around?" Vanessa groaned. "For real, M.?"

Mikaela knew how ridiculous that sounded. How humiliating it would be to cede an entire eight-hundred-thousand-square-foot megamall to one man, but she was prepared to do it. "I can't."

Vanessa shook her head, her heavy breath a puff of white smoke in the chilled air. "Okay, how about this. You wait here with these. I'll run back through to the C-lot and get the car? Be back in five."

Waiting out in the cold wasn't a much better alternative, but as she stood there Mikaela wasn't sure of another choice, unclear if it was the temperature or the sight of Cameron that had her trembling.

She nodded and Vanessa dropped her bags and took off running back into the building.

Mikaela hugged herself. She'd left her coat in the car and it was actually very chilly. She played with her feet, awkwardly moving from heel to toe and back in her high-heeled boots. The moon had risen high in a crystal clear night sky and she could hear crickets chirping off in the distance. Every time the doors opened, numerous shoppers spilled onto the sidewalk, fanning out into the darkened lot in search of their cars. Intermittent strains of Merry Christmas classics leaked out with them along with bursts of warm air that kept it from getting too uncomfortable as she waited.

"Mikaela?"

She winced hearing her name coming out of Cameron's mouth again.

Balling her hands into fists, Mikaela turned to face him. His nose was red and his cheeks were ruddy. Cameron breathed laboriously as if he'd been outside a while. He stepped toward her before putting his bags at his feet. Just staring.

"You ran."

"I'm sorry," she lied, with a disingenuous smile, "for, ah, not stopping to say anything in there." She tipped her chin toward the mall doors. "But I didn't realize it was you. Vanessa had to tell me."

He cocked his head to the side, disbelieving.

"So, uh, how are you? I heard you guys moved back home to Larkspur after the baby was born?" She breezed on, keeping her tone cordial. "Congrats, by the way."

"Thanks. We're good. You?"

The small talk was quickly excruciating.

"I'm good." She searched for some sign of Vanessa. "At Columbia Law now."

"Makes sense. You were always gonna get in anywhere you wanted." He paused. *"And I knew you'd stay up North."*

Mikaela clenched to absorb the blow of that unspoken accusation. It was as if he was more hurt by all this than she was, which she knew was not physically possible. She shook her head, placing fingers to her lips to stifle the wave of nausea that flooded her just looking at him.

They stared at each other for another long moment. The grief in his eyes agitating her.

"Kaela, please." Cameron's voice broke. If possible, he sounded as fragile as she felt. "Say something."

A distant owl's solitary hoot resounded in the silence between them.

"Like what?" Mikaela spit back then, her voice thick with fury.

"Was I wrong to think you didn't care? You didn't respond to a call, a letter, anything for months!"

"Yes! Yes, you were wrong!" The dam in her cracked open, breaching her reserve. "And you know it! Don't you try and blame this on me!"

"How many times do I have to say this?" he asked through gritted teeth, clenching his jaw. "It was *one* time!"

A small group exited through the doors behind them, catching them unawares. The people skewered them with disapproving looks. Cameron closed their distance, stalking all the way up to Mikaela, nearly overwhelming her. Knowing they had an audience, Mikaela didn't react, only rolling back on her heels. She followed the group with her eyes, giving the women little reassuring smiles and praying no one would call mall security.

"That's Bio 101, Cameron. That's all it takes!" She spoke in a scathing whisper to his chest, to a distant spot over his shoulder, anywhere but his face.

"*Once*, Mikaela!" He threw up a finger as if to illustrate. "It happened once."

She focused on avoiding his eyes. The usual visions of Cameron and Julie together returned to haunt her, simultaneously making her ill while also igniting a blue flame of rage so hot her brain sizzled.

"I'm sure it's been plenty of times since then."

"That was cheap."

"I don't care!" she snarled, before catching herself as more people exited. Finally, locking eyes with him, she hissed, "You were supposed to be friends! I trusted you both! There shouldn't have been *any* times!"

"You left." Cameron's shoulders fell, some of the bluster dissipating.

"I went to *school*, you mean?"

"No, school, I could handle. School, I expected. *You left me.* For two years! Without giving me any indication of where we stood. After begging me to take care of her."

"'Take care'!" Mikaela's voice rose again. "Was impregnating her how you did that? Is that what you're saying? You loved me so much somehow you just couldn't control yourself?"

The mall doors opened and more shoppers filed out. Cameron glanced over his shoulder. Grabbing all their cumbersome bags, he pulled Mikaela by the arm away from the doors inelegantly as she found herself holding his large teddy bear.

"I was lonely, Kaela!" he growled in her ear, gripping her tightly. "What was I supposed to do, become a monk?"

"Of course not. *I didn't*," she lied, aiming for injury. And by the way he blinked rapidly at her words, she succeeded. "But why her?" Mikaela glared at his fingers wrapped around her arm.

"You don't know what it was like." He released her. "To miss you constantly, want you but instead have her, the closest thing *to you*, always there." Ribbons of emotion made his voice waver. "Always around. Always available. Always on me. Talking about you, reminding me of you." His voice dropped to a near whisper. "I think I told myself that maybe that's what you wanted?"

"You thought I'd want you to *fuck* my best friend?" She shoved the comically large bear back at him.

There was a long pause between them, where he looked dazed by her bluntness and shrugged.

"Let me help you—I didn't."

The stars were visible now that they stepped away from the entrance lights and night truly fell around them. It made Cameron's expression more inscrutable, cast in shadow by the sparing lights around the building.

"I don't really believe you thought that." Mikaela shook her head. "That's—" She crossed her arms to hold herself up, brace herself. "That's crazy."

"Is it?" Cameron asked, mirroring her, sounding genuinely confused. "Didn't you push us together after her dad died?"

"Yes! Because I was away! Because you had things in common and you went to the same school! And I needed someone to look after her. Be kind to her. Not, *for the record*, because I wanted you to *sleep* with her!"

"Why me?" he pressed. "She has other friends. *You* have other friends. Shit, you could have asked one of those twins. Corey, he went to Georgia too, right? But you chose me. Why?"

He whispered the question like an entreaty to share a secret between them. And despite Mikaela's anger, it took everything in her not to launch herself at Cameron. Wrap her arms around him and beg for his forgiveness.

She'd asked herself that same question a lot in the time that passed.

"I don't know. To help her?" She shook her head. "I didn't know how to help you. I didn't—"

"Don't tell me any bullshit!" he snapped. "I might have believed it once but I know now that's garbage. Somewhere inside you must have wanted this. So, just admit it!"

"No! Her dad had just died. And she *needed* so much, so much attention…" Mikaela couldn't adequately articulate a thought that she'd never before fully allowed herself to have. "And you were so sad over your mom. It was just like you both wanted so much of me… And well, I don't know… I—I didn't want to leave you both but I needed to get—"

Cameron inhaled sharply before letting go of a shuddering sigh. *"To get away from us?"*

"No, it wasn't like that!" she insisted, though she knew she was equivocating.

Mikaela hung her head, nearly touching Cameron's chest. Even though he radiated anger, just smelling his familiar combination of soap and cinnamon undid her.

"I just didn't know what to do! How to give you what you needed from me. And I wanted…"

"Just say it, *to get away from me*," he repeated, over her objection. "The guy with the sick mom, and no real prospects, right? Bet there's more and better in New York, right?"

"No!"

"I don't believe you," he said, skewering her with a disdainful glare.

"What does any of it matter when you got *exactly* what you wanted anyway?"

"What *I* wanted?"

"I mean you lost your dad, you were losing your mom. Let's face it, all you *really* wanted was a family. *Any family.* So, you just started one with her, you married *her*. Don't pretend now that I mattered at all!"

"Is that what you've been telling yourself so you can sleep at night? That you set us up because you thought that I had some plan to trap you here in Georgia with me?"

"Cameron, that's not what I said!"

"You might as well have." He pushed.

"I GOT PREGNANT!" Mikaela screamed into the night, dropping her arms at her sides. "And it scared me!"

It was still difficult even now to say those words and think of those awful months. She was shocked she'd allowed him to goad her into revealing something not a single soul, besides her dorm-mate Penny, knew.

"What?" Cameron stopped, pulled up short, angling his head to reach her eyes.

Mikaela shook her head, closing her mouth, dreading this. Why had she said that? She cursed herself. What possible good did this knowledge serve now?

"Mikaela, what did you just say?"

She licked her lips, suddenly dry and quivering.

"Look at me!" he demanded.

She squeezed her eyes shut as his voice rose.

"Kaela. Look. At. Me!"

But she wouldn't. She grabbed her face, willing herself not to say any more, covering her mouth, trying not to cry.

"You were pregnant…with *our* baby?" His voice dropped but it had a raw edge. "When?"

She dragged her hands away. "After that Christmas."

The faint strains of cheerful holiday music emanating from mounted speakers along the exterior of the building made those words particularly offensive.

"Wha— Why?" He faltered, almost incoherent, squeezing his eyes shut. "Why didn't you tell me?"

"I didn't know what I wanted to do."

It was unreal days of denial turned into weeks of inaction, with Mikaela praying for a solution to magically present itself…and then being terrified when it did.

"What did you do?"

The quaver in Cameron's voice begged for an answer different than the one she might provide.

"I lost it," she answered, putting him out of his temporary misery but resenting the relief that appeared on his face.

Even years later, Mikaela was still riven with a profound guilt for her relief. The kind that came after rushing to a city emergency room at the unexpected but not wholly unwelcome sight of blood. That night had been like being painfully pulled apart but then sewed back together. *Changed. A patchwork of her former self.* And this new self bristled at Cameron's mournful little sigh.

His eyes grew watery. "Why would you go through that alone?" His voice cracked. "I would have—"

"You would have *what*? Done what you did with me instead of Julie?" She glared at him and he shut up.

But the torment on his face threatened to undo her.

"I couldn't say anything." She eased. "I didn't want it to be happening. I was afraid."

"Afraid? Of what I would say?" He was incredulous. "Afraid of me?"

"No." Mikaela hesitated. "Afraid you'd want me to keep it. And afraid I'd want to, to make you happy." The truth ripped from her chest as if he'd badgered her for it. "Or that I wouldn't and you'd hate me for it," she finally admitted.

"How can you say that?"

She'd never allowed herself the fully formed thought, although it had always hung there in the shadows, lurking, seething, taking up space in the furthest corners of her mind.

The silence that grew between them now created a chasm deeper, larger...*impassable.* Something disappeared from Cameron's eyes, an emotion Mikaela hadn't realized existed there until it vanished.

"So, here's the thing I don't think you ever understood." Cameron leaned in by Mikaela's ear, his words severe, tone incensed. "Since apparently all you saw in me was some poor, desperate orphan…"

"That's not true."

"I would have had ten kids, or no kids. Tomorrow or twenty years from now, if that's what you wanted. I'd have waited forever. Would have done *anything* to make you happy. If you'd only just *told me* what you wanted. Because all *I* wanted…*was you*."

The single tear rolling down his cheek threatened to rip a hole in her chest. Mikaela couldn't meet his eyes.

"Goddamn it!" he cursed, his voice laced with scorn, brushing more tears back from his face with his forearm.

She jumped at his outburst.

"Julie is absolutely right about you! You *are* just like your mama! Just a shitty, selfish person who can justify anything. And as always, you're right. You're gonna make a great lawyer, *Mike*."

Mikaela shrank away from him.

Talking about her mother was a spectacularly low blow but the idea that Julie and Cameron talked about her, picked apart her life and choices while sharing a bed, was what really unraveled her. Hot tears slipped down her cheeks one after the other. She didn't wipe them away as Cameron grabbed his things, preparing to disappear into the darkness.

Selfishly, she couldn't allow that to be the last word spoken between them. "Cameron!"

He paused, turning. And a truth she had for so long tried to deny was written all over his crumpled face.

Cameron was as devastated by all of this as she was.

Holding her gaze, he stalked all the way back, leaving his things lying forgotten in the road. Cupping the back of her head in his hand, he drew her in and kissed her, hard. Mikaela's heart raced at being this close again. Stealing her shallow breaths, claiming them as his own, his mouth over-powered her. He devoured the tears on her lips, tongue lick-ing them away, groaning as she dragged her fingertips across his nape, holding him there. She anchored herself to him, desperately gripping his jacket in the fist of her other hand for balance as Cameron's arm crushed her against his body. They prolonged this kiss beyond reason and when Mikaela attempted to pull back, he pressed forward unwilling to re-lease her, and when he tried, she clung to him too.

The fact that this would be the final time Cameron touched her caused pain to radiate through her chest, making it ache, cracking it open as her breath quickened. At last, he pulled away. Peeling her hands from around him, he dropped them at her sides with a savage sort of finality, then fell back, panting, ireful. With himself or her, she couldn't tell.

"It's never really gonna be finished between us, is it?" It was a statement filled with more frustration than anguish. Cameron retreated, swiping his things from the ground as he went.

Headlights from a car parked in the fire lane illuminated suddenly, blinding her.

It was Vanessa. She hopped out of the car, running up to Mikaela.

"Kae, you're shivering," Vanessa said.

"How much did you hear?"

Vanessa sealed her mouth shut, avoiding Mikaela's eyes. "C'mon."

She loaded their bags into the trunk. Mikaela wobbled on unsteady legs back to her car, putting one foot carefully in front of the other. She braced the hood when she got there while Vanessa jumped back into the driver's seat.

"You okay?" She hung her head out the window, her face a map of concern.

Mikaela nodded for fear of more crying, or likely, sobbing.

"Let me get the heat on," she said as Mikaela finally came around the car and got in.

Vanessa started up the engine as something snapped off the key chain into her hand.

"Ugh, you and this damn thing. Here, take it," Vanessa said, putting the flat little broken metal bulldog squarely in her hand. "You don't even go to that school. I don't get the fascination."

Mikaela closed her hand around the broken key fob and leaned back in her seat, squeezing it in her hand until its sharp edge made her palm hurt.

thirty-four

On a Wednesday night, Mikaela found herself back at Cameron's gallery exhibit again.

She wound around the space, contemplating the divergence of their lives and what they'd both managed to accomplish in all that time. Then after evasion and delay, she stood before the thing that represented the beginning of it all, both then and now.

The picture that caused all the fuss.

Mikaela nipped at the side of her lacquered fingers, gazing up at the large photo. Without any context, the photo looked totally innocuous. A simple photo of two girls on a swimming platform. The girl in the foreground faced the camera, her mouth forever forming a word, the expression on her face hovering somewhere between amusement and censure. The wind carried her mane of wavy hair away from her face in a way that made her look stunning, like a naiad on a sunning rock. Beside her, in the background unaware of the camera, was another girl peering into the murky depths of the lake with her leg outstretched, toe pointing to an unseen horizon. The water shimmered around them forever and the sun shone on them in perpetuity.

Mikaela was barely noticeable in profile—Julie's wild, windswept hair took care of that. Still, anyone who knew her then would recognize her now. A large, distinctive scar on her shoulder confirmed it. They, but mostly Julie, looked young, beautiful and joyful even. Quite possibly, the photo represented the epitome of the typical summer day for a particular type of American teen...and a snapshot of her own youth, most definitely. Which was clearly why it had appealed to *Glamazon* so acutely, who even cosponsored this retrospective.

"Do you still like it?" Cameron came up from behind, catching her off guard. He was so close she could smell his aftershave, but he didn't touch her...*thankfully.*

Mikaela stepped forward, turning on her heel to face him while putting some distance between them. She was dismayed to realize that the gallery had nearly emptied out during the time she'd spent staring up at this picture. Only a few stragglers remained.

"I think it's fabulous." She smiled up at him. "All of it. Really, Cameron, I'm so proud of you! I saw a couple of pieces I could even buy for my house."

"Don't do that." He shook his head, crinkling his nose.

"Why not?" She was genuinely perplexed by this response. "I want to give you the support."

"You're the reason some of these pictures exist, directly or indirectly."

Mikaela glanced around, weighing that.

"I couldn't charge you for them. You just point out any

one you like and it's yours." He nodded his encouragement, looking around.

"Anything?"

"I'm serious."

"I believe you," she said, walking toward the next picture. The price tags alone on some of them indicated that Cameron would be a moron to do this.

"No, you don't," he said, following her.

"You a mind-reading photographer now?"

"Nope. I just know you."

"No, you don't," she parroted, then clasped her hands behind her back and moved on to inspect the next photo.

Behind the bar, the cater-waiters pulled their gear together.

Cameron followed her eyes. "Don't worry. I have a set of keys. I can lock up."

She did not want to be all alone with Cameron...nothing good could come of that.

"Tell me about this one..." Mikaela deflected.

Cameron turned where she pointed briefly, then back. His eyes roaming her face, instead of the picture.

"What?"

"I just can't believe I finally have you here." He smiled more to himself than to her.

"Just focus on the pictures, Mr. Murphy." She nodded, moving on.

Cameron followed Mikaela around the gallery offering descriptions of his work. But Mikaela found herself watching his mouth more than listening.

"You see anything you like yet?" he asked, breaking into her wandering thoughts.

She paused, knowing that her immediate answer would not have been about his artwork. Few things on display were as captivating as him. Casual in a dress shirt tucked into a pair of blue jeans, with his rugged five-o'clock shadow and his hair a little overgrown and tousled, he looked inordinately good for just a regular weeknight.

"I'm thinking on that one of Robin and Julie in the sand. It's nice." Mikaela pointed out one of the triptychs that had caught her eye on her last visit, since they hadn't reached it in their tour yet.

"That's actually Kit. Juliette didn't want to cut his hair until he was two. Superstitious…but I understood, at that point we needed all the luck we could get," Cameron explained. "Robin wasn't with us on that trip. She was spending some time with her father."

Mikaela's heart felt as if it had stopped.

"Wait, wait," she said and paused on their turn around the gallery. "Her *what*?"

Cameron just nodded for a moment, leaving it all for Mikaela to digest.

"It's not something we discuss anymore because with every atom of my being she's undoubtedly mine. But she's not biologically mine," he babbled.

"But her eyes, her smile…" As she said the words, Mikaela knew they sounded moronic.

"Juliette's mom, Miss Liza, has blue eyes too. You remember that?"

"Of course."

"And, Robin's BioDad—*that's what we call him, Robin's BioDad*—he does too." Cameron said it so calmly, it left Mikaela baffled. "*Et voilà!* The miracle of genetics. A daughter with blue eyes."

"But, Cam—"

"Juliette claims she didn't know. I mean, she suspected, I'm sure, but she didn't know. Not until Robbie got sick and we needed his bone marrow. Listen, as both my therapist and later my divorce lawyer were good enough to explain to me, it's better that I make the choice to believe her. So, I guess since she wanted it to be me, and maybe I needed that a little myself, it is better. You know, after everything."

He gave an inconsequential little shrug.

"Excuse me?" Mikaela frowned, not being able to help the small swivel that came to her neck.

She had never forgotten the tongue-lashing Cameron meted out to her the last time they saw each other all those years ago. The one in which he'd basically accused her of deliberately saddling him with a wife and child.

"What does 'a little' mean?"

"Well…" Cameron swallowed hard, his Adam's apple bobbing in his throat. "Those were the things I could have seen myself having with you eventually. But I had them with her instead."

The statement, so casually offered, was like a dagger in Mikaela's chest. She remained ambivalent about children but to be considered so ultimately replaceable was…

"Cameron, I was nineteen years old! You were twenty-two."

"Yeah?" He shrugged. "Still, people did it all the time. Half our classmates, I'd bet. My parents, your parents."

"My parents?" She gave a guttural grunt that resembled a laugh. "And look how well that went for them. I had a lot of life I wanted to live before any of that. And look at all the things you've accomplished! We couldn't have done that together. We'd have been trapped!"

"You certainly thought that…" he mused, looking around the gallery as if it was a million-dollar consolation prize.

"Did you forget? I didn't think, *I knew*!" She paused because making even indirect reference to that long-ago "accident" was still hard.

"I haven't forgotten," he said in a low voice.

"For you and me, it would have been babies, marriage and Harmon, but neither of us *truly* wanted that."

"I guess that's where we part company 'cause I wanted that."

"Clearly…" She trailed off, gesturing toward the photo of Julie and Kit. "You think that. But one look around shows that's not all. You wanted a *life*. One we wouldn't, *couldn't* have had together."

"So then, maybe you're right." Cameron shrugged again. "I guess it all worked out."

Mikaela choked back unanticipated emotion, clearing her throat. She ran a finger along her lash line to stave off tears. But not sad tears—she was angry. And her anger was fueling her in ways the other confusing emotions she was feeling were not.

"So, lemme get this straight…are you saying you're happy you married Julie?" Mikaela searched Cameron's eyes for some alternate interpretation of his words as he sighed, his shoulders falling.

"I was just doing the 'right thing' initially. But, to have the children we had, whom I adore, to have raised them? Yes, I can honestly say I don't regret it," he answered in a hesitant way, as if picking his words carefully, "now."

Mikaela had spent too many years thinking it was a mistake, *her mistake*, that led to all of this. She reeled with these revelations, literally dizzy and nauseated.

"So, I guess, it is just as well," he concluded, looking pleased in his complacency.

"Just as well, huh?" she nearly shouted. "You know what, Cameron, fuck you!"

He blinked and her eyes scanned the room, but there was no one else there by then.

How did he keep finding novel ways to piss her off?

Cameron hesitated for a moment, bewildered. "Listen, Mikaela, whoa—"

Mikaela stopped him, holding up a hand. "Do you know how long this has torn me up inside? Gutted me? Made me angry with myself? Berate myself? Blame myself for the part I played? Then you come back now. Swoop into my life. Disrupt things. Make me think that we could still—" She stopped, the humiliation of false hope shutting her down.

He stood there waiting, his almost amused passivity only making her angrier. "Mikaela, you don't underst—"

"So, this whole thing, the last few weeks have been what? You toying with me? A very elaborate and juvenile little screw-you? *Revenge?* Some mind game for you and your ex-wife? What?" She stopped again, nearly breathless, trying to calm down. "Well, screw you both!"

I've allowed him to upset me again, she chastised herself. Mikaela had prided herself on the fact that few people could do that now, yet he'd already done it more than once. Cameron should not have been capable of it. *Not anymore.*

"Are you done?" He crossed his arms over his chest like she was an overbearing child he was indulging.

"I sure am." Mikaela spun on her heels, footsteps echoing across the concrete as she headed for the door.

"Mikaela!"

She stomped away. She wasn't sure what she had expected from tonight, some form of catharsis, or closure perhaps. And it could have been argued this was it. Just not the way she'd planned it, not the settling of accounts she'd hoped for. Still, she was free. She wasn't even on the *Glamazon* team anymore, so there was absolutely no reason why their paths should continue to cross. She could finally be rid of Cameron Murphy and that niggling little voice over the years that had forever whispered, *What if?*

Now she knew.

He'd all but said it. She had been entirely interchangeable. He'd claimed to want her, but Julie had been a better-than-fine substitute. Despite his professions of love all those years ago, Mikaela had been right all along. Cameron didn't love her, *not particularly*, and ultimately, he and Julie had done just as well together.

She was released. So why didn't it feel that way? Why did it feel all wrong?

With his long legs, Cameron beat her to the front door, leaning back against it when she got there, his hands behind his back holding the knob, blocking her way.

"You gonna let me out?"

"I don't know. You gonna hear me out?"

"I think I heard you fine."

"No, you didn't." He frowned.

They both took a beat.

"Okay, fine." Mikaela rifled through her tiny clutch. "I have mace."

Cameron stood straight up and threw his hands into the air. "You're perfectly safe with me. But perfectly welcome to leave if you want."

"I want to go now."

He stood aside for her.

"Then go, Kaela." His voice softened in defeat. "But after all these years, I think you owe me the courtesy of hearing me out, instead of jumping to conclusions."

"I don't owe you shit!" She reached for the doorknob.

But Mikaela knew, if she dared to admit it, this wasn't the way she had wanted it to go, why she came tonight. Truly, she had wanted to know he pined for her as much she had for him all these years, feeling incomplete and unsatisfied with all subsequent relationships. Was it sensible? *No.* Selfish? *Yes.* But it was what she wanted… And exactly the thing, in the moment, he denied her.

"Mikaela." Cameron's expression grew more somber. "Listen to me, and really hear me now. When I said it was just as well, it's because it *was* just as well." He stated this with a sigh. "It didn't take me long to realize I had made a huge mistake. But you had been gone for so long. I think that's why I slept with Juliette that first time, as an act of despair. It was me finally giving up on the idea that you might come back."

"But I did come back." Indignant tears welled in her eyes as she admitted this. "I even applied to Emory Law."

"You did?" His voice broke at that.

She nodded.

"Too late," he lamented. "By then, I'd lost you and destroyed our relationship. So, you understand, I couldn't allow my decision to stay with Julie, to marry her… I couldn't let that be yet another mistake. It just could not be a mistake—Robin *needed* to be mine. And whether I originally liked it or not, I wanted to be Robin's father too. I wanted to be there for Julie and be the father to my child my dad was to me. I had to do it, otherwise what the fuck had I done?"

Mikaela bit her lip, feeling the truth of that. Still, the memory of returning home to the news of Julie's pregnancy was seared into her memory as the single most painful moment in her entire life. Cameron's subsequent visit to her house begging for her forgiveness being a close second. He was right. All that pain couldn't, in the end, be for nothing.

"And now, she's this amazing young woman that I'm grateful to have in my life…regardless of how she got there."

"I understand that."

"Do you?" He placed his hand over hers on the doorknob.

Mikaela thawed, with her hand in Cameron's as he intertwined their fingers. And he smiled that smile again at her that almost distracted Mikaela from the ache in her chest.

"You're a good man, Cameron. You always were. Of course, I understand."

"Well…" He paused. "Don't canonize me yet. When I found out Robin wasn't mine, I was upset. No, I take that back. I was enraged. But then it occurred to me that maybe it was a sign, instead of a punishment. Or, whatever it was, it was mainly an out. By then, things were so bad between Juliette and me and had been for so long that I couldn't think of anything else to do but run. So, I came and saw your father. Did he ever tell you about that? That he saved my marriage… at least temporarily?"

"*My* dad did?" Mikaela brushed at her lashes, moisture smearing her mascara, and sniffled. "No, he never told me. You weren't exactly his favorite person."

Showing up on her doorstep in the middle of the night, drunk on Jim Beam and loudly pleading for her forgiveness, had not endeared him to J.D. Marchand.

"Yeah, I could've guessed that." Cameron gave her a wry smile, shaking his head and leading her from the door. "But he was really decent to me this time. I came by, asking after you. You understand, I was desperate to find you. To try and salvage something. But instead, he brought me in and stopped me from making a terrible decision. I told him about Robin's illness and what Juliette had done. And he helped me think things through. Then he told me about how you were so happy interning for some ritzy law firm and how when you called him, you sounded so sophisticated."

Mikaela sighed. Knowing which magic words her father had imparted to keep Julie and Cameron's marriage afloat for six more years wasn't highly desirable. Yet this was Cameron's story, so she let him tell it when what she really wanted to do was go have a word with her father about meddling in her affairs.

"He talked about how ambitious you were, like your mom."

She winced.

"How, like everyone else, he could always tell that you had been made for bigger things."

"And that stopped you, right?" Mikaela cut to the chase, thinking of the years apart her father's unilateral decision cost her. "Stopped you from trying to reach out to me? The things my dad told you?"

Cameron nodded.

"I wish he hadn't done that," she muttered more to herself.

"Well, I'm glad he did," Cameron answered anyway.

Mikaela didn't know what to do with that. But perhaps it was true. Maybe everything happened the way it was supposed to happen. And maybe she needed to know this now so she and Cameron could forgive each other and finally move on with their lives…separately.

She reclaimed her hand and folded them both over her chest to keep them away from him. Trying to remind herself that just a moment before she'd wanted to eviscerate him with a dull soup spoon.

"So that's a photograph of Kit?" Mikaela changed subjects abruptly to short-circuit the melancholy this whole conversation brought on. It was better when she was just pissed with him; she didn't know what to do with the feelings she had now. He nodded, following her eyes.

"And this?" It was the monstrosity at the center of the room which somehow had not stopped causing her problems.

"That is my favorite photo that I've ever taken."

She raised an eyebrow and stepped over to gaze up at it.

They were back where they started.

Cameron moved in behind her, mouth hovering just behind her ear. "What do you see?"

"Billable hours."

"Kaela."

"What?" she snapped before relenting. "Fine."

"Okay, what?" He laid his hands on her shoulders. They seized, then relaxed under his grip.

"Youth." She offered after thinking about it for the millionth time. "Summertime."

"Try again, be more literal, less metaphorical." He squeezed her gently as she cut her eyes at him over her shoulder.

She turned to regard the photograph again. "Um, Julie, swimmers, a platform on a lake…"

"Step back from it." He took her by the elbows and pulled her one large step backward.

She inhaled. The heat of his body behind her made her sharply aware of how much she had always loved being in his embrace. But she wasn't done being annoyed yet, and that irritation helped inure her to all the butterflies and warm feelings being this close usually gave her.

It was true though; the photo did look better from farther away.

Even metaphorically speaking, Mikaela needed distance to appreciate it as others did. The two young women on an old wooden swimming platform having carefree fun. There was Julie, the way Mikaela remembered her, exuberant both inside and out, joyful before their anger. She saw herself as she had been then too: a little awkward but thoughtful, exuding untapped potential, yet lacking in confidence, still seemingly content despite it. They were both beautiful in their irrepressible vibrancy.

"Happiness?" Mikaela's eyes roamed the picture then seeing all the little details she had missed.

The assortment of arms and legs of the other people who were also on the platform that day—*these were cropped and photoshopped out of all the high-gloss versions.* The heads and shoulders of swimmers in the water wading off in the distance, a hawk overhead captured a second before it climbed out of the frame, the way the sunlight glinted off the water's surface and just about a dozen other things she had never even noticed before.

He shook his head.

"I really don't know—a large canvas, your future, a big lie?" She shrugged, fed up with the guessing game.

And deathly tired of this picture and all the angst their mutual history bound up with it.

"No, Mikaela, what do you *see*?"

"Just tell me."

"*It's you.* The only reason I allowed them to use this picture, and yes, to wallpaper the City with it, was in the hopes that you would see it. Not to taunt or harass you, but so you could see the photo again and think of me. Maybe want to see me," he confessed in a whisper.

Mikaela was overcome.

"And that's because this is a picture of me, *looking at you.*"

Mikaela turned to Cameron, looking into his eyes, then back at the photograph.

It was all right there. Mikaela just stared, words feeling inadequate. They had been so wrongheaded...about everything. All of them, but especially her.

She was speechless.

Mikaela stood still as Cameron slowly bent forward then. Feeling a bit outside herself, she watched as he grazed her closed mouth with his own. Just the smell of him, mixed

with the musky cedar, bergamot and sandalwood of his co-
logne, did things that upended and confused her. His deli-
cious mouth and those soft lips over hers made her forget
every question she'd had about them over the past eighteen
years they'd been apart and what went wrong. Cameron
gathered her into himself, brushing his cheek and nose past
hers, first across one side, then the other. His five-o'clock
shadow prickled her cheek and galvanized nerves not just
on her face but all over her body. The sensation pulled her
back into this moment they were sharing. Finally, *again*, after
all these years.

Her heart skidded, a little syncopated beat, delighting at
his touch. And she inhaled as his tongue skimmed the seam of
her lips, sending a jolt through her that coaxed them to part
for him. He bit her bottom lip lightly then licked it before
slipping his tongue into her mouth. Mikaela rejoiced at the
discovery that even after all these years he still tasted faintly
of cinnamon. It made this all too familiar and good to be
true. His arms encircled her further and her hands itched to
reach out for him. Yet she didn't, indecision keeping them
locked at her sides.

"You have no idea how much I've wanted to do this." He
spoke the words against her lips.

Barely giving her time to think or the space to breathe,
Cameron reclaimed her mouth, their kiss deepening. His
tongue engaged hers, tempting and teasing with each pass,
making her savor every lick and nip at her lips until she
sighed wistfully and he groaned in response. She still resisted the temptation to embrace him. But something close
to a needy whimper escaped from her and both their eyes
fluttered open, mutually surprised and aroused at the sound.
Mikaela balled the hem of Cameron's shirt up into her fists
to steady herself, holding him. And soon, their kiss made

her forget everything until she lost all sense of herself but for him and them together.

Then, just as quickly, it was over.

"Will you stay?" he whispered into her lips.

"Stay?"

"I'm subletting an apartment from the gallery owners, upstairs."

"Cam, you know I can't. Not with your case and everything. How would it look?" She said it but knew after that kiss they'd just shared this rationale couldn't hold sway for long. Still, she pulled out of his arms.

"You're not on my case anymore."

"But still…" She resisted, if only barely.

"Mikaela, there's so much we still need to say." He took up her hand and kissed it. "Just to talk, I promise."

She didn't believe that and didn't honestly think he could either. Every time they looked into each other's eyes now, embers of what should have been long-extinguished fires glowed there. "Okay," she relented after an extended silence.

He gave her an achingly sweet and triumphant smile.

"But." She raised a finger. "Only if we stay down here… and only because you haven't finished giving me the tour."

thirty-five

"I bought me these shoes from a drug dealer, okay?" Mikaela's stepfather, Luke Franklin, looked to make sure she was following.

Mikaela nodded, listening as Luke unfurled his latest dad joke.

For her, essential to the humor was the fact that he was always already laughing before he could deliver the punch line.

Mikaela smiled, waiting.

"I don't know what he laced 'em with..." Luke guffawed, pulling his glasses off his face to wipe tears from his eyes as Mikaela chuckled along with him. "But I was trippin' all day!"

They were standing, stationed in the massive lobby of the palatial Lotus Fifth Avenue hotel as her mother, *the woman of the hour*, held court with dozens of her friends in the banquet room nearby. Mikaela and Luke stood outside acting as ushers for any guests that got lost in the immense reception area. With conventions, weddings and other events happening there simultaneously, it would be easy to lose a lamb or two. And as usual, Mikaela's stepfather, being unsure of what to do with himself once his wife got with gaggles of her friends, went in search of an occupation...which as usual, led him to her. Mikaela remained astounded by how many of her mother and stepfather's people had been willing to fly all the way up to New York to celebrate Natalee's sixtieth birthday lavishly, when they could have just as easily thrown this party in Atlanta, where they *actually* lived. But that had always been her mother's style: extravagance at every opportunity. Mikaela's father could never have hoped to support that epicurean lifestyle. This birthday party was only the most recent example of that.

"That was a good one. Okay, which one gave it to you?"

Mikaela referenced his two youngest grandkids, Charlotte and Amir.

"Amir," Luke answered proudly. "I don't know where he comes up with them!"

Even after all these years, Mikaela still found Luke's marriage to her mother remarkable...though not for the same reasons as before. He was balding, bespectacled and as round as a potato with a big, infectious laugh as perhaps his most attractive feature. Once upon a time, he had seemed to be stiff and uninteresting, with a bland manner and a terminal lack of charisma. Now, Mikaela bitterly regretted those early judgments because she was wrong on all counts. A doting husband, father and grandfather, Luke was sweet and gregarious. A slightly older widower when he and her mother first met, he'd seemed an odd choice for Mikaela's young vibrant mother then. But he had fallen hard for Natalee and smartly, she never let him go. He was steady and practical where she was flighty, and deeply caring where she could be frequently callous. Ultimately, to Mikaela's surprise, it had been Luke who helped create the bridge in her twenties that finally allowed her to reconcile with her mother...and in that way, he had also become one of her favorite people.

"Okay, now what does a vegetarian zombie eat?" He snickered even as he asked.

Mikaela shook her head. "I have no idea..."

"GRAAAAINS!" Luke howled as Mikaela giggled too.

Luke continued on as Mikaela scanned the hotel lobby making sure that they didn't miss any stragglers. It was dead boring but still preferable to sitting inside with her mother, sister and assorted family and friends.

"Okay, Lottie gave me this one. A termite walks into a bar and asks," Luke started, already giggling as Mikaela watched the door, "'Is the bar tender here?'"

Mikaela's smile widened but not because of the joke.

"Get it?" He tapped her with his elbow but she was transfixed by the sight of Cameron, Robin and Christopher stepping into the lobby.

"Gimme a sec, Luke," Mikaela said, already moving away from him.

Robin and Christopher saw her first, coming across the large, busy grand lobby as Cameron's eyes still cast around.

"What are you guys doing here?" Mikaela asked, her grin growing outsize, wrapping her arms around Robin.

"Vanessa invited us," Cameron said as Mikaela hugged Christopher too.

She looked at them all wide-eyed, unbelieving.

They were clearly dressed for the party with Robin in a yellow polka-dotted party dress and her dad and brother looking preppy in pastel oxfords, ties and trousers.

Cameron pulled Mikaela into an embrace, putting his lips to her cheekbone.

"You look amazing," he whispered, making her cheeks burn.

She hadn't seen him since the night at the gallery, but

they'd spoken nearly every day since. He never once mentioned coming. They walked up to Luke with Cameron's arm looped around her waist. She reached for his hand, pinning it to her hip, not wanting to let go.

Mikaela made quick introductions.

"Oh, I remember you, young man! *The artist*. Would you believe I've been following your career since then?" Luke asked, shaking Cameron's hand vigorously and shocking the hell out of Mikaela.

"You have?" Cameron asked, appropriately astonished. "It's been almost twenty years."

Luke nodded. "I knew when I met you that you had something. I mean, you had a good eye and good taste, *clearly*." He beamed with fatherly pride at Mikaela.

Cameron squeezed Mikaela's hand on her hip as they both grinned at each other and Luke.

"But, honestly, it was Nat that recognized your name about ten years ago, and then we saw one of your pieces up here at PS1 about two years ago now." Luke spoke of the Museum of Modern Art's Queens outpost.

Again, Mikaela was appropriately impressed, looking Cameron over as he appeared abashed. But she couldn't help feeling simultaneously shocked.

Her mother really *had* remembered him.

"And I said to her then, 'I wonder whatever happened to Kaela and that guy?' And now here you are!" Luke said, pleased with himself. "We're honored."

Robin and Christopher grinned proudly at their father too.

It was amazing to Mikaela that Cameron had not lost his nearly absurd level of modesty. He cast his eyes down and reddened, genuinely embarrassed by Luke's mild praise.

"I hope you all brought your appetites, these girls got us

a buffet extravaganza and a carving station you have to see to believe!"

"She doesn't eat meat," Cameron said at the same time Robin spoke for herself.

"Just like your mom, huh?" Mikaela remarked smiling.

Robin nodded. "He'll eat anything that isn't nailed down though."

Christopher shrugged, copping to it.

"Like his uncle Gabe; the more things change the more they stay the same, I guess," Mikaela remarked to Cameron, who chuckled.

"Lemme take you in and introduce you around," Luke offered, excited by the prospect of new young people to take under his wing, as was his way.

The kids followed Luke into the banquet room leaving Mikaela and Cameron behind.

"Hi." Cameron turned to her, speaking softly. His fingers were still intertwined with hers at her hip.

Mikaela's cheeks ached. She'd been smiling since they arrived.

"You didn't tell me you were coming."

"Your sister wanted it to be a surprise. She asked Suze to get in touch with me."

"I bet she did."

Vanessa had not changed one iota in their entire lives. She was still absolutely a troublemaker.

"Well, I am surprised."

"Pleasantly?" His eyes searched her face.

Mikaela nodded. "Very."

She hadn't known how much she wanted to see Cameron until he was there, stepping into the lobby from the street. Just seeing him standing there set her heart to a gallop as it had when they were kids. It was the same giddy way she felt eons ago when he called or she knew they would be meeting. Reminiscent of when she'd sneak out in the dead of night and race down the darkened streets of Harmon to meet him, exhilarated and vaguely reckless.

Cameron smiled back before leaning in and kissing her, right there out in the open. Mikaela was surprised but not perturbed like the last time, enjoying the feeling of being in his arms. He pulled her closer, pressing her body into his, as he surged forward, feasting on her lips and tongue.

Yet as good as it felt, to be with him and in his arms again, as comfortable and strangely right as it always felt, they had not come to any decision about one another. They'd spent the rest of the night at the gallery talking as they agreed. And though Cameron knew about her breakup with Rashad, this still felt unprecedented.

Mikaela pulled reluctantly out of Cameron's arms as he attempted to enfold her further.

"Whoa, whoa," she said, laughing at his enthusiasm. "Wait a minute, Mr. Murphy. What's happening?"

She took a half step back, wiping her top lip with her thumb. Unthinkingly, she reached out for him as she used to. And the corners of his lips rose as he held still while she thoroughly removed all traces of her lipstick from his mouth.

"I can't be happy to see you?" he joked, reaching for the hand against his lips, but she moved evasively out of his grasp.

Mikaela tried to approximate a serious expression. "There's happy to see me and there's this. *This* is something else."

Cameron let out a heavy breath. "Monica says Juliette might be willing to settle. They're drawing up another offer for her lawyers now. This could all be over by next week."

"That's wonderful news!" Mikaela smiled, allowing Cameron to pull her back into a congratulatory hug, though she wasn't sure how she truly felt about it.

Of course, as one of the last strings holding up the *Glamazon* portions of the overall Altcera business, this was hoped-for news. It stung a bit that it had happened under Todd's watch but a victory for one was a victory for all, Mikaela repeated to herself. The other part, however, was more complicated. It had been an unexpected challenge to have Cameron in and out of the firm's offices. But now that it was almost over, Mikaela acknowledged, seeing him again was also one of the best things to happen in a long time.

Cameron worked in New York but was not based here. It had been the confluence of the lawsuit, Robin's acceptance into the ballet program and his retrospective that had kept him in one place for over two months. But with two of the three things soon to be done, his life of traveling the world no doubt called to him. And Mikaela couldn't think of anything else that could compare, even in her life, to that sort of siren song. She dreamed of traveling the world as extensively as Cameron did in just the course of a few weeks. In short order there would be nothing keeping him here, with her. Yes, his appearance had disrupted her life and helped to upend her existing relationship, but she wasn't entirely sure she was ready for this to be over just as it was beginning.

Mikaela struggled to keep the smile on her face, like the sudden weight of this news dragged on the corners of her mouth. She was pleased for him, she had to remind herself more than once. Maintaining that limp smile, she took Cameron's hand, pulling him toward the banquet hall doors. "C'mon, let me reintroduce you to my mom."

Cameron dragged Mikaela to a stop, bending slightly to wrap both arms around her waist and pull her back to him. With his mouth right at her ear, he whispered huskily, "That is *not* who I want you to reintroduce me to."

And if for a moment she had misunderstood his meaning, right then it vanished with his body flush against hers.

Mikaela gasped, scandalized...but excited. Falling back slightly to look into his eyes, she asked, "The case?"

"Is almost over. Next week," he insisted.

"I—I can't just disappear." It was the only other rebuttal she could think of as Cameron's eyes were already stripping the clothes from her body.

"Think of something. I'm going to get a room. Meet me by the elevators in ten minutes." He let her go abruptly and walked away.

She stood there frozen, indecisive, confused by what was happening and undone by the promises in his expression.

"Kaela!"

She turned at the sharp whisper of her name echoing through the high-ceilinged space. Cameron stood a couple of yards away staring her down. His eyes widened as he fished his wallet out of his pants pocket.

"Now!"

Mikaela startled to life obediently, heading back into the banquet hall.

thirty-six

M ikaela wasn't sure what she said, and even less sure what her sister believed as she asked for an hour or so of coverage. Vanessa wore a half-knowing smile as she promised Mikaela no one would come looking for her for at least the next sixty minutes. Mikaela didn't bother with being too coy. Historically speaking, she'd been bad at keeping what was happening between herself and Cameron a secret from Vanessa anyway.

Now Mikaela stood on the opposite side of a crowded elevator from Cameron as he stared holes into her. She bit at her nails to occupy her hands. She didn't even know why she was that far away other than she wasn't entirely certain they wouldn't have begun pulling each other's clothes off in public if she was any closer. They watched each other restlessly while guest after guest stepped off the elevator, which seemed determined to stop at every floor.

At seventeen, with the majority of the other passengers gone, Cameron slid across the car behind an elderly couple and a bellman, who rode along with them and their bags, and took Mikaela's hand in his, interlacing their fingers. His hand enveloped hers, squeezing some kind of message into her palm like he used to, his fingers drumming across the back of her hand with impatience. He pulled her close to his side, so their bodies touched, looking like an overgrown kid that had secreted away a candy. Only now he itched to peel back the wrapper and feast...*and she was the candy*.

"I hope you have a *very* pleasant stay in the City," Cameron wished the couple at twenty-four, when the doors slid open, pulling her out. "Lots of fun to be had here!"

They nodded, exchanging glances with each other and Cameron as the door closed between them all.

Mikaela swatted him on the arm for being so obvious a moment before he pushed her up against the wall beside the call button. He buried his face in her hair, inhaling deeply.

"Oh God." His moan in her ear made her legs wobble. "You feel the same, you even smell the same as I remembered."

Cameron's hands roamed her body, groping her through the fabric of her dress, dragging the hem up her thighs toward her waist.

"But I'm not. I'm not the same person you remember. You get that, right?"

Mikaela pushed him back when her words didn't seem to pause his hands or take root in his consciousness, snatching the key card from him. She checked the number on it, pulling herself away and following the signs until she found their room. She opened the door and slid the card into the reader, illuminating the space, before sitting on the corner of the king-size bed inside. For something that was going to amount to a by-the-hour situation, Cameron had forked over a pretty penny. Even cast in an unflattering artificial light, it was a nice room. Great views of Central Park sprawled below them and Midtown off in the distance peeked from between the curtains. Nearby, a plush couch and stylish low-set end table sat off to the side.

Mikaela crossed her arms and legs primly, waiting for Cameron to pull up the distant rear.

It would be a shame if he'd done all this for nothing.

Which was what this was beginning to feel like. Still, she took off one heel and then the other, casting them aside and shimmying out of her pantyhose.

Cameron looked as if he realized that too when he finally pushed the door open with a few fingers and came inside.

"Tell me this hasn't been about you recapturing the past? It's not about you trying to find that naive, silly little girl you used to know?" A profound disappointment ached inside her. The idea that she had to even ask that question rankled her. "All this time, it's been what? A stroll down memory lane? About wanting to be that boy again and dredging up that girl?"

The door clicked shut before Cameron spoke. He pulled the card out of the reader and the room was dark again. Only the half-light from the partially open curtains gave his face any aspect. But his jaw set before he spoke. He wrestled with his tie, loosening it at the collar, and sighed.

"Would it be so bad if I was? She wasn't silly. She was the smartest, boldest, funniest and most remarkable person I'd ever met, from the first moment I laid eyes on her."

"When you *helped them book me*, you mean?"

"Yes!" Cameron's voice rose in exasperation. "Can you imagine how crazy that was for a moment? From my perspective? Small-town guy, never been farther away than the seventy miles to college. And this beautiful girl, I didn't know it then, but easily the prettiest I'd ever see, is arrested doing cartwheels on a crowded football field in a full stadium without a speck of clothing on. Completely unashamed!"

He crouched in front of her, placing his hands flat on either side of her on the bed. "It was like witnessing the birth of a star, a new galaxy! Try to imagine something you couldn't even conceive of before you saw it. *That was you to me.* You were already bigger than that town then. I was there, I saw you—even after they ran you down and threw the jacket over you, you had this big ole smile on your face. Like you knew something, *some secret*, the rest of us hadn't worked out yet. I rushed back to the station for the chance to see you. I knew I would never meet another person like you again. *Ever.*"

"Ah, Julie was there too." She tugged at his tie until it came apart, gathering it in her lap. "She did the exact same thing."

"No." He shook his head with vehemence. "Juliette did it because she likes attention, but you did that for *you*. Declaring your space in the world. There's a difference. And it was obvious, you sparkled, like diamonds versus glass. Then to find out you were not at all reckless or impulsive or, yeah, silly. That it wasn't just some senior prank for you, it was a statement you were making. It was inspiring."

"I don't know about all that." She waved his words away.

"You were young, but already so mature. It was almost bizarre that you were so driven, even back then. You already knew what you wanted to do with your whole life when most of us were still so lost. Juliette worshipped you."

Mikaela scoffed again, turning toward the windows to avoid the plaintive expression on his face.

"Believe me. *I know.* I've known Juliette for twenty years now. I've heard her talk about you, I've seen her when other people talked about you. She dreamed of being like you. You were older than your years, so discerning and humorous…

droll, really. Your daddy doted on you, Vanessa looked up to you, your friends admired you. I don't think you realize how clear it was to everybody that you were going places."

Cameron sought out Mikaela's eyes as she tried to remain unmoved by his words.

"Anyone could see Harmon was just the first stop on your journey. That your star was rising. But can you imagine what it was like for me? I just wanted to hitch a ride. And when a girl like you looked at me the way you did? *I felt seen.* Maybe for the first time. Definitely for the first time since my dad died. A girl like you saw something of value in me?"

Her eyes drifted back to him. "Cameron, you're extraordinary! There was nothing to see. I mean, nothing that wasn't already apparent."

"Maybe to you but do you understand how improbable it was for me? I had no reason to ever imagine more for myself. My dad worked construction, my mama was a florist. I had no reason to believe there was anything beyond Larkspur or Harmon in my cards. *But you saw more.* You saw more for us both."

Mikaela's hand itched to stroke Cameron's cheek, soothe the creases forming in his forehead. She forced herself to remember that she was angry, instead using her hands to pull out the pins that held her high, tight bun in place. Her braids tumbled down around her shoulders as he watched.

"Sometimes when you looked at me back then, it was like I hung the moon," he whispered. "And that felt scary. Honestly. Like a big deal, like I was special. Earning your love became a responsibility that I took seriously. Like I *had* to be great because you believed I was."

His lips curled slightly at the recollection and she did touch him then. Mikaela ran her fingers through Cameron's hair, and he closed his eyes as her nails skittered across his scalp.

They both fell silent for a moment and only their breathing and the sounds of a knock on a door down the hall filled the space between them.

Cameron swallowed and when his eyes opened again, Mikaela nearly gasped. She was plunged into the icy depths of his wide, tear-filled and impassioned eyes. She shivered. He was baring his soul to her, openly pleading for her understanding.

"You respected me, respected my work. It was the first time I really believed I could be a photographer, for real. It was because of you that it didn't feel crazy when Jacqueline came along and said the same thing. You saw me as a photographer even when I had to go into that awful station and sit behind that goddamn desk every day. It was intoxicating that you saw me the way I wanted to see myself..."

He stood.

"And then you just left."

Mikaela sighed heavily.

"Don't worry. I'm not doing that again or anymore." Cameron shook his head, opening his collar as he paced away. "You did what you had to do. I understand that now. But I decided to punish you—*and myself*—for it anyway. For daring to hope things could be different. I wanted to hurt you for leaving me. And myself for believing that somehow you were going to rescue me from my life."

Mikaela's eyes stung as he spoke. Water filled them until she could barely make out his wavering figure moving across the room toward the windows, pushing the curtains farther apart and bringing more natural light into the darkened space.

They both squinted at the blinding sun beam, splitting the room into halves, his in light and hers in shadow.

"I'm so sorry, Cam," Mikaela added somberly.

She got up from the bed then, meeting him at the window. He shook his head as she reached to cup his cheek in her palm. It was moist and he averted his gaze, embarrassed by his tears.

"It's okay." Cameron sniffled, dragging a hand roughly over his face. "Because when I finally decided to leave Juliette, it wasn't as some knee-jerk reaction to the way my life had fallen apart. Or because I wanted you instead. I did it after first trying to salvage things with her. Individual counseling, couples counseling, anything, *everything*. But I knew I owed it to *myself*. By then, I realized I couldn't make Juliette happy and myself happy at the same time. We were too incompatible. I needed to find out what sort of life I wanted… for *me*. I needed to discover who *I* was. Who I wanted to be."

There was so much in his eyes, pain but also far more profoundly, pride. Cameron took Mikaela's hands between his and squeezed them. His trademark earnestness almost too much for her heart, thrumming in her ears, to bear.

"I'm not talking about the past, Kaela. Finding you now isn't about trying to recapture who you or I used to be, at least not totally. It's about being ourselves, *who we are now* and finding that, improbably, we're both still the same *together, to each other*." Cameron's voice dropped deeper, his arms encircling Mikaela's shoulders, hugging her to him. "What I said by the elevator was just my realization. That as much as we've both changed in these years apart, we still fit the way we once did. It was just acknowledging that despite everything, I wasn't wrong. You were molded to fit me in the same way that I know I was made to fit you."

thirty-seven

When Mikaela rose to the balls of her feet, kissing him, Cameron's mouth tasted salty with tears. Her tongue lapped at his, pulling his bottom lip into her mouth. Her hands spanned the sides of his face, holding him there as his arms tightened around her back. He breathed her in, gorging on her open mouth, mating his to hers. A growing heat ran the course of her body with him this close, touching her again. It was all she could remember ever wanting: him, her *and this*. When their lips parted, Cameron pulled Mikaela up into his arms and she wrapped her legs around his waist.

"We were made for each other, Mikaela," he whispered, crossing the room to lay her on the bed, stretching out beside her. "That's what I meant." He stared into her eyes, pausing. "It's what I believe—we always were."

Cameron moved closer, poised above her. His avid gaze ran the length of her body, making her feel like she was burning from the inside out. His lips grazed her nose, cheeks and chin before sliding along her jaw to her neck. He dragged her dress down, uncovering her shoulders, while his mouth blazed a sizzling path over her hot skin. He caressed her with a reverence that eased the self-consciousness so many years apart gave. And true to his word, being in his arms was like coming home.

"Cameron," she breathed, sighing his name into the air.

"I'm yours," he answered, licking her bare breasts and savoring her hardening nipples, lingering there, kneading and palming them. Filling his hands and his mouth as she moaned, her nerves aflame. "You were made for me," he repeated, his voice reverent and prayerlike. "And me for you."

Taking his head between her hands again, she brought his face back up to hers. As she gazed into his eyes then, many unspoken but always known things, feelings that had never changed in all these years, passed between them.

"Yes." Mikaela nodded.

The solid heft of his body over hers, his spicy, lush mixture of sweat, soap and aftershave, the feel of his hands and mouth on her, all aroused her. Her movements became frenzied as Cameron's arms tangled with hers. His shirt sleeves caught at his wrists as she struggled to tug them off. He held her close as if fearing to be separated from her even for the moment it took to relieve him of his clothing.

"Clothes. Off. Now." She growled in frustration when stripping him further proved difficult.

She used her hands, legs and bare feet to push his trousers down his hips when he wouldn't let her go. Cameron laughed at her enthusiasm. Kissing her before lowering his head, he lavished more attention on her breasts.

"You taste so sweet." He again sampled her pearled nipples before trailing downward.

Diving beneath her dress, Cameron ventured between her legs with an eagerness that made her giggle. His hands impatiently tugged her underwear aside and fingers explored her, spreading her wide while his stubbled cheeks abraded the supple skin of her inner thighs. His tongue glided through her folds, lingering until she arched upward, currents of electric pleasure tearing through her, buzzing the length of her nerve-endings. He stayed there applying pressure, sucking on her sensitive, swollen bud, ministering to it until she trembled, crying out his name. She exclaimed it again and again like a chant, quivering, twisting her fists into the top cover of the bed as he gorged himself on her. Muscles tensed all over her body as waves overtook her. She grew louder and louder, building to a screech in release that sounded foreign, even to her.

He resurfaced, a self-congratulatory grin painted across his face. "That's new—" his mouth and chin glistened with evidence of her approval "—and nice."

Mikaela rolled her eyes, feigning irritation. "C'mon. Help me out of this dress."

They both giggled as he assisted her in pulling at the mass of blush-colored, draped satin bunched at her midsection.

"This is gorgeous but what the hell is it?" he cried in frustration, sitting up on his haunches between her legs and searching for a zipper lost among the ruched, asymmetrical fabric.

For a moment she stilled, distracted by the sight of him, his wide, lightly freckled shoulders, strong tanned arms and broad bare chest. Long-ago memories of moments like this one, in the garden, at night by the lake and in his bed years before, flooded her. All the scenes of furtive meetings and secretive giggling as they hurriedly stripped out of cumbersome clothes. Their struggle to achieve the same shamelessly lustful ends under similar time constraints, all returned.

"Stop starin' and help me before I rip you outta this thing," he warned with mild impatience.

She reached between them and finally locating the small hidden zipper, eased it down. Cameron started to peel her out of the dress slowly, like unwrapping a precious gift. Then, in a single fluid motion, he pulled the dress up and over her head, tossing it to the floor, before falling over her again. Her prior knowledge of him guided her movements as she touched him. His breath hitched in his throat as her hand slid slowly from his abdomen down between them. Taking him into her hand, she stroked until the grin fell from his face. Soon, he sounded much the same as she had, grinding out her name through gritted teeth repeatedly as his whole body tensed over hers. Grimacing as he looked down between them, watching her work him in her fist. She panted in time with his moans, bringing him to within a hairsbreadth of climax before guiding him to her entrance.

"Oh Jesus, Kaela, don't move," he groaned, holding perfectly still, trying to compose himself just there.

"Cam," she urged in a needy whisper, raising her hips to meet him and letting him feel how ready she was.

"You want me?" he asked, when he fully regained the ability to speak.

She nodded, having lost hers.

"Say it." His voice was gravel deep and dipped in sin. *"Tell me."*

"Please…"

She didn't need to say more.

She groaned, missing his closeness as Cameron moved away to grab a condom.

He returned within a moment, answering her call, sharing an intimate, knowing smile just between them. They held each other's gaze and sighed in mutual satisfaction as he entered her. Mikaela's whole body tensed then relaxed, the feeling first a trepidation then a kind of soul-deep relief only Cameron had ever given her. The welcome familiarity of his body soothed her remaining anxieties and preoccupations. She yielded to him, her toes curling and flexing with relish at each stroke. Straining on one elbow, his fingers digging into her fleshy thigh, gripping her, urging her open, he repeatedly seated himself, then retreated. She ached to somehow draw him closer, as if for this one moment they could somehow occupy the same skin.

Linking her legs around his, she clung onto him as he thrust against her again and again until they were both keening. Mikaela drove her fingers through the moist hair at his crown, her whole body quaking as he moved.

"Christ, Kaela, you feel so good," Cameron said, echoing her thoughts in a strangled whisper by her ear. He slid in and out, grasping her hands to pin above her head, against the headboard.

They were not each other's firsts, but because they had learned together, experimented to hone and refine sex together, they still knew each other unquestionably. So as Cameron moved, he confidently made Mikaela's nerves sing and skin burn with his expert touch. And at that moment, she knew he was right: they were eminently compatible. It was all still there, the chemistry and insatiable passion for one another. But though this was wonderfully similar—*their feel, rhythm and compatibility with each other all very familiar*—it was *definitely* not the same. There was no comparison even. These many years later, their mature bodies were far more knowledgeable, experienced and adept at giving and receiving pleasure than they had been all those years ago as wide-eyed kids awkwardly fumbling around. And this was far, far hotter and better than anything they had managed back then.

"Oh God, yes!" Mikaela moaned, her body almost rising off the bed to meet Cameron's, her inner walls throbbing in time with his pace. She whimpered as he moved faster, tormenting her until she cried out, begging for either release or reprieve.

"I love you so much!" His voice was muffled, his head buried in her neck, biting into her shoulder then laving the pain away with his tongue as he continued within her.

Still, that was enough. It was enough that he'd said it and enough that she'd heard him. Her eyes popped open, pulling her back from their shared fantasy to reality.

She pushed him onto his back and moved over him then, their sweat-soaked bodies slipping past one another. Mikaela saw a slight furrow form across Cameron's brow as she assumed control. Still, he did nothing but grunt as they worked together, rhythmic and bound. She hovered over him and their gazes met, holding as they moved, both driven by an insatiate yearning. Then closing her eyes, she threw her head back, losing herself to the moment, her hips rocking as it intensified. Pinioning his shoulders to the bed, her nails sank into his corded muscle and she rode him toward a destination she would never reach, where there could ever be enough of this, *and of him*, under and in her. They both hissed as he wrung a cascade of blistering orgasms from her. Then kissing, their tongues twined and voracious, she came in pulsating waves as he chased her over the cliff.

At last Mikaela sank onto his chest, spent, as Cameron held her to him. Both sated and gasping, and unable to speak. But in the silence, her brain misfired, still replaying his words and anxious to break free of his embrace even while he remained inside her.

He had been right, of course. *This was still good.* And yet she could already feel it. If she wasn't careful, she was going to fuck it all up...*again*.

Mikaela was on her stomach and half off the bed when she opened her eyes. Her body ached, but it was a good pain, the kind she appreciated, that made her feel alive in ways she hadn't in years. Their two rounds were hardly enough. This was a feeling that she would happily repeat again and again, given the opportunity.

And she fervently hoped Cameron would be giving her plenty of opportunities from now on.

She was tired but also exhilarated. Mikaela squinted up at the dusky skyline with sunset reflecting off other buildings and peeking through the curtains. A tangle of bedsheets and items of clothing lay in heaps on the floor. Underneath a pile, in the dimly lit room, something glowed.

She glanced to her side where Cameron slept beside her, supine, one arm thrown across her back and the rest of his large nude body taking up the majority of the bed. She eased up, letting his arm slide away, and reached into the pile of things for her flashing phone.

Padding into the bathroom, she closed the door quietly before checking the screen.

Vanessa: WHERE R U?!?

The same message appeared three times in a row. There were others from her mother and Luke that Mikaela swiped away as she dialed her sister directly.

thirty-eight

Mikaela smoothed down her dress for the tenth time as she stepped out of the cab. It was entirely possible that she didn't look as freshly fucked as she felt but looking over at Cameron as he jumped out on the other side, she doubted it.

His aqua shirt was rumpled and half tucked, his tie hung untidily out of his pant pocket and his hair still stuck out in spiky points no matter how many times she'd tried to flatten it. Mikaela didn't know what she looked like, but it could barely be better as he took her hand and they ran through the emergency room's sliding doors.

Cameron spoke with the intake nurse as Mikaela clung to his elbow, her eyes scanning the room for faces she recognized. When he was done, he pulled her through the triage area, flashing the visitor's passes he'd just been given, to reach the innermost parts of the department.

"Dad!" Robin said, exhaling as she saw him coming down the hall.

She ran to him and he finally let Mikaela go to hug his daughter. Mikaela stepped to the side, the embarrassment of the whole thing finally descending on her. What were they doing while his son was going into anaphylactic shock?

Fucking like teenagers, without a care in the world.

"I'm so sorry, Dad," Robin said into Cameron's chest.

Vanessa rose from a seat behind the curtain accompanied, to Mikaela's surprise and mortification, by their mother and Luke. It was just moving from bad to worse. Being there meant her mother's party, her sixtieth, the event she had gone on about for at least the last five years, had ended with a child nearly dying. Natalee frowned as she looked Mikaela over. But Vanessa stepped forward and hugged her fiercely anyway.

"Girl, it was the scariest thing I've ever seen! The boy turned blue! I mean as blue as a berry. And they had the nerve to call us 'colored,'" she whispered in Mikaela's ear. "That's it. I'm carrying an EpiPen for my students everywhere from now on."

Christopher sat up in bed with a cannula in his nose feeding him oxygen. He watched the gaggle of adults around him intently. If he hadn't been in a hospital bed and looked like he was recently run over by a car, swollen and red, he might have seemed fine.

"They had these little egg roll thingies that I think were fried in sesame oil," Robin explained as Cameron ran a hand over Christopher's head, kissing the top.

He frowned down on him. "Egg rolls, Kit? C'mon, buddy."

"They said they were Mexican, Dad! I didn't know!" Christopher's voice was a hoarse rumble.

Cameron looked at Robin.

"He'd already eaten three by the time I saw him." She shook her head, cutting her eyes at her brother.

"But he's fine now, he's fine," Luke said, his usual cheerful self, taking his turn to ruffle Christopher's hair lightly like he was a toddler and not an overgrown thirteen-year-old.

"We couldn't find you, Cameron." Natalee spoke directly to him, a shade less judgment in her countenance than in her tone.

Vanessa held on to Mikaela's shoulders as if bracing her. A second later, she knew why.

"The ambulance told us we needed a parent to meet us at the hospital."

Mikaela's stomach dropped into her feet as her mother went on.

"So, we called Julie."

And as if conjured by incantation and a puff of sulfur and brimstone, at that moment Julie returned, rounding the corner holding a four-coffee caddy and a spare in her other hand. The mild look on her face hardened to stone as she saw Mikaela and Cameron there.

Together.

Dressed in jeans, a T-shirt and ballet flats with her hair pulled up into a ponytail and a clutch tucked under her arm, Julie looked as effortlessly chic as she always did. As if even in a crisis, she knew the exact dress code.

Meanwhile, Mikaela was pretty sure by the way Vanessa tugged at the back of her dress, that it was on inside out.

Julie shook her head as she came closer, offering everyone their drinks.

"Juliette, what are you doing here?" Cameron asked, although the answer seemed pretty obvious.

"They called me!" Her hazel eyes bugged wide and indignant.

Cameron huffed and Mikaela fought the impulse to reach out to him. Calm him.

"You know what I mean."

"The better question is, where were *you*?"

"What the hell is that supposed to mean?"

"That if you were where you *said* you'd be when you left the apartment with my children, we wouldn't be here." She took a long look at Mikaela as she said that, dragging her eyes all the way up her body.

Mikaela grabbed Vanessa's hand, knowing her sister was apt to do or say anything if she believed Mikaela was being insulted. Eyes went in a million different directions as everyone saw an argument igniting.

Cameron caught Julie lightly by the elbow and pulled her away as Robin followed them. "Can we not do this here...?"

"Why'd you even bring them, huh? If you couldn't even spare the time to make sure they were safe?" Julie said before they got too far up the hall to hear.

Mikaela turned then and to her surprise saw her mother doting on Christopher. Her hand was under his chin as she gently spoke with him.

Vanessa cleared her throat to catch Mikaela's attention. "Listen, I have to get back to the hotel and finish up there. Take them back." She eyed their mother and stepfather.

"I am *so* incredibly sorry, Nessa." Mikaela's face would have been crimson if possible.

"Pshaw...it happens."

"Does it? In your experience?" Mikaela smirked. "This *exact* thing?"

Vanessa pursed her lips, shaking her head, jokingly contrite.

"I'll go back with you."

"We all will. Seems like a crowded house now," Luke admitted.

Vanessa patted Mikaela's hand. "Shouldn't you, I don't know, *stick around*?"

"*This* is none of my business," Mikaela said, shaking her head, eyes still trained down the hall. "In fact, I think my presence might be making things worse."

As she spoke, Cameron had his back to them, shoulders shaking as he argued, while Julie glared at her.

thirty-nine

"Tell me again why you left?" Vanessa asked through the cell phone's speaker.

Mikaela sat at her desk turned toward the broad picturesque view of the Hudson River emptying into the Atlantic Ocean in the far-off distance. "You saw Julie's face."

"No doubt. Tensions were high at the end there."

"High?" Mikaela pinched the bridge of her nose. Vanessa was her little sister. And she loved her to a breadth and depth that rivaled the ocean in front of her, but while occasionally comforting, Vanessa's tendency to trivialize the important frequently tried Mikaela's patience. "Did you not see that she wanted me to burst into flames!"

"Well, you *were* getting your back blown out by her ex-husband while their son was having a medical emergency," Vanessa quipped.

Mikaela covered her face and chuckled against her better judgment. Head shaking at the recollection of it, properly abashed now. The mischievousness in her sister's tone made Mikaela smile when by rights she should be guilt-ridden.

"He's been divorced for five years." As she thought about Cameron, her eyes were drawn to the picture frame, which sat in its normal spot on the credenza.

"So, you'd think Julie'd have gotten a life by now."

Mikaela snickered. "According to Cam, she's had plenty of lives since then. A decent amount of them on his dime. Julie just doesn't like to lose. Never has."

"I certainly remember that." The line went quiet. "So, Cameron's really a thing again, huh?"

Mikaela waited for Vanessa's gloating to begin. She *had* called that weeks ago.

"So? You're the one that invited him to Mama's party!"

"I know but…well, that's certainly ancient history repeating itself," she mused. "You sure you're not just rebounding?"

"Why would you say that?" Mikaela sat up from her slouch in the chair.

"Um, Rashad? How are you sure that's over?"

"'Cause it's been over for a while, we just didn't realize it. His words, not mine."

"I did too, but that's a whole 'nother…" Vanessa muttered.

"Well, if you did, then you coulda warned a sistah," Mikaela snapped. "Saved me the wasted time."

"Hey, remember Jahlil?"

Mikaela frowned at the non sequitur, but played along. "Um, your ex-husband? I think so. I recall buying an expensive bridesmaid's dress."

"*Him.*" Vanessa's residual disgust was evident even through one word and a telephone line. "Did I tell you that I ran into him and his newest little girlfriend at brunch the other day?"

"No!"

A quick knock preceded Suze's head, now topped in a crown of serpentine golden-blond braids, poking in from behind her door, as she pointed at the watch on her wrist.

"The nerve!" Mikaela said, giving her assistant a thumbs-up, pulling her shoes back on from where she'd kicked them under her desk.

Suze disappeared as silently as she'd turned up, while Mikaela stood to check herself in the full-length mirror by her bookshelf.

"We haven't gotten to the nerve part yet. So, he corners me on the way to the bathroom and tells me that he regrets the way it ended!"

Mikaela gasped with theatric volume for Vanessa's benefit as she freshened up her lipstick in the mirror. "I know you told him to get gone!"

"Well, that's the thing. I was about to. It was gonna be so good too! That this corny-ass, cheating-ass, anal-retentive who conned my behind into marrying him, could fix that lying-ass mouth of his to tell me that he wanted me back. Girl, I told the muthaf—"

"Shut yo' mouth!" Mikaela played along, giggling.

Vanessa laughed, then sighed. "But the thing was. That's not what he was saying at all."

Mikaela paused. "So, wait, what did he mean?" She sat back at her desk, facing the phone where she'd left it.

"He was saying, he regretted *how it ended*. He realized he'd elevated me onto some pedestal. Believing that being with me would magically make him a better version of himself. But when the magic fizzled, *as it must*, the relationship failed. Now he realizes he's constantly done that. He'd gone from Marie, to me, to the child bride…"

Mikaela shook her head. Five years later and Vanessa still couldn't bear to use her ex-husband's subsequent, far younger ex-wife's name.

"…thinking each time that somehow he'd lucked into the

mystical woman that really only existed in his head, who made everything perfect."

"He is such a jackass. So, you mean to say, he only just discovered that the perfect woman doesn't exist? Boy bye."

Vanessa snorted. "He apologized for not being able to see then that I was never going to be able to make him happy. Because what he was *really* looking for, was something that prevented him from committing to anyone fully—a figment of his imagination."

"You're good. I might have asked him to get out of my face...with my fist."

"You know..." Vanessa's voice took on a dreamy quality and she sighed again. "I've realized this is actually a mistake lots of people make. Since Jahlil, I might have used a relationship or two to prevent me from moving on. Used old wounds to protect me from getting any new ones..."

Mikaela paused assembling her papers, listening. Vanessa was silent on the other end. Ever since she'd found therapy, every story she told and situation she encountered suddenly had to have an additional and greater meaning. "An emotional truth," Vanessa's therapist called it.

Mikaela just called it annoying. Nothing was ever just juicy gossip or a funny anecdote anymore.

"Nes, act like it's not Cameron. Imagine I'm dating someone else. Someone totally new. That I really, *really* like. And so far, it's good, so, I'm not interested in revisiting old wounds."

There was nothing wrong with her. She'd just been waiting for the right guy. And what if that was Cameron all along?

"But it's *not* someone new. It's Cameron, so 'old wounds' are gonna be inevitable."

"Maybe. Maybe not. I don't know. We agreed to leave the past in the past."

Suze appeared at the door again, stabbing at her wrist with a finger, miming a vigorous and elaborate reminder that Mikaela would be running late for a meeting soon.

"But what if you don't?" Vanessa asked. "Are you ready for that?"

"I think—" Mikaela shooed Suze away, miming back at her, arms flailing.

"Particularly when you've used him all this time to disqualify everyone that has had the misfortune to not be him... What if he doesn't work out either?"

"Wow, that's not fair. We're happy just dating—can we please just do that before you get existential on my ass?"

Had she been using a comparison to Cam as a reason why she wouldn't commit? It was true that she had not yet been able to find anything comparable elsewhere since. Had she done that to Rashad?

Mikaela picked up the silver frame with Cameron's picture off her credenza and examined it closely. Only the two of them would ever have known it was him in their garden. The sun created a halo effect behind him that prevented his face from being visible. One of her misjudged shots when she was learning. Still, she'd always looked at that picture and seen him with clarity. In one form or another, nearly every day since she'd found that picture, she'd looked at him.

Did that mean she'd been looking *for* him too, in every subsequent relationship she'd had? And if so, was that really so bad?

Yes, it had all gone desperately wrong in the end. But while it worked, it had been singular, and it was neither the glow of halcyon days that made it significant nor the inexperience of her youth that made it special. It was in the way they had loved each other. The purity of it, the power of it and the depth of it. It was unmatched in her life, still, to this day.

"You realize if y'all get serious enough, you're gonna have to be vulnerable again…at some point." Vanessa's words cut through Mikaela's thoughts, resounding crystal clear and pointed in the quiet of her office, through the miracle of modern technology…and abundant self-righteousness. "If you have any chance of working, you do get that, right?"

"Of course."

"And you're gonna be able to do that without dealing with any of the old shit?" She was dubious.

"Nessa…" Mikaela sighed heavily. Didn't she owe herself this opportunity to find out what this could be?

"Fine," Vanessa relented. "Just promise me you're gonna take care of yourself and remember this conversation?"

"I will."

"Now—" Vanessa lost the austere tone a second later "—we've been on this phone what? Thirty whole minutes? How many times has Suzukea tried to come in and get you?"

Mikaela chuckled. "I don't know what you're talking about."

forty

Mikaela stood at her door waiting for Cameron to climb the two flights to her floor. She leaned against the doorjamb rubbing the top of one bare foot with the sole of the other, her whole body vibrating with nervous energy.

Recently, she'd discovered that dating Cameron was only moderately easier than dating Rashad, though this was mainly her own fault. Other than Cameron carving out some time to slide into her bed or for her to fall into his, for the first week and a half, they weren't able to see each other as frequently as she'd hoped. Mikaela remained uncertain what was happening between them, but she was sure she didn't want whatever they were to morph into just another booty-call situation. As a result, they had largely kept their distance, meeting sporadically for a meal here or there but talking on the phone daily. Still, the inability to see each other consistently was driving them both crazy. So tonight, with both their schedules clear, Mikaela had invited him over promising dinner, a movie and sex…although she wasn't certain in which order they'd occur.

When Cameron finally reached her landing, Mikaela saw what was taking him so long. He was lugging an extra-large square frame wrapped in brown paper and twine with him.

"Aha! She awaits me!" he declared on the top step, breathy and triumphant.

"What joy is joy, if Kaela be not by?
Unless it be to think that she is by...
Except I be by Kaela in the night,
There is no music in the nightingale!"

"No." Mikaela rolled her eyes. "What you're *not* gonna do is be out here butchering Shakespeare in my hallway. Come inside, please."

"You disapprove of my attempt to woo?"

"You are so incredibly corny," Mikaela laughed, moving aside as he entered. "You get that I'm a sure thing tonight, right?"

On her tiptoes, she gave him a kiss on the cheek as Cameron came in and deposited the frame on the floor, propping it up against her coat bench.

"So that means I shouldn't even try?" He grinned, kicking the door closed with a foot and gathering her into his arms.

"What's this?"

The wrapped package on the floor beckoned until Cameron tipped Mikaela's chin over in his direction with a finger.

"A present for you," he said before moving his mouth to her neck, already beginning to bedevil the small space behind her ear.

They were like kids again with the same almost insatiable need to be near each other and touch each other. The days since she'd last seen him were never-ending. Even at work, it had been hard to concentrate and at home, idle, it had been nearly unbearable. Explicit visions of them together had fevered her dreams, disrupting her conversations and derailing whole trains of thought. When he finally buzzed downstairs tonight, it was all Mikaela could do not to be waiting at the door for him, naked.

"I guessed that from the wrapping."

Cameron kissed her, pushing her back against the door and pulling one leg up to hook around his thigh. But her eyes popped open, focusing on the wrapped square again.

"Cam, what's in the package?" Mikaela asked again as soon as his mouth moved from hers back to her cheek and ear.

"Which one?" He grinned, moving her hand from his waist to cover the stiffness in the front of his jeans.

"Ha ha. The one on the floor."

"I told you, a present."

"I want to see it," she demanded, intrigued.

"Now?" He pouted.

"Why not now?"

"'Cause, right now I want you. I've been hard for the past thirty minutes, just thinking about you. The least we can do is do something about it!"

"Thirty minutes? You took *this* and that on the subway?"

"Uber was surging. It would have cost me fifty bucks to take a car," he murmured against her ear.

"*Cheapskate.*" She laughed until he covered her mouth with his again.

Then she momentarily forgot what it was they were talking about. She moaned as he eased his hands into the back of her yoga pants, gripping her bottom in both palms.

"No, no," she still insisted. "I want to see...now."

"Fine." He released her with exasperation and truthfully, she was nearly as disappointed as he was. "At the gallery, you never picked a photo."

"You were serious about that?"

"Aha! I *knew* you didn't believe me. Yes, I was." He turned to her as he unknotted the twine and pulled the heavy brown paper from around the frame. "So, I picked one for you."

He tore the last of the paper free and hoisted the large frame up, turning it to face her. Mikaela's heart thumped as she came closer to examine it.

The large photograph was another moment from her life frozen in amber, just as potent and poignant as the photograph up in Times Square. Mikaela's chest ached, recognizing the moment it was taken. On a deserted shore by the lake, lying in his arms, their last day like that, the last time they'd made love before she left for her sophomore year. Before she'd left him a final time. It had been one of his seemingly haphazard, taken-on-the-spur-of-the-moment shots.

On its surface, it was a literal study of contrasts, both bright and dark. Within the white space was a close-up of Cameron's face. He was young, with the same cherubic look he sometimes got when he smiled broadly. But it was only half his face, awkwardly angled—*what was now called a selfie*—with the camera so close that the entirety of his features didn't even fit in the frame. Primarily, it showed the faint outline of one bright, crystal-blue eye, his nose, dimpled cheek and the beginnings of the gigantic, magnetic smile that had always made Mikaela feel a little off-kilter. But the image was so totally blown out that he almost wasn't there.

The white space of the picture was blindingly white. It added to his almost angelic look, making him more like a specter, an afterthought, though he occupied the majority of the foreground of the frame. But, in the shadow cast by his body, behind him but close, so close, there she was. Not all of her, just her lips, smile and the area from her chin to her breastbone. Not even her nose was visible behind his face.

It was as if one image had been superimposed over another. However, unlike with that other, more famous photograph, there could be no doubt about who the focus of this one was. *Mikaela*...and them as they were. There was no other context to the photo than that.

Her smile and them, together.

Teetering on her feet, she sat on the floor, speechless. Standing behind the huge frame, Cameron didn't notice, still holding it up.

"Didn't you say your personal work was always black-and-white? This photo is actually in color. It just seems monochrome." She rolled her eyes trying to keep tears at bay, clearing her throat, hoping it would distract him.

What he hadn't been lying about was that a lot of his work featured her.

"What are you doing on the floor?" He set the picture frame down, coming over to her.

She bit into her upper lip, holding a trembling hand over her mouth and blinking back the tears that threatened to slip past her lashes.

Cameron put his arm around Mikaela's shoulders, pulling her toward him so they could admire the picture together. "Actually, only my personal photos of you are in color. I made a whole series with them. There's only a few I'd ever choose to show though. I don't want anyone asking me to buy them. But this one has always been yours. Even so far as to be bequeathed to you in my will..."

"Cam—"

"Okay, I have a confession to make. It wasn't so much that I *allowed Glamazon* to use that other photograph...as much as I knew what they were looking for and I sort of *led* them to it, deliberately. I bet Jacqueline's kicking herself for listening to me now."

Mikaela smiled wryly, but her eyes remained on the picture. Cameron used his thumb to catch stray tears, stroking his knuckles across her cheek.

"All that?" she asked in disbelief, more tears escaping her lashes. "Just to get my attention?"

He nodded. "I said I was trying to woo."

She burst out laughing, turning into his body to kiss him. But once their tongues touched, things became more fevered. Mikaela threw her leg across Cameron's lap, placing her arms over his shoulders, cupping the back of his head. Straddling him, she wrapped her calves around his waist. With her body flush against his, grinding in his lap, his erection butted against her, making them both moan. She raked her fingers across his scalp, shamelessly teasing him with her tongue. He groaned. Tracing his lips, she offered then withdrew to frustrate him as he tried to feed on her mouth. He grabbed the back of her neck finally to hold her still, parting her lips with his tongue.

They divested themselves of their shirts. And Cameron yanked Mikaela's bra down, using his wide palms to push her breasts together so he could greedily feast on them both at the same time. He gorged himself on her nipples, kissing and licking, showering attention on them. Her eyes glazed over as she mewled in response. He reached behind her, and with a dexterous ease her bra strap popped, freeing her to spill into his hands.

"Why can't I get enough of you?" He put the question to her, his voice laced with real frustration, as if she could possibly provide the answer. She only knew she felt the exact same.

"I need you." Her voice was high and pleading, as he palmed her breasts, kneading them until she moaned into his upturned mouth.

"The bedroom?" He paused, voice strained as if even that moment taken to ask tested his patience.

She nodded, dreading the moments it would require to get them there.

"C'mon." He rose to his feet with surprising ease, still holding her up as she clung to him.

He glanced around as she pointed over his shoulder at the stairs on the far side of the living room in case he'd forgotten.

"It's too far," Cameron fretted in her ear and she agreed.

He walked her straight through a pair of French doors directly behind them into the empty formal dining room and deposited her on the polished walnut dining table, knocking a chair aside. In the darkened and sparsely decorated rectangular room, the sounds of their panting bounced off the high ceilings, bare walls and parquet floors. But even in the dim light cast from the other room, he held her gaze. Spread out beneath him, lying back against the hardwood surface, Mikaela could just make out the contours of Cameron's body. Things she missed due to their frenzied and frequently rushed assignations, she savored now. As he pulled her pants and underwear off, Mikaela took him all in. His body was still magnificent, more muscled than when they were younger. His shoulders and chest somehow broader while his waist was not as trim. But it was still all built on what she had always recalled as a rather generous endowment and thick, sturdy thighs. Running her hands over him, she pulled him closer by his belt loops to ease his zipper open fully. Then helped push his jeans and boxer briefs down over his hips.

"You are so beautiful." Desire thickly coated his words, making his voice deeper.

Cameron's eyes moved over Mikaela, somehow glittering in the low light. An almost appreciative caress that ran the length of her. In their years apart, she'd grown even less modest, and more prideful about how her athleticism had kept her toned, yet she'd remained ample in the places she always was. And in a lasting holdover from that football game many years ago, she'd discovered that she enjoyed being watched. Cameron's eyes on her, even now, turned her on.

"I think I want you more now than I did then," he said.

Interlocking their fingers, he used their clasped hands to pull her to the edge of the table, before dropping to his knees. He threw her thighs over his shoulders, kissing the soft flesh there, methodical in his journey to her center. She gasped as delicate kisses became more fervent, ravenous, making love to her core with his tongue as deftly and ardently as he had to her mouth. She squealed as he held her with firm arms looped over her thighs that prevented her from moving or scrambling away. Her nails scratched at the table, insensible to the damage she might be doing to its polished surface. Expletives streamed from her mouth.

After a nearly unbearable interval where the fingers of one hand fisted through his hair, holding his head in place as the other pounded with a flat palm against the table, Mikaela's whole body tensed. Then she came hard and thunderingly loud. The sound echoed through the room and quite possibly, the whole apartment.

Cameron rose slowly from between her still-quaking thighs looking as sated and pleased as a cat who ate the cream. And wearing a smile that was just as smug.

His eyes roamed the room as if seeing it anew. "There's nothing in here."

He stepped away, flicking on the light switch, bathing them in light and giving her the first good, unobstructed view of him in his totality.

Cameron was even better than the darkness had hinted at. Still golden tan and sinuous, lean in all the right places but now thicker in others. And most importantly, at that moment, still sporting the prodigious hard-on he had once promised her would always be hers.

Mikaela propped herself up on her elbows, catching her breath. "I don't use it. I had a choice—make it an office or a dining room. I plan to host dinner parties when I make full partner, for the young POC associates. To help them on board and for firm leadership on occasion. So, I decided, a dining room. But I have a laptop and a pad. I mainly just work upstairs in my room."

"Lots of plans. But why aren't you using it now? High ceilings, curtained French doors, it's a beautiful room. There aren't even things on the walls."

"Never got around to it, I guess." She shrugged a little. "But I'm not an artist, I don't have that eye." She stretched in leonine fashion, arms extended above her, legs elongated, feet flexed to a point, and shuddered. "Later, I'll hire someone to come in and do some decorating, when I have the time."

"Later? How long have you lived here?" His eyes tracked her closely, darting between her breasts and face. "It's like you're just stopping through."

"It's been a while," she admitted. "And sometimes I do feel like I'm just passing through. I work so much. But that'll change once I make partner. Plus, so what? Your apartment is sparse too."

"That's 'cause it's not mine. I *am* a visitor."

At that precise moment, she didn't care for the reminder.

"Well, I don't have the time to do it now."

"We'll have to do something about that," he said.

"But it's not something we're gonna have to do *right* now, right?" She spoke pointedly to him as he touched himself, stroking, almost absently.

He smiled, shaking his head.

She yawned, giving a petite, feminine roar.

"You're not getting tired on me...already?" Cameron turned to her in surprise from again traversing the nearly empty room with his eyes. Thought bubbles seemed to pop above his head as his focus narrowed to her alone.

"It's been a long day." She yawned again to his obvious dismay. "Perhaps you shouldn't have done what you did, if you didn't want to wear me out." She uttered the rejoinder full of snark, not expecting his response.

"Kaela." He said her name in all seriousness, tone demanding her sole attention. "I haven't even *begun* to wear you out."

He came back and she sat up to receive him. He lightly brushed his lips across the bridge of her nose, before wordlessly directing her. At his urging, she slid off the table, dropping inches lower in her bare feet, not even clearing his shoulders.

"Turn around."

As he said it, one hand reached for her stomach while the other held her at the base of her spine. He spun her, leaning her over the table on her elbows. Cameron's hands and mouth traveled the length of Mikaela's spine, creating a trail with his lips and tongue that made her shiver. His large palm pressed her down so she was splayed before him. And she trembled when his erection brushed against her as he squatted to retrieve a condom from his pants on the floor. She could feel him, a rumbling, lascivious hum emanating from his throat as his nose just barely grazed the crack of her ass. He separated her legs, pulling them apart as anticipation made him rougher and turned her into a furnace, giving off heat, ready for him. Bracketing her hips to hold her still between his wide palms, he kissed and nipped at each of her cheeks and she gasped, her pulse quickening. Then sweetly, he kissed her core once more before greedily lavishing the bud of her sex with his tongue and nose, raking the sensitive folds lightly with the edges of his teeth, fraying her nerves and making her cry out. There was a pause followed by the crinkling sound of the foil square that made the silent wait for him worse. Cameron rose to his feet again, tilting her hips slightly upward to meet him, giving her an abrupt push forward on the table. Rising up to her toes put her on display before him, titillating her.

"Hang on," he instructed ominously, cupping and directing himself into her in one fluid motion. There was a sharp intake of breath between them, despite both knowing what was coming.

"Oh Christ," he exclaimed, as he slid into her.

Cradling her hips, he began. Using leisurely movements that allowed her a moment to acclimate to his force, he thrusted. Slow and smooth at first, he gradually picked up speed, retreating fully before slamming all the way back into her. Mikaela whimpered, bracing herself against the table. Cameron ran his hand down one silky thigh, hooking it under her knee and bringing it up to rest on the table. Up on one tiptoe, she held on but the effect was disastrous for any composure she tried to maintain, guttural snarls escaping her mouth.

"Fuck!" she groaned.

Holding her by the nape of her neck, Cameron denied her attempt to inch away from the exquisite torture of his body in hers. And eventually, leaning over her, as he did, he eased them both onto the table. With him hovering over her, she lay flat against its cool surface. Gripping the edge, Mikaela rested her forehead against the table's unyielding surface and gasped. Eagerly accepting his barrage, she pushed back into him at every stroke until he groaned too. She bit her lip, as her nerve endings juddered like they were going to ignite and burn her to ash. For minutes, their moans, connecting flesh and arduous breathing were the only sounds echoing throughout the room, bouncing off the walls. It was an obscene melody that also proved a powerful aphrodisiac. Mikaela cried out encouragements, at first coaxing, then urging, then begging him to go harder, deeper, faster, and Cameron obeyed until she could no longer speak at all.

"Baby, please," he moaned, similarly inarticulate, beginning a sentence he couldn't finish as she turned slightly to catch a glimpse over her shoulder of him straining behind her, undone by her eyes briefly connecting with his.

He bent to kiss her, covering her whole body with his and slowing to an indolent, teasing stroke that kept Mikaela's remaining coherent thoughts at a frustrating distance. His heaviness above her was welcome, anchoring her when the sublime sensation of them joined threatened to drive her completely out of her mind and body and send her soaring up into the stratosphere. Yet Mikaela reached for him anyway, grabbing at the hand that pressed her down and the fingers sunken into her hip. She slid hers through his, twining them.

"Oh yes," she hissed, pleading. "Yes."

Cameron eased onto his side then, keeping Mikaela fit to him, his large body spooning hers. They still moved, locked together like the matching pieces of a puzzle, writhing together. She guided their intertwined hands down, between her thighs until they both moaned as he touched her. Fingering the sensitive lattice of nerves there, he pushed her toward a raucous climax. Rubbing in time with each and every fevered thrust of his hips into the cushion of hers, soon Mikaela came with a ululating cry. Her eyes were open but unseeing, only registering stars, pinpricks of light and halos around everything. She hooked her arm around Cameron's neck to bring his mouth down over hers as her whole body quaked with the force of her orgasm. Insatiable, her mouth devoured his moans hungrily as her inner walls throbbed, pulsating wildly and pushing him over the edge as well.

Later, well after their heart rates had returned to normal and Mikaela was sure her full faculties had returned to her, she raised her head from Cameron's cool, damp shoulder. The framed photograph still sat across the room, facing them on the floor where they'd left it by her front door.

"So, you left that to me in your will?" Her voice broke their extended mutual silence.

He nodded. It was the only part of his recumbent body that moved as she lay almost directly on top of him.

"How did you plan to explain that if we'd never found each other again?"

"I wouldn't have had to." He smiled, hands tucked behind his head and eyes fixed on the small chandelier that floated above them. "I'd be dead, remember?"

She hit him lightly on the chest. "I'm being serious."

Cameron shifted, causing her to slide off to his side as he got up on his elbows. "Mikaela, did you think Robin and Kit had no idea who you were when you met them?"

Mikaela blinked. "Uh, yeah." She moved onto her side, propping herself up on her elbow to face him, one leg still draped across his stomach.

"Oh no." He shook his head. "Well, Robin, more so than Kit, knew that the girl in those pictures was a very dear friend. An extremely important person to me. I had told her that years ago, when she first found some of those photos in my basement. But I mean, she loves her mom and I'd never have complicated things more than that for a twelve-year-old. So, I didn't go into detail. We didn't have the type of conversation we would need to in order to fully explain the provenance of the pictures. But everyone knows who you are."

"Everyone?" she repeated, shell-shocked.

"By that I mean they know you're the girl in that photo, in those photos. That's why when you showed up at the gallery, Robin recognized you. In fact, that's what she said to me that day you came by...*the day you ran*."

He skewered her with a disapproving frown. "You keep running away from me."

"I didn't run." Mikaela avoided Cameron's self-righteous smirk by focusing on the picture again. "I just remembered I had somewhere else to be...urgently."

"Have you honestly never figured out that I can tell when you're lying, Mikaela? You do it so badly." He leaned forward and smacked her bottom sharply.

She gasped as the sweet sting of his palm across her hip and cheek resounded in the room. But he followed it up with a caress of the same spot, soothing the tingling warmth that was spreading across her skin. Then he reached for her, urging her onto her back, poised above her, staring down into her eyes.

"Anyway, my daughter's a very astute young woman, so I think she's figured it all out by now. She knows how important you were to me then...and she definitely knows how important you are."

"That I *am*...to you?"

"That you are, *present tense*." He settled in between her legs. "That is something that has never changed."

Mikaela gave a short inhale as he entered her, followed by a long, jagged exhale. Holding his gaze, she smiled, overcome by a rush of feelings, both in her heart and elsewhere.

The truth be told, try as she might have to deny it, this was something that had never changed for Mikaela either.

forty-one

Cameron's apartment was situated above the gallery featuring his work. So, every time she visited now, Mikaela found it interesting to walk past the place where this had all begun again. Coming straight from work that night, she was eager to see him for the first time in a couple of days. And considering the apartment was just a large studio, not a cavernous manor, Cameron took longer than expected to answer the door as voices came from behind it. Mikaela was surprised to find herself standing outside for minutes, then taken aback by a face creased with frown lines when he finally answered. Still, he broke into a welcoming smile upon seeing her.

"Hey there." She stepped through the doorway into his arms, kissing him. "Are you okay?"

"I have company," he said with urgency, in a low voice a second before the person called out.

"Cam, do you have any wine in here?"

"Julie?" Mikaela pressed her forearms into his chest to break out of his embrace. "Julie is here with you?"

"Soda?" Julie called out again.

He nodded, then sighed as if bone weary.

"No, I don't!" he shouted back, still looking at Mikaela. "There's water and beer, that's it!"

"Are the kids here too?" Mikaela asked, searching for understanding.

"No."

A complete sentence, as they say. Mikaela almost chuckled.

There was silence between them as she waited for him to explain in greater detail.

"I'm sorry, she just showed up."

"And you let her in?"

Cameron made a face and she knew the question was beneath her. Mikaela sighed.

"We have some stuff to work out."

"I understand that."

And she did...intellectually, but it didn't make the central question any less relevant. "But I mean, why is she here *now*?"

He crossed his arms over his chest. "Does it matter?"

"Since I thought we had plans ourselves, I think so."

"She turned up on my doorstep, unexpectedly at—" *he checked his watch* "—nine thirty tonight. But, Kaela, I knew you were coming. You remember that, don't you?"

"What I remember is that you've been cursing her name. And not too long ago you were castigating me for making nice with her. What's changed? Or are those only rules for me while you do whatever?"

"Oh, Kaela, gimme a break! You aren't alone, I have things going on in my life right now too, *including dealing with my ex-wife occasionally.*" He jabbed a thumb toward the living space behind the wall, pursing his lips as if holding back more. "We have to discuss the end of the summer and start of the school year for the kids. And I have a flight tomorrow morning. I'm going to Paris to meet a few people and sign some papers on a grant I just got. That I need."

Mikaela was acutely aware of what Cameron wasn't saying—*he was busy*. The reality was he was too busy for her and whatever it was she imagined was going to happen tonight.

Mikaela gathered her thoughts, searching for magnanimity.

"Congrats." She tried to keep her tone light and her irritation at bay. "What—what grant?"

"Le Prix Taillefer pour Arts Visuels et Métiers d'Art."

She was envious of how fluidly the French flowed from his lips. Yet more evidence of the full life he had lived without her.

"Oh my God, Cam!" As ignorant to the ways of the art world as she was, even Mikaela had heard of the Taillefer Prize. She grabbed his hand, squeezing it and smiling at him. "The Genius Grant?"

This grant was awarded annually to artists considered extraordinary in their field, innovators, visionaries and industry leaders. More practically, it was also one of the highest honors a visual artist could achieve. It came with a nearly-one-million-dollar stipend. Still, Cameron shrugged, impervious to her enthusiasm.

"Yeah well, it'll go a long way toward covering my expenses." He tipped his head toward the other room. "Especially, her regular alimony payments…not to mention damages if this thing takes a turn."

"Don't think that way. You'll win. Todd says it looks good."

"Does he?"

Cameron sounded unconvinced. The proceedings had already dragged on long past their last proposed settlement, Mikaela suspected as a way to punish Cameron for their recent indiscretion at the hospital. Then just last week, Julie's team had requested a short continuance Todd didn't even bother to challenge. It concerned Mikaela but Todd claimed he wasn't worried. Still, Cameron fretted, rightfully to Mikaela's mind, that Julie's lawyers had something else up their sleeves. Julie was petty but also shrewd, and if the proceedings were being held up deliberately, as he suspected, Mikaela knew there had to be a damn good reason. Even though neither of them could figure out what the hell it was.

Mikaela thought she spied movement through the archway behind him. Cameron glanced over his shoulder, then extended his arm urging Mikaela back outside his front door. She couldn't help it; her eyes widened in indignation.

"I don't want her overhearing us," he explained.

"Why does that matter?" Mikaela nearly shouted.

Cameron quirked his mouth to the side. Contrite, she acquiesced, stepping back into the hall with him right behind her. He pulled the door shut. "Mikaela, she and I just have stuff to hash out."

This brought Mikaela back to the awkward moment she now found herself in, standing with her—*What? Lover? Boyfriend?*—outside his door. Twenty years later, and Julie had somehow managed to remain the constant unspoken thing between them.

"Well, is she leaving soon?" Mikaela asked, trying her best to seem reasonable and understanding.

Cameron opened his mouth to respond when the door opened and Julie's head popped out. "What are you doing out here— Oh hello, Mike!"

Julie sounded surprised, though her face didn't seem surprised in the least. Cameron's mouth set and his eyes went dark.

"Hi, Julie."

It was as if the deposition and the hospital never happened.

Julie smiled warmly. Cameron had not been wrong about her; she turned on a dime.

"Are you coming in?" She inspected Mikaela, sizing her up as she had at the hospital. But unlike the last time, this time Mikaela was raring for a fight.

"Considering it," Mikaela lied, cocking her head.

Cameron smirked.

"Cam and I were just doing a little reminiscing. You'd be a perfect third wheel for a little of that."

"Juliette." Cameron's expression hardened and his tone advised caution, watching her out of the corner of his eye.

Mikaela glanced from Julie to Cameron, waiting to see if he would say anything more.

He didn't.

"I don't think so but can you excuse us anyway?" Mikaela asked instead.

"Sure, good to see you as always, Mike." Julie dipped back inside as if she was in her own home while Cameron just stood there, still watching Mikaela.

"What the fuck is this?" Mikaela was galled now. Even if she had wanted to be an adult, rational and not accusatory, that was all gone. Incinerated in a flash of white-hot anger.

Mikaela waited for the explanation Cameron was denying her, that she now felt owed.

"If I wanted to be with Juliette, what exactly do you think would be stopping me?"

"I don't think you want to *be* with her! I just don't want to see her manipulate you."

"It's your buttons she's pushing not mine." Cameron sighed, coming up to Mikaela as she pouted. "C'mon, rain check?"

In his bare feet and her ridiculously tall heels, their faces were very close. His mouth hovered over hers, teasing her.

As it always had, Cameron's proximity alone defused some of Mikaela's anger. Which he clearly knew, pulling her closer. Still, it pulsed like electrical currents at her temples just thinking about Julie inside his apartment, as she stood relegated to the hallway, but Mikaela's annoyance was dissipating.

As he slid his large palms past her blouse, into her skirt and over her hips, Cameron's eyes widened when he felt her skimpy underwear, and a small smile crept across his lips.

Mikaela grinned in spite of herself, nodding, gratified by his lust. "See what you're missing?"

He nodded, pouting.

"When will you be back?" She slid her hands up over his shoulders.

"On Friday," he answered, brushing his nose lightly across hers. "Maybe we can go somewhere for the weekend?"

"Like a vacation?" Mikaela's eyebrows rose. It was a foreign concept. "This weekend?"

"Wait, do I need to clear it with Suze first?"

She rolled her eyes. "I think I can clear my own calendar."

"Can you?" Cameron teased.

"In fact, I'll take care of *all* the details. Just be ready for me…next time," she sniffed, giving him a light swat on his backside.

forty-two

"Robbie is gonna hate that she missed this. But ballet's more important… I guess." Cameron sat across from Mikaela at the sidewalk café. "Kit, what do you think?"

Christopher, seated beside her, pushed his plastic, tortoise-shell Wayfarers farther back on his head and squinted out at the crowded but slow-moving thoroughfare called Circuit Avenue. "I mean, New York is very cool. I like it a lot. But yeah, it's slower, nicer here. Definitely more of Robin's vibe. Mine too."

Cameron winked at her. "Children after my own heart."

Mikaela shrugged.

She hadn't been back on Martha's Vineyard since she, Vanessa and a few friends had pooled their funds to go in on the purchase of a summer house near the Inkwell. Located near the legendary generationally black beach, the house was an investment property that could double as a vacation home. But the closing was the one and only time Mikaela had ever braved the packed Interstate 95, interminable Route 28 and a ferry ride to make the long five-plus-hour trek to it. Still, when Cameron had wanted to take a spur-of-the-moment, long-weekend trip, this place was Mikaela's first thought. And after a little strong-arming and horse-trading with her co-owners, she'd made both the trip and a far shorter, one-hour flight directly from New York happen.

"It's really beautiful, Kae," Cameron said, for the fourth or fifth time before reaching across the table for her hand. "Thank you."

Mikaela grinned, sitting back in her chair, basking in a self-satisfaction that helped make the weather better, the sun brighter and her food tastier. She stretched for him without moving and they both giggled when she failed to reach, wiggling their fingers at each other from a distance.

"I'm gonna have to be rolled onto that flight on Monday, I see it already."

The many picked-over plates sitting between the trio attested to that fact.

"Maybe if you don't keep having dessert after *every* meal while we're here, I'll be able to fit you into a seat?" Cameron's eyes lit with mischief.

"Mad Martha's ice cream requires my fealty." She shrugged. "I don't make the rules, right, Kit?"

Cameron turned to his son, who was people-watching, catching his attention. "Kit?"

"Huh?"

Cameron and Mikaela shared an amused look.

"You have plans for the afternoon?" Cameron asked. "Or you want to join us?"

"I'm thinking first, a tour of the gingerbread houses at the Methodist Camp Meeting Grounds. Then maybe, what do you think, the MVCVA Art Gallery?" Mikaela asked.

Cameron nodded, elbow on the table, furrowing his eyebrows and covering his mouth with the heel of his palm as Christopher's face grew increasingly horrified.

"Um, I'm gonna head over to the Flying Horses carousel and meet up with the kids staying in the house next door. See what's good with them. They talked about heading out to… Little Bridge, they called it?" Christopher excused himself and vacated his seat hurriedly.

Mikaela nodded as Cameron stifled a snort.

"Keep your phone on. Be back by four." Cameron sobered, putting on his sterner dad voice. "We're going to check out the lighthouses in East Chop and Edgartown later… What?"

His son's aggrieved face told a whole tale of forced labor and unjust servitude.

"We're having dinner in Edgartown, so we need to get started early. Eight-o'clock reservations."

Mikaela's eyebrows rose, impressed with Cameron for making plans on his own.

"Fine." Christopher huffed, shuffling off, a lumbering mass of gangly limbs.

Mikaela laughed, imagining his father at that same age.

"So, Ms. Marchand." Cameron turned to her as soon as his son was out of earshot. "What are we *really* doing with the next four hours?"

She grinned wickedly.

Cameron's arm draped across Mikaela's shoulders as they stood waiting for their table by the hostess desk at the restaurant that night.

Christopher stood a few feet away peering into a lobster tank near the door, tapping lightly on the glass.

That was where they were when Todd and the whole Hoover clan, including two tan-faced, elder-WASPs Mikaela could only imagine were his in-laws, found them as they exited the restaurant's dining room.

Cameron's lips were affixed to Mikaela's temple whispering filthy recollections of their afternoon together under his breath, just as Todd's wife, Anita, spoke.

Mikaela froze at the sound of her name.

"Nita!" She choked out the words. "Oh my gosh! Hi!"

Cameron's arm slid off her shoulders and he stepped back as she nudged him, placing space between them.

"Mike, look at you!" She took Mikaela by the hand, raising it slightly to better display her simple, but elegant daffodil-yellow maxi dress. "I almost didn't recognize you."

She and Anita Hoover were not truly friendly enough to be this familiar, but in the moment Mikaela was too discomposed to react. Her stomach did revolutions like she'd been pitched downhill and had not yet stopped tumbling… and that's what it felt like, totally off-balance. Todd glanced from Cameron to Mikaela and back, his lips curling into a gross reptilian smile as realization came to him.

"Mike." Todd stepped forward and kissed her on the cheek as if they hadn't just seen each other three days earlier when she closed her office door in his face. "Mr. Murphy," he said formally as they shook hands.

"Todd."

The men made the numerous introductions, including between the kids, and even Todd's leathery, toast-colored in-laws, the Forsyths.

"*You* come to the Vineyard, Mike?" Anita said, her voice lilting but puzzled as if she was pleasantly surprised to discover Mikaela ran manned missions to Mars on select weekends. "My parents have a place in Chilmark. We try to come out at least once a summer."

Uniformly looking like they were ripped from the pages

of *Town and Country* magazine, the Hoover-Forsyths, according to Anita, were always on the Vineyard for a month or more. Unfortunately, ofttimes without Todd, who was so frequently and inconveniently chained to his desk back in Manhattan.

Mikaela fought a snort. It was more accurate to say Todd's associates did most of his work so he was free to practice his golf swing at the Chelsea Piers driving range.

"Oh, I love your hair down like this!" Anita reached a marauding hand out, to bounce the curled braids that fell freely over Mikaela's shoulders. "You should wear it this way more often…"

Mikaela inched out of her grasp, her chest tightening, heart thudding.

Meanwhile, Anita's eyes darted between Mikaela and Cameron trying to make out more than the plainly obvious as she rambled.

"Mikaela owns a place out here too," Cameron interjected on her behalf, irked.

Mikaela bristled at his no doubt well-intentioned defense but still, words failed her, beyond the simplest pleasantries. A panicked half smile remained plastered across her face.

"Oh?" Todd's eyebrows rose.

"Just a share," she answered finally as the Hoover collective nodded. "With friends."

"In Oak Bluffs," Cameron offered up.

Mikaela groaned, wishing he'd keep his mouth shut. As her dad always used to tell her, *"Never let white folks figure out what you've really got…or they'll want to pay you less."*

"Mr. Murphy? Party of three?" The hostess appeared, relieving the tension like a spigot and sporting a confused look at the group of ten that stood before her.

"Well, twice in one summer," Anita observed, reaching

over for another hug and feel of Mikaela's hair. "Am I lucky or what? Then probably again in October at the partnership dinner, right? Fingers crossed!" Anita spoke like she didn't know Mikaela was her husband's direct competition. "If you want to have lunch while you're still here, give Todd a call, okay?" she added cheerily.

Mikaela pressed her lips together, nodding, willing a small smile into existence.

"Puppy, I bet they've got to be back in NYC on Tuesday like me," Todd corrected his wife. Deliberately calling attention to the inappropriate tryst-shaped elephant standing among them. "In fact, we have that meeting next week, don't we?"

Cameron nodded, smiling thinly, Todd's implication not lost on him either.

"Fast ferry?"

"Ah, flight," Mikaela answered with continued reluctance.

Todd's eyebrows rose again, impressed. "Guess I'll see you both back there then."

Mikaela smirked, feeling as if she'd been blindsided by a sledgehammer.

"Kaela, breathe." Cameron bent to whisper in her ear as the group cleaved into two and the Hoover-Forsyths left.

Mikaela allowed Cameron to steer her by her shoulders through the lively dining room, steps behind Christopher and the hostess.

"He's gonna say something to Art." Mikaela's hands began to tremble.

"You aren't on *Glamazon* anymore, so, it really doesn't matter. You told me that yourself. Besides, he wants us to win the case too."

Cameron spoke into Mikaela's hair, his voice acting as a balm, a soothing murmur in her ear. Still, her shoulders remained rigid in his grip, unable to shake off the dread of what now awaited her Tuesday morning.

"It doesn't matter. It *looks* bad."

The hostess placed their menus on the table, excusing herself as Cameron and Christopher sat. Mikaela hesitated.

"I have to say something," she announced.

She didn't know what to do or how she could mitigate this. Wasn't the truth that she and Cameron were seeing each other? There was no way to clean that up. What would the partners think?

"Mikaela, don't." Cameron shook his head. "Our relationship isn't his business, isn't anyone's business."

"Your wife made sure to make it their business," she snapped.

Christopher looked up from his menu in surprise as Cameron's eyes narrowed on her.

"Oh, Kit." She took a shallow breath, then cleared her throat. "I'm sorry."

He shook his head, but his brows knitted together as he returned to a thorough examination of the menu in his hands.

"Mikaela." Cameron scowled at her. "Calm down."

Her blood boiled at his words. She resented being turned into "just another irate black woman" anytime she was upset.

"You know how much I hate being told that."

"I do, I apologize. But pleas—"

"I have to say *something*, Cam!" She gripped the back of her chair, her heart racing, pleading. "I can't claim that I have the best interests of the firm at the forefront when I'm sleep—" *Cameron glared at her* "—sl-slipping up here," she stammered, correcting her reckless tongue.

"Buddy..." Cameron turned his attention to his son. "Why don't you go pick out your lobster?"

"I'm not having lob—" Christopher began before glancing up at his father's expression.

"I'm so sorry, Kit," Mikaela repeated as he rose and excused himself without responding.

"Kaela." Cameron's words were slow and deliberate as if he was dealing with an irrational person, which annoyed her further. "They don't pay you for, and aren't entitled to, all of your time and energy. They don't get to dictate who you spend it with either."

"But they do…"

Cameron's words hung at the periphery of her thoughts. Foremost, she decided, she needed to find a way to disarm Todd.

"Until I make partner, they do."

"That's asinine. But you explain this to them and I'm telling you, they'll definitely think so." Cameron was emphatic. "In fact, you say anything to them and you'll be telling them they're right."

What was asinine was giving Todd Hoover the power to walk into their office on Tuesday and detonate a bomb on all her aspirations.

"Sit down." Cameron pulled out her chair as she stared blankly down at it.

"I'm gonna call Art when we get back to the house." The time on her phone screen read eight fifteen.

Could it wait that long?

"No," Cameron said firmly, startling Mikaela.

"You're right, maybe I'll just pop out to the parking lot for a second and do it now."

"No, it can wait an hour. Sit down!"

Mikaela frowned at the presumption in his tone.

"Sorry, sorry." Cameron sighed heavily, shaking his head

at himself. "Just…can we…can we please, *please* just stop and eat something first? Before you spin out about this?"

"This is my job, Cam… You know how important it is."

A sullen darkness transited his face at her words, his brow furrowing and mouth becoming a flat line.

"Fine, Mike. If that's what's most important to you right now, go do it." He picked up his menu, dismissing her. "Can you send Kit back in when you see him, please?"

"Two seconds, I just need to handle this," Mikaela muttered, already turning on her heels toward the exits, dialing.

forty-three

"Morning, Mike."

Mikaela barely caught the elevator, sticking her hand in the closing doors to step in. She plucked her earbuds out, to acknowledge the speaker. "Oh hi, Peg. Morning, how are you?"

She hated running into her coworkers outside of the office, even when she was only in the elevator. Before she got her game face on, people were liable to see anything. Like today, a starry-eyed half smile inspired by the rest of her weekend away, where she and Cameron had spent much of their remaining time making up. And which was painted widely across her face until a moment earlier.

"I'm good," senior partner Margaret Tillerson answered, looking her over.

Mikaela turned to face the door, lightly touching the bun in her hair and smoothing down her dress.

"Do you think I can grab a little of your time?" Margaret asked as they both watched the floor numbers rise on the panel above the door.

"Sure." Mikaela woke her phone up and checked it. "What's three thirty look like for you?"

Margaret chuckled. "Oh no, dear. I mean *now*. Do you have a minute?"

Her face was perfectly serious, but a small smirk suggested something more. Mikaela could count on her hands how many times in her entire tenure at the firm she'd had a private conversation with Margaret. In fact, when she'd first become a junior partner, Mikaela had hoped to mentor under her but Margaret was uninterested. Preferring to be the only female senior partner of standing and disinterested in blazing a trail for other women to follow. Not that she wasn't pleasant or quietly encouraging, just not mentor material.

"Sure," Mikaela said, stepping off the elevator when the doors opened.

Margaret followed silently all the way to Mikaela's office, only nodding at Suze as they walked by.

"Boss, just a reminder. You have a call with Ms. Dampierre at eleven." Suze, now sporting a burgundy pageboy, said, watching the two women walk past her desk. "Good morning, Mrs. Tillerson."

Mikaela's anxiety screamed like a siren in her head, her heart thumping like a jackhammer. Margaret surveyed the room as she crossed to the couch, obviously impressed. She'd never been in Mikaela's office before and her eyebrows rose and fell as she scrutinized the decor.

"So, Mikaela…" Margaret sat down, sighing as if she was just relieved of a heavy load. "Tell me, what is it you want?"

Mikaela took a deep breath, stepping farther into the room, remembering that this was her space, and trying to reclaim it. She sat in a chair near her desk and turned to her guest. "What do you mean?"

"I mean, you've been here for twelve years and I've been

extremely gratified by your rise. I like to think I helped you with that."

Did she really? Mikaela could have laughed at that. *How, by standing by and watching?*

"You're focused—no husband, no kids—*not that I'm finding fault with that.* Because Brian and the kids definitely slowed my climb—added at least ten years to it." She propped her elbow up on the armrest and crossed her legs at the ankle getting comfortable. "But you? You've been smart about it and now you're almost there. So, I'm here to pick your brain, what do you want?"

Almost there? Mikaela held in a smile.

"After partnership? Well…to implement a pet project of mine that I think the partners will really like…that will benefit the firm, of course." She detailed the broad strokes of the more robust Diversity, Equity and Inclusion Program she'd created.

Margaret nodded all the while. "Sounds good. Anything else? Anything extracurricular?"

Mikaela frowned, confused.

"Anyone special? Work-life balance and all that?"

Had Todd already opened his big mouth? Mikaela straightened in her chair. How many had he told?

When she reached Art on Saturday night, he had barely seemed interested. After an extended silence, he advised her that because she and Cameron had a preexisting relationship, it negated some of their legal exposure. And the fact that Mikaela was no longer directly in charge of the *Glamazon* case eliminated the rest.

"A doctor…?" Margaret specified.

"No, we broke up." Mikaela relaxed, shaking her head.

"Oh. I'm sorry."

"Um, but, there's someone else."

Mikaela didn't know why she'd volunteered that. Other than wanting to talk about Cameron, claim him, if only obliquely.

"It's not serious though," she amended.

Margaret's eyebrow rose, her green eyes widening.

And why had she said that?

"Well, good," Margaret said, getting to her feet, satisfied.

By what? Mikaela wasn't sure.

"You're in the home stretch now, Mikaela."

Mikaela got up too, the unspoken question on her face.

"Some advice—don't get distracted. Not now."

Mikaela found that unnecessarily cryptic. Was this the word coming down from on high, a little hint from the partners?

"Especially not by a man."

Mikaela smiled politely, a tight grin over a closed mouth. Everyone in this office knew, she ate, slept and dreamed Wexler, Welford and Bromley.

"Now don't get me wrong." Margaret countered herself, as if she'd heard Mikaela's thoughts out loud. "I've watched you, Mike. And I'd be a hypocrite if I suggested you shouldn't have a life outside of work. In fact, *you* need one. But there's plenty of time for romance afterward. *Now, focus.*"

forty-four

"So then, I let her take a picture of me as a kind of even exchange and promised to send her a copy of each," Cameron explained to Mikaela.

Mikaela reclined against the kitchen counter. Large frames lined the opposite wall. Cameron stood topless inspecting the newly printed photographs. The images occupied his mind as they both inspected them.

When she came last night, he'd been able to set them aside so that they could enjoy themselves but as usual when the sun rose, both their priorities shifted away from one another.

Still, having been not quite finished dressing for work earlier when Cameron waylaid her for round three on the counter, Mikaela now stood in his tiny kitchen in only her blouse. And for the first time in a while, she was late for work, but found it hard to leave.

Despite it being a studio, Mikaela liked it there. Cameron's sublet was spacious, with a front door foyer, a dedicated living room space and a small bedroom alcove with a Murphy bed that they made good use of overnight and again early in the mornings. Though not his, the whole apartment fit his aesthetic, in that it was spartan, simultaneously large yet cozy and the furniture was attractive but utilitarian. Mikaela enjoyed hanging out there with him. It made them spontaneous and youthful, in a way that her more well-appointed apartment with its king-size mattress and luxe furnishings didn't. Reminiscent of their old days.

As Cameron spoke, Mikaela reached up on her tiptoes and ruffled the hair on the side of his head with the tips of her fingers, before pushing it behind his ear.

He didn't say anything, holding still until she'd stopped.

"What was that?" He laughed.

"You need a haircut. Quick, gimme a pair of clippers. I could do something with this. You know, like guys used to do back in the day when they got shaped up?"

"Like Vanilla Ice?"

"No. Ugh." She rolled her eyes at him. "Not like *Vanilla Ice*. Like the cool guys that used to cut designs into their fades."

"Oh so, you mean *exactly* like Vanilla Ice," he teased. "Or maybe MC Serch?"

"Forget it," she said, pulling her skirt off the back of a nearby chair and stepping into it.

Cameron laughed at her. "So, when am I gonna see you again?"

"Well, I've been swamped," Mikaela hedged with her back turned, Margaret's words coming to her. Cameron always wanted so much of her time and she was surprised to find she frequently wanted to give it to him too.

"I had to beg you to come over last night or it would have been almost a week since I saw you last." Cameron came up from behind and hugged her to him.

"I know. But I have to put this Zenigent contract thing to

bed. Once Jackson and I can get that memorandum of understanding banged out and ratified by their rank and file, I'll be free and clear."

Mikaela squirmed in his arms until Cameron let her go and walked back over to his photos, examining them. "Well, we know that's not true."

"What? You know I'm chasing that promotion. I have to give—"

"I know, one thousand percent," he recited, "because they don't see you as a valuable asset. And they take you for granted."

"Whoa, whoa. I didn't say all that." Mikaela sniffed, her chin rising.

He turned back to her. "You don't have to say it, I have eyes. They don't value you or fully appreciate what you bring to the table."

She blinked, frowning. "Why are you saying this?"

"I think I'm jealous." Cameron put one of the frames down and came back to her, putting his hands around her waist. "I want all the time you give them. And I know I can show my appreciation better than they do."

His smile made Mikaela feel like her panties were going to melt off her body.

"You work a lot too." She gripped him by the wrists, fingers pressing into his skin, to make him remove his hands.

"I do." Cameron released her with a kiss to her temple, heading back to his work. "But I play hard too."

Mikaela took a deep breath. Her body could certainly attest to that.

"The simple fact is, they don't deserve you."

"I appreciate your faith."

"It's not faith when I know it to be true." There was no

flattery in his words, not even looking her way as he said them, like an incontestable truth.

Mikaela smiled, grabbing her pantyhose from the floor where they'd tossed them the night before. She crisscrossed the room reconstituting the elements of yesterday's outfit, stuffing them into her gym bag.

"We're not gonna keep this up, are we?" Cameron broke an extended silence to ask.

"Are you not enjoying yourself?"

"I am. But I want to do more than just 'enjoy myself' a couple nights a week."

"Well, since you have Kit in this apartment without any bedrooms, I didn't think you'd want me here *every day*."

"You know that's not what I meant. And Kit splits his time in the City between me and his mother's rental, so don't use that as your excuse."

"*Excuse?* I don't need an excuse. I have a plan and I'm right at the finish line. Please don't try to make me feel guilty for putting that goal first."

Cameron glared at her, his jaw clenching. "Have I *ever* made you feel guilty about putting your goals first? Better yet, has there ever been a time when your goals didn't automatically come first?"

Mikaela was stunned, standing in the center of the room, her mouth agape. "What are you even talking about? We've only been dating a few weeks."

"You're absolutely right, Mike. I don't know what I'm talking about either." Cameron walked into the bathroom, slamming the door behind him.

forty-five

A week later, Mikaela sat at her desk squeezing the bridge of her nose. In her boredom, the contract in front of her had become a jumble of clauses and subclauses.

At least the *Glamazon* portion of Altcera's business had had a little drama.

This Zenigent labor contract stuff was brain numbing and never-ending. And the union rep handling it for the workers was a snooze too. Sometimes those guys could be a hoot, full of piss and vinegar from years of working with their rank and file. This guy, however, had never been more interesting than he was, some anonymous business agent from the union's collective bargaining unit. Listening to him drone on with their labor litigator on her speakerphone was like a sedative. She fought sleep, desperate to stay engaged.

"This seems fairly simple, gentlemen," Mikaela interjected. "There are floating holidays, three of them, that your members are free to use for their birthdays."

"We're accustomed to a separate dedicated-day provision delineated in the holidays clause of any new contracts..."

Her door easing open caught Mikaela's attention.

Yet it wasn't Suze's currently rose-gold and cotton-candy-like bouffant Mikaela expected sliding through the crack, but Cameron's face there instead. She'd left him asleep in her bed that morning but somehow was still overjoyed to see him at her door. She could imagine herself getting accustomed to this arrangement.

She brightened, holding up a finger to her lips as he opened his mouth to speak.

"Simon? I'm sorry to cut you off. Jack, you there?" Mikaela stood while speaking into the phone to her associate on the floor below. "Can you take over? Something just came up. Simon, I'm going to leave you in Jackson's very capable hands. We'll circle back to this point in our next call."

"Will do, Mike," Jackson said through the phone.

"I really want to get this sorted for the membership as soon as possi—"

"Jack's got you covered, Mr. Skillman, I promise."

Mikaela's finger hovered over the disconnect button until Jackson began to speak again then she pressed it.

"Sorry." Cameron frowned.

She brushed it off coming around the desk hurriedly as he walked in and reached for her.

As they kissed, Mikaela caught a glimpse over Cameron's shoulder of Suze, sitting at her desk with the chair turned toward them. Her expression was all happy endings and sunsets and rainbows, breasts heaving a sigh, eyes misty like she was watching her favorite romantic movie. Mikaela rolled her eyes at her love-struck assistant, sidestepping Cameron to close her door before the girl actually swooned in her office chair.

Cameron was on her again before she could fully turn back to him.

Something was off.

"What's wrong?" she asked as he pulled her into him.

Mikaela held Cameron's face between her hands, staring into his eyes, the blue darkening like a tumult at sea.

"We lost." He sighed, his chest becoming concave.

"What?" Mikaela pulled herself out of his arms as he let her shift dress slip through his fists.

"Juliette got affidavits from those damn Douglas twins and Nicki Henderson stating that they were with her the day she signed the model release."

Hearing those names was like an echo from her past. Mikaela hadn't spoken to or thought of Corey, his brother Rory or their friend Nicole in years. Particularly since Julie had gotten them all in the dissolution of their friendship like a marital property division.

"I don't understand." Mikaela led him to a seat. "So, they admitted she signed it, just like you've always maintained? Did you remember that?"

"I don't know, maybe. But Julie produced what she claimed was an original, so that's moot." Cameron fell heavily onto Mikaela's couch, shielding his eyes with a hand. "Apparently, her mother had it. Is that possible? I don't know. Technically, we never lived with Miss Liza and she never lived with us. But for whatever reason, the original form was supposedly up in some storage space at her retirement home. Gabe and his husband searched and found it in with some of our old shit."

"So, what was the problem?"

"It's undated. But they all swore under oath that it was signed before Julie's big birthday party that August."

Mikaela leaned back against her desk, folding her arms. She remembered that summer. If true, it *was* before Julie's eighteenth birthday…when she was still a minor, legally incapable of entering into a contract with anyone.

Meaning that Cameron did not have the right to license that photograph to *Glamazon* without the subjects' permission…precisely as Julie's lawyers asserted.

"Todd, Monica and Celia don't think it's worth continuing on now."

"We'll probably send someone down to properly depose Nicki and the guys, but truth is, Todd's right," Mikaela admitted dejectedly.

Cameron's head bobbed in reluctant agreement. "Now her lawyers are talking about making a motion or something?"

"Yeah, for summary judgment." She sighed.

"All I understood was that they're going to start hashing out very favorable settlement terms with her lawyers. So, it's just a matter of how vindictive she plans to be… And judging from her attitude in there, I'd say very."

"Do you think the release was real? That she had it all along? That she knew?"

The thought had occurred to Mikaela already that this whole lawsuit was in pursuit of something else entirely.

"I think it's possible."

"Then why wait to drop that bomb?"

"For this." Cameron threw a hand up, motioning around the room. "The drama and spectacle and aggravation it'd cause. Like I said, Juliette is not who you remember. And seeing us together drives her up the wall. This was probably her nuclear option, employed as a final play to screw me."

"Like I screwed you," Mikaela finished.

Cameron's eyes flew to her face. "What?" He rose from the couch and came to her.

"C'mon, you know we antagonized her. Our relationship, seeing us back together again. First, we make a scene at Robin's recital, so she embarrasses me in front of my colleagues and then we're together at the hospital in front of your kids, so she prolongs things. We take Kit to the Vineyard with us and now this. All because I can't stay away from you."

Was Mikaela behaving like a child ruled by her hormones where Cameron was concerned? Most of the time all she knew was she wanted him as much as he wanted her. But because of that, had Mikaela helped Julie's cause and damaged Cameron's?

"No." Cameron drew Mikaela up by her elbows from leaning against the edge of the desk, trading places. "Juliette is just being a spoiled brat."

Seated on the corner of her desk now, he held Mikaela in his arms. She hugged him back, tucking herself under his chin, in a funk.

"Too many people have catered to Juliette in her life. Her mother, her father. God, even I did it for a decade! Now I won't anymore, it just makes her crazy. She believes that she's entitled to everything she wants."

"And she gets it, doesn't she? She wanted you and I stupidly pushed you right into her arms. Now, she wants the proceeds from this license and because of me, you have to give in to her."

"Because of you?"

"Because of us, *this*," Mikaela hissed, irritated by his semantics. "Can you even afford this lawsuit?"

He swatted at the air. "I think I can swing it. But it's not your problem anyway."

She'd come to understand that Cameron was successful, and quite comfortable, but legal damages were likely to be in another stratosphere of expense. Plus, whatever he'd have to pay *Glamazon* back directly to recoup his part of their legal fees—*an indemnification clause she knew any lawyer worth their salt put into Cameron's licensing agreement*—was liable to put Cameron thousands of dollars in the hole, if not more.

"Don't dismiss this, Cam," Mikaela warned, stabbing at his chest with her fingertip. "This is bad."

"I'm fine."

"No, really," she insisted, easing back to see his eyes.

"Is this about me and you, or you and her?" he asked, suddenly tetchy himself. *"Or is it actually about this deal with Altcera and your promotion here?"*

"Wait?" Mikaela pulled herself away. "What does that mean?"

"Look, I'm done with it all." Cameron mimed dusting his hands clean. "I don't really care at this point. Fuck this lawsuit and fuck Juliette." He said it as if repeating a personal mantra. "If I knew then what I know now, the *only* reason I would even bother fighting her at all is because it allowed me to find you again. As far as I'm concerned, that makes all this shit worth it."

"Why?" Mikaela was genuinely puzzled. This loss was potentially financially crippling. She needed to find a way to help him navigate it.

"Really, Kaela? Because I love you."

Oh please. "Not right now."

Cameron grimaced, cocking his head to the side. "What?"

"Let's do that another time. That's not what we're talking about right now."

"But that's what *I'm* talking about."

"Then try and focus, please."

She hadn't meant that to sound so harsh, so offhanded like that. There were just more pressing things on her mind. Her love life was the least of it. Things like Cameron's potential financial ruin for one. *And* her falling fortunes at the firm for another… Standing idly by as *Glamazon* lost this case was not a good look for her, particularly given her personal connection.

"You know," Cameron began as he braced one hand against the corner of the desk and smoothed his tie straight with the other. "Even as I watch the words come out of your mouth now, and you're absolutely clear, I still don't want to believe."

"I'm not saying I don't care." Mikaela came back to him, throwing her arms over his shoulders as he leaned against her desk. "Cameron, c'mon."

"Then why does it sound that way?"

"You're hearing things…" But instead of looking at him, Mikaela glanced over his shoulder, at the floor-to-ceiling windows behind them, glimpsing her own reflection in the glass.

The woman reflected back was so successful, so accomplished. In many ways, she'd become exactly who she dreamed of being since last they knew each other. She'd worked hard, *so hard* to get there, to let go of that insecure girl who basically ran away from home, leaving heartbreaks and thoughts of inadequacy behind. But for better or worse, it just took seeing Cameron again to bring it all back. And when he said he loved her, she suspected that despite what he claimed, he still saw the "old" Mikaela and it was like coming full circle.

Not in a good way…

It frightened her. Like a regression, like he saw past the facade she'd so painstakingly constructed over the years, through "new" Mikaela to that girl underneath. And when he said these things so easily, every time he did, she wondered who he was speaking to? Did he see *her*, or just the ghost of her former self? So even when he said it and it filled her with an almost indescribable joy, questions still lingered: Was it real? Lasting? Or even enough for her?

And could it be anywhere near enough if the rest of her world fell apart?

Mikaela stepped back from the aggravatingly tolerant look in Cameron's eyes.

"You don't get to decide what's important to me. Just like I can't dictate to you that you should be far more worried than you are right now—*because between Julie and Glamazon, they could bankrupt you.* I can't tell you how to feel, and you can't tell me, okay?"

"Fair enough." Cameron shrugged, his hand sliding over his tie again as if he were stroking a beard, listening.

"Is everything this easy for you? 'Cause, it scares the hell out of me how this is all rolling off your back! It's so effortless. Like everything is just that simple."

Cameron chuckled, the sound like a deep rumble in his chest.

"So is everything a joke to you?"

"If you don't laugh, you'll cry. I've had to learn that."

"But you've always been that way! Everything in stride… Well, I'm not like that. I worry and stew over things. And I need time to process this."

"Honey, I know this about you," he said easily, disregarding her words…*again*. "And it's gonna be okay."

Everything was on the verge of toppling, like dominoes. How was he so unfazed?

Mikaela shook her head. The specter of losing this promotion now hung over her like the end of her world as she knew it.

"Stop being so cool about everything!" Her voice rose in exasperation. "In fact, stop acting like just because you've seen me naked and can rattle off a few of my vital statistics it means that we know each other. I already told you, you don't know me now." She shook her head, stopping him before he could rebut. "We have something, yes. But it is based on *two* summers, twenty years ago—you have no *idea* who I've become."

"You're wrong," he said, stunned. "I'm in *awe* of who you've become."

"W-well," she stammered, flustered and frustrated as if he'd deliberately said that to undermine her. "Well, what if you realize you don't *like* the person I am now, let alone love her? Will this lawsuit still seem 'worth it' then?"

"I definitely don't know if I like how you're acting now," Cameron muttered, pushing off from her desk.

He moved toward the window. Pausing in front of her credenza, he spotted the silver frame. He was older and more self-possessed than he had been the last time they did this— the day that picture was taken in fact—but his silence, absolute stillness for a moment, didn't bode well.

He picked it up, studying it. "Okay, so if you don't trust my judgment, do you trust your own?" He shook the picture. "*We* chose this time. And now I want to make even more room in my life for you, but I can't if you won't let me. So, do you love me, Kaela? Let's start there."

"What?"

He came back her way. "You are always showing me that no matter what, I can't have you. Back then, it was Juliette, then it was school—" *he raised his hand to preempt her objection* "—which, of course, I understood. But now it's this case and *it's fucking Juliette again*! There's always something. Some excuse. Like is there a point here that I'm just stupidly not getting?"

"You were the one in that hotel room telling me to leave

the past behind." She glared at him. "Why would you ask me this right now?"

"*That's why I'm asking.* I'm so tired of you using me and Juliette and what happened before as an excuse. Yes, we all made mistakes. But are we gonna continue to allow that to hold us hostage?" He sped up, agitated, while Mikaela's chest caved in at his words. "This is not a hard question. Do you love me now? Do I matter to you?" He paused. "Or maybe it's just that I never did?"

"Cameron…"

"Okay, easier question, when is there *not* something more important than me? *Than us?*"

Mikaela took a moment to compose herself. "You're being really melodramatic."

"The question, Mikaela, answer it! Do you love me? Now? *Ever?*"

Her mouth opened then abruptly closed as nothing came out.

The silence spoke instead. Stretching out, making the room somehow smaller. Filling in the spaces between them like white noise until she was certain all she could hear was her own heartbeat thrumming in her ears.

"Oh, wow. You don't. Is that it?" Cameron's chin set and shoulders fell, heaving one gigantic, shaky sigh as if he'd had the wind knocked out of him. Then he nodded. "Got it."

She frowned, unable to speak as he turned and walked out, leaving her door wide open.

"*Yes,*" she finally mumbled to the empty room, just before Suze stepped into the doorway looking as bewildered as Mikaela felt.

forty-six

"That *Glamazon* business was just a bad beat," Art said, roaming the room, making Mikaela anxious with his restlessness.

Just the fact that he was in her office gave her pause. It was a rare occasion that Art took a meeting in her office and not his own.

"I agree," Mikaela contributed, although Art was only talking, not listening.

"I spoke with Proctor, he's disappointed in the outcome." He turned to her. "Of course, no one blames you, Mike."

Mikaela bit the inside of her cheek. Though they said they didn't, she did. Her inappropriate behavior pushed Julie, right when she'd been willing to settle.

"I hope they don't blame Todd either," Mikaela added.

Just because she blamed herself didn't mean she was foolish enough to let them lay this all at her feet, especially when she wasn't even overseeing the case anymore.

Art's head bobbed a little, then he shook it, a little too vehemently. "Oh no. No."

Suddenly, he justified her having said it.

Something was about to happen.

As if on cue, Art took a deep breath and spoke. "It's Todd's year."

He paused in front of her and gripped the chair back he was supposed to be sitting in until his knuckles turned white.

"We're gonna announce it in the meeting, but I had to let you know ahead of time. The equity partners discussed it at length. I went to bat for you, of course…"

"Of course."

Art liked to use the words *of course* as a cudgel to beat people into submission then drag them into line. He did it now to convince her that this decision somehow made sense. And at any other moment she'd have believed him. She was his *pet* after all.

Her office was the proof of it. And all the hard work he entrusted in her, the countless important jobs he'd given her, institutional responsibilities he'd shared. It was all because she was worthy, *right*? Yet, here she was *again*, being passed over, *again*, as Todd failed upward…*again*. Suddenly, even the wording of that thought, *Art's pet*, disquieted her.

"But it was decided that we couldn't pass him over again, of course."

Mikaela blinked.

That hadn't been an issue the two previous times that others, less senior, had gotten the equity partnership offer instead of Todd? Mikaela had actually begun to think Art preferred to keep Todd where he was, as his perpetually subservient right hand. Was that the position he hoped that she would now fill in Todd's stead? Negating the fact that Mikaela had been Art's de facto right hand for as long as Todd had held the honorary title?

Art droned on in explanation as Mikaela surveyed her office.

For so long, this office stood as her symbol. Of the inevitable attainment of all her ambitions. Now it occurred to her that perhaps this office was not the promise she'd believed it was, but just Art's way of placating her. Her very own gilded cage. She thought of the lifestyle she had, the salary she earned, the things she'd acquired over her quite satisfying, if sometimes frustrating, rise. She was proud of herself, the little brown girl from Georgia with the outsize ambitions.

Yet there had always been that small tug at her. The tiny question of what she'd given up for all this...*stuff*.

Up until this very moment, had anyone asked, Mikaela would have said it was worth it. The equity stake she'd coveted for so long was worth the nights working late, the vacations with friends she skipped, the dots on the map still undiscovered, the dozens of lovers jilted, the lack of anyone or anything in her life that was more important. But now she knew that it hadn't mattered. Not to the firm. And in fact, it didn't even matter to her that she hadn't gotten it.

Because what else was there afterward? Who had it been for? And what had she sacrificed in its service?

Her inner hard-core, militant feminist refused to believe it was marriage and kids. She abhorred that idea for herself. Having witnessed her parents' marriage implode and what that had meant for her and Vanessa, Mikaela had never truly seen wife but especially not mother in her cards. Still, life, *a real life*, of fun and freedom, friends and family? Of adventures filled with the sights and sounds of foreign places? Of different people far afield from her small town in Georgia? All that had featured prominently in her imaginings of her future long ago.

And what had come of that? What the hell happened to any of that?

Academic success had begotten professional success, which begot—New York real estate success?

'Cause she could admit her little duplex, classic six-room condo in Park Slope for under a million was a genuine coup bordering on miracle.

But the happiness and adventure parts that she had sworn to herself as a kid also, what happened with that?

"And you know, after that business with Murphy—" Art's monologue enumerated excuses but that one caught her attention.

"Excuse me?" Mikaela cut him off not even sure what he'd been saying anymore.

"Well—" he slowed down, eyes wandering around the room as if searching for delicacy but still missing it by yards "—it's no secret you're in a relationship."

"Because I told you," she clarified.

"Yes, you're dating him now, right? I mean, Mike, far be it from me to comment on your personal life…"

But he was about to.

"We *both* know, you haven't been exactly discreet in the past couple of weeks."

"He's only come into this office specifically to see me two times in the last month! And you said it didn't matter, since we're not legally exposed."

"Yes," Art hemmed. "But appearances…"

"Appearances," said the man married to a firm receptionist, twenty-four years his junior.

Mikaela realized then that Cameron had been absolutely right on the Vineyard. She was the one that had made their relationship fair game.

Who had given them the right to think they could judge her?

She had.

"What happens outside of this—" Mikaela began, actually blinking at the blinding epiphany before her. Then she chuckled, realizing she already knew *exactly* what she needed to do. "No, you know what? That's fine, Art. Because I've been thinking of scaling back anyway."

It was Art's turn to blink rapidly with confusion. "What?"

"Yeah, *way* back." Mikaela rose from her couch where Art had asked her to sit.

They were supposed to be pretending they were friends as opposed to coworkers, sitting across from each other. But Art had never sat down, instead looming over her as he broke this news which shattered any illusions she'd had about their standing with each other.

He was her boss and close colleague; it had never truly been anything more than that.

"Yes, I think starting next month, I'm going out on sabbatical. I've been working here for twelve years and I've never had one of those."

"Now, Mike, hold on," Art stammered. "We don't want you to view this Altcera business and Todd's offer as a knock against you. Of course, we love you."

Mikaela smiled. Art only started using the royal *we* when he needed political cover.

"And I love you too," she said sweetly. "That's why there are absolutely no hard feelings, *of course*, Art. I mean I'll certainly feel the firm's appreciation of my efforts in the fourth quarter, won't I?" She licked her lips like a cat sizing up its dinner. "After all, our acquisition of Altcera's North American business interests will still be going ahead. And it counts in my win column when the yearly billables are calculated, right? Zenigent is a done deal, as soon as the contract is ratified. And the membership vote is tomorrow. I know Todd is finishing up with Celia and Monica, having talked the plaintiff's lawyer down significantly from their initial settlement request. Mark Slocum's made meaningful headway with the Splendure litigation. And Frank and Max fly up to Colorrblur HQ in Quebec next week to do the final walk-through at their new site for the closing."

Art's eyebrows rose at Mikaela's accounting, not realizing, she supposed, that naturally she would be keeping a close eye on everyone's progress. That's why he loved her, for her meticulous attention to detail, right? And in this instance, it all reflected on her and the reputation she had striven to create with Mr. Proctor and the Altcera higher-ups. She'd have been an idiot to let Art slide in and poach that relationship from her. She couldn't even honestly believe he thought she would have allowed him to do it.

Or maybe she could...*now.*

Mikaela had spoken to Proctor, *and even Jacqueline*, a number of times since her move over to Zenigent just to make sure they were still happy with the firm.

"I have a call with Proctor in about—" she tapped her cell phone to awaken it "—ten minutes, and I'll break the news to him myself. Don't worry, Art. I'll maintain contact with them during my break. And the rest, I'll hand over to Jackson in my absence."

Art's eyes widened, his cheeks getting that after-cocktails flush, as Mikaela rounded the chair to put her hand on his shoulder.

"Let's call it, maybe a partial sabbatical? Suze will stay on my desk and act as point person. And *when* I'm needed, I'll make myself available. Now according to the company manual—" *a document Art himself had tasked Mikaela with revamping three years ago* "—I'm entitled to one month of leave for every year of service."

"But—but, Mike, that's a whole year!" he cried, alarmed.

"It is," she agreed and smiled, taking a beat to twist the knife a little. "But I'm only going to take five months of it to start… Never know when I might need to recharge again."

She walked him to her door and opened it. Suze looked up at them both, her eyes darting from one to the other, trying to read their faces.

"We'll hammer out the exact details over the next couple of days, okay?"

She patted Art's back easing him out. He looked unsure of what was happening. He nodded as she accompanied him, both stopping in front of Suze's desk.

"Well, I, I just want you to remember you're a valued, um, *cherished*, member of the Wexler, Welford and Bromley family."

"Of course." Mikaela nodded, leaning against the desk with a hand on her hip.

Art deflated before her eyes, his wide shoulders bending slightly inward. He paused, peering closely at Suze's shoulder-length, black-to-silver ombré tresses before turning to walk away.

"We still have that dinner date with Countess next month, don't we?" Mikaela called after him.

Art acknowledged her with something approximating a smile and waved over his head like he was swatting a fly.

Five months…long enough for her contributions to be missed, but not long enough to become replaceable.

When Art had finally disappeared down the long hall, she turned to Suze.

"Everything okay, boss?"

"Should be, after you get Burt Proctor on the phone. As soon as you can. Tell his assistant it's an emergency, if you have to. Then, can you call Cam, uh, Mr. Murphy, and tell him I need to see him?"

Suze smiled, shaking her head while picking up the phone.

"Suzukea, you have *got* to stop looking at me like I'm the girl on the cover of a romance novel or something."

Suze laughed as she began dialing. "Stop acting like the heroine in one and I will."

Mikaela shook her head.

What I need to do, she thought as she walked back into her office, *is stop giving Suze fodder to work with and get my life together.*

Maybe Cameron could help her with that?

Mikaela waited until she was inside her office and had closed the door behind her before dropping the nonchalant facade. She bent forward and gripped her waist.

What the fuck had she just done?

forty-seven

Mikaela tightened the belt around her raincoat as she caught the door to Cameron's apartment building from someone walking out. She had never done anything like this before and was terrified. Her heels clicked against the lobby tiles echoing as she fussed with the knot at her waist, climbing the three flights to his floor. Her hands fiddled, tugging and straightening something that could not be made more straight or secure.

It was because of her sister that she had dressed like an extra in a pornographic film in a diaphanous, black lace teddy with an assortment of cutouts, a plunging neckline and little else, under a raincoat. She was a walking cliché: wearing nothing but thin straps to call clothing as she stood in front of Cameron's door. She pulled a chilled bottle of expensive champagne out of her tote, sweeping her long thin braids over one shoulder before letting herself in with the key he'd given her. As she came through the foyer, he glanced up from a spot on the couch, eyes traveling from head to toe, as if he had no idea what to make of her.

"Hi." The hopeful half smile she'd worn a second before fell.

Cameron divided his attention between the television and papers on the coffee table in front of him.

"Sorry, am I disturbing you?"

"Not really, but you could have asked before you came." He didn't elaborate, only shaking his head as if warding off the question.

"Are you saying I just showed up unannounced? 'Cause you know I didn't, I had Suze call."

"No, I mean you automatically assumed I'd be available whenever you were ready. It's been days, Mikaela."

She stared at him wide-eyed, taking a step back.

This was supposed to be her moment. Like in a movie, she was certainly wearing the getup for it, *or not wearing it*, as it were. This was about her triumphantly sharing her news that she'd reclaimed her life and she was finally, at long last ready to try and make some room in it for someone else.

No, not *someone* else, as if it could have been anyone at all. No, to finally make room for *him*. Instead, he was accusing her of taking him for granted.

She pulled her raincoat closer around herself. He noticed her motion and frowned.

"I specifically asked for your permission to come," she said, indignant. "But if you're too busy I can come back?"

"You could." For the first time that she could remember, Cameron avoided her eyes, focusing on the television.

"What aren't you saying?"

"Summer's ending," he sighed, gathering the papers into a stack. "Juliette's taking Kit home soon. It's his final year of middle school. And I agreed to let Robin hang out in Savannah with me for a few days before she goes home to start her junior year."

"So, you're leaving again?" Mikaela let the tote slide off her shoulder onto the floor before dropping into a chair near her.

"I am."

"And you're not coming back." Mikaela tried to discern his words from his expression...but he wouldn't look at her.

"Fashion Week is a month away. I'll probably be back for that."

Mikaela snorted, less with humor than scorn. "For work then, but not for..." She trailed off.

"What's the difference if I say I'm coming back?" Cameron finally faced her.

"The difference is you've been busy trying to lock me down but now you can't even commit to when you'll be in the City next?"

"I'm not trying to *lock* you into anything. I said I would be back in September. That sounds pretty definitive to me."

"You mean you didn't hear yourself just say 'probably'?"

"I meant *probably* unless *Glamazon*'s offices burn to the ground or Jacqueline gets hit by the cross-town bus or Bryant Park suddenly falls into a sinkhole," Cameron retorted derisively. "I mean definitely, *barring an emergency*, I'll probably be back in September."

"How old are you right now? 'Definitely probably' is not an adult response."

He chuckled as Mikaela's eyes narrowed at his moronic obfuscation. Then one of his shoulders rose and fell infinitesimally, in the most lackluster of shrugs. But as an unspoken statement of indifference, he couldn't have been clearer.

"Then I don't know what to tell you, *Mike*," he answered.

Mikaela had never heard Cameron so cavalier, seen him be so coolly evasive or felt him so remote as he was just then. And she recognized that he only called her Mike when he was aggravated. Still, she didn't understand what was happening.

She felt very naked and very silly. She stood, retrieving her tote bag from the floor, and got to the door before Cameron seemed to even notice her retreat. Behind the wall, he sighed. And she hung there waiting for him to say or do something to stop her.

"Is this your way of punishing me for the other day?" She stalked back into the room.

"I'm not punishing you for anything. I can't force you to say something you don't want to." Cameron was decent enough not to pretend that he didn't know what she was talking about. "And I don't want you to say anything you don't actually feel."

Despite the fact that one part of her recent epiphany was that every time she saw Cameron *I love you* were the first words on the tip of her tongue, Mikaela couldn't say it now either. Even though she showed up tonight in her skimpy lingerie with expensive champagne and the express purpose of finally telling him, again, the words refused to come.

Mikaela licked her lips then bit them, struggling.

She didn't want to say it glibly as a guilt trip, *either his or her own*. Not because she felt bad that he had been waiting for her to say it. Or because, somehow, she knew that if she did, it would make a difference now.

"I don't feel forced, I—I just," she stumbled, trying to gather her thoughts into coherence from the maelstrom of emotion they were in their current form.

"Just don't feel anything at all?" He finished for her as she stared at him aghast. "For me, at least. *What a fool believes*, right?"

Cameron had an epiphany of his own. Right in front of

her. Mikaela would have gasped if it felt like there was any air left in her body.

"Don't do this," she warned, her voice barely above a whisper. Her eyes ached from the pressure building behind them.

"I'm not doing anything but putting two and two together. I said in your office that we chose this together, but we didn't, and that's my fault. I keep pushing you. I realize I did that before too. Back then, you kept telling me in different ways that all you wanted was a fling. A secret little thing that you could take off to college with you. And I stupidly spent that same time believing I had met the love of my life. Even after you passed me off to your friend, I crazily tried to justify it instead of just seeing it for what it was."

"I was young and stupid and desperate to make everyone happy. I—"

"'I, I, I!' It's always about you, Mikaela!" Cameron stood, shaking his head.

She pressed her lips closed.

"Sorry, I know you were young." He stopped himself and a momentary silence enveloped them.

"Ultimately, you are always going to do what's best for you. I can't blame you for that. I did it too. When my mom and dad died, I felt lost. I had very little family. Even fewer who actually cared about me. So, I guess you weren't wrong when you accused me of searching for family. And *I* chose how I handled that. *Not you.* Despite what you apparently think.

"But this…" He motioned between the two of them with an upturned finger. "This shouldn't have happened this way. *Not again.* This time, you warned me. I can't pretend that you didn't. You told me that you did not want this to become a thing. And even when you didn't say the words, your actions were more than clear. Yet somehow I ignored them…again."

She was mistaken, this was no recent epiphany; he'd been thinking about it.

Mikaela slumped against the wall behind her, hugging her tote to her chest, mortified to hear the stupid celebratory bottle clinking against the ridiculous flutes inside. Grabbing at her face in one palm, she tried to hide as tears began overflowing her lashes, running down her face. She squeezed her temples between her fingers but the teardrops were already causing trails down her face, dripping off her chin. She was sure with all the makeup she had on, she'd soon resemble a raccoon.

"Mikaela…" Cameron turned off the television, moving from the couch.

She shook her head. She was crying in front of him…*again*.

"Kaela, *please*," he called out to her in a way that ruptured a million additional fissures in her heart. "I'm trying to apologize to you."

"Is that what you're doing?" She sniffled, brushing the tears back from her face with her sleeve and taking a deep breath. "'Cause this feels very accusatory."

Cameron's expression went soft; in fact, he appeared pained too, which made it all the worse.

"What I'm saying is, I'm sorry for pushing this so hard. It's just that from the second I saw you again, it all came back. All those feelings that, yes, I was trying to recapture," he spoke, trying to make sense of it himself. "So, I guess I lied about that too. Maybe you were right in the hotel, maybe you and I only exist in my head. Or we're too different now. And I get it. It's not like I haven't had a life. It wasn't like I haven't had others—people I loved, *but more importantly*, people I didn't."

"No. I—"

"I know you care about me. *I know that.* Just not in the way *I need.* And I would love for that to be enough. To not want you in the way I do. But it's just not."

"What are you saying?"

"That we should look at this as an opportunity to step back. Both of us. I've got a lot going on, you do too."

She quirked an eyebrow.

"With the partnership and everything?"

She hadn't even told him she didn't get the job. Strangely, there was a part of her so excited by the prospect of her sabbatical and all the time that would mean she could spend with him, she'd almost forgotten.

"So, I'm thinking, maybe we both take this time…"

"And just…be friends?" Her heart sank but she'd take it. Take anything that wasn't the banishment he was working up to. She couldn't bear that.

"No," he whispered. "You know I can't just be your friend, I lo—"

"Don't say it. Please."

Not if she couldn't say it back when he needed to hear it, and not if it was only in service of brushing her off.

He acquiesced, pursing his lips.

Finally. After all these years, Cameron Murphy was leaving *her* for once, instead of the other way around.

He shook his head, as if he knew her thoughts, stepping closer. And despite her dejection, she allowed him to enter her space. She pressed herself flat against the wall.

"So just go our separate ways then?"

His face wavered in her watery sight.

"Maybe for a while," he whispered with a grim nod. "Give it some time."

Some time for him to get over her?

"You're not wearing anything under this, are you?" he asked suddenly, gaping.

He reached out and her eyes followed his hand. Two fingers lightly touched her lapel, peeling it back to expose her bare skin underneath.

"Very little," she admitted, her face burning. "It was supposed to be part of my apology."

The corner of his mouth rose as if he was teasing her for her stupidity. For so completely misreading the moment.

She looked down at her costume. And though she was aware enough to realize that it wasn't his intent, that didn't stop the feelings anyway. The immature, insecure phantom emotions of a girl literally half her age, returned to ache in her chest.

Cameron leaned in, tipping her jaw up, and inched forward until their lips touched. Tenderly at first, before her fingers slid up and around his neck, growing possessive and grasping. She pulled him closer and he pressed into her. Capturing her lips and tongue while anchoring his forearm against the wall as their mouths hungrily collided. Their imminent separation seemed to add to the urgency, intensifying it.

Like when they were young and known to one another, they both did things without asking. Touching here, caressing there to stoke the fire that even in these final moments still raged between them. Cameron's hand slid under her knotted belt, palming her heated skin. Her nails raked through his hair until he growled into her mouth.

Even if nothing else worked, this always did.

He had been right on that score. Whether or not they were compatible in any other way, they were indeed made for each other physically. Mikaela sighed into his mouth, her whole body melding to his as he feasted on her lips. Their mouths vied for dominance, tongues twined, eyes closed, breathing in sync, their pulses racing in tandem. And as usual, it was Cameron who broke away first, looking shamefaced and overwhelmed.

He opened his mouth, no doubt to apologize for starting something they couldn't, *shouldn't*, finish.

"Let's not say anything else." Mikaela stopped him.

He was right. She'd hurt him, being callous. She was determined to be better for once, not reactive. Despite being upset with her, he'd been gentle. Without doubt, he was letting her down easy. Being careful was the least she could do in return. Not dragging this whole thing out with maudlin displays of anguish or anger.

She *had* to give him that.

She fished his key out of her coat pocket and placed it in his palm, grabbing her tote off the floor.

"See you around, Cam." She broke the silence at his front door, opening it, with him right behind.

She slid her hand down his shoulder, along his arm and into his open palm, squeezing it. And he held on for a second longer before letting go.

She stepped out then without looking back, moving down the hallway to the stairs. Back on the ground floor, she slipped onto the street, into the general bustle of things, smoothly hailing a cab despite feeling disjointed. As if parts of her hadn't just been painfully torn away. And while knowing that this time, unlike all previous, Cameron would not be coming after her.

forty-eight

It was her father's influence, she was sure of it, that made Mikaela compulsively clean when she was upset.

So far her "sabbatical" had been a wash.

She was restless, hating her sudden idleness. Mere days into it, Mikaela was ready to go back to work. She still checked her email regularly and spoke to Suze multiple times a day. It had been a rash decision, made to punish Art and the partners, to teach them a lesson, but she was the one learning something.

Mikaela had no life without her work.

Dressed in a pair of half-done-up overalls, Rashad's old, oversize Brown sweatshirt and a kerchief to cover her braids, Mikaela had become a woman obsessed...*with dirt*. She ferreted it out of every nook and cranny of her apartment. Every grain of wood or pane of glass, or piece of crystal that could be polished, was. All week long, she moved from room to room, spraying, dusting, wiping and washing every inch in which a speck could fall.

Now, Mikaela was in her half bathroom, on her hands and

knees scrubbing the grouting between tiles when her door-bell rang. She got up gingerly and trudged to the intercom panel that controlled the downstairs bell, pressing the button to open it. Vanessa had been threatening to come over all weekend. Mikaela left the front door slightly ajar before returning to her pitched battle with a spot she was certain was the beginnings of mildew.

"Hello? Mike?"

The soothing and almost rhythmic sound of the scrub brush against the floor tiles nearly drowned out the words.

"In here, Nes!" Mikaela called out, up on her haunches, wiping her forehead with the back of her forearm.

But it wasn't Vanessa that appeared in the doorway moments later.

There, dressed in heeled mules, black high-waisted gauchos and a black-and-white-striped sleeveless blouse, stood Julie. Her hair was sideswept and pushed back off her face by a pair of white sunglasses, despite the fact that the entire weekend had been overcast. Mikaela ran a hand over her head, dismayed at what she must look like by contrast.

"Julie, what are you doing here?" she asked, easing from the floor.

"Hello, Mike."

Julie backed up to let Mikaela out of the small space. Mikaela led her back through the house, past the den, into the kitchen, offering her a seat wordlessly.

Perhaps, as Vanessa had always maintained, leaving the door open for guests wasn't a best practice, despite the many ways in which Brooklyn had gentrified in recent years.

This was clearly how riffraff got in.

Mikaela went to her front door and closed it before peering around the corner into her open-floor-plan kitchen, just to make sure she wasn't mistaken. Julie was indeed seated comfortably at her kitchen island, waiting. Mikaela glanced at herself in the large full-length mirror in her hall and shook her head with annoyance. Washed-out and puffy from crying intermittently for days and dirty from all her cleaning, it wasn't possible for her to be caught looking worse than she did right then. She took a breath and walked back into the kitchen.

"How did you know where I live?"

Julie's perfectly plucked eyebrows rose. "Is that the lawyer in you or have you just forgotten your manners up North so long?" she sniped, placing her purse up on the counter to search through it.

Mikaela opened her mouth before pulling it shut again like a drawbridge, keeping the foul things inside. Julie wasn't exactly wrong.

She licked her lips, trying again. "Why, Julie, bless your heart! You came all the way to Brooklyn to visit me? Now, what could I have done to earn this pleasure?"

Julie flashed a wry smile at Mikaela's heavily accented sarcasm. "The kids and I are flying back to Charleston tonight, but I had something that I wanted to give you." Julie rifled through her purse until she found what she was looking for.

"Give…" Mikaela repeated. *"Me?"*

Julie pulled a small sketchbook out of her bag.

"Well, you or Cam."

Julie opened the book and removed a photograph. Placing it facedown on the island between them, she slid it across the smooth granite surface under a manicured fingernail. Mikaela eyed it with curiosity but paused before touching it.

"It won't bite ya," Julie verified, nodding at it. "I just thought y'all might like that."

Mikaela picked it up and recognized the image immediately.

"When we moved from Larkspur to Savannah, we gave a couple of boxes to my mama for safekeeping. Cam never could keep track of details like that. And when Mama sold the Dogwood Lane house in Harmon, she musta packed it all up and took it to Gabe's in Arizona with her. So when I asked him to look for the release, I guess he found this picture too. 'Cause he sent them together. I'm figuring someone else should have it, because it really belonged to Cameron... and you."

Mikaela dropped onto the chair nearest her, shaken.

The matte photograph was in color; Mikaela ran her fingers over the smooth surface of it. Her first year away at college. Her and Cameron on the Bow Bridge in Central Park. On Christmas Day.

In her recollections, they were never so young, making all the life-altering decisions they did. But seeing them in old photographs reinforced how young they were, truly just kids.

Mikaela shook her head amazed at how Cameron looked at her, how they looked at each other.

"You guys looked good together. I'd never seen that," Julie said.

Mikaela sighed at how difficult she'd made things for herself and him.

If they so clearly loved each other, why couldn't they have made it work? It was a question for then and now.

Mikaela examined the photo more closely.

In it, they were slightly turned toward each other, talking, an outtake from the actual photo they'd asked the jogger to capture. Their expressions saying enough to show that this boy loved this girl and vice versa. It was astonishing to see years later. And for Mikaela, it was a beautiful thing to have in her possession. An artifact to add to the chronicle of her and Cameron's short but intense relationship. Still, given that, she couldn't imagine what would have possessed Julie to want to pass it along.

Mikaela shook her head, befuddled.

Julie took a deep breath then. "Look, Mike," she started.

Mikaela raised her hand to stop her.

"No, *you look*, this has been a rough week for me." Mikaela waved the photo at Julie, like a white flag. "And I don't have the energy to readjudicate this. This is *twenty* years old! And I just cannot do it right now."

Julie shook her head, chuckling. "Honestly, I agree. That wasn't the meaning behind the picture. I just wanted you to have it." She shrugged. "There's no need for us to be sworn enemies or anything. To act like complete strangers. That was the purpose of the picture, just to say that."

A peace offering?

Mikaela was confounded, Cameron's words at the recital returned to her, making her suspicious.

She's playing you.

Mikaela exhaled, leaning back in her chair. Julie had done enough recently to prove she didn't have Cameron's best interests—*or Mikaela's, for that matter*—at heart.

After all these years, she and Julie need not be anything more than what they were currently: near total strangers. Why would Julie suddenly want anything more than that anyway? Especially not after seeing a photo of her ex-husband and her former best friend as lovers.

"I don't get it. You were married to Cameron five years ago. I don't understand what you're doing now?"

"Did you somehow miss the fact that we have children together?"

"Yes, of course you have to speak to each other, but you guys aren't friends. And this thing you've done with the lawsuit, was just…mean." Mikaela took a breath trying not to lose her temper. "So, I ask again, what are you *doing*?"

"How did I know you would try and throw an olive branch back in my face?" Julie raked a hand through her hair and shook out the ends in frustration like she used to. "I knew you would do this! You've always been so damn binary!"

"An olive branch? I'm being binary because I don't think it can all come down to an old picture and suddenly, we're what? Besties again? Because I won't pretend with you?" Mikaela retorted. "When I wanted to act like adults, you made a fool of me. So no, I'm sorry, I'm no longer willing to pretend that you didn't end up married to my boyfriend."

Julie sighed with exasperation. "Do you hear yourself? Way to hold a grudge, Mike. You just said it—it's been years! How is it *still* your version of events that *I* married *your* boyfriend? How about the fact that you're sleeping with *my* husband, right now!"

"*Ex*-husband."

"Ex-husband," Julie corrected, glaring before she continued. "Have you forgotten your role in that? Or are we going to pretend that you didn't have one?"

Mikaela swallowed hard.

She constantly beat herself up over what happened between the three of them—*more so in the past couple of months than she had in years*—but she wouldn't be playing the blame game now.

"Do you mean my part in your pregnancy or your sham marriage or the subsequent divorce? Which? 'Cause it seems like you both did a great job of ruining things all on your own."

When Julie spoke again it was with a level of composure Mikaela could almost admire.

"How about the part where he never got over you? Or the part where we never had a chance because of you?" She rolled her eyes. "At first, after you left, Cameron and I spent our time together getting over you. Yes, it turned into something else later, in the year before Robin was born. But we bonded initially over both being abandoned…by you. Did you not think we missed you? That *I* missed you?"

Mikaela was taken aback.

"*You* were our connection, M.," she said softly, voice thickening in her throat. "We had loving *you* in common and that was the glue that held it together at first. 'Cause, at first, he was just a friendly, familiar face at school. But I was smitten in a way I'd never been with a boy before. And when Daddy died, Cameron and his mama were so kind, and I was so lonely and heartsick. So, a little crush one year turned into a bigger one by the next. Then you disappeared and his mama died and we were there for each other… And well, I fell in love, it's just that simple.

"Okay, and so maybe I was being *a little* petty." Julie rolled watery eyes at Mikaela when she scoffed. "But I wanted him, and you so clearly didn't! And having him became much more important to me than whether he actually wanted me back," Julie said, avoiding Mikaela's gaze.

"So, when I got pregnant, and you found out and left for good, *forever*, it left Cameron and me alone, together. Having to figure out a way to navigate parenthood and a relationship with this giant Mikaela-shaped crater blown all the way through everything. But by then, having each other at least felt like *something*, like a relief, like having a life raft to cling to."

Mikaela's mouth twitched, the space behind her eyes burning. Cameron once said something like that to her, admitted the same thing. But she hadn't heard him. Didn't understand.

"We were happy for a time. We had Robbie, then Kit. It did work for a while." Julie closed her mouth, holding back tears. Unveiling a completely different face, vulnerable, wholly unlike the person who sat there a moment before. "Before it didn't."

"Okay, but that wasn't my fault. So, what do you want from me...or him, now, Julie?" Mikaela cleared her throat, trying to dislodge the lump forming.

"Well, I certainly don't want anything from *you*," Julie snapped, returning to form.

"Then, I don't know what to tell you. You've wasted your subway fare because I have no influence over Cameron."

"Don't you?"

"I don't know what you thought you saw at the hospital, but Cameron and I are not a thing." Mikaela dreaded admitting it, her chest hollowing out at the words.

"If we're being straight with each other—" Julie's eyes narrowed, nostrils flaring "—then at least give me a little more credit than you did back then. Don't lie to my damn face! The hospital where you were literally hand in hand was the least of it!" She rolled her eyes, her disdain evident. "How about at Robbie's showcase, when he could barely keep his eyes off you? Or the deposition, when you kept staring at each other as if I wasn't sitting *right there*! For God's sake, you just took my kid on vacation with you! Give me the courtesy of not insulting my intelligence!"

Mikaela braced herself, unable to speak for a moment. In the next, she decided to just be honest. "I'm not suggesting that *nothing* happened. I'm only saying it's over."

"Huh." Julie sat back and propped her elbow along the back of her chair, eyeing Mikaela. The indecision about whether or not to believe, written all over her face. "Interesting. Does Cameron know that?"

"I would think so, since he's the one that ended it."

Julie smirked in the snide way that made Mikaela's blood pressure rise.

"Well, I suppose that's no surprise. He was so sure that if you ever found your way back to each other again, he wouldn't muck it up. I tried to tell him you would. Ya did, didn't ya?"

Mikaela felt run through. But it was true, wasn't it? She'd ruined things, yet again.

"I did—" Mikaela said, not looking for sympathy but perhaps something closer to courtesy, at least the courtesy to not gloat "—what I thought would help back then."

"So you said. And I think you did what you thought would help alleviate your own guilt. You wanted to not feel bad about leaving and the easiest way was to set us up together and then cry victim when it worked."

Mikaela pursed her lips, slightly more aggravated by that shot than the last.

But was it true? She had run off without much of a backward glance at the emotional chaos she'd left in her wake. There was little point in arguing that now.

"You think I deliberately did that?"

"I've *always* thought it. And for a while, even Cameron was convinced...just long enough to marry me." Julie pointed at her. "But he's always had a blind spot for you that prevents him from seeing you for who you really are."

"If it's been so horrible living in my shadow all these years, Julie, then why the hell would you do it?" Mikaela sniped with as much venom as she could manage.

"I could've asked you the same question, couldn't I?" Julie stated. "For me, the answer was always simple—I wanted him."

Mikaela blinked at Julie's bluntness.

406   NOUÉ KIRWAN

"I knew that from the moment I first saw him. My mother told me it was the same for her with The Judge. Like a lightning bolt." Julie slid out of the bar stool, her eyes appraising Mikaela again, before wandering around the kitchen.

"But you have the Robertson family trust fund. You didn't need him. Cameron had nothing."

"You're wrong. Cameron has *heart*. I didn't really care about the money! And unlike you, it didn't take me long to realize how rare a find he was. Cameron is a faithful, hard-working, caring, responsible man who's only ever wanted the best for our family and adores our children. He took excellent care of us." Julie ran a finger along the countertops. "Now, maybe you think that grows on trees 'cause you got lucky out the gate. But lemme tell you, you find that, and you hold on to it with both hands for as long as you can. The death of my father confirmed that."

"So, is that when you decided? After The Judge died?"

Julie peered at her fingers inspecting them for dust. "Decided what?"

"Decided to take him?"

"Oh, grow up, Mikaela," Julie sighed with peevish exasperation. "Contrary to what you—*and I guess maybe even he*—believes, you *gave* him to me. I decided to *keep* him when I realized what a skillful little liar you were. You both were."

It made Mikaela a little ill speaking about Cameron like a prize to be fought over. But it was clear, for Julie, he was... *even now*. "This whole thing, the suit, everything was all a reconciliation attempt, wasn't it?"

That's why her presence had infuriated Julie so much.

"I never wanted that divorce. I just wanted him to want *me*." Julie set her mouth. "I didn't see why we shouldn't reconcile... in due time."

Mikaela frowned.

"Plus, our sex life was always at its best when we were at each other's throats." Julie shrugged, nonchalantly, as if an attempt to bankrupt a man was no different than sending him a perfumed love note. "You miss a hundred percent of the shots you don't take, right?"

Julie headed for the front door. She paused in the foyer in front of the large photo of Cameron and Mikaela that now hung prominently on that wall. And Mikaela got a juvenile thrill from witnessing Julie's short intake of breath and the tiny tick in her jaw as she inspected it.

"Well, I'm sorry that I wasn't able to give you whatever it was you came here to get." Mikaela opened her door but Julie didn't immediately step through it.

Julie wrinkled her nose, finally peeling her eyes from the picture to cock her head as if breaking some unfortunate news. "Oh, but in a way, you did."

"Really?"

Julie stepped into the threshold then, turning to face Mikaela. "I came to offer *that*," she said, nodding her head at the picture Mikaela didn't even realize she still held between two fingers at her side, "to my children's new stepmother."

Although the prospect of becoming that permanent a fixture in Cameron's life quietly thrilled her, Mikaela was staggered by the logical leap such an idea entailed. "To manipulate me?"

"*As I said*, I came to extend an olive branch. But according to you, I needn't have bothered. So, if that's not in the cards, then you can say, you gave me—" Julie shrugged again indifferently, though she was obviously enjoying herself "—the satisfaction of peace of mind."

Mikaela gripped the doorknob, praying for the strength to not slam it in Julie's face.

"Goodbye, Juliette," Mikaela responded, finally understanding why Cameron had told her this wasn't her Julie anymore.

Julie still had all the trappings: the flawless beauty, the stylish clothes, even her hair looked glossy despite the dreary, wet weather and the even drearier lighting in Mikaela's foyer. It was as if she still walked between raindrops. And though it could be argued Mikaela now possessed all those things too, she found it somewhat unnerving and wholly unfair how even when Julie lost, she still somehow won, learning nothing from the experience. But that wasn't Mikaela's concern anymore. Julie was not the person she remembered, at least, not *in the way* Mikaela had wanted to remember her. And Mikaela had to finally let that old Julie go.

The Julie who encouraged her to cartwheel naked across a crowded football field and brightened every room with her infectious laugh and mischievous nature. Who encouraged The Judge to bring Mikaela along to court and helped her pick out a junior prom dress when she had no mother to take her shopping. The Julie who never once let her down for each and every time that Natalee did.

"Take care, Mikaela," Julie said in a way that made it sound more like a warning and less like a salutation, ambling down the short hall to the stairs. "Enjoy the picture."

Mikaela slumped behind the closed door afterward and examined the photo at length from a spot on the floor, wondering how this had all gotten so colossally messed up.

forty-nine

"Hey, stranger."

J.D. Marchand was lying on the couch reading his newspaper when Mikaela walked into the living room.

Three weeks into her sabbatical and Mikaela was back where it all started. New York City wasn't really a place for deep introspection, solitude or soul-searching. There were always too many distractions—free end-of-summer concerts, street festivals and Sunday brunches with girlfriends, or block parties, things happening at all hours of the day and night. In order to turn inward, as her therapist, Ximena, had suggested, to regroup, Mikaela decided to go home, to her dad's...*to Harmon.*

J.D. gazed at Mikaela over his bifocals and smiled at her before going back to the paper.

At that moment, her father looked older than his sixty-seven years, which was what Mikaela hated about those glasses. Even in his advancing years, J.D. looked at least ten years younger, with smooth chestnut skin and boyish freckles dusting his cheeks that could have appeared odd on a man of his age, but looked cute on him. The glasses though, provided him with a visual expiration date when she most wanted to see him as immortal.

Tonight, however, they mainly just made him look mature and erudite.

Mikaela collapsed into the sofa chair opposite him as she used to, throwing her feet up over the armrest. It was good to be there and just be J.D.'s little girl again for a few days.

He lifted his eyes from his paper again, giving her one raised eyebrow.

"You still going to that show tonight?" Mikaela asked when their eyes met, referring to the custom car show that her father had been talking up for weeks, every time they spoke.

"Why? You got some hot plans somewhere?"

Mikaela and J.D. exchanged smirks.

"I just might," she said.

"Maybe you should have stayed at your mama's. 'Cause here in Harmon, miles from the Atlanta, there ain't no nightlife. It's gonna have you bored to death within hours. I don't even know what y'all kids used to do back in the day," he chuckled, looking back down on his paper.

"Oh, I think you do."

J.D. dropped the newspaper again, shaking his head. "Lawd have mercy, Mike."

Mikaela giggled, pleased with herself for having scandalized her father. She stared up at the exposed beams in the living room ceiling.

As much as she hated to admit it in New York, she missed this. If not Georgia or Harmon itself, she missed this house. From her apartment in Brooklyn, when Mikaela closed her eyes, she saw the timber support beams and exposed brick of this fireplace. Its quaintly rustic charm and many happy memories. As a young couple, Mikaela's parents had worked on this little house with their bare hands, sanding down beams and floorboards, varnishing woodwork to a shine, painting, polishing and nailing every stud where they wanted them. Even all these years later, J.D. left everything just as it had been when her mother cared for it, down to the arrangement of the colorful ceramics she'd placed on the mantelpiece years ago.

And if Mikaela was another sort of person, a naturally sentimental one, she'd have found that all terribly romantic. How even so many years after she'd remarried someone else, it seemed painfully obvious that J.D. still carried a torch for his ex-wife. But instead Mikaela felt almost unbearably sad for him. She couldn't help but think every time she came for a visit, that her dad had spent the bulk of his adult life alone…pining.

Was that what awaited her too?

"How's your retirement treating you so far?" she asked just to make conversation.

"As well as can be expected, I imagine. Made better when my oldest comes down to visit me though." J.D. smiled over the bent corner of the newspaper at her and Mikaela grinned back.

"It really is good to see you, Sugar Foot. I always hope you'll come see me more often."

"Well, with no partnership offer, I'll certainly have more time."

She'd never considered that but it was true. The career chase had preoccupied her for so long, she'd willingly sacrificed everything, even a closer relationship with her father, to that altar.

"What you're saying is, now you can come 'cause you don't have anything better to do?"

"Don't be that way," she said. "I love visiting."

"You do?" he asked, an eyebrow raised.

"Of course! Only the demands of work kept me away."

"You hightailed it outta here eighteen years ago and have been scarce ever since."

"Okay, fair." Mikaela frowned. "But it's not because I don't love seeing you. You were a good dad."

"*Were?* Wow. When's my funeral? I wanna make sure I'm late."

"You know what I mean. When I was a kid and are currently," she clarified with a laugh.

"Well, if you're only just figuring that out now, I'm in trouble."

"Daddy, what I'm saying is, I love you. I'm sorry if I haven't said it enough or shown it."

Her father's evident pleasure at her words made Mikaela imagine that she must not have.

"You butterin' me up for sumthin'?"

"C'mon! I'm being serious," Mikaela said, laughing.

"Then you're thinkin' about Cameron again, aren't ya?"

Mikaela folded her arms, turning her eyes back to the ceiling. "No." Mikaela fidgeted on the couch. "I'm actually thinking about Mom. I spent five straight days with the woman in July and I don't understand how y'all made it fifteen years."

J.D. didn't answer but did grin, closing his newspaper to lie flat on his stomach.

"Well," she said, waiting.

"Well?"

"Everybody else has weighed in. But I have yet to hear from you."

"How do you mean?"

"Everyone has had something to say about my love life and

what I'm doing wrong and what I need to be doing right, I thought you might have some ideas too. In fact, I'm sure you do. So, spit 'em out!"

J.D.'s eyebrows rose.

"Sorry," she groused, but more respectfully. "It was just annoying hearing all these people, *including someone named Natalee*, telling me how I should feel and what I should be doing to make things work." Mikaela sighed heavily, pursing her lips for a moment. "The man just doesn't love me."

"Mikaela Diahann Marchand, you didn't even believe that when it came out of your mouth just now." Her father pushed his glasses down his nose, skewering her with a look. "I don't know nuthin' about nuthin' and I know Cameron Murphy has loved you since he was just a pup come up on my porch beggin'. You know that boy showed up here more than once, right?"

"I do." Mikaela nodded, as her father spoke.

"I'm talkin' 'bout even *after* you were long gone. Used to sometimes park across the street like I wouldn't notice! Then when his marriage was on the verge of goin' bust, had the nerve to come back sniffin' around." J.D. rolled his eyes, still affronted all these years later.

"I know, he told me."

"Did he, now?" Her father's mouth made an O-shape. "Tell you I sent him on his way too?"

"He did, actually. Thank you for that, by the way."

"You're welcome." He sucked his teeth. "Y'all didn't have nuthin' to offer each other back then."

Mikaela frowned. "You think?"

"*I know.* He didn't have a pot to piss in, nor the window to throw it out of. And you were too busy with yourself."

"Are you saying I was too selfish, Daddy?" Mikaela gasped, mildly offended.

"That, and too young."

"Cam's daughter was three, maybe four then, so I was, what, twenty-seven? Hardly too young."

"Too young to support Cameron the way he would have needed. *Yes.* Too young to commit the way you would have had to, to a man with a family going through a crisis. *Definitely.* You are so capable, girl. You don't do anything halfway and I honestly think you'd have given it all up if he needed you to. Your life and everything you wanted for yourself. Diminished yourself to be everything everyone needed."

Mikaela sobered. "Mama was younger than that. She was twenty-one."

"*Exactly.*"

She was offended now. "I am not my mother."

"Kaela, darlin', you *are* your mama, tip to tail. Only smarter... Smart enough to avoid the crash before you was in it."

Mikaela hung her head. It was like a knife in her belly to hear her father say that.

"Driven, gifted, ambitious, brilliant, accomplished. All the best parts of her," her father continued in his soft tone. "...And so damn hard on yourselves."

"What?"

Her father's eyes stayed on her, smiling. "Your mother was also hard on herself. When she got that job, the one with the accounting firm that had her commuting to Atlanta, she killed herself to be home for y'all. Would arrive at night too tired to do anything but eat, sleep and turn back around. Until it became obvious that she couldn't do it anymore."

Her father had always made excuses for her mother. Excuses about where she was and what she was doing. He had always said she had a good job, making good money for their family but Mikaela never had any real idea what that meant. Other than the fact that her mother was never home. It had always seemed like a poorly constructed excuse for her mother's questionable decisions.

"So why didn't she just quit?"

"Her job? We needed the money!" J.D. laughed. "You think good jobs where black women can make what they deserve grow on trees?"

Mikaela pressed her lips closed.

"Plus, she needed the space to grow. Being the housewife to a small-business owner is no walk in the park. Her getting that job kept us solvent."

"But she left us. Why weren't you *ever* hard on her for that? She ruined your life."

"Excuse me?"

"I mean, the life you planned for yourself."

"Young miss, you think I couldn't have remarried if I wanted? Meg Whatley and I were an item for quite some time."

"What?" Mikaela sat up, as her father nodded, laughing. "Miss Meg from the diner?"

"Sugar Foot. I am not 'hard' on your mother because it's not for me to judge her decisions," he said softly. "And honestly to indict her is to lay a lot of blame at my own doorstep too, you know?"

Mikaela listened. She had heard the story of how her parents met many times, sometimes as a story of breathless, young love and sometimes like this, as an excuse for bad behavior.

"Nat was only seventeen when she and I first met. But I was twenty-four, grown and in my mind, ready to settle down. She wasn't and the truth is, even though we waited a few years for her to finish school, I knew that when we got married. But we were so in love. Pretty quickly though, you could see, it was destroying your mama. She never got a life before me and you and us and this." He waved around the room. "It was a lot for a young girl."

"A lot that *she* chose." Mikaela worked hard not to roll her eyes in front of her father.

"Nope, a lot that *I* chose. That I convinced her we chose together. *Not her.* Her mistake was loving me so much she believed it."

"So then was the love not real between you two?" Mikaela asked. "That's what you're saying?"

"Hardly." Her dad smiled to himself, evidently tickled by the question. "It was *very* real. Too real, maybe even. Like a roller coaster. Got two beautiful girls out of it though. And we loved each other fierce for a time, but your mama wasn't ready. We met at the wrong time and ultimately, you can't force a situation to fit. I couldn't force your mama to be happy in a situation where she just wasn't."

Memories of crying and arguments behind closed doors came back to Mikaela. Things she tried not to remember...

"No matter how much she beat herself up over it. It wasn't working. Like you, your mother has a hard time with the concept of not being perfect. She does everything full-bore. But if I had forced her to quit her accounting job and come back to Harmon to play Happy Homemaker again instead, that would have been worse. And I didn't want y'all to see that."

"But then we didn't see her at all. Was that better?"

Her father spoke simultaneously. "That's why in the end I had to divorce her."

"Wait? *You* divorced *her*?" Mikaela's foundations shook; she actually braced the couch beneath her. "What? I thought she— I thought you just said you loved each—"

"That's not how humans work. Love is wonderful, love

makes the world go round and all that. But that's not enough. Love is not fuel, baby, it's a fire! It consumes, and you have to hope you and your partner have enough kindling: friendship, hopes, dreams, goals, desires to keep the fire burning between you when stuff gets dark. Ultimately your mother and I didn't recognize that we didn't have the stamina to keep the fire burning," her dad finished quietly. "I hope you'll remember that. It'll save you a lot of grief and heartache in the long run."

"So, what are you saying? Are you saying that Cameron and I don't have enough of that stuff to make it?"

"I don't know that. 'Cause I'm not *talking* about you and Cameron. And when you're dealing with *your* love, you shouldn't be comparing it to your mother's and mine anyway. Or anyone else's. That's part of your problem—making decisions in your life worried about what happened in ours. It's apples and carburetors," he said in the low authoritative tone that since childhood had given Mikaela the tenets she lived her life by. "Now I'm gonna run upstairs and get changed to meet the fellas."

She nodded as he got up from the couch.

"Mikaela, I really want you to be happy, baby girl. But only you know what that looks like," her father added, crossing the room to her. "With Cameron or without. You can't go studyin' somebody else's past to determine your future." He bent and kissed her on the forehead as she sat, brooding. "Think on that," he reiterated.

"I will, Daddy."

"That's my Sugar Foot."

Mikaela didn't move as her father walked away, just turning to the assortment of her mother's small knickknacks still occupying pride of place on their mantel.

Mikaela had spent so many years of her life blaming her

mother for a situation she never truly understood. But as her father said, her parents' relationship now and forever had been *theirs*. A part of a shared past they'd both clearly made peace with. It seemed that Mikaela was the only one who had allowed it to dictate so much of her present.

So now, as her father had asked, what did she want her future to look like?

fifty

"Mikaela, darlin', welcome!" her mother said as soon as she stepped off the private elevator into the apartment. "Luke's off playing golf. He'll be sad to have missed you. Maybe you should stay the night? Then we can have breakfast tomorrow."

Mikaela smiled. This was her mother's way, always trying to extend her visits. She wouldn't be surprised if she'd deliberately sent her husband away for that express purpose.

"Interesting choice." Natalee reached a hand into Mikaela's halo of hair, freed from microbraids for the first time in a year. Natalee teased the tight curls out with her fingers like a stylist, bouncing and patting it as Mikaela stood still. "Love it!"

This sabbatical was a gift. It had just taken Mikaela a few weeks to realize it.

It was the first time in a long time she was freed of a lot of things—the constant need to conform chief among them. Leaving New York and coming home had reminded Mikaela how enduring and oppressive her desire to please others had been, how acute her concern for their opinions was. Normally, she was preoccupied with propriety, how her bosses might feel about her being out of touch, using Suze as an intermediary. But she and Ximena had been working hard during this break, and for once, Mikaela didn't worry. Not about how her abrupt departure had apparently created a stir in the office. Or about the strict beauty regimen she normally was a prisoner to. Not even about her preoccupations with who people believed she was or what she looked like. How she appeared without makeup or how much shorter she was without her trademark heels. For the first time in a *very* long time, Mikaela was who she was. As free as she had been for those two hundred and eleven seconds on that football field.

So, while her mother's approval was appreciated, for once, Mikaela honestly didn't care.

Natalee led her down three steps into the expansive sunken living room. As usual, words died on Mikaela's lips, taking in the view. One wall entirely made of large, floor-to-ceiling windows offered sweeping views of the downtown Atlanta skyline. She also noticed there were new Adirondack chairs out on the wide terrace that wrapped around the corner of the building.

"You want to sit out there?" her mother asked, following Mikaela's eyes.

As the sun began to set, the windows framed a dazzling deep orange-and-blue-and-purple watercolor vista. The glass of other neighboring buildings refracted the light brilliantly, making it difficult to look out without shading her eyes.

Mikaela shook her head. "Too bright."

"I'm glad you came at this time of day," Natalee said. "I call this the Golden Hour, when the view is at its most spectacular. Sometimes I just go out there and watch the sun set.

On nice days, I take a book out and laze away hours just taking it all in."

Mikaela nodded. That's what she would have done with a view like this too. Just another way in which she was her mother's clone.

"Sit, please," Natalee instructed, extending an arm toward the cream-and-gold-colored jacquard settee near her. "What a surprise! Your daddy told me you came to visit him, but I was afraid to hope you'd swing by."

The two women lapsed into an extended silence as Mikaela's eyes swept the room.

It never failed to confound Mikaela. Atlanta's Natalee Franklin was just not the Nattie Marchand of Harmon.

Even all these many years later, Mikaela mourned the woman she remembered. That woman made griddle cakes and cheese grits for midnight breakfast. She got on her hands and knees in their front yard every fall burying bulbs in preparation for spring flowers. That person enjoyed co-hosting women's auxiliary bridge games and playing spades with the family. Seeing the old Rambler bench in the community garden and eating funnel cake and kettle corn during the Fourth of July carnival. She loved it when her husband bought out the entire Ferris wheel for one ride alone with his family, every year.

And twenty-five years later, Mikaela still didn't know what had happened to her.

"Where'd you go?" Mikaela spoke into the quiet.

Natalee frowned. "I beg your pardon?"

"Daddy told me *he* divorced you," Mikaela answered. "Why'd you let him?"

"Ah, he finally told you." She sighed, crossing her wrists over her knee delicately.

"Why didn't you?"

"Oh, I tried. *Many times*. But there was no way to do it that didn't make him the bad guy. I didn't want that. I was already the bad guy for leaving, why make us both? And I'm glad he did it, honestly. I can say that now. But when you girls were younger, it was hard. I didn't know how to say it or what to do. It wasn't working. Me here, y'all there. And having you come to me was a no-go for both of us. If I had wanted you two to be latchkey kids, I could have fought to raise you here. But John and I *chose* Harmon because we wanted a house and a big lawn for you girls to play in. A safe community where we wouldn't have to worry. So, I never pushed back when he said no. But make no mistake, *I wanted you with me*."

"But then why'd you leave?" Mikaela's voice broke in frustration.

"I needed to work, Mikaela! I would think you, *of all people*, would understand that. I needed to use my degree and my brain for more than planning your meals and bookkeeping for your father," she said defensively. "But here, I worked sixty, seventy hours a week, plus long weekends."

Mikaela remembered when her mother had first moved away for that "good job in the city," all Mikaela had wanted was to go with her. She also wanted to say goodbye to small-town life and being singled out as part of one of the only black families in town. Mikaela was tired of being a spectacle, particularly once that also meant being known as the only family around without a mother at its center. Back then, Mikaela ached for her mother and was thrilled every weekend when she came home.

But slowly every weekend became every other weekend and every other weekend became once a month.

Still, at first, Mikaela had refused to fault her mother, seeing how whatever charms the city held could outweigh visiting Vanessa and herself weekly. Her mom always seemed slightly outsize in taste and personality for Harmon. To a girl who dreamed of Atlanta, identical little houses and life on a suburban cul-de-sac could easily be an ill fit. Mikaela recognized that, even as a child. So, her mother's move to the city made an odd sort of sense, even as it hurt, because she understood her mother. She was *like* her mother, though she never admitted it. And she loved her mother enough to see how life in the big city made her happy, much happier, than their tiny life did.

"But then where were you on vacations?" Mikaela sniped. "When you said you would come to visit and you still didn't? Was it more important to have all this?" She gestured around.

"You must know Luke and I didn't happen until later. I need you to believe that. Your father and I had already fallen apart."

"I love Luke, I'm not talking about Luke! I don't care about any of *that*…now."

"I changed but your father changed too. We ended up wanting different things."

"*Stop!* What he wanted was a wife and a mother to his kids, but you wanted this!"

"You don't remember how you were back then. So angry with me for leaving. The time just went so fast. One minute you were thirteen and calling me all the time, and then the next thing you're seventeen and you wouldn't even pick up the phone if you knew it was me. Being with you was *hard*."

Mikaela sighed.

That was true, and it was mutual. And it wasn't as if her mother hadn't constantly told them how much she loved them both. Their answering machine used to be filled with unlistened-to messages saying that. There were shoeboxes in the back of her closet in Harmon, even now, filled with greeting cards for virtually every occasion saying the exact same thing as well. But Mikaela couldn't hear it for so many years.

"Your father and I were young…and stupid. The one thing we did right was you two, but we also made mistakes. Mistakes doing what we thought we should. I thought I should make him happy by being the person he wanted me to be, and he thought he should pretend to be happy with that version of me. But here's the thing, *I couldn't and he wasn't.* I'm sure he told you that himself. That 'wife and mother' Nattie wasn't the girl he fell for. She was a shell of herself."

"Having a family to care for hollowed you out is what you're saying?"

"I didn't mean it like that. You misunderstood me."

"I don't think I did. That's what *shell* means."

Natalee sighed. "Then I used the wrong word."

"Likely story."

They both chuckled awkwardly despite the tension, gazing off the balcony at the sunset.

"Being *that* kind of wife, doing what my mother had, living where we did, going through those same motions—women's auxiliary, chamber of commerce, garden club, church council, bake sales, Christmas pageants, carnival committees—*that* hollowed me out."

"So, you got bored."

"Kaela, that's not fair. Not with you and your sister, no—"

"What if I'm the same? What if I only have a little while in me? What if I'm no good after that? What if Cameron's not enough?" Mikaela looked at her mother, pained. "What if we end up like, like—"

"Me and your daddy? What if you burn hot and then fizzle out, ruining everything around you?"

Mikaela brushed away the tears crowding her lash line

and cleared her throat. "Well, I wasn't really going to put it like that."

"You know back when you came to visit and I met young Cameron, and I saw you two together, all I could see was history repeating itself. Then I came to Harmon for The Judge's funeral and I saw you both there. You were *so* in love. I even called J.D. afterward terrified for you. So, no one was more surprised than me when I heard that you'd broken up. But I was proud too. Proud you'd made the choice I didn't, that I couldn't."

"I think it's more accurate to say that I made a hash of things with Cameron and Julie then and I'm in the process of doing it again. I'm just incapable of trusting myself, or him enough. I don't think I can give him what he needs. So, I guess maybe it is *exactly* you and Daddy all over again."

"Listen, you wanna know my secret?" Natalee put the question to Mikaela abruptly, ignoring her little dig. "Why I'll stay married to Luke when I couldn't make it work with your daddy?"

"I think that's what I'm asking," Mikaela said, unable to check the barbed sarcasm in her voice.

"Simply, because I am who I was meant to be now and I committed from that place. After all the mistakes your daddy and I made. I made a conscious decision to love Luke. It's nothing we just 'fell' into. Luke and I *chose* our life together fully aware of who we are. And we keep choosing it. *Every day.* I wake up and make the decision to commit myself to my husband and my marriage. *Every day.* You just have to believe that you're capable of it and that Cameron is too, then do it."

Mikaela nodded, fighting the tears welling in her eyes. "Just like that?"

"You're adults now. You've decided you want to be together. Why wouldn't it work once you trust yourselves enough to give it a chance?"

Hadn't Cameron been asking her the same question?

How was it possible that Mikaela still wasn't sure she knew the answer?

"I hear you, Mama, I do. And I want to try. But what if it's too late? I don't think Cam wants to do this with me anymore. And I don't blame him. I think we've burnt ourselves out."

"Now I know you don't believe that. Otherwise, you wouldn't be asking your daddy and me for advice all these years later. But, darlin', I can't tell you what to do." Natalee smiled warmly. "And I know you wouldn't listen to me anyhow."

Mikaela smirked; she was her mother's daughter after all.

fifty-one

Mikaela stood at a porch screen door two days later wondering if this was the dumbest thing she'd done yet. She'd been thinking it the entire drive from her mother's house in Atlanta to Cameron's home in Savannah. Still, she rented a car and did it anyway.

In the few past weeks of increasingly random decisions, this being number one was really saying something.

She pressed the doorbell once and got no answer. She pressed it again, and then again.

Several minutes of repeated rings later, she was greeted by a slightly agitated Cameron in a Sting and the Police tee and jeans.

"Mikaela." He didn't seem surprised by her being there, but he didn't seem pleased either. "I was in the backyard, not across the country."

Cameron stepped out onto his porch and glared at her.

Already, this wasn't the reception she'd hoped for. Normally, anywhere else, with anyone else, Mikaela would have apologized for her lapse in judgment, offered hollowly to come back—*without any true intention to do so*—tucked tail and run. But thanks to months of therapy and the fact that running home was a little difficult to do eight hundred miles south of Brooklyn, she stood her ground.

"I'm sorry. I know I should be giving you the space you asked for. But I'm here to plead my case," Mikaela spoke rapidly in case he tried to stop her.

"Well, you know what they say about lawyers who represent themselves."

"I love you. I need you."

She didn't waste time. She'd been working on this with her therapist. Mikaela just had to put it out there like they were the three most important words in English or any other language…because to her, for him, they were.

Cameron only snorted and without exactly inviting her inside, turned to head back in, the flimsy screen slamming shut but his heavy front door left open.

Standing on the porch of Cameron's craftsman bungalow, Mikaela was acutely aware of her situation: unexpected, uninvited and separated by more than just the screen door that stood between them. Still, she persisted, following him inside as he stalked off. She slowly wandered through the house, sidestepping flattened moving boxes on the floor in the hall. The furniture was simple but well-built, and the walls of each room, in warmly complementary shades of beige, gray and taupe, made the interior cozy.

But what she noticed most was that every single wall and open space was covered with art. There were lots of photographs: daring, colorful and evocative, both his and those of other artists. Paintings were interspersed with sculptures and on one wall, quite boldly, there was a relief over the fireplace in his living room.

If Mikaela didn't know better, she would have sworn it

all suggested the sure hand of a decorator. *A refined taste.* But Cameron had been a fine art major in school. Curating a stunning home collection was as much in his wheelhouse as lawsuits were in hers.

Still, she was unsettled by the way everything, down to the burnished bronze lamp on a mahogany credenza in his hall, suggested a completeness in his life that actively negated her presence. The neat and tidiness of it and the attractiveness stole her thunder, making her feel even more superfluous to him.

It was nothing like she expected. For some reason, Mikaela had imagined Cameron in a slick and sparse bachelor pad befitting his itinerant photographer's lifestyle. Like the borrowed apartment in New York. But this was a home. It very nearly stopped her short as she wondered: *Had she made a mistake?*

Ximena, Vanessa and Suze were of the impression that all she needed to do was say her piece and Cameron would somehow be persuaded. Persuaded that, despite her own doubts, theories and actions to the contrary, she did indeed have a place with him in this life. One she was finally willing to take up. One she wanted; she saw that now.

She'd come here determined to tell him so.

Mikaela heard the sound of water coming from the back. She stepped out of his kitchen, through the sliding glass doors and onto his backyard deck.

Cameron stood barefoot in a small, muddy puddle in his grass, spraying his impressively verdant lawn as if she wasn't even there. He didn't even look her way.

"Cam," Mikaela said, "I swear I am going to give you the room to do whatever you need to once I say this." She took a deep breath, bracing herself to finish the rest of it as if she'd rehearsed it...*which, she sort of had.* "I know I have done a terrible job of speaking from the heart before, for which I'm sorry."

"Mikaela—" He finally acknowledged her.

"No," Mikaela interrupted, afraid of losing her resolve. "Let me say it. I love you. Not only that, but I have always loved you and never stopped, not in all these years."

Cameron straightened, turning to her and finally dropping the hose. Yet, his face retained a scary indifference. He crossed his arms as if putting a physical barrier between himself and her words. "What are you doing here?" He sighed, getting straight to the point. "I thought we both agreed to take some time?"

"*You* decided that. Besides, it's been a few weeks, right?"

He didn't smile at her attempt to lighten things.

Mikaela cleared her throat. "Like I said, I came to apologize for making you doubt. For not being able to say this to you before," Mikaela continued. "I didn't know how—how to say it and actually mean it. The words terrify me, always have. I've never said it and meant it, to any man. Until now."

Had she kept him waiting too long? Exhausted his last shred of goodwill? Hoping someone would wait while you took months—years—to straighten your head out was a lot. No matter how willing they seemed to be to do it.

"So, you came all the way to Savannah to apologize? To little ole me?"

She averted her gaze for a moment. "Well, I visited my dad and mom too."

"So, you're here on vacation then?" He sobered, reaching down for the hose. "From all your work stuff? Your partnership chase? Altcera—"

"It's a sabbatical, I'm taking a little break from all that."

He paused, his eyes searching her face. "Why?"

It was like being under a microscope, Cameron examined her face so closely. Mikaela rubbed her lips together, licking them.

She took a deep breath. "I didn't get the partnership offer."

"Oh, Mikaela, I'm so sorry." He frowned, genuine sadness on his face.

She tipped her head up, shrugging. "No, it was good. I realized that, though I thought I was on the verge of getting everything I had ever wanted, I wasn't. *Not really.* Everything I ever saw for myself…" she rambled nervously trying to marshal the fortitude to keep going. "But it wasn't that."

"Uh-huh." Cameron's shoulders fell in on themselves, his brows furrowing further in confusion.

He didn't understand what she was trying to say yet. She was talking without truly saying what she needed to. That the truth was ever since he'd appeared at that baseball game, she'd been unsettled. Seeing him had put her on the back foot for the first time in forever. It was as if his turning up like a long-lost item unexpectedly revealed an assortment of missing pieces that had always been there to begin with.

"Well, that all sounds great." His mouth formed an almost polite half smile.

"It's not enough, it would never be enough," she blurted out to his blank face. "So, I came here…for you."

A cardinal sang in the trees high above them.

"You know," he laughed, more of an irritated bark than levity, shaking his head. "When you do this you make me feel like a real sucker."

"What?"

"You say 'jump' and I do. I *always* do, it's always been that way. I mean, how many times are we gonna do th—"

"Cameron, please. I said—" she started, as their words trampled over one another.

"No! You please!" he ground out. "You must think I don't

have feelings. 'Cause here I am, the idiot, wearing my heart on my sleeve and I'm the only one paying the price. You love me, need me. So?" He shrugged, his eyes back on her as if in challenge.

"So?" She didn't know how one followed that up.

It occurred to her, she had never said those words, bared her heart, to anyone who wasn't Vanessa Elizabeth or John Darnell Marchand. But it was time to place her faith in the fact that Cameron did love her. And if she was capable of reciprocating... despite an entire adulthood spent hedging her bets or outright betting against love, this *could* work.

"So...that's great. But what am *I* supposed to do with it, Mike?"

"I thought you'd say you loved me too. Needed me too," Mikaela admitted.

Cameron rolled his eyes. "Apparently, whether or not I love you is irrelevant, given how many times I've said it, to whether you actually believe me. Tell me, what's different now? Would you even be here if you had gotten that partnership offer?"

This was not going the way she hoped it would...again.

"That's not fair."

"Isn't it?"

"I was afraid!"

"Of what, Mikaela? You already know I adore you! That I have *always* adored you! There has never been anyone else but you. God forgive me for saying that considering I was married before, but it is what it is."

"What do I have if I don't have my work? I mean, you say you love me but what if loving me wasn't enough to make you stay when it counted?" She'd finally said it, unloaded her deepest fear and the one true thing she'd known since childhood, feeling laid bare as the words left her mouth. "I don't know how to make anything last long-term. I'm afraid I'll mess it all up. That you loving me and me loving you isn't enough to keep us together!"

Despite people's best intentions, things fall apart, people leave. They change, grow apart, move on, break up, divorce...how much they loved each other in the beginning seemed largely irrelevant to whether they stayed together in the end. Her parents' story was her living proof of that.

"And I'm doubly afraid," Mikaela continued, "that my constant fear of you leaving will just drive you away faster. I mean, it already has, hasn't it?"

"No, it hasn't," Cameron countered, with a frustrated groan. "Kaela, I will *always* want you, but the fact that you're still questioning that, how I feel about you—*after all this time*—that really scares me. It's what makes me afraid you'll be the one doing the leaving, chasing the next thing... I mean, you've done it before."

Mikaela was quiet for a moment, skewered by his words, plainly spoken like an inalienable truth. And the anguish in his voice cracked Mikaela in two. The last thing she ever wanted to do was hurt him, especially not again.

"I'm so sorry," Mikaela said. "For then. And now. You are within your rights to want nothing to do with me."

"Is that what you just heard me say?" he asked with a long, exasperated breath. "Be honest with me, is that what you think I want? Or is that just what you want?"

"Well," she scoffed, "obviously not, Cameron. I came all the way to Savannah. I want you to love me. *I'm ready now.* That's why I'm here."

"Great. You're ready...but?"

"But?" She parroted back before she realized what he was doing.

It was that infuriating therapist thing that Ximena had

been doing for months. Repeating all Mikaela's questions back to her because she remained confident Mikaela already knew all the answers, even when Mikaela herself wasn't.

"But…how can I know for sure that this time would be any different than you and me before, or you and Julie, or even my parents? How do I know this time it'll be forever?"

"What a completely ridiculous question!" Cameron laughed, throwing up his hands and rolling his eyes exaggeratedly.

Her eyes widened at his outburst.

He paced the length of the deck steps. "How do any of us know anything? What makes *you* so special that you deserve some kind of cosmic reassurance no one else gets? I've learned, in life, unpredictability is the only certainty. I'm no blade of grass blowing in the breeze, but life takes its course, and you can either bend with it or you'll break. As my dad used to say, 'People make plans and God laughs.' You see, there's no magic equation or special trick for it. There is no celestial alchemy. There's just constancy. Just you and me deciding *every single day* that 'us' is enough to try and stay together for. I can't give you any more reassurance than that, cosmic or otherwise. I have always loved you, *Mikaela Marchand*, since I was twenty-one years old! And I can only promise you that you had my heart then, you have my heart now and you always will. That's it, that's all."

But wasn't that everything?

Just like her mother had told her: *she* had to decide.

Mikaela could either choose to continue to see the pittance of that offering and its inherent insecurity or see it as an abundance tendered with its amazing possibilities. To reject that uncertainty or draw comfort from his reassurance. Was it enough, after spending her whole life wagering against love, to build a foundation on? Cameron had now repeatedly offered her this, his heart, the essence of him, even when she pushed him away. And frankly, he'd always had her heart too. So, what was really the problem?

He made no ultimatum, but Mikaela knew she had to finally decide, right there, right then, if it was enough.

His eyes fixed on hers and held. In that moment, she saw the boy she first met twenty years ago, who took pictures that offered glimpses into his soul, and she knew. There was no one else with whom she'd ever be willing to make such a gamble.

It had always only been Cameron.

She swallowed. "Okay."

"Okay? Just like that?"

She nodded, more for herself than him. "If you'll still have me?"

"You're kidding, right?" He swept her into his embrace, swinging her off her feet and into him.

"Yeah, actually I am."

Cameron laughed and pulled her up onto her toes as she lay her arms over his shoulders, cupping the nape of his neck. His hands slid around her waist, and he placed his lips to hers, beginning a blistering kiss that nearly lifted her out of her sandals.

"I love you," Mikaela said when he finally retreated. She tested out the words, as if tasting for mouthfeel.

They still felt foreign. *But not wrong, said to the right person.*

"I love you too. *Always.*" He grinned at her. "What?"

She tried to decipher the triumphant look on his face. "So, were you teasing me before? Holding out? Or were you really going to let me go?"

"No, not teasing. Giving you a taste of your own medicine."

"Ah, so then I guess you'd have been really upset if I called your bluff and left."

"I knew you wouldn't—not this time."

"That's really confident considering, as you said, I'd done it before."

Cameron scrunched up his nose. "Well, this time your sister and your assistant were blowing up my phone all day. Telling me you were coming. Warning me, on pain of death, that I had better listen up to whatever you had to say."

Mikaela sucked her teeth, shaking her head. Vanessa and Suze truly were physically incapable of minding their own business.

"And I suppose if it doesn't work out between us, there are always other women you could call. I'm sure Jacqueline could hook you up with a model or two."

"Didn't you hear me? You're it for me. Us or bust." He shook his head. "Plus, Jacqueline likes you. Still, I wasn't that worried. I always believed it was gonna work out for us."

"You couldn't possibly have known that."

"You think so, huh?" Cameron smirked, reaching into the back pocket of his jeans to retrieve a key chain.

She grinned. "And what's this?"

"Keys to my apartment...in New York." Cameron placed the keys in Mikaela's hand.

"Wait, you're moving? There? Now?" Mikaela's eyebrows shot up.

"Yup." He nodded. "Fashion Week... And 'cause it seems the girl I love lives up there."

The boxes in the hall.

"You *were* coming back. I jumped the gun, didn't I?"

He gave her a self-satisfied smirk.

Mikaela glanced around. "And what about this place?"

"I'm putting it on the market. By the way, those are actually yours." He gestured with a nod of his head toward her hand.

Attached to the keys in her palm dangled a small pewter

bulldog. "Oh my God." She laughed out loud, marveling. "It's Uga!"

"Well, not quite. More like Uga IX. He's been through a lot." He shrugged. "But Uga still knows."

"Knows what?" She fished.

Cameron rolled his eyes knowing what she was after. "Knows that my life, my last, best and only chance at true happiness was always gonna be wherever you were."

"If Uga thought so, then I don't know why I ever doubted." Mikaela chuckled as Cameron nuzzled her nose tenderly with his own.

"I don't know why you did either." He smiled.

He leaned in and kissed her then, a light brush of his lips across hers like their very first time.

Well, she thought confidently, *starting today, neither of us will ever have to doubt again.*

★ ★ ★ ★ ★

acknowledgements

My editor, Lynn Raposo—there aren't enough words of gratitude to express how I feel (that says a lot coming from a wordy writer!). You saw potential in my little story when it was still germinating. You found it, you read it, you made a case for it, you nurtured it, you refined it. Did I already say you read it? *Over and over and over again.* I'm so sorry, LOL! Still, if there's one thing I know for certain, it's that no one loves Mikaela and Cam more than you do! And for that, I am forever grateful.

My agent, Jill Marsal—from literally day one and that first call, I felt like it was kismet the way we found each other! THANK YOU for proving me right, for all you do, for being a font of information, guidance and experience. Thank you for tolerating my constant worry, doubt and incessant questions—basically, thank you for being a nerd-whisperer.

Samira Ellis—my mentor, my adviser, my coach, my fan, my consigliere and my own personal Henry Higgins (is that inappropriate to say?). The one person who continues to make logging on to Twitter worthwhile. You took a lonely little story with a cute moodboard and one "like," and helped turn it into something people (besides me) could love. You saw something where I worried there was nothing. Among my first writing cheerleaders. My appreciation of you is boundless.

Risa Edwards and Ashley Jordan—for steamy scene boot camp. Savants of Sensuality, Goddesses of the big O. Y'all should give masterclasses! I ♥ U!

Tanisha Mathis—thank you, thank you, thank you for talking me off many ledges, reading a million pages, indulging both numerous flights of fancy and pity-parties, being my first PR person, celebrating every success and sticking through every disappointment. Thanks for bringing your organization, discipline, knowledge base and drive into the life of possibly the laziest writer to exist, and lighting a fire under my butt! You are without question THE best critique partner turned close friend a girl could ever hope for! I am humbled by your friendship.

My LATTIS group writing partners par excellence: Sara Moran (MSU-4-eva!), Tamara Golden and Lee Rigoux— brilliant writers in their own rights who take time out of their schedules bimonthly to bring me up onto their level. And who always show me how it's done. I'm in awe of you ladies. And I *cannot wait* to hold your books in my hands!

My wonderful family: Mom, Dad, Ma'am, Cyle & Alyssa, Amin & Felicia, Carl and all the kiddos—for your inexhaustible patience, love and support for your poor relation, the dreamer. You guys have been waiting for this (even when I had no idea). Thank you for your unwavering faith. You already knew it, thanks for helping me figure it out.

Jerneeka S.—my Ace, the Queen of the Romance Novel, genre goddess, fellow bookworm, "Happy" Club co-president and the leader of my "squad," who knew all the rules (when I knew none) and has shared her expertise enthusiastically whenever I asked. We've now known each other for longer than we haven't. Can you believe it? I still say we're too young for that, LOL! Love you, girl!

Simone P.—girl, words cannot express my love for you. Head of the Cheering Section. The Queen B. We've been ridin' for twenty years now and your joy is mine. Thank you for making my joy yours.

The Cheering Section:

My fellow Witches of Amherst: Amora M.P., Zandrina A., Lina A. and Shalini R.—together, we can still do powerful things! See? I love you guys so much!

Femi L., Yvette T.W., Ada A., Kay and Celia P.—for their staunch support, love, faith, laughter. Did I already say love? Yeah, an abundance of that! I adore you ladies.

A special thank you to Linda Mayo-Perez and Jimmy Williams, my MV/SC connection without whom I'd know nothing about the beautiful shores of the Vineyard or the Low Country. Two special places and times in my life that have become cherished memories. Thank you for sharing your homes with me.

To Jessica Watterson & her MSA writing group, and to my book's fairy godmother, Ann (A.H.) Kim, in the moment of magic and manifesting that was the Romancing the Runoff event—these folks that have no idea how valuable I found their precious time, that they so freely gave. But hopefully now they do! Thank you for sharing so much with me, helping me to refine my words and discover my ending.

To three people who have no idea they're about to be thanked here:

Catherine T.—for preventing me from entirely butchering American jurisprudence. (Though please don't fault any other lawyers included in my thanks for the places where I did, LOL!)

Brittaney-Belle G. and Patrick W.—for your steadfast support and indefatigable optimism. Y'all kept me going and believing. Thank you.

The wonderful, loving and indomitable women of Maclean House at Princeton University during my time there, who, without reservation, believed I could do this without ever reading a single word I'd written. LOL! Ladies, you're the best! XOXO

And last but not least, a very special and profuse thanks to the entire team at HQN Books who worked so tirelessly on my book and whose specific and essential contributions to my labor of love are largely unknown to me. I don't see you but I know you're there and I appreciate you.